W9-AVX-643

Before I Say Goodbye

BOOKS BY
RACHEL ANN NUNES

Before I Say Goodbye

A Novel by

RACHEL ANN NUNES

DESERET
BOOK

SALT LAKE CITY, UTAH

This is a work of fiction. Characters and events in this book are products of the author's imagination or are represented fictitiously.

© 2011 Nunes Entertainment, LLC

All rights reserved. No part of this book may be reproduced in any form or by any means without permission in writing from the publisher, Deseret Book Company, P. O. Box 30178, Salt Lake City, Utah 84130. This work is not an official publication of The Church of Jesus Christ of Latter-day Saints. The views expressed herein are the responsibility of the author and do not necessarily represent the position of the Church or of Deseret Book Company.

DESERET BOOK is a registered trademark of Deseret Book Company.

Visit us at DeseretBook.com

Library of Congress Cataloging-in-Publication Data

Nunes, Rachel Ann, 1966– author.
  Before I say goodbye / Rachel Ann Nunes.
      pages cm
  Summary: After a twenty-year absence, Rikki Crockett has come home to Utah, to the same house where she grew up. When she left, she was young, hurt, and angry—abandoned by her parents and her best friend. When the worst happens, home is the only place she might still find a future for herself and her two children.
  ISBN 978-1-60641-425-5 (paperbound)
  1. Homecoming—Fiction.   2. Mormon women—Fiction.   3. Domestic fiction.
I. Title.
  PS3564.U468B44 2011
  813'.54—dc22   2011019748

Printed in the United States of America
R. R. Donnelley, Crawfordsville, IN

10   9   8   7   6   5   4   3   2   1

To all the people in my past and current wards
who have reached out to our family over the years.
Thanks for being there!
Ward families do make a difference.

Acknowledgments

Publishing a book is always a group effort. A big thank-you to Cátia and Gretchen, whose comments on the manuscript resulted in many clarifications and two additional chapters. To my family, who constantly encourages me. To Suzanne Brady for her editing suggestions and for always making me feel like a pro. To Jana Erickson for loving the story, and to Sheryl Dickert Smith for a cover I love. Thanks also to the great staff at Deseret Book for helping my book reach readers. It's rewarding to work with such fabulous people.

CHAPTER ONE

Rikki

Mountains loomed on all sides, some closer, some in the distance, but always there. A presence that exuded safety and permanence and hinted at something deeper, something I couldn't explain but felt deep in my being. My soul. If I even had a soul, which I wasn't betting on.

I hadn't remembered the mountains like this, how they made me feel. I should probably have come back before now, at least to attend my mother's funeral. Except that I might not have been able to escape a second time—and back then, escape had been all that was important.

Well, not all. Dante Rushton had been important.

I couldn't think of him because it wouldn't change what had happened or why I was returning to Utah after all these years. The Dante I'd known twenty years ago had nothing to do with it. Who that boy had become, however, was another story.

"I can't believe you're forcing me to move to this . . . this place." Kyle's lips twisted in disgust.

My daughter looked so much like I had at her age it was uncanny—white-blonde hair, thin, willowy figure, heart-shaped face

1

that was trying to look older than the thirteen years since her birth. Her eyes were bluer than mine, taking after her no-good father who'd cut out on us, but the shape of them was mine, as was the light smattering of freckles on her face. "I mean, look at it, Mom. This place is a cave. All these mountains staring down at us, like they're going to fall and crush us to dirt. Maybe it'd be better if they did."

"They look like kings from a story," James told his older sister. His first name was actually Dante, after that first Dante I'd known as a child, given him in that magic euphoria that follows birthing. Except I soon found I couldn't call him Dante on a daily basis. So I called him by his middle name, James, which had been his father's last name. Since I hadn't married either of their fathers, both my children officially shared my maiden name, Crockett.

Kyle groaned. "I'm going to miss all my friends and the ocean. It stinks!"

"This is where my job is." I wiped beads of perspiration from my forehead. The air-conditioning in my pickup wasn't working well and had made the trip that much more joyful. "We have no choice."

"It still stinks!"

"Yep, it does. Big time." She had no idea how much, but I would have to tell her soon.

"Leaving California for Utah. To live in an old house that no one has lived in for years. It's as bad as moving to Idaho and farming potatoes or something."

"I think it's p—uh, nice," James said.

"Ha! You were going to say it looks pretty, weren't you?"

James blinked at the viciousness in her tone. He shrugged. "I know boys don't say that, but, well, it is kind of pretty." He was utterly defenseless, and I wasn't surprised to see all the fight leak from my daughter. James had that way with people. I hadn't found anyone who could derive pleasure from hurting him for any length of time. Not that I had any doubts this would eventually change. The world never stopped kicking. His seven-year-old innocence was one of the reasons I had to come home.

"I guess," Kyle said dully.

"And we get to have a dog." James's smile was back. "I've always wanted a dog. We never had a dog at our apartment."

Tears burned in my eyes. He could have all the animals he wanted, so long as it made him stay a little boy that much longer.

"I'd rather have a rabbit," Kyle said, relenting just a little. Enough.

"That's fine," I said. "But you'll have to figure out how to take care of it."

• • •

The old house in Spanish Fork looked nothing like I remembered. In my memories it had a much larger, darker presence. A being of ominous silence, of cringing at the screaming, of talking to only when talked to, of chores and wishing myself away. Now the house and its half acre were run-down, but it didn't hold the darkness. In fact, with some white paint and red trim, it would look nothing like the house I'd grown up in.

"This is it?" Kyle said with another groan.

Her pain pierced me but more for what would come than for what she felt right now. There was nothing I could do about any of it. I'd run out of places to hide.

James was careening all over the yard, exclaiming at the treasures he found—a rusted truck, a half-broken wooden spoon that made a lovely sound when beaten upon an old pot, some rope, the rusted front wheel of a bike, a nest of mice under the narrow cement porch. Best of all was an old tree house in the backyard, probably built by some renter in the years since my father's death; it had never been mine.

"Stay off until I check it out," I said, pulling him down from the wooden steps nailed into the tree. I climbed up, and thankfully the structure seemed sturdy enough. What wasn't could be fixed by a few carefully placed nails.

"Bring the tool box from the truck," I yelled down to Kyle.

"You gotta be kidding. You're doing this right now?"

"Why not?" I asked.

"Hurry, get it!" James was jumping foot to foot on the weeds below. "Mom, can I come up?"

"Sure!"

Kyle returned, and soon we were all banging away with hammers and nails. Kyle hit her finger and swore.

I caught her hand. "Hey, I said no more of that."

"Well, it hurt!"

"So? A lot of things hurt. Small words mean a small mind." I'd heard that before, but I couldn't remember where. Maybe in church as a child.

"I don't see what the big deal is. You always swear."

"Not anymore I don't." She couldn't either. That might ruin the plan. "Now toss me another nail."

We pounded until I felt it was safe enough. "Just don't lean too far over that window." Even as I spoke, I knew that a really responsible mother would probably board it up. But doing so would completely ruin the fun of having a tree house.

Kyle quickly leaned through the window to check out the danger. "Not that bad. He'd probably only break his neck if he fell."

"I'm not stupid enough to do that," James protested.

"Wait." I held up a hand until I had their attention. "I just thought of something really cool. The best thing about this place is that if the house is too ruined, we can live up here." The kids stared at me, smiles spreading across their faces.

"Really, Mom?" James bounced with unconstrained energy.

"Of course."

"I get dibs by the door!" Kyle laughed, and that set the rest of us off. Maybe, just maybe, this would work.

"Okay, people," I said, pushing past Kyle and starting down the wood rungs. "Let's see what the house looks like."

I had the key, sent to me by the realtor who'd been trying to either rent or sell the place until I told her a month ago that I'd be coming home. Since I'd cancelled her contract, no one had been here. I'd called the utilities to start service, but they hadn't been sure it would happen before we arrived, and I could only hope I had no broken pipes when things finally got up and running. A Sunday wasn't the best time to move in, especially if I didn't have water or electricity, but I'd packed a few bottles of water to get us through. I needed a shower, but that could wait.

Thankfully the electricity was on, though a lot of light bulbs needed replacing. The house had undergone a few changes in the past twenty years—a wall shortened here, a built-in bookcase added there. A gas fireplace instead of the old wood one. Wallpaper that didn't look half bad graced the tiny living room, but the remains of what looked like a fire blackened one wall of the kitchen. The kitchen cupboards had been painted at some point, and the stove looked nearly new. I liked the addition of the shelves on either side of the window that overlooked the backyard.

I turned on the tap. Nothing. The water bottles would come in handy.

Kyle ran her fingers through the thick layer of dust on the Formica countertop. "Nice," she said, rolling her eyes.

"I can draw on the counter!" James quickly made a huge smiley face, and soon Kyle and I were laughing again.

"It'll be nice once it's all cleaned up," I said as Kyle started down the hallway. "We won't have to worry about turning down our music or smelling the neighbor's cooking."

"Or hear the yelling, or smell that awful smell in the stairwell." James wrinkled his nose.

"But there's only two bedrooms." My feet retraced the steps to where I'd slept for nineteen years of my life. Unlike the rest of the house, these rooms seemed unchanged, except for the color of paint in the small master bedroom. I stepped inside the smaller room, and it was almost as though I'd stepped back in time. Memories slid through my mind, some more vivid than others, and not nearly so black as I expected. The closet was where I used to play with my dolls, and that space near the left wall was where my bed had been and where my mother had occasionally read me stories. The window was where Dante had come to rescue me when I could stand no more of my father's yelling.

I'd have to paint the room, if there was time. Decorate it for James. I'd read to him in the bed, and I'd help him sneak out of the window so we could pretend to run away to the tree house. But I couldn't unpack anything from my truck or the rented trailer I was towing until I cleaned at least enough space for the mattresses. Maybe we'd spend the first night in the tree house after all. James would love that.

The next thing I knew Kyle was tugging on my arm. "Mom, did you hear me?"

I shook my head. "You and I can share the bigger room. James can have this one."

"Did you zone off again? I'm trying to say that I went downstairs, and there're two more rooms there that are really tiny but are painted kind of nice, and a bigger room that's not exactly finished but it would be okay if we put down some linoleum or something.

If we could find it cheap. It'd be good for practicing my dancing. Can I sleep down there in one of the rooms?"

I grinned, glad for the motivation in her voice. If there was one thing Kyle loved besides everything she shouldn't do, it was dancing.

"Sure. You can sleep in the basement, and if you get too scared, you can always come into my bed."

"I'm not going to be scared."

"Okay, then if I get scared, I'll come find you."

She laughed. "Come see."

Apparently my father had made progress on the basement before he died six years ago. He'd had the rooms framed long before I left and put up drywall in one of them, but I'd thought he'd never actually finish. Either he had, or a renter had finished the rooms at a later date.

That the house had been a rental was clear. There were dings in the walls, a few holes in the doors and in the carpet, two missing doorknobs, only minimal light bulbs, and towel rods missing from the bathrooms. None of this mattered. It wasn't as if the children would be staying long enough to grow up here.

I should have come back before.

The thought wouldn't leave me. I should have come to see my mother when she was sick before she died. Tell her I loved her and that I didn't blame her for not protecting me, even though I did, a little. I knew now what I should have done, but it was useless to worry about the past, about things you couldn't fix. Life was too short for that. Tomorrow was what really mattered. I had to plan for tomorrow.

I stifled a yawn, thinking longingly of a hot shower. I'd slept a few hours last night on the side of the road, but it wasn't enough. It was never enough; I'd felt as though I'd been tired for years. All the choices of my life creeping up on me.

I clapped my hands before I could feel sorry for myself. "We'll save the unpacking for later. Right now we have somewhere to go."

"Where?" Kyle said.

"To see an old friend." I grinned at Kyle's scowl. "First you need to change into that skirt I bought you."

"Aw, Mom!"

"I know where my nice pants are," James said. "But I'm a little hungry."

"We have granola bars and chips in the truck. We can eat on the way." I tossed Kyle the key to the rented moving trailer we'd hooked to my truck. "Hurry and get your skirt, Kyle. I'll get the water. I need to brush my teeth. Oh, and take out that nose piercing."

"I'm not taking it out."

"Please, honey. I need you to make a good impression."

"On who?" She swore under her breath.

"You'll see. Just do what I say. I mean it." My tone still worked on her for now. Maybe because I didn't use it much. I wouldn't now if it weren't so important.

"I can't believe this!" Kyle stomped from the house, but I yelled after her. "You'd better fix your hair. There'll be boys."

James snorted at that, and we burst into giggles.

CHAPTER TWO

Becca

Getting four children up and ready for church by myself was easier now that meetings didn't begin until eleven, but the belated start only meant that much more time without Dante. He'd moved his other meetings later as well, which was nice because he could sleep in a bit for change, but all too often that meant he'd stay later at the church holding interviews.

Not that I'm complaining, I thought as I dragged a brush through my shoulder-length hair a bit too vigorously, pulling out several brown strands in the process. I'd known the returned missionary Dante Rushton had leadership potential when I'd met him—he'd reminded me a lot of my father in that respect. I'd learned at my mother's knee that a man was only as great as the woman standing beside him, and I'd been determined to help us both reach new heights.

Only sometimes I didn't feel great. I felt tired and irritated and that life was somehow passing me by. I had everything I'd planned to achieve in my life—a good husband who was strong in the Church, beautiful children, a house, two cars, and a calling as second counselor in the Primary, which I adored. While Dante didn't make a huge salary at his job as a technical writer for a software firm, we weren't in debt except for the house. I was good at managing a budget, and Dante was a hard worker. Once the house was paid off, we planned to go on a cruise, just the two of us. Or so we said.

Why did I feel incomplete?

Maybe we should have another baby. I'd found myself wishing lately that we'd done it years ago because I wasn't as young as I used to be, though my teenagers' friends seemed to think I was one of them, if the way they hung out constantly at our house during the summer was any indication.

"Mommy, should I wear the red dress or the blue one?" Lauren asked.

I turned to look at my eight-year-old, who was wearing only her underclothes, the shirt a bit tight since I bought it last year. Her siblings had chosen their own clothing long before age eight, but she was the baby and found it difficult to do anything without approval. She had Dante's brown eyes like the rest of the children except Travis, but she had my dark hair, cut with bangs because we'd both tired of dragging hair from her eyes. Her skin was smooth and made me want to rub my cheeks against it. Fortunately, she wasn't above cuddling yet, and we got in our share during morning scripture study.

"Which one do you like the best?" I'd been trying to get her to make her own decisions lately. Heaven knew she'd have to make enough in her lifetime—important decisions that would affect her entire future. Better to start small.

Lauren's forehead crinkled. "I like both. Can't you just tell me which one *you* like the best?"

"I love red. It's my favorite color."

"You do? I never see you wearing it."

She was wrong, of course . . . wasn't she? "You need to choose now. You can think while I do your hair."

"I'm sick of bangs," she said, coming to stand in front of me. "We should cut them all off."

"That's not the way to get rid of bangs. You have to grow them out, and I'll have to put an elastic pulling them to the side, if you want them to stay out of your eyes while they're growing out."

"Okay."

Her hair was usually six inches longer, but she'd begged to cut it last year and it had been so much easier combing through it that I'd kept it trimmed. Even so, part of me missed the longer length.

Lauren primped in the mirror while I finished brushing her hair and pulled the red dress over her head. "You look beautiful," I said, adding a red clip to her hair.

"Thank you, Mommy. I love you!" Lauren hugged me, smearing my lipstick with her hair.

"I love you, too." I hugged her tightly, and for the moment there was nothing I was missing. Nothing at all.

There was always the mad dash at the end, even on this later schedule. "Hurry," I called to Allia, my fourteen-year-old. She'd recently discovered makeup, and if we were late, it was usually her fault. She came flying from the bathroom. "Nope," I said. "That eyeliner is too thick. I've been telling you that for the past two months." Allia would never believe it, but she was more beautiful without makeup. She had the same smooth skin Lauren did, thick eyelashes most girls achieved only with mascara, and long, thick hair. Her biggest problem was plucking her eyebrows, which she wasn't skilled at yet.

"I tried to make it lighter."

"I didn't say it was too dark. I said it was too thick."

She blinked, her brown eyes widening. "You mean make it

thinner? Oh, that's what you've been trying to say. Well, that's easy." She dived back into the bathroom.

Sixteen-year-old Travis rolled his eyes. He was the only one of our brood who had blonde hair like their father, and except for the blue eyes, he almost exactly resembled the pictures of Dante as a boy. I was glad about that. "Good thing we got that straight. She's starting to look like a raccoon. Right, Cory?" He slugged his younger brother in the arm. Cory, newly turned eleven, grinned. He worshipped Travis and would agree with him if he said the world was flat.

"You guys stop being mean." Lauren put her hands on her hips and faced her brothers. "Allia's more beautiful than you two, even if she does look like a raccoon."

Her brothers giggled, and Allia poked her head from the bathroom. "Thanks, babe, but you're not helping."

"She agrees that Allia's a raccoon!" Cory slapped his leg.

"Mom!" wailed Lauren.

"Out to the van—now," I said in my I-mean-business voice. "Or you'll all be grounded, and you'll eat tuna casserole every day this week."

Grumbling, the boys and Lauren obeyed, grabbing their shoes from the racks I'd installed in the garage by the door.

"Allia, I'm leaving. You'll have to walk—and explain to your father why you're late."

That had the intended result, and Allia flew outside as I was backing out the van. "Much better," I said, glancing at her face. "That's the right way to put on makeup. If you had lighter hair, you'd have to use a lighter brown, but for your coloring, that's perfect."

"I didn't understand what you were saying before. Thinner, not lighter." Allia flipped down the mirror and studied her eyes. "It does look better."

I was glad the whole eyeliner thing had been a misunderstanding. I'd honestly begun to worry about my daughter, who was usually more conservative. I didn't want her to look like, well, like those kids who sluffed school and lit up smokes whenever they thought people weren't looking.

We made it barely in time, our bench seat in the middle section of the back row standing vacant for us. I exchanged smiles with our ward members. I'd been dubious when Dante had wanted to move back into his old ward, but now I knew why. I loved it here. The ward had changed over the years, of course, but many of the older members remained from Dante's childhood. His father no longer lived in his old house—a couple with three children lived there now—but the old man had never attended church anyway. The longtime members were what was really home to Dante. They were the reason he'd come to church and the reason he put in his mission papers. That he was now the bishop of the ward that had nurtured him was an irony that escaped no one, and Dante worked even harder to save each youth because of it.

Dante smiled at me from his seat in front, and I tipped my head, giving him a return smile. He held my gaze. I knew it was silly, but here like this, staring at each other across the room, I felt as close to him as if we were alone, curled in each other's arms. I didn't always feel that close to him. Especially of late.

Lauren began fighting with Cory over the hymnal, and the moment was lost. No, not lost. Stored with all the other moments I had with Dante. The stitches that made up who we were. Or who we were becoming. I wondered what he'd say if I told him I felt unsettled, that I was thinking about having another child at the great old age of thirty-eight. Or about returning to school. Or traveling. Something. Anything.

We'd sung a hymn, said amen to the opening prayer, and Dante was greeting the congregation and taking care of a few items of ward business when Allia leaned over Lauren and tapped my knee. "Who are they?" she whispered.

I followed her gaze to the door behind us to our left where a woman with long, flyaway blonde hair, dressed in a flowing red skirt and tight black tank top was leading her two children to the only open bench seat—the soft seats, as my children called them. There were always plenty of hard plastic chairs set up in the overflow, but they weren't comfortable. The woman was pretty and petite and near my own age, though she was far too thin. She wore little if any makeup that I could see, and the determined look on her face was emphasized by the dark circles under her eyes. She hesitated a moment, looking up at Dante, her children bumping into her from behind. A second later, I wasn't sure I'd imagined the pause as she marched on.

Like the woman, the two children were petite and blond. The little boy could have been any little boy in the ward, though his hair was a bit long and uncombed. The girl, however, was something else, and I was sure it was she who held Allia's attention. From her size, she looked eleven or twelve, Cory's age, but the heavy makeup made her look far older and worldly. She wore a white tank top, and her short black skirt would probably show flashes of her underwear when she sat. I'd have expected ratted hair with that ensemble, but her hair was flattened down over her forehead and covered most of her face. Not ugly but unnatural-looking. The only good thing about the girl seemed to be that she wasn't developed enough physically to make the tank top obscene.

I shook my head at Allia as the newcomers settled into the left section, up a row from us, for which I was glad because my boys might have seen more than I wanted them to. We weren't the only ones who'd noticed their arrival. Every eye in the chapel was fixed in their direction.

"Talk about a raccoon," Travis whispered. Cory giggled, and I had to shush them.

Even at the pulpit, Dante faltered, his eyes wide. He blinked once, twice. That wasn't like him. I looked back at the woman, saw her hand lift in a little wave.

She knew Dante? Could this be a family the missionaries were working with? No, he would have told me. My mind rushed over all the reasons this woman could know my husband, but nothing seemed satisfactory.

Maybe she didn't know him. Maybe the wave had been an apology for her interruption.

Dante was talking again, smoothly, as though nothing had happened. Everyone was paying attention again, and the whole incident might never have occurred.

Yet there was something. Sister Gillman, one of the old-timers, was whispering to her husband. Both of them kept glancing around at the woman and then at Dante. More whispering. Several of the other old-timers were doing the same thing. What was going on?

Surreptitiously, I studied the woman, or what I could see of her from my position. Untamed hair, a pale cheek. Not much to go on. A coldness entered my breast. There was something about her, about the way everyone reacted to her. The woman's face moved, scanning the ward, and I saw her gaze occasionally linger on someone before sliding on. She wasn't paying attention to the first speaker, who had finally taken over for Dante.

Her eyes fell on me—and stopped. Now I could see the whole of her heart-shaped face, which was unlined and innocent, belying the age, the knowing I saw in her eyes. She smiled. Not tentative, but whole and more than a little vulnerable.

Who was this woman? This woman who would let her young daughter enter a church dressed for a nightclub. She might as well be wearing a swimming suit for all the cover the skirt and tank gave her. The girl would feel horribly out of place in Young Women—if they stayed that long.

She continued to smile, her eyes locked on mine. I wanted to turn away, to shun her and protect my family, but all the teachings of a lifetime rose to the forefront of my brain. She was a daughter of God. That horrific girl and that sweet-looking little boy were all children of God, and He loved them. A rush of warmth blotted out the coldness in my heart.

I smiled back. She dipped her head and at last looked away. The little boy next to her buried his head in her lap as Lauren was doing to me.

I looked up at Dante to find him staring at the woman. There was a tightness around his mouth that I recognized. Worry. The woman felt his gaze and smiled. The tenseness relaxed.

What did that mean?

I slipped my arm around Cory and tried to catch Dante's eye. But he was staring in the other direction now, toward the back of the chapel.

It's nothing, I told myself. But I knew I was wrong.

CHAPTER THREE

Dante

I'd never even imagined how it would feel to see a ghost, but I found out when Rikki walked into the chapel. She was a ghost to me. Long dead and gone from my life. Yet suddenly alive.

Everyone stared, though that shouldn't have surprised me. Everyone had always noticed Rikki. Of course, the tank top and her daughter's getup were so out of place in an LDS ward that anyone in their place would have been stared at.

She looked almost the same, though twenty years had passed, and up close there would surely be differences. She knew me, too. Our eyes met, and I forgot completely what I was saying, which is embarrassing for a bishop at any time but even more so when it's because his old flame walks into the room.

Not that anyone was listening. All eyes were on her as she gave me a little wave.

I looked back at my paper and found my place. "We've called Julene Tuft to serve as a Primary instructor. Those in favor, please raise your hand. Any opposed? Thank you. We'll now turn the time over to our first speaker, Brother Jerry Sagers."

I scanned the ward, purposefully avoiding the place where

Rikki and her children sat. They had to be her children; they looked enough like her. I was curious about what she'd been up to all these years, but at the same time, the old hurt and resentment reared their ugly heads. Guess some things aren't easily forgotten.

In the back of the chapel, three of the ward youth slunk in. Two boys and a girl. Good. I'd been after them to attend. Now if only the teacher could keep their interest. Shouldn't be hard—I'd given the youth all the best teachers. I didn't want to lose any more young people.

Something tugged at me, and my eyes were pulled—not to Rikki but to Becca. My wife was watching me, her forehead slightly drawn. No one else in the ward might have noticed my bumbling at the pulpit, but she would have. A protective urge swelled in my heart. No matter what, I wouldn't let Rikki's coming touch my wife. Rikki had nothing to do with here and now or with what Becca and I had built together.

A rush of gratitude filled me. Every day Becca gave me strength. I never had to worry that she would leave or that her example would push our children away from the truth. On days when I felt I couldn't stand one more meeting, hear one more confession, or solve one more problem, her quiet determination and support encouraged me to rededicate myself.

My father had been right all those years ago when Rikki gave me her ultimatum. I'd thought at the time I would never recover, and that fear had almost been enough to keep me from letting her go. In the end, I'd been wrong, and my inactive father, whose regrets stretched wide enough to fill the state of Utah, had given me a final gift I never could repay.

He gave me Becca. He didn't know it then, and I didn't know it, but I still thanked the Lord for her every single day.

Becca smiled, her face coming alive. She was beautiful in a classic way that made her grow more and more beautiful with every passing year. When we were seventy, she'd look like a refined sixty, and I'd be just an old man.

I wouldn't let Rikki touch her. I would have to greet Rikki—politeness and my position as bishop demanded that, but I wouldn't let her near my family. She had a way of hurting those she touched. Of using them up.

Still, I was glad she looked okay.

Why was she back? The last time I'd seen her, she'd told me she was finished with Utah, with her parents, and with the Mormons. I understood why she wanted to get away from her family, and I even understood why she'd want to leave Utah, but being LDS had helped her survive a difficult childhood. The ward had been her family—and mine—in the way that our parents never had.

I'd known she would turn her back on me, but it surprised me that she'd also left everyone else. As far as I knew, no one had heard from her in all these years, except for a letter or two in the beginning.

After the meeting concluded, the older ward members surrounded Rikki as though drawn by unseen cords. Sister Giles, Sister Bunk, and Brother Warner, who'd taught us in Primary, Brother Flemming, who in his role as second counselor in the bishopric had filled in at the father-daughter activities, and Sister Lundgren, who'd been the Young Women's president. Other older members of the ward gravitated to her as well, but I couldn't remember their role in Rikki's life.

Rikki was hugging them all, even the brethren, who didn't look a bit unhappy about it. Her face was bright and excited. Her game face, I recognized. It hadn't changed in all these years. Rikki was uncomfortable but holding her own. Pretending.

Becca also headed toward Rikki, and I excused myself quickly from Jerry Sagers so I could meet her there. Unless the years had tempered her, Rikki was unpredictable at best. With the onslaught of members, her stress level would be high. I hoped no one told her how inappropriately her daughter was dressed. Looking at the child now, I felt a sweeping compassion. So young, so hard. What had Rikki done to her?

"Ah, Bishop, look who's back." Charlotte Gillman flashed me a pointed look. Her narrow face made her aquiline nose more prominent now that she'd lost weight with her recent bout with cancer, and though I'd visited her almost every day in the hospital, it still shocked me. By contrast, her rotund husband seemed almost flat-nosed. Sister Gillman glanced back at Rikki. "This brings back so many memories of Sunday School class. Remember when you were both sixteen and I was your teacher? Where have you been all these years, Rikki?"

Rikki laughed a little too loudly for the chapel, and everyone cringed. "Oh, here and there. I've seen the world."

"What brings you back?" asked Brother Gillman.

Rikki breathed in. "The fresh mountain air, that's what." She laughed again. "Actually, work. These are my children, Kyle and James."

"They look like you." There was a hint of disapproval in Sister Gillman's gaze as she eyed Kyle's miniskirt, but Rikki didn't seem to notice.

Her eyes fell on me. "Well, Dante. How have you been? You still writing?"

I felt more than saw the members of the ward slipping away to their classes but not without casting last lingering looks at Rikki and me.

"I work as a technical writer," I said. "For a software company. I don't have to beg magazines to take my articles anymore." Up close she didn't look like I remembered her at nineteen. Then she'd worn makeup—a lot of it. The way she was now reminded me of before eighth grade. She had aged, of course, but not nearly as much as I'd expected. An odd ache formed in my stomach, though it had nothing to do with Rikki so much as it had to do with growing up, with leaving home and losing parents.

I put my arm around Becca as she moved into the place vacated by Sister Gillman. "This is my wife, Becca, and two of our four children, Allia and Lauren. Becca, this is Rikki Crockett. She grew up in this ward, like I did."

"We're old friends," Rikki added.

"Nice to meet you." Becca held out a hand. She was taller than Rikki by at least three or four inches, which surprised me. In my memories of Rikki, I didn't recall her being so short. Shorter than I was, yes, but not this tiny.

"Are you in town for long?" Becca asked.

Rikki nodded. "I'm moving back into my parents' house for now. Looks like we'll be in your ward."

"It's all dirty!" Rikki's little boy spoke up. "And there's no water. But there's this really cool tree house. We were fixing it up today. I might get to sleep there."

Rikki laughed. "This is my son . . . James." Her hesitation was odd, given that she should know her own child's name. "He's seven. And this is Kyle, who's thirteen."

"Kyle?" Lauren repeated. "That's a boy's name."

Kyle stared at her without replying, resentment plain in her eyes. Or maybe that was all the makeup. Underneath the hardness there was a distinct vulnerability I recognized from my interviews with wayward youth. She might as well have been Rikki all those years ago. Could I help this child? I hadn't succeeded with her mother, but I'd been younger then and vulnerable myself.

"Kyle isn't only a boy's name," James said. "'Cuz it's my sister's name."

"You don't have water?" Becca's eyes went from James to Rikki.

"They haven't turned it on yet is all." Rikki tossed her head. "My fault. I wasn't sure when I'd arrive."

Becca looked at me. "There has to be something we can do. If they've turned off the meter, they already read it, so they have a record of where to start charging. Someone should be able to turn it on."

"I'll ask around in priesthood."

Allia glanced toward the door. "Uh, I need to get to class. I thought maybe she'd want to come with me?" She looked at me as she spoke, and I felt pride in my little girl. "Since I'm a year older, we're not actually in the same Sunday School class, but it won't matter for today."

"That's a great idea," I said. "If you're staying."

"Sure." Rikki gave Kyle a little nudge. "Go with—"

"Allia," Becca supplied.

"Allia to class," Rikki said. "Go on." Kyle gave Rikki a perfected teenage look that quailed a lot of parents, but Rikki only laughed. "There'll be boys."

We watched the girls leave, Allia with her normal bouncy gait and Kyle looking small and wilted and defensive. Could Allia sense her discomfort, or was all she saw a rebellious teen who wore too much makeup?

"She'll be fine," Rikki said brightly. Too brightly, but only I would notice.

"Guess you gotta come with me," Lauren said to James. "Mom?"

"You and James go ahead. I'll be there in a minute." Becca smiled at Rikki. "I'm in the Primary, so I'd better get in there, but it really is nice to meet you, Rikki. Look, would you like to come over for dinner after church? Without water it's going to be hard to make any kind of dinner at your house, much less clean up. Besides, I bet you're buried in boxes."

The Rikki I knew would have laughed at that. Dirt was not an issue. The queen of making the best of any situation, she'd probably throw up a tent and call it camping. One thing I knew for sure, she didn't like being at the mercy of strangers.

"I'd love to have dinner with you," Rikki said. "If you're sure there'll be enough."

I stared at her, experiencing a strange kind of inevitability about the situation. After all, I couldn't undo Becca's invitation.

Becca smiled. "There's plenty. I'll find you after church, and you can follow us over."

"You're not in your dad's house?" Rikki's eyes swung to me.

"Oh, no. We sold that house after he died. It was a little small for four children."

"What he means is that it was too old and run down at the time, and we didn't want to renovate. We built a house on a lot the next street over." Becca squeezed my arm and backed away. "See you later."

I wished she hadn't gone, but we had a hundred and twenty children in the Primary, and she was needed there. Besides, she loved the calling, and I wouldn't begrudge her the fun.

"She's nice," Rikki said. "Looks like you did okay after I left."

It hadn't been that easy, but it was also not something I wanted to talk about after all those years. The time when Rikki and I had known each other well enough to talk about anything had long passed. "Becca's wonderful," I said.

"Good Mormon girl?"

"Yes."

"I'm happy for you."

I could tell she meant it, even though she was still using that fake brightness, the one she used to hide pain. *Why are you really here?* I wanted to ask. But that was one more familiarity time denied us. I didn't know this Rikki, for all that she appeared the same.

23

"Sunday School is in the Relief Society room. I'll show you where it is, and we'll catch up at dinner."

She waved her hand. "I think I remember where it is."

Well, she hadn't remembered that Mormons didn't wear tank tops. Once I would have pointed that out, teasing her without mercy. That wasn't appropriate now. As her bishop, I would pray a lot, give her time to see if she adjusted, and maybe talk to the Relief Society president for ideas. It might come to the point of talking to her, especially about Kyle's manner of dressing. But hopefully not.

Sometimes being a bishop was all about waiting. Waiting and praying.

"See you later." Brushing past me in a cloud of scent that reminded me of springtime, Rikki went down the aisle, her long red gypsy skirt billowing out behind her. That was Rikki for you. Brilliant colors that screamed either "Look at me" or "Please keep your eyes on the color and away from what I'm trying to hide."

For a brief instant, I experienced the old loss I'd felt when she left twenty years ago, pulsing like an open wound. The next minute, it was gone as though it had never existed.

Why are you here, Rikki? Why in all the world and all the wards have you come here?

Through the door I caught a glimpse of the three teens who'd come in late to sacrament meeting. They should be in class right now, so apparently they needed an escort. I hurried out the door to give them a hand.

CHAPTER FOUR

$\mathcal{B}ecca$

The little boy's name wasn't just James, I soon found out, as I questioned him for our Primary records. His name was Dante James Crockett, and he was seven years old, turning eight later in the year. Dante. The woman had named her son after my husband. What had he meant to her?

In seventeen years my husband had never mentioned the name Rikki Crockett. I knew he'd had a girlfriend before his mission, but it had never seemed important. Had Rikki been that girlfriend? Or had they simply been friends growing up?

I shook my head. Dante was a beautiful name, and there was no reason why Rikki couldn't use it. Dante, the Italian poet, who had loved a woman from afar, a woman who'd been the inspiration for much of his work.

I frowned, not appreciating the image. My Dante hadn't been pining after anyone.

Not as far as I knew, anyway.

This must be one of those strange coincidences. Only last week, I'd run into an old friend of my brother's I'd had a huge crush on as a teen. When I told him about the children, he'd reminded me that his sister's name was Lauren, too. Coincidence.

Rikki seemed nice enough, and James, well, he was too sweet for words. Despite his rumpled looks, he'd taken immediately to folding his arms, singing the songs, and raising his hands at any obvious question, answering with thought and seriousness.

There he was, at it again. "Yes, James?" asked Mayra Godfrey, our Primary president, her narrow face wrinkling in concern.

"How do you get baptized? I never saw anyone get baptized before." His ignorance was starkly clear to everyone in the room, even the youngest children, who gaped at him in amazement.

"James, you don't know anything." Lauren's clear voice rang out, accentuated by giggles from the other children. "I was baptized after my birthday. I got to do it twice, since my toe poked out."

"Cool," James said, unperturbed. "So did you have to stick your head under the water? Was it scary?" More giggles at that.

Lauren shook her head. "Your daddy holds you so you don't have to be scared."

"I don't have a daddy."

"Lauren." I drew her away from James and the other children as Mayra stepped in and began to answer James's original question in her easily understandable way that made her a favorite with the children.

"What, Mom?" Lauren frowned at me.

"Please don't tell James he doesn't know anything. That's hurtful."

"But it's true. He didn't know about John the Baptist or about the dove. He doesn't know any of the songs."

"That's because no one ever taught him. He never went to Primary before." If Rikki and her daughter's clothing had left any doubt about that, James's ignorance cleared it up. "You know that hooked rug Allia's been working on? How would you feel if everyone in this room knew how to do it, except you, because Allia hasn't taught you yet? And what if someone teased you or said you didn't know anything and all the kids laughed?" If there was one thing Lauren hated, it was her siblings laughing at her for not knowing something. She was the youngest, so that happened a lot.

"I wouldn't care. Rugs are stupid." But the line on Lauren's brow told me she was thinking about it.

"I mean it, Lauren. Be nice to James. Pretend Jesus is sitting right by you. How would you act?"

"Okay, Mom, I get it." A phrase she'd recently picked up from her brothers.

I let her go back to her seat next to James, who already had his hand in the air again. "What's resurrected?"

Once again the kids laughed, but this time Lauren rounded on the biggest offenders behind her. "Would you laugh at him if Jesus was sitting in that chair?"

Everyone looked at the chair.

"I don't see Jesus," James said. "Is He invisible?"

"Yes. He always is," Lauren said.

Mayra clapped her hands for attention. "I think it's time for another song, and then we'll talk a little about resurrection and what it means to all of you."

During the song, Lauren was leaning over and whispering to James. I was about to have another chat with her when I realized she was whispering the words so he could sing the song. That was my Lauren—bold and sassy one minute and tender and kind the next.

James didn't refuse her help or hold a grudge against her and the other children. He listened with an eagerness that tugged at my heart. I wondered if his mother knew how special he was—and how much in danger he was of losing that willingness if his curiosity wasn't met or if one day he was hurt too deeply.

Before the children went to class, Lauren slipped over to me. "Mom," she said in a whisper I could barely hear. "James can't read. Not even a little."

I tried not to show my dismay. "You read for him, then, okay, sweetie?"

"Okay." Lauren ran back to James and marched with him from the room behind their teacher.

Curiosity driving me, I slipped out to the hallway and down to the Relief Society room and peeked through the partially open doors. The sisters were singing a hymn, and Rikki was smack dab in the middle of the room, her bright skirt a radiant flower among the calmer pastels. Several of the old-timers sat next to her. Our ward was great about welcoming new people, so I wasn't surprised.

What I hadn't expected was the welling of jealousy in my chest. Jealousy that this woman could flounce into an LDS chapel wearing a tank top and a flowing red skirt without even a hint of embarrassment. Why I'd be jealous at such a ridiculous thing made me wonder if I was hiding something from myself. What?

A longing for something.

Frowning, I turned away, feeling as though I left something behind me in the room.

CHAPTER FIVE

Rikki

S trange how I could feel so at home in a place I hadn't set
foot in for twenty years. Everything was familiar, like a long-
owned piece of clothing I'd set aside and forgotten. Not that
everything was comfortable. I sensed disapproving stares, and I realized I was the only one who wasn't wearing sleeves. Oops. I'd
forgotten the Mormon dress code. Was it more strict than it used to
be? Probably not. I'd been a teen when I left, and teens had more
options and received more leniency. I hoped Kyle was getting along
okay in her classes.

In retrospect, I realized I should have come alone the first time
to check out the place and the clothing. If the truth be told, I'd
been a little nervous, not at meeting all these people but at seeing
Dante again. Having the children with me helped. I could be bold
and brave in front of them.

I hated the selfishness in me that insisted they come along.
Well, I'd make it up to them. Or at least add it to the pile of stuff I
would never have enough time to make up to them. Despair arced
through me, but I wrestled it down to that corner where I hid all

the dark things in my life. I didn't matter now. I could only try to do my best for my children.

Dante.

He'd aged well, as I'd always imagined he would. Tall, broad-shouldered but not overly muscular, his face carved with laugh lines that made me feel glad and angry all at once. Blond hair that hid any gray, compassionate and compelling brown eyes. Wisdom, yet still that little flavor of innocence that had surrounded him as a child, a determination to do good. It was this that had taken him away from me, and it was this I would rely upon now.

I'd met a few men like him over the years, men who'd been willing to take care of me, fight my battles, but they weren't Dante and had only reminded me of what I'd lost. My fault. I knew that now. None of them had been as handsome as Dante. No, men who looked like him were always snatched up and held tight. Instead, I'd gone for dark and dangerous. I knew it was wrong, but it made me feel something to be with them. For a long time that had been all that mattered.

Not now. Kyle and James were my entire existence. All that re-mained. All that would ever be. I would lose them too soon.

I'd pinpointed Dante's wife easily in sacrament meeting, sitting in the middle, one row back from us, near the young man who resembled the Dante I had known, except for the blue eyes he'd apparently inherited from his mother. Becca wasn't pretty or flashy, but she was attractive in a truly beautiful sense, with caring blue eyes that were quick to see every need. I knew her type. Many had tried to save me over the years, and I'd scorned them all. She was exactly the woman Dante needed. What I needed now.

Relief Society ended, and I had little idea what had been said. That was a problem I'd always had—my thoughts, the images in my head, always burned so brightly they took all my attention.

"So nice to have you back," Charlotte Gillman was saying to me. "Next time you might wear something a little warmer, though."

I grinned, unable to resist baiting her. "August is so hot in Utah."

"Oh, but the air conditioning makes it a little cold in here sometimes."

Not today. Today was stifling, and I was probably the only one the least bit comfortable. "I'll try to find something warmer," I said. "We've been living in California, you know. Mostly, I go around in my bikini top, it's so sweltering."

Her eyes widened, and I had to look away not to laugh aloud. She was too easy a target.

"Well, that won't work for church," she said quickly.

"Oh, right. I think I remember you teaching something like that in Sunday School." I hadn't really, but a flash of memory came to me now, making me feel woozy. Or maybe that was the new medication my doctor had given me for the migraines. "Well, see you next week."

I made my way past the throng of sisters and down to the foyer where an angry-looking Kyle was waiting, her arms folded over her chest like a protection. For a moment she was me, as I cowed under my father's biting words.

"Hi, sweetie," I said brightly. "How was it?"

She leaned into me. "Horrible. The boys are all snobby and preppy. Everyone is so, so . . ." Apparently, she didn't have enough words, or maybe she was trying not to swear.

"What about Allia? She seemed nice enough."

"I guess. But I'm not really supposed to be in her class since I don't turn fourteen until next year. I'm not ever going alone. Please tell me we don't have to come back here."

Her voice was loud enough that people I didn't recognize were paying attention to our conversation. "We'll talk about this later."

"I'm not coming back! And I'm not wearing this stupid skirt ever again."

There was nothing wrong with the skirt that I could see, though now that she mentioned it, some of the looks we were getting seemed to be directed at Kyle's clothing. Maybe the teens here weren't like I'd been. "We'll get you another skirt." I didn't know where the money would come from until I got paid. I didn't know how I'd even get Kyle anything new for school before it started this week. Maybe they had a secondhand store nearby. I wondered if I dared use the food money. I wasn't often hungry these days anyway.

"There you are." Becca appeared behind me, moving with an ease I envied. "Dante has to stay after for a bit, but he'll be home for dinner before he comes back for interviews."

"Interviews." I wrinkled my nose. "Weird to think of Dante doing interviews."

She laughed. "That's what he says. Come on, kids."

"Can James ride with us, Mom?" asked Becca's little girl, whose name I couldn't remember.

"He'll have to ask his mom."

"Please, Mom." James smiled up at me, and I nodded even though I didn't want to let him go. I didn't want to share my boy with anyone. Except I knew I'd have to. That was the plan.

"That's fine. We'll follow you in the truck."

Outside, Becca eyed my old blue Ford. "I didn't realize you still had all your things loaded."

"We haven't had time to unpack yet. There's a rented trailer, too, that I unhooked, but I want to get things cleaned at the house first before I bring anything in." I grinned. "I was thinking we'd spend tonight in our tree house."

"Yay!" James bounced up and down, and I felt the kind of happiness that came only from making him happy.

"You have a tree house?" Lauren asked. "I have a slide and fort that my daddy built, but they're not in a real tree. Mom, can I sleep in our fort? I bet the boys would sleep out with me."

"No." Becca rolled her eyes. "Go to the van. Now."

"Aw, Mom."

I laughed. Funny how alike kids were.

A brooding Kyle and I followed Becca's van to Dante's house, less than a block from the church. It wasn't at all like a house I'd expect him to build—brown stucco, dark gutters and trim around the eaves, lighter trim around the window, exactly spaced trees, a manicured lawn—but then maybe my dreams of our future house had never matched his. I'd have wanted bright colors, numerous pine trees in the yard even if their needles killed the lawn, a pond with ducks and goldfish. Thick brush that could house birds and squirrels or feed deer. A place you could let down your hair and have parties your neighbors couldn't see through the trees. I wouldn't at all be comfortable in Dante and Becca's house. My friends wouldn't be comfortable here—if I had any friends left. Only the flower beds, spilling over with a riot of colors and blossoms, were my kind of landscaping. It reminded me of something breaking free.

As I thought about it, I decided the impulsive boy who'd come to my window at night wouldn't have been comfortable here, either, but this place radiated the man he'd become, the man he'd started to be from the day he'd made the choice that had me packing my bags to leave Utah. It wasn't a bad house. In fact, it was welcoming, beautiful, organized. A place I wish I could be comfortable in. It might not be too late for my children to feel comfortable in a place like this.

"Nice house," Kyle said, her frown slipping for the first time since we left church.

I shrugged. "Yeah, but they don't have a tree house, and I bet you have to eat breakfast every morning. Pancakes, maybe."

She grimaced. "Or oatmeal. Then again, it could be bacon."

"Every morning? I don't think so. They'd all be fat."

Kyle's non-frown turned into a grin, and the next second we were laughing. Our glee didn't last long, though, and Kyle's sullen expression returned the minute she jumped down from the van. I made a silly face at her, but she didn't respond.

"Come on, come on, come on!" I heard Lauren shouting to James as we went into the garage where Becca had parked her van. "Come see my fort."

"Not until you change, Lauren Michelle Rushton."

"Mom!" Lauren whined, but she closed the garage door to the backyard and headed up a short flight of stairs into the house.

I'd never have gotten away with that. My kids would have had me out to the fort so fast and involved in some game that I'd never remember about Sunday clothes. Who cared about clothes? All they did was cover you, right?

The air-conditioned coolness in the house felt a little too cold against my bare arms. I wasn't accustomed to air conditioning. The swamp cooler cost too much at our old apartment to use for very long. I didn't know if my father had installed air conditioning in the old house, but even if he hadn't, we'd probably have only one uncomfortable month before fall and cooler weather. I didn't plan to be around here another summer.

We passed through a mudroom and into a kitchen. "Make yourselves comfortable," Becca said. "We do crock pot on Sundays, so all I have to make now is a salad. Allia!"

"Right here, Mom." The girl appeared from the hallway. "I know. I'll help."

"Cory, set the table."

He groaned. "Where's Travis? He's supposed to help. I always have to do everything."

"Everything?" Becca laughed. "Oh, so it was you who put

everything in the crock pot this morning—and who made the pancakes for breakfast."

I gave Kyle a smirk at the mention of pancakes, but she didn't respond. I knew she felt out of her comfort zone, but she would have to get over it—sooner rather than later. The thought threatened to dump depression over me like a bucketful of mud, but I'd made my choices, too, and Kyle and James would have to live with those choices.

"Anyway," Becca continued, "Travis had to stay for a meeting with the priests, so"—her eyes fell on Kyle—"maybe Kyle will help you set the table. Kyle?"

My daughter's eyes widened slightly at the request, but her sullen expression eased. "Sure," she said, which is kid talk for "If I have to."

"The dishes are over here," Cory said, smiling. His eyes were the brown color of Dante's, but otherwise he didn't look much like his father. "Come on, I'll show you."

The inside of Becca's house was a lot like the outside. Not elaborate but well-kept with a touch of elegance. The stainless steel refrigerator was what I liked best, not for the smooth finish or because the freezer was on the bottom, but because of the numerous drawings, papers, and magnets. It reminded me of the overflowing, riotous flower beds.

I smiled.

"I know it's a mess," Becca said, seeing my gaze, "but with so many of us running here and there, I have a tendency to forget if it's not on the fridge. And Lauren likes to draw pictures—a lot of pictures."

"I like it," I said. "Is there anything I can help with?"

"Oh, no. Allia and I'll take care of the salad. That's all we have left."

"Come outside with me, Mom." James took my hand. I glanced

at Becca, who tipped her head toward a sliding glass door that led to a wood patio outside the kitchen.

Lauren blew past us, still in a dress, but one that looked more casual. A play dress, maybe. "I'll show you."

We hurried after her. The heat felt oppressing after the coolness inside, but my arms were thankful for the change.

"I'm so lucky you guys came," Lauren said. "Mom never lets me come out here and play on Sunday. Only when my cousins come over, like when I got baptized. Race you!"

"Just try to beat me!" I said, going into a sprint.

Lauren laughed. "I'm going to win!"

She didn't because my legs were longer. Casting me a scowl, she climbed up a rope ladder into the little fort. James struggled up a short wall with handholds. I took the slide.

"Hey, you're not supposed to go up the slide," Lauren said.

"Is that what your mom says?" I asked.

"Yeah, but I do it anyway. She doesn't really care. Except if kids are trying to come down."

"Look at this slide, Mom!" James poked his head in a tunnel entrance. "Cool." He dived in and disappeared. Lauren tumbled after him.

I lay on the floor of the fort, my arms out. Maybe I could have been comfortable in a place like this after all. It was too late, of course. Too late for me—with Dante or without him. Too late for me with the children. But they wouldn't make the same choices I had. I would see to that.

I shut my eyes and floated, letting my brain drift. The children's voices and giggles lulled me into a peaceful state where I didn't have to worry about unpacking or working or anything else.

"Your mom's cool," I heard Lauren say from a long distance away. "I wish my mom would sleep outside with me."

"Yeah, my mom's the coolest."

I wasn't. Cool moms always took care of their children and didn't leave it to others. If I was really cool, James would be able to read. Somehow I would have been able to reach past his problems and help him.

I give him what I can.

Too bad that was so stinking little.

I shut my eyes tighter, and a tear squeezed out. I let myself drift into the darkness until the children's voices faded completely.

"Rikki?"

My eyes opened, and I rolled my head toward the sound of Dante's voice. It wasn't my Dante, though. It was an older man with Dante's eyes. Becca's Dante.

Not the dream, then.

I pushed myself to a seated position. "Oh, hi."

"Dinner's ready. You okay?"

"Sure." I smiled to show I was. "Nothing like driving all night to make you sleepy. Must have dozed off."

Dante laughed. "Since when did you start sleeping outside?"

"I never stopped. I always sleep wherever I want."

His face froze for a moment before relaxing. "I'd forgotten that."

Was he remembering the time I'd slept in the bushes outside his house? We'd made the small space up with blankets and a tarp so it wasn't too cold there even for November. By the time the snow fell, my dad was calm enough for me to go home again.

"Need help?" he asked, his voice gentle.

"I'm okay." No way I wanted him touching me. Not that I was still in love with him or anything—I was long past needing him that way. I just didn't want him to sense the truth. Not yet. He'd know soon enough.

"Well, everyone's waiting. The kids were calling for you, but I guess you didn't hear."

I gave a huge yawn and straightened my clothing before going down the slide, feeling only slightly dizzy. My skirt went up a bit, but Dante had predictably averted his eyes.

Everyone was at the dining room table off the kitchen. The dark wood of the table matched the baseboards and the frames of the family portraits on the wall. I didn't believe in pictures because the people they portrayed didn't exist. They changed and moved on before the picture was even printed.

My eyes went to Kyle so we could share a smirk, but she was gazing at Dante's oldest son, her expression completely entranced. Uh-oh. I hadn't counted on that. I didn't blame her, though. Travis was Dante in miniature except for the eyes—handsome, teasing, and polite even to a thirteen-year-old obviously nursing a crush. Could he ever be interested in Kyle, given the worlds that separated them? Either way, her infatuation might mess up my plan.

Back then Dante and I had come from the same world. Both of us had been poor, lost, alone, and without parental guidance except for the adults in the Church who had taken us in. We'd been stronger together; neither of us would have survived without the other. I wanted that stability for Kyle and James but not from Travis. He would never need her the way she would need someone.

"Shall we pray?" Dante looked at Becca, who nodded.

"It's Travis's turn."

The food was good, and Becca hadn't stretched the truth when she'd said there'd be enough. She and her daughters ate little, and while Kyle, James, and Travis more than made up for their lack of interest, there was still plenty left over. I wasn't hungry, but I forced down a few bites for politeness' sake. I was grateful the children would be fed and I wouldn't have to scrounge up anything more tonight.

"So, you mentioned a job?" Dante said before drinking the last of his milk.

I shrugged. "Nothing special. Data entry. It pays the bills."

A smile tugged at his lips. "I never figured you for data entry." He turned to Becca. "This is the girl who hated computer class so badly she kept dreaming up ways to put a virus on the school's computer. Unfortunately, all it ever got us was detention."

"Detention?" Allia's eyes went wide. She was beautiful with that dark hair and Dante's brown eyes.

"My fault, not your father's," I said. "He was trying to protect me." He'd always tried to protect me.

"Wow, Dad. Detention." Travis grabbed another roll.

"Don't get any bright ideas," Becca warned.

"I get detention all the time," Kyle took her eyes off Travis long enough to say.

I kicked her under the table. "Kyle."

"Well, I do. I'm not exactly ditching class all the time, either. Sometimes I'm taking care of James."

"I can take care of myself." James let his fork clatter to the table. "I do it all the time."

Kyle rolled her eyes. "Sure you do. Anyway, school's a waste of time."

Silence.

Becca looked at Dante and he looked back at her before his gaze shifted to me. Right, I was the parent of this renegade child, the one who should correct her before she corrupted their perfect children.

"Well, it is a waste sometimes," I began.

Travis barked a laugh. "You won't be able to sell that in this house." He stood, scooping up his dirty dishes and heading for the kitchen. "If I sluffed school, I'd be grounded for a week."

"A month," Allia corrected.

Nodding and grinning, Travis disappeared, and we heard the dishwasher opening and closing. Cory jumped up and followed his brother with his own dishes. I wondered how Becca got them to do that. Kyle and I had a tendency to use every dish in the house before we bought ourselves a couple of chocolate bars to help us tackle the mess.

I could feel the weight of Dante and Becca's stares. "I meant, well, like who cares where Benin is? Have you ever heard of that country before? I didn't before I had to do a report on it, and knowing about it never once helped me get a job." I didn't think I was doing myself any favors, but I had to continue. "I don't even remember where the, uh, country is, so it was a waste of time."

Kyle grinned at me, and I knew she'd noticed me swallow that cuss word. Probably Becca and Dante didn't miss it, either.

I needed another nap.

Dante cleared his throat and looked at Becca again. She stopped chewing her lip and said, "Well, I guess there are some things that have questionable value in a classroom, but for the most part school prepares you for the future. Regardless of what you are learning, doing hard things trains you for real life."

"Exactly," Dante said. "I learned more about finishing large projects when I did them than what the project was actually about. It's what gets me through those big projects now." He arose and leaned over to kiss Becca's cheek. "I'll be back as soon as I can, honey. I don't have many interviews."

"I'll see you later then." She handed him the suit jacket from the back of her chair.

The affection between them was obvious, and the years of living together had made their movements complementary, from the way they handled their children to the way she passed him the jacket.

If I'd stayed, would we be like that now? I didn't think so. I'd never have been happy living in one place. I liked to move. I liked to get out and discover. Live. But there had always been something of permanence in Dante. He was who he always would have been—without the crazy girl leading him astray. At least that's what I was depending on.

Dante picked up his dishes and started for the kitchen.

"Oh, I might not be here when you get home," Becca called to him. "I think I'll go over to Rikki's and see if I can help her." She looked at me. "If you don't mind."

"You don't need to do that," I said. "We're really fine."

"Mom, let her help." Kyle's mouth was stuffed with roll. "The place is a mess. It'll take hours and hours to clean."

Dante paused. "That reminds me, Rikki. I talked to someone who has a brother who works for the city. They'll come out to see about the water. Might have already stopped by. You'll have to of-ficially talk to the city on Monday, of course, but that'll get you through tonight."

Dante to the rescue. "Thank you," I said.

With a kiss blown to Lauren, he was gone. We heard the dish-washer open and a minute later the back door shut.

Becca sighed. "Okay, kids. Everyone help with the table."

They did, including Kyle, which surprised me. Even the boys reappeared to put away things like the butter and the milk. Becca smiled at each one, and I knew they did it because they loved her.

"They do it because they don't want to be grounded," she told me when they'd all disappeared again. "The girls would probably help anyway, but if I tell Dante the boys didn't help, they won't have access to electronics for the week."

I laughed. "So that's the secret." Becca was still busy working, setting things right. Did she ever take a break? I doubted it.

"Your house is so clean," Kyle said, rubbing her hand along the granite countertop. Her nostrils flared, and I knew she was tak-ing in the clean scent as well. A twinge of jealousy surprised me. I wanted a house like this for Kyle. I wanted the steadiness of this life for her.

I didn't know the hurt I'd feel going down this road. It would all be harder than I'd thought, and what I'd thought had been difficult enough.

"We'd better get going," I said.

Becca threw down her dish towel. "I'll need a few cleaning supplies. I was thinking we'd do enough to get you settled for the night, and then tomorrow we could get a few other women and finish up."

"Oh, no. I can do it. Kyle will help. She doesn't start school until Wednesday, and I don't work until then, either."

Becca's face flushed. "I'm afraid I already told Charlotte Gillman, and she said she'd get together a bunch of ladies you knew when you lived here. I volunteered to bring a snack."

Kyle laughed at the horror on my face. She knew how I hated to be a project. I didn't mind free food, hand-me-down clothing, or other tangible gifts, but my space, my freedom to live the way I wanted, was untouchable. I'd rather live in the dust for weeks.

"I can call and tell them no," Becca said. "But they really want to help. I think you should let them."

"We were going out to get some clothes tomorrow," I said. "Kyle needs a new church skirt."

Becca's eyes flashed to Allia, who was seated at the smaller kitchen table next to where Kyle was standing. A clear message, though I didn't know what it meant.

A wave of tiredness came over me. "Oh, let them come." I edged toward the door and my escape. One day I could endure, and it was only dust after all. They wouldn't be frowning over my friends because I didn't have any here, or about the way I dressed my children because they themselves should be in scroungy clothes for cleaning.

"We'll be over in a minute, then." Becca said. "I know where the house is. Would it be okay if Lauren came with me?"

"Sure. She and James can play together."

"They could stay here with Travis, if you want."

I should let James stay, but I wouldn't because he was mine for a bit longer. "No, he should help with his stuff."

"Okay, then." Becca walked me to the door.

"See ya in a bit," Allia said to Kyle.

Kyle lifted a hand. I saw her scan the hallway, as though searching for something, and I knew she was looking for Travis.

Out in the truck, I rested my head against the steering wheel for a few seconds as the children buckled their seat belts. "Are you okay, Mom?" James asked, nudging me.

"She drove practically all night," Kyle said in an old voice. "She's tired, and now that lady is going to come over and make us clean."

"I like that lady. She smells nice."

She did smell nice. I swallowed hard and started the engine. "Kyle, what was it with you and the goo-goo eyes?"

"What?"

"I saw you looking at Travis. Little old for you, I think. He's what, sixteen?"

"Who cares? He's hot."

I laughed. "Looks like his father did at that age."

"Were you in love with his father?" Kyle sounded dreamy.

"He was my best friend, and I needed him. We were too young for love." The truth. I had loved him, but I didn't know it was love until I'd given birth to Kyle. I hadn't slowed down enough to examine my emotions, and by then it was far too late. What I felt for Kyle wasn't exactly the same as what the girl I'd been once felt for Dante, but it had been every bit as strong. Maybe that was the way you felt about someone who'd saved your life.

"Well, Travis is off limits," I said.

"Why?"

"Because, that's all."

Kyle folded her arms in a pout.

"Please," I said more softly. "I have a good reason."

Kyle glared at me. "Whatever."

On that fine note I drove to my parents' house and parked in the driveway. She'd hate me more before this was over, but I hoped someday she'd forgive me.

CHAPTER SIX

Becca

Rikki's house had a lot of dust, and by the time I'd vacuumed the entire upstairs, I knew it'd need to be done again once we got the walls, shelves, and closets cleaned. But that could wait until tomorrow. Allia and Kyle were in the kitchen, supposedly washing out cupboards to hold the dishes Rikki had brought in from the truck, but mostly they were laughing and throwing wet rags at each other. James and Lauren had disappeared into a tree house out in the backyard, and in the back of my mind I worried it wasn't safe, even though Rikki assured me it was.

"I'll call Dante and have him and Travis help us bring in your mattresses and a few of your bigger boxes," I told Rikki as she came inside with another box. We could probably do it ourselves, but she was looking paler by the moment. She hadn't eaten much dinner. Poor thing needed sleep.

"Even if he brings in the mattresses, I'm going to have to sleep in the tree house, you know," Rikki said with a grin that lit up her face. "James has his heart set on it." She sat down on the living room floor against the wall. I knew her black tank top was probably dusty from the contact. On the bright side, the wall would be marginally less dusty.

The other reason, maybe the real reason, I wanted Dante to come over was so he could look at the tree house to make sure it was safe. Apparently, there was no man in Rikki's life at the moment to take care of that kind of thing.

"We'll also need to check the cord on that refrigerator. Hopefully it's not plugged into the outlet and that's why it's not working."

Rikki jumped up. "We can do that ourselves. I haven't needed a man for something like that for a long time." She paused. "In fact, I can just about pay someone to do anything I'd want a man for, and I don't have to cook his food or do his laundry." She winked, and I laughed.

I understood what she was saying. There'd been far too many times when Dante was busy at the church and I'd had to pay a handyman to install or repair something. I told myself I didn't mind, but lately I did mind all too much.

To our daughters' amusement, we pushed and pulled at the fridge until we exposed the back—and inches of dust. "Wait," I said, hurrying to the living room. "Let me get the vacuum."

"But I'll never see it," Rikki protested.

"Not good to breathe in, especially for kids." I approached with the wand outstretched. "Out of the way!"

The girls and Rikki giggled. "You worry too much," Rikki said. "But go ahead. Knock yourself out." She slumped down next to the cupboard to wait while I expunged the dust. I doubted it had been cleaned in a decade or more. The refrigerator was at least that old. Might even be the same one Rikki had used as a kid.

When I was finished, I shoved the plug into the outlet. "Okay. All ready. Help me, girls."

"Sorry, they went down to Kyle's room. With any luck, Allia

will clean it, because Kyle never cleans anything." Rikki stood, and together we pushed the fridge back into place.

I frowned. "Guess we should have checked to make sure it worked before we pushed it back."

"The moment of truth!" Rikki pulled open the door. "Well, the big light isn't working, but these smaller ones for the temperature are."

"The bulb's probably busted." Squeezing in next to her, I unscrewed it. Sure enough, the filament inside was broken.

"Better leave it in there until I'm ready to get a new one," Rikki said. "Otherwise I'll lose it."

"If you put it in your purse, you'll have it with you when you remember."

"I guess so. But I'll be honest with you, Becca, I don't really care about the light. I'll probably never replace it." She shrugged. "Lights aren't a priority with me." She leaned against the counter.

I palmed the light and stood next to her. "Lots of things more important, I suppose. Like the children and work—" I was wondering how to bring up James and the fact that he couldn't read. Did she even know? How could a mother not know?

"Dancing, seeing the sights, meeting new people. Sleeping under the stars." The longing in Rikki's voice made a hollow ache grow in my stomach.

"Must be hard coming back here after all these years."

She sighed. "It's something I never thought I'd do."

"Where else have you lived?"

"California, Mexico, Oregon, Nevada, Boston, New York, Florida. I even stayed a year in Spain. I went to Morocco while I lived there, and France. Boston was probably my favorite place, though."

"What'd you do in all those places?"

"I danced. I tended bar. Whatever I wanted. I was a secretary once and a waitress at a place where the tips were phenomenal. Sometimes I didn't work and just lived with . . . friends."

"What about the kids?"

"Well, it was easier before Kyle was born, but she went with me. Mostly."

"Mostly?" That worried me. James was too young to be without his mother, and Kyle needed more guidance than apparently even her mother could give her.

"I had to leave the kids with friends a few times." Rikki shrugged and pulled herself up to sit on the counter, which the girls had left more or less clean. "Only for a few months. Sometimes you can't take kids certain places, you know? But they're usually good to go wherever I need to be."

I couldn't imagine leaving my children with "friends" for a few months or even with Dante for that long alone. But I would have loved to see those places she talked about. And others. My sister and her husband went every year for a short vacation together. I knew because I watched her children for the week. I'd never felt I could leave mine that long, even if Dante's work, with its odd deadlines, had been more conducive to vacation. His extensive church callings only added to the scheduling problems, and we were lucky to take the kids somewhere for a few days each year.

"So you liked to dance," I said, pulling myself up to sit on the counter near her. The counters were in good condition, so they must have been replaced in the last decade. I wondered if Rikki was as bothered as I was about the peeling wallpaper in the living room and the old paint on the other walls, especially here in the kitchen where it looked like something had caught fire.

Dante didn't notice little things like peeling paper, faded curtains, or chipped wood, not even in our old house, but I had grown up in a house where things were replaced or repaired on a regular basis. My parents hadn't been exactly wealthy, but they had enough funds to make sure where we were living was inviting. I'd learned it had more to do with attention and time than actual dollars.

Rikki smiled. "Once dancing was my life. I did shows and clubs and plays. It was all a lot of fun. But I also wanted to sky dive and travel. I wanted to climb tall mountains. I wanted to swim in blue oceans. So I did."

"Good for you."

"Kyle's like I was." Rikki's freckles looked dark against her pale skin. "She's always dancing. I'll have to find a place for her to take lessons after we get settled."

"There are a few places in town. My girls used to take classes, but they didn't want to continue."

"What about you? What did you always want to do?" Rikki asked, crossing her legs. "Or what do you want to do now? Dante can be a little time-consuming, if I remember anything about him, and the kids are, too, I'm sure, but what do you do in your free time?"

"What free time?" I didn't think the occasional walk with my friends every morning after the kids went to school qualified. Every day I meant to do something different, but the house and yard needed work, there were errands to run, and the children were demanding. Even after school started, my time wouldn't be my own. Cory had experienced some difficulties last year in the fifth grade, and I'd decided to homeschool him for a time to see if we could turn things around. I'd done it with Travis in the seventh grade, and it had made a world of difference.

Rikki frowned. "Well, what would you do if you had free time?"

"I'd finish college."

"Ohhhhh," Rikki groaned. "Something fun, I mean."

"I loved college." I thought a moment. "Okay, how about this? I guess I've thought that someday when the children are older, I'd like to design landscapes. Flower beds, that sort of thing. I'd like to visit famous gardens and see what landscapers do and how it feels." I felt stupid telling her this. It almost seemed disloyal because I was happy with my life.

"Did you design your flower beds?"

I nodded. "Dante thinks they're rather much, but I love them."

Rikki's grin widened. "Why, Becca, I think we have something in common, because I love your flower beds, too. They're wild and voluptuous." She laughed. "They must be the real you."

I giggled and shook my head. "Thanks. I think." Why it should mean so much to me that this stranger should care about my flower beds, I didn't know or care. Come to think about it, I still didn't know who Rikki was to my husband.

"So," I prompted, "you and Dante grew up together."

Her smile faded. "We were sort of the odd kids out, you know. Everyone else had two parents, mostly members of your church."

"Your parents weren't members?" I knew Dante's mother had been an active Mormon, but she'd died before he started kindergarten. Dante's father had been an inactive member. The story went that he'd converted so Dante's mother would marry him and that his heart and faith and will to live had died when she did.

"My mother might have been once, but she didn't go after marrying my dad. He was . . ." Rikki paused, her face completely without expression. "He was the worst . . . Let's just say, I wasn't unhappy when I learned he'd died."

In that instant, my feelings toward Rikki shifted. Under my mask of politeness, I'd been jealous, worried, and a bit resentful, but in that moment, I glimpsed the lost little girl in her, the child who had still not come to terms with her own past or her choices. For the first time I felt pity and compassion. "I'm sorry," I said.

Rikki grinned. "It doesn't matter. I stopped caring about my father a long time ago. I only hope there is actually an afterlife so he gets what he deserves."

I thought of my own father, newly retired and serving a mission with my mother in Africa in the same country where he'd once been mission president. As some children of mission presidents were permitted to do, I'd served my own mission at eighteen during his time before I returned to the States to attend BYU, where I met Dante, also a freshly returned missionary. My dad was everything I could ever want in a father. I wondered what Rikki might be like if she'd been raised in a house like mine.

"Well, there is an afterlife," I told her. "Of that I'm sure."

Rikki's brow rose. "Oh? Do tell."

"Later, maybe." I rubbed my hands. "I feel like I've been bathing in dust."

"You have." She laughed. "You know what? That reminds me of the time I went to some mud hot springs in Florida. Lovely place. I'd never seen so many practically naked, wrinkled old people in my life. Made me vow never to wear a swimsuit in public after turning sixty-five."

"Thank goodness. I have a way to go then."

We laughed.

We laughed, but there was something odd between us, something I couldn't pinpoint. Not so much in what we said, but in the way Rikki studied me when she thought I wasn't looking.

CHAPTER SEVEN

Dante

The sound of children's voices drew me around to the back of Rikki's house. I let myself follow them instead of going inside where I knew from her text that Becca was cleaning. Old habits die hard.

So odd to feel the old reluctance at even the idea of going to the front door. How many times had I first checked to make sure Rikki's father wasn't around? He hadn't liked me. He hadn't liked any of Rikki's friends. As far as I knew, I was the only one who hadn't let that stop me.

"Whoa," I called. James was hanging out of a wobbly window in the tree house that threatened at any moment to dump him onto the hard, weed-covered ground below.

"Hi!" James waved.

"Daddy!" Lauren appeared in the doorway. "This is a cool house, but it has lots of nails, and I scraped myself." She showed me her hand.

Glad that I'd left my tie and jacket in my car, I climbed up the wood rails, some half grown into the old tree and several loose or threatening to fall apart. I'd have to assign Rikki a home teacher who knew about being a handyman.

Unless she had a husband. I realized I'd forgotten to ask. After all, she had children, and that likely meant she had someone in her life. Or had in the past.

The tree house was fairly large inside but not in good repair. A pink toolbox lay open in the middle of the room. Someone had obviously tried to fix a tilting wall and the wobbly window, but it was a haphazard job. What I needed was more wood and a saw. The broken pieces of that shelf might serve for the time being.

I reached for the shelf, tugging at it to remove it the rest of the way. "Lauren, hand me the hammer in that box."

"You need nails, too?"

"Yes, please."

"I got some big ones." James pulled a handful from his pocket. "Can I help? That's okay if you say no. But I can help if you want me to."

The need in his voice called to me. "Sure, James."

"Me, too, Daddy?" Lauren extended the hammer.

"Sure. Both of you can help." It would take longer with their help, but that was the point of a tree house. It reminded me of when the children were little and Becca had insisted they take their own plates to the dishwasher after each meal. I'd argued that it was faster for us to do it, but in the long run she'd been right.

It was starting to grow dark when I was finally satisfied that the window and wall were secure. I climbed down the ladder and this time made it to the front door, which, to my surprise, was ajar. I pushed it open. "Hello?"

"In the kitchen," Becca called.

I followed the laughter into the kitchen. Rikki and Becca were seated on the counter looking younger than their years. Travis slumped in a chair with a bored expression on his face, and Cory perched on another nearby. "Are we going to move the beds or what?" Travis asked.

Becca hopped off the counter and gave me a kiss. I felt Rikki's gaze, and my arm tightened around my wife.

"Travis said your car was here," Becca said. "I called him to help. I'd wondered where you were."

"I heard the kids around back." I met Rikki's gaze. "That tree house isn't as sturdy as it should be."

With a small, worried sound, Becca started for the door, but I stopped her. "Don't worry. I fixed it—at least temporarily. Someone left a tool box out there with a hammer and some nails. The kids aren't in any immediate danger."

"I should have checked."

Rikki waved a hand in dismissal. "It was fine. I put a whole bunch of nails in earlier."

I grinned. "That explains the pink toolbox. But it was still kind of wobbly."

"You've always been such a worrywart," Rikki said with a laugh. "Guess that hasn't changed."

Silence fell over the kitchen, and I wondered if it was because she'd spoken with such familiarity. Becca caught my gaze. I briefly wondered how I'd feel if someone from Becca's past appeared out of nowhere. I doubted I would have invited him to dinner and helped him clean his house. Becca was incredible.

"So where are these beds?"

Rikki slid off the counter, hardly more than a scrap of a thing. I'd have thought the years would have put a few pounds on her, since both her parents had been a healthy size, but apparently not. "Out in the trailer. I'll show you."

I decided to set up the bed frames as well, since it'd have to be done anyway. The Savior believed in service, even on a Sunday, and so did I. Becca and Rikki helped Travis and me screw the metal frames to the wooden headboards. The furniture was battered, and the ease with which Rikki threw the pieces together made me suspect she'd done this before, and maybe even by herself, though she wouldn't have been able to carry in the headboard alone—or the queen mattress.

"Is there any other big furniture?" I asked when we'd finished.

"A couple of dressers. Everything else is in boxes.".

"No appliances?"

"Nope. We'll have to use the laundromat for a while."

"Come on, Travis." We carried in the dressers, while Becca, Rikki, and Cory stacked boxes in the living room. Though Rikki had only meager belongings, I was beginning to wish I'd invited a few neighbors to help. Thankfully, Allia and Kyle appeared from wherever they'd been, and we put them to work on the boxes as well, emptying the rest of the trailer in good time.

"There," I said. "Now you won't be stuck with bringing all that in."

Rikki sat on a box, which caved a bit under her weight. "It'll save me money to get that rental trailer back tomorrow. I really appreciate it."

"We'd better let you get some sleep." Becca caught my eye pointedly, and I knew she could see the bags under Rikki's eyes. She looked about dead on her feet.

"Come on, kids," I said.

"I'm taking off." This from Travis, who'd driven over on his own.

As I headed to my car, the girls piled in the van with Becca while Rikki and Kyle watched us from the door. I felt uncomfortable, but I couldn't pinpoint why.

"That girl, Kyle, is a bit strange," Allia said as we entered our own house a few minutes later.

"Strange how?" Becca asked.

"Well, first of all her clothes are, well, kind of slutty, and she has everything pierced—her nose, her belly button. She says her mom made her take off the nose ring, but she says she's going to keep putting it in at night so the hole won't close. She showed it to me, and it looks so funny, like the ring Brother Warner put in the nose of one of his problem cows to control her. We went there for Young Women, and I thought it was really sad."

"You should have told her she looked like a cow," Cory joked.

"Ah, no," Becca said. "You both need to be nice to her."

Cory shivered. "She gives me the creeps. She's small, but she's old-looking, too."

"She's thirteen," Allia said. "And I don't think she's the kind of person you want me to hang out with. She's more boy crazy than Cydnee."

"She doesn't seem that bad," Travis said. "I mean, yeah, too much makeup, but she seems nice enough."

I hadn't missed her longing glances at him—I looked for those things in my role as protector of the ward youth. Maybe he hadn't missed it either.

"Well, I love James," Lauren says. "He's my best friend now."

"That's only because he does everything you say." Travis bopped her on the head. "Don't think we didn't see you ordering him around like a slave."

"He likes to do what I say," Lauren protested. "He likes me."

"Okay, that's enough," I said, clapping my hands to cut off the discussion. "We'll discuss this tomorrow in family night. Everyone come for prayer." Exhaustion always fell over me on Sunday nights, and the extra effort at Rikki's had added to the weight. Becca and I would have to discuss Kyle at length and pray about her influence before we decided what, if anything, we should do regarding her possible friendship with Allia.

Later, after the children were in bed, I changed into my pajamas with a sigh of relief and headed to the bathroom connected to our bedroom to brush my teeth.

"She seems happy to be back home," Becca said, pulling down the blankets on the bed.

She was talking about Rikki, and I knew I still had some explaining to do before I could rest. Becca was going to hear about it sooner or later, and I'd rather it came from me. I set down my toothbrush and turned in the doorway. "She may act all bright and happy, but she's in a lot of pain, and she's angry."

Becca arched a brow. "Is that some sort of bishopy wisdom, or just you?"

"Not inspiration. I knew Rikki for almost half my life, and I can see she's hurting. I wonder why she's really here. It's the last place I'd expect her to be."

"I think you're right." Becca sat on the bed. "She's sending out some weird vibes."

"She didn't say anything when you were there today? You two looked pretty cozy in the kitchen."

"The only thing I learned is that she's lived all over and that sometimes she's left her children for extended periods with friends. Not sure why. She wasn't specific. She's an interesting person, though, I'll give you that. Why do you think she's really here?"

"Maybe she has regrets. She missed the funerals of both her parents. Perhaps she's come to say goodbye."

Becca's lips curved in the hint of a frown. "She didn't seem to have any love lost for her dad."

"He wasn't an easy man, but she loved her mother. Unfortunately, her mother wasn't very strong." What I meant was that Rikki's mother hadn't kept her husband from emotionally abusing their daughter, but that wasn't my story to tell, not even to Becca. Not now. "But Rikki was never one to worry about the past, what she couldn't change. Maybe she's trying to turn over a new leaf. After all, she was in church today."

My wife was silent for a long moment and then asked, "What was she to you?"

I studied her in the light coming through our bathroom. I noticed the dusky shadows under her eyes, the faint lines at the corners. The curve of her cheek. Her eyelashes. I wished I didn't have to answer, but I'd held this back from her for long enough. Not purposefully but because I hadn't thought it mattered. With Rikki back in town,—for whatever reason—she needed to know.

"I told you we grew up together, and that's true, but before my mission, Rikki and I were engaged. I was torn between going on a mission and staying home to marry her, but the bishop and my father"—I swallowed hard—"urged me to do my duty."

"Your father?" The surprise was evident in her voice.

Yes, my inactive father, whom I'd always thought joined the Church only because of my mother. We'd been sitting across from each other in our small kitchen, the stark light from the afternoon sun shining onto the table through the open window. He'd looked at me with solemn eyes, with the face I'd rarely seen laugh. "There're a lot of choices in life, son, and this one's going to affect you forever. You could stay and marry Rikki, but if you do that, you'll always regret it. I know it might not seem like that to you now, but it's true, and believe me, regret is not the way to live. I've lived an entire life of regret. I haven't been a good father to you, but if you ever choose to listen to me, I hope you'll do it now. You don't want to spend the rest of your life living in the past. You've taken care of Rikki long enough. She can fight her own battles now. If she's right for you, she'll know how much this means to you, and she'll wait. You need to stop depending on her and make your own choices."

My inactive father hadn't been there my entire life, except as a shadow, a caretaker who'd given me shelter and clothes and food but otherwise had been missing. For that moment he'd been real. It's how I remembered him now. I could never repay his advice of that day.

"Yes, my father," I answered Becca slowly. "He knew I had a testimony and that I wouldn't be happy if I denied it, so in the end, I chose a mission. Rikki wasn't excited about my choice. She left."

"She broke up with you?"

"It wasn't a surprise. I knew what the choice meant when I made it."

"You chose the Lord." She said it firmly, almost proudly. Her confidence vanished a second later when she whispered, "Do you ever regret it?"

Back then I thought I would. I'd feared my father was letting me down one more time.

Memories assaulted me, and for a moment I felt drawn back into a past that only I could see. "I'll miss you," I'd told Rikki when she'd left. She'd been my best friend since kindergarten, and I wasn't sure I could go on without her. What kind of missionary could I be without her support?

"Of course you will." Her eyes flashed a blue promise. "You'll miss me every single day, and you'll regret everything. But I won't miss you, Dante. I promise, I won't. I'll be having too much fun."

I believed her, and that hurt more than anything. I was sure at that moment I'd made the wrong choice.

Yet in the end, it was Rikki who was wrong. I missed her those first months, but afterward I'd been too swept up in the sweetness of teaching the gospel, and only when I'd see someone who looked like her would the old pain return. Not too often. Never after meeting Becca. Until today I hadn't realized there was still a part of me that missed Rikki. A part of me that clung to childhood and had no place in my future.

Tears started in my eyes, tears I hoped Becca didn't see. "That choice brought me you." I pulled her into my arms, where she fit as if she were a vital part of me. "Becca, you're the best thing that has ever happened in my life. I absolutely don't regret my choice then or any choice since that brought you to me."

"Good answer, mister." She snuggled her face into my neck, and quite another emotion rippled through my body, pushing away the exhaustion. I tilted her face to mine, kissing her slowly and then with more passion.

Time stopped.

CHAPTER EIGHT

Rikki

I lay in the tree house so I could see the stars, wishing I could hold on to this moment forever, with my children lying close to me, their small bodies warm against my sides. Innocent, protected, and all mine.

I'd slept at least a couple hours, judging by the ache in my bones from the hard floor, but despite my seemingly permanent exhaustion, I couldn't sleep. I never could sleep through the night anymore.

Dante a bishop. It was hard to believe, and yet on the other hand, it wasn't. Even when we were children, he'd taken the religion thing more seriously than I had. Maybe because his mother had drilled it into him as a small child. Or maybe he'd been born that way. Maybe he'd found a peace that eluded me. I'd known people who'd found peace, and they'd come from all backgrounds and religions. I didn't know what that meant for me. What was truth but an extension of ourselves?

I hadn't known about his being the bishop of the ward, though I had searched him out on the Internet and found out where he lived, so I knew which ward to attend. I wasn't surprised to find him back here. He liked the comfortable, the familiar.

What I hadn't suspected was that I'd like it, too. These people had known me as a child of promise, regardless of my questionable background. They didn't know where I'd been, that I hadn't been married to the fathers of my children, or that I'd been married twice, once six months after Dante left on his mission, and once when Kyle was five. Neither experience had been enjoyable.

I didn't regret anything. All the experiences in my life added up to the person I'd become, to the people my children were becoming. To regret meant to wish them away.

What I regretted was the future.

I closed my eyes and tried to hold back the sobs, as tears rolled from my eyes and down into my hair.

It was okay, this nightly ritual, because it helped me be strong for the children during the day.

Kyle's white cheek was illuminated by the moonlight. My little girl, trying so hard to grow up. My fault in a big way, but I was hoping to rectify that. If only she hadn't started falling for Travis.

If I'd married Dante, our son could have looked like Travis, with my blue eyes and Dante's good looks and strong build. He might have been Kyle's sibling instead of Allia's.

Imagining did not mean regret. It was simply the path not taken.

Becca and Dante were good people, which meant Dante hadn't changed all that much from the boy I'd known. If their inviting us to dinner and helping us move in wasn't enough, the box of clothing Becca brought had proven it further.

"Some of Allia's outgrown things," she'd said casually. "Kyle seems to be a size or two smaller than Allia, so if she can use them, we'd love for her to have them. They're all pretty much in style, and they probably won't be by the time Lauren could wear them. Oh, and Allia's discreet. Kyle doesn't have to worry about her saying anything to embarrass her."

I'd snorted. "If Kyle were embarrassed at hand-me-downs, she'd be going around naked." That had startled Becca. "What I mean is," I added, "thanks. I'll show them to her later." At least now I understood the look between mother and daughter at their house. They either weren't impressed with Kyle's clothing at church or suspected how poor we were. Either way, I didn't mind. For now I wouldn't tell Kyle where the clothes came from. She didn't need to know her benefactress was so close.

Or that I intended for her to get a lot closer to the Rushtons.

Stifling the little hole that thought carved in my heart, I started making plans.

Becca was good. Maybe too good, though, because I'd felt the ache in her voice when she said she'd wanted to visit famous gardens and *feel* them. She needed to do that, at least a little, so I'd have to help her with that. Before she could help me. She needed to have a release that wasn't wrapped up in Dante and the children.

So loosening up Becca would be my first goal. And Dante? Well, I wasn't sure what was going on with him, but couldn't he see that Becca was suffocating under all she had to do? Not exactly because of him and the children but because she didn't put herself on any of her to-do lists. And Travis. I'd seen the way the boy hungered for his father's attention. Very much the way Dante had hungered for his father's. Maybe that's why I recognized it when neither Becca or Dante seemed to notice. Travis was heading for trouble. I knew that in the same way I knew Kyle was heading down a similar road. I couldn't save her alone. I didn't even know how to save her. She was slipping toward the same kind of hole I'd fallen into after leaving Dante, and I hadn't been able to save myself. But Travis, that was different. I might be able to help there. Not for him or for Dante but for my children.

I'm nothing if not selfish.

I sighed. When did things become so complicated? When I was young, all I had to worry about was staying out of my dad's way, making it through school, and planning what Dante and I would do for the weekend. I'd thought that was huge then, but what I now faced every day was off any scale I'd ever known.

A shift in Kyle's breathing told me she was awake before she spoke. Had she heard me crying?

"Mom?"

"Yes, baby?"

"I'm not going to fit in, you know. I don't belong here."

"You and Allia seemed to get along okay."

"Are you kidding? Did you see the way she dresses? I'm a thrift store reject compared to her. She's so beautiful. I could never look like that."

"You're beautiful, too, Kyle. In a different way. That's all."

"She's not gonna want to hang out with me. Girls like her never do."

"She's not like other girls."

Kyle rose up on her elbow. "Why?"

"She's Dante's daughter. He was my friend."

"So because of that he'll make her be my friend?" Kyle snorted. "That's not going to happen."

I couldn't tell her the truth, so I said, "Can't you just wait and see?"

"There's something you're not telling me. I want to know what we're doing here. You hate data entry. You liked that restaurant you worked in."

I wasn't ready to have this conversation. "I needed a change. We all did." I put my arm around her and stroked her hair until she stopped resisting and snuggled closer.

"Take it a day at a time for now, okay? I promise it will all make sense later."

She sniffed. "Okay. I guess. But I'm going to need some new clothes if you're gonna keep dragging me to that awful church."

"I know."

"The only thing good about it is that Travis will be there."

"In this culture, you can't date until you're sixteen. So I'd look for someone closer to your own age."

"Sixteen! That's forever away. Are they like hillbillies or something? Or those religious fanatics like on TV?"

I smiled. My daughter was creative, I'd give her that. "Not exactly."

"Well, I don't care. I like him."

I didn't reply. No use making things worse. The more I disagreed, the tighter she'd hold to her crush.

I stroked her hair long after she drifted off to silence.

•   •   •

I took my pills from my purse and gulped them down at the sink. I was having to take the ones for my headaches more often now. I hated how they made me dependent, how they changed my senses. Stupid to think that once I'd taken similar pills for recreation. Another pill from a different bottle followed the first, this one smaller but every bit as necessary.

Kyle squealed from across the kitchen as she looked in the box of clothes Becca had left. "These are cute. I mean, some are a little boring, but I could put these tops with some cooler jeans or shorts, and these jeans would look good with my white-and-red-striped tank, don't you think?"

"I think you'll look great in all of it."

Kyle held up a dress and frowned.

"Maybe not that." The dress had a nice blue plaid skirt, but the ruffle around the neck of the attached white blouse looked decidedly juvenile. "Unless we cut off the skirt and put in elastic."

"Could you? I like the plaid."

I laughed. "I think I had one just like it when I was your age. It shouldn't be too hard to make it work. I'll need to buy elastic, though, and I'm not sure we have thread that color."

Kyle came around the counter and hugged me. "You're the best."

If I had money, I'd never attempt any sewing, not even a simple hem by hand. I was lucky I even knew how to use a needle.

Wait. I remembered learning to sew. It had been in the Mia Maid class where we'd made pajamas and frilly aprons. I'd worn out the pajamas, but I still had the apron somewhere. I'd saved it in a box, always planning to give it to Kyle one day along with some other mementos. I shouldn't wait too much longer.

"Mom, someone's at the door." Kyle's voice penetrated my thoughts. "I bet it's those women from church that Allia's mom said were coming."

I put on a cheerful face. "Good. Because you haven't been much help with unpacking." In fact, we hadn't made any headway, except for the small TV James had plugged in all by himself. That morning I'd come in from the tree house, eaten a bit with the kids, run to city hall to see about the water, stopped by the grocery store, and then fallen on my bed and slept for a few more hours. Driving had wiped me out more than I expected, and I had to work in two days.

I pointed to the box of hand-me-downs. "Why don't you take those downstairs, and I'll get the door?" She hadn't questioned me too closely about where the clothes had come from, and I decided not to tell her. If Allia showed up with her mother today, I hoped she'd keep quiet.

When I opened the door, Becca, Allia, and Lauren stood on the porch, and behind them stood three other women from the ward. I recognized Charlotte Gillman with her hooked nose and sagging cheeks and Debra Lundgren with the bright patches of blush, both of whom had introduced themselves the day before. The other woman I'd also seen yesterday but I hadn't caught her name and she didn't seem familiar. All the women were carrying cleaning supplies and containers filled with food. I didn't believe in God anymore, but at the sight of the food, I wanted to.

As I said, I'm nothing if not selfish.

"Hi," Becca said. "We're all here, ready to go."

Was it my imagination, or was she a bit cooler toward me today? "Come on in. Thanks for coming." Very gracious of me since I didn't want them here. Well, except for the food.

"You probably know everyone," Charlotte said, "but let me make the introductions just in case. It's been a long twenty-odd years. I'm Charlotte Gillman, one of your old Sunday School teachers, as I told you yesterday. This is Debra Lundgren, who was the Young Women's president during your time but who is now the first counselor in the Relief Society." Debra still had poofy, shoulder-length brown hair, obviously dyed. Except for a few lines on her face, she didn't look much different from the way she'd looked twenty years ago. Her makeup was perfectly applied but dated. Practically no one outside the modeling circuit wore blush these days. I guessed both women to be in their early sixties.

"And I'm Teri Bunk," said the woman I hadn't recognized. She had short gray hair tightly curled under, a deeply lined face, pale sunken cheeks, and huge green eyes covered by tiny round glasses. Late sixties or early seventies. "I taught you and Dante in Primary. Such a handful you were. Always with the questions."

"Oh, yes, I remember you now." She'd been thin even then, but her face had been much softer and less lined. The green eyes were the same, with the exact intenseness as when she'd borne her testimony about some principle or another. "Can I carry that for you?" I gestured toward the casserole dish she carried with hot pads.

"No, no. That's fine. I remember where the kitchen is. I used to be your mother's visiting teacher, you know."

I hadn't known that, but she must have come when I was in school in order to avoid running into my dad. Mother would have never allowed him to know that anyone from the Church had been in our house. She might even have kept it from me, in case I let it slip, just as I'd never told her about going to Primary.

Or maybe she knew all along. Sister Bunk would have likely mentioned me. I frowned. That didn't go with my memories of my mother. We never talked about the Church. I didn't know why.

I'd never know.

No looking back, I reminded myself.

"Well," Charlotte said after everyone set the food dishes on the counter, in the oven, or in the fridge. "Where do you want us to start?"

I looked around a bit helplessly. Everything needed attention.

"The walls," Becca said for me. "And probably the ceilings, especially the corners. I brought my vacuum with a long extension, so Allia and I can do those and the tops of the walls. We also brought a ladder, if we need it."

"Good thing you're here, dear," Teri said to Allia. "I may be a spry old lady, but I don't think I'm up to vacuuming ceilings."

"I've never even heard of anyone cleaning a ceiling," I said.

Charlotte took a bucket to the sink and began filling it. "I do it with a damp mop. Once a year or so. Not all of it. Mostly to get the cobwebs."

"Mom," Lauren said to Becca, "James wants to go outside to the tree house. Can I go, too?"

I marveled that she asked. I mean, it was in the backyard. Why did she need permission? I made James ask only if he was going farther than our neighborhood.

"Sure, sweetheart. Be careful."

"Have fun," I added. Hey, you're only young once.

"Here," Becca said, shoving something into my hand. "A light for your fridge."

"Thanks." I had to work to swallow the sudden lump in my throat.

They fell to work, my own little cleaning crew. We had to open the windows because of the dust and redo everything several times. Finally, the dust quit flying, and we began to unpack the boxes in the living room. Those went fast simply because I didn't have much. I'd moved too many times to collect many household items, and I didn't have money to buy again for each new apartment. We kept what we really needed and did without the rest. In fact, Kyle had more boxes for her room than James and I had for our rooms combined, but she wouldn't let anyone open them. I wasn't sure what was inside.

When the women were finished with all but a half dozen boxes of things I didn't know where to put yet, three hours had gone by and it looked as though I'd lived in the house for months. Well, except that it was clean.

Was I grateful? Yes. But I didn't like feeling that gratitude. I didn't want to be indebted to anyone, even though I knew they would have done it for any stranger.

Would I have?

Once, maybe. But after a lifetime of being used and abused, I'd grown a bit tough inside. I wasn't prepared for the tenderness I felt for these women. I didn't want to feel it.

"Food time!" boomed Charlotte. Though she'd lost a lot of weight since my Sunday School days, she still talked in the theatrical voice that had matched her former bosomy figure. I wondered what had happened to her. Fad diet, an illness, an operation?

Becca brought out paper plates, cups, and utensils from somewhere, we said a prayer, and the women began dishing up. Becca took plates outside for James and Lauren. I hadn't been imagining her coolness, though I probably wouldn't have noticed a difference if it had not been for our warm, laughing exchange on the counter yesterday. We'd been almost friends. Today she was reserved and wary.

Dante told her about our being engaged, I thought. I wasn't proud of deserting him, but he'd done it first. What did it all matter to Becca? Twenty years had gone by, and while I'd chosen Utah in part because he was here, I didn't entertain any thought of reviving our childhood romance. Besides, even if I had, I couldn't offer him even the tiniest part of what Becca could give him. For that alone I was glad I'd left. Glad he'd left.

At least that's what I told myself. There is always that sliver of doubt. Of wondering. But it didn't control me. I'd done what I'd wanted for most of my adult life, and if I'd stayed in Utah, I would certainly have far more to wonder about than what would have happened if I'd stayed.

"Nothing like a bit of work to give a woman an appetite," Debra said, her face flushed beneath the rouge.

"Not me," mourned Teri. "I never feel hungry much anymore. I suppose that's my body's way of shutting down. Getting ready to pass on."

Charlotte clicked her tongue. "Oh, shush, now. You're not dying. Not any time soon. Besides, so what if you do? Your husband and parents will be excited to see you. And your sister."

"Well, it's just, I haven't done everything I wanted," Teri said.

Debra blinked. "Like what?"

"Like skydiving. I never got to do that."

I laughed. This was too funny. Never in a million years did I think I'd be in my parents' kitchen talking with three older ladies about skydiving and dying in the same breath. "You ought to do it," I urged. "I would if I were you."

"Ridiculous!" Charlotte said. "She'll break all her bones."

"Maybe, but she'll know what it's like to go skydiving. It's not as if she can do it after she's dead."

"Well, we don't exactly know that," said Debra. "Maybe heaven has something better than skydiving."

"Star diving?" suggested Teri, lifting her wrinkled hands and arcing them as though diving into water. Charlotte laughed, and the others joined her.

Whatever they wanted to believe was fine with me, but I still thought Teri should do it now and not wait for a future that might not exist. That probably didn't exist. I didn't think there were any laws against seventy-year-old women going skydiving.

Becca came back in then and called down the stairs to where Kyle and Allia had disappeared. "Girls, we're eating!"

Leave it to her to think of telling them. I'd always been of the opinion that children would eat when they're hungry and didn't need prodding. If they ate lying down, in the car, or in a bathtub at odd hours, that was okay. How did Becca stand on the issue? Did she force kids to the table at each mealtime? Did she hover over them to make sure they ate their peas?

If she did, maybe that wasn't a bad thing.

Kyle and Allia came up the stairs. "Can we go shopping now?" Allia asked Becca.

"Sure. After we eat."

Kyle cast me a pleading look, but I wasn't about to invite myself along. I didn't have the kind of money they did. Better to visit the second-hand stores ourselves. I wondered if Allia had seen what was in all of Kyle's boxes.

The other women were already finishing. "You keep the rest of this casserole," Teri said. "I won't be able to eat it all myself. Bring the pan to Relief Society when you're finished."

"Thanks." My kids weren't picky, and the chicken and broccoli casserole was rather good.

"We'll leave everything." Charlotte put an arm around me. "That way you won't have to worry about cooking for a few days. We're so glad you're back, Rikki."

"That's right. Call us if you need us," Debra added. "I brought you a ward list and highlighted our names. I didn't see a phone here, though."

"I have a cell phone." It was the one luxury I allowed myself.

"What's the number?"

"It's probably long distance," Teri put in as all the women jotted down the number. "You should ask for a local number, so those of us who don't have cell phones can get a hold of you."

"Good idea." I wouldn't be around long enough to need the change, but I couldn't tell her that now. Besides, just because I'd gone to church yesterday didn't mean I wanted to get all cozy with these ladies.

"I'll tell Lauren we're going," Allia said, taking her plate of casserole and vegetables with her to the kitchen door.

"She could stay, if you wanted," I offered. "They play so well together."

Becca shook her head. "I wouldn't dream of intruding. You have enough to deal with getting settled. Besides," she added as I opened my mouth to protest, "I need to get her a few more things for school."

Decision rendered, Allia moved out the door but without letting the old screen bang shut behind her as I always had. Kyle stared after her for a moment and then clomped down the stairs, taking nothing but a roll and a handful of chips with her. Becca didn't say anything about her leaving without real food, and I almost wished she had.

I walked the ladies to the door. I could hear Becca in the kitchen putting things away. As I returned to the kitchen, she hung the dish towel on the oven handle, picked up her vacuum, and started to move past me.

"Thanks," I said.

She shrugged. "They really enjoyed themselves. Thank you for letting them come."

Becca was polite, I'd give her that.

"Look," I said. "Is something wrong?"

Becca bit her lip. Her face seemed pale against the shiny length of dark hair that seemed almost black in the sparse light coming through the small windows. "I'm just thinking that you don't seem the type to be happy in this town among these people." She dropped her eyes before continuing. "I know about you and Dante, and I'm wondering if why you're here has something to do with my husband."

There. It was out. I'd hoped not to challenge her this way.

"Don't worry one more minute about that, Becca. I promise I don't want anything from Dante, except as a friend," I said. "And a bishop." That ought to be okay, given her faith.

Her lips quirked in a smile that didn't reach her eyes. "Why do I get the feeling you don't believe in God?"

"I don't know about that, but I do know that growing up Mormon is the safest thing I've seen for kids."

"God does exist, Rikki, and the proof is all around if you open your eyes." She crossed to the door. "I'll see you on Sunday."

I nodded, but she couldn't see me, so I wasn't surprised when she looked around at my face to check my expression. Whatever she saw made her brow furrow.

I watched her drive away with her daughters. I wanted to hate her, but her largeness of spirit prevented that. She'd given me exactly what I needed, though she couldn't possibly know I'd needed it. I hadn't known it myself. Much as I dreaded coming here, I felt a belonging I couldn't deny. I didn't know if it was Mormonism, or the people, or Dante, or even Becca, but I was supposed to be here—and not only because there was no place left to go.

Or maybe home was simply where you landed when you reached the end of the line.

CHAPTER NINE

Kyle

I knew Allia had only come because of her mother. I wanted to hate her for that, but she was so nice that I couldn't find anything really to hate her for. She didn't laugh at my band pictures that I tacked to the wall after we'd run a wet rag over them, or tell me my shorts and halter top were inappropriate, though I could tell from how her eyes widened that she didn't approve. She admired my new hand-me-downs in the box and agreed that the plaid dress would make a better skirt.

"You could cut off the trim on the sleeves and make a scrunchy," she said. "We learned how in Mutual."

"Mutual?"

"That's where we teenagers meet at the church to do activities during the week. It's a lot of fun. You should come. We aren't having it this week because of school starting, but next week we're doing baptisms for the dead, and the week after that we're going to Sister Flemming's to learn how to make her special chili and bread sticks. It's on Tuesdays."

"Cooking?" I grimaced, deciding not to get into how weird being baptized for dead people was. One of the teachers had explained the process on Sunday, but the only thing I really understood was that it wasn't something I could do since I wasn't a member of their church. Fine by me. "You think that's fun?"

"I love Mutual. It's always fun. We end up laughing a lot. I like learning about cooking because then Mom lets me do it at home."

"My mom doesn't cook much. She's mostly working." Or sleeping, but I didn't want to say that. Mom seemed more and more depressed lately, and I wasn't sure what was wrong. At first I thought it was because she'd broken up with Tony, her last boyfriend, but he was kind of a creep, so I was glad he was gone. The only reason I hadn't run away to live with my friends instead of coming here to Utah was because I was worried about who would take care of James and Mom.

"Well, you could cook. I have a lot of easy recipes. You can copy them."

There she was being nice again. I wanted to say something to hurt her, to let her know I knew she was fake, but I didn't want to make her angry. After all, if I pretended to like her, I might get to see more of her brother, Travis. "Thanks," I said. "Good idea."

"Want me to show you how to make a scrunchy? If you have some scissors and thread and a little elastic, it'll only take a minute on a sewing machine."

"We don't have any elastic or a sewing machine."

"Well, I can make one and bring it to you later, if you want."

"Sure." I went upstairs, and after a bit of a search, returned with a pair of scissors. With decisive movements, she cut out several rectangles from the trim on the sleeves and stuffed them in her pocket. "I'll give it to you on Sunday, okay?"

"Okay." I wondered if I'd ever see it. Not that I really cared all that much.

Allia busied herself with sweeping away the spider webs in what I planned to make my dance studio in the basement while I unpacked some of my special boxes. One held my dance clothes—leotards and tights of many colors. Another box held my shoes—jazz, ballet, tap. I kept everything related to dancing, even the clothes and shoes I'd outgrown. Mom hadn't always been able to afford dancing lessons, but I practiced on my own when she couldn't. I'd sometimes show up at dance lessons even when I wasn't enrolled so I could watch and practice the moves at home alone. I hoped I was doing them right.

Another box held videotapes of dance performances, either from our recitals or the television or the recitals of friends and their siblings. I watched them only when I was alone.

Other boxes held my clothes, even some favorite outgrown ones, knickknacks, old toys. I saved everything. I would keep the old clothes and toys in the box in my closet; it was enough to know they were there. I'd given James a few things that weren't only for girls, but knowing the rest were there comforted me.

Another box held cake mixes and cans of food I'd swiped from friends' houses. Those too would go into the closet for a rainy day. Another small box hid several albums of pictures that my mother would laugh about if she knew I had them. She didn't believe in pictures. But I did. I loved remembering the people we left behind. I didn't care that they'd moved on or were different. I wanted to remember them exactly as they had been.

I had a picture of my dad and James's, too, which I would show him one day. I even had an old one of Mom and her friend Dante. I'd found it in the garbage years ago when we'd been packing for another move. I hadn't been more than James's age. I didn't know where the photo came from but figured Mom had found it in a junk drawer somewhere and tossed it. If I squinted my eyes a bit, it could almost be me and Travis in the picture, and I was glad I'd saved it.

"What's that?" Allia had come into the room, and I stifled the urge to slam the album shut and throw it under my bed.

"My mom and your dad, I think."

She sat down on the floor beside me. "Wow. That was a long time ago. Do you think they were in love?"

I shrugged. "Mom says they were friends."

"That's weird."

"I know. Now he's a pastor."

"Bishop."

"Whatever."

"So, you aren't a Mormon?"

"I don't think so."

"You weren't baptized?"

"Not that I remember."

"Interesting." She had a gleam in her eye that made me uncomfortable.

"Look," I said, "don't tell my mom about the picture. She doesn't like pictures."

"Okay. She looks a lot like you."

"I guess." I thought she looked rather pale and lifeless, and I hoped I didn't look a thing like her.

"She's really pretty. Look at her smile." Allia moved to get a better view of my face. "Yep, you look like her. Well, you would without the makeup."

She said it casually, but I chose to pick a fight. "What's wrong with my makeup?"

"I was just saying you'd look more like your mom without it, that's all."

"I need to wear more than you do since I'm so pale."

She nodded. "Can I see the other pictures?"

I started turning the pages, telling Allia about my old friends and other people I'd known. It felt good to tell someone.

"You've been to a lot of interesting places," Allia said. "That's really cool. Oh, look, here's your little brother. He's adorable." Her finger traced the words under the photo. "His name is Dante James?"

"Yeah. Dante James Crockett. I've never even heard the name Dante before, except for my brother."

"My dad's Dante, too. My mom says he was named for an Italian poet from the Middle Ages, but Dad jokes about it coming from a character in a science fiction series. Mom said the movies weren't out when he was born, so that means Dad's wrong. It's weird, though, because the character also has a son named Travis. I've never seen the shows, but it's pretty funny how my parents joke about it."

"That is weird," I said. "But not as weird as your dad having the same name as my brother." In fact, it was so weird we stopped to think about it for a minute. "They must have been really good friends," I said finally. "Anyway, we've never called James anything but James."

Allia's mother called us up to eat, and Allia jumped to her feet before I could object. "Mom's taking me school shopping this afternoon. I'd better get up there."

"Do you always go running right when your mom calls?"

Allia blinked. "Why not? I like my mom."

"I like my mom, too, but that doesn't mean I don't need my space."

"I don't need any space on shopping days." She laughed and I did, too, as I followed her up the stairs.

• • •

Mom and I'd been to two second-hand clothing stores, and already I was sick of the smell of other people's clothes. It had never bothered me before, but today it made me depressed. Maybe it was because Mom kept overruling my choices when she'd never put her nose in my business before.

"What's up with you?" I asked as she put back a miniskirt.

"You already have one of those. Remember the one you wore to church on Sunday? Look, it's going to be a lot colder here in the winter, and we need to buy things that will last all year long."

"You sure you're not just trying to get me to look like Allia?" I was making a jab, but the way she hesitated made me suspicious. "This is all because of your *friend* Dante, isn't it? You're so pathetic. He's married now, you know."

Her eyes turned icy, and the coldness in them made my stomach hurt. "I have no designs on Dante, not in the way you're meaning. He's a friend and a spiritual leader, that's all."

I snorted. "Since when are we spiritual?"

"You need guidance, Kyle, just like I did at your age."

"You think those old women and your old boyfriend can give that to me? You're so lame. You never used to be this way." I would have added a couple of cusswords to emphasize my point, but I didn't want to freak her out anymore. She looked so frail at the moment, an old lady, not like my mom at all. The pain in my stomach cranked up a notch.

"Are you finished behaving like a two-year-old? Look, there's a lot of things I did wrong in my life, and I don't want you to make the same mistakes. I want you to have an education, something to fall back on."

"I'm going to be a dancer!"

"That's fine. As soon as I get a paycheck, I'll enroll you again, but only if you don't sluff school and you keep your grades up."

I glared at her. "I don't know who you are anymore. My mistakes are mine to make. You always said that's how you learn."

"I was wrong."

That stopped the other words in my throat. Oh, I knew logically that my mother wasn't perfect, but she'd always taken care of us. Maybe not like other mothers who were home more or who had normal jobs, but even when there was no money and things were crazy, she acted like she knew exactly what she was doing, like there was some plan in the end that she'd always been able to see. Take that box of clothes she'd pulled out of nowhere this morning. She made things work. But to have her admit now that she was wrong make me feel afraid. It made me wonder what was making her cry in the night when she thought no one else could hear.

I turned away. "Can we go somewhere else? Wal-Mart, maybe? Can we afford at least one thing someone else hasn't already worn?"

I could tell I'd hurt her with that comment, but I didn't care. I was too afraid she didn't know what she was doing. For all I knew, we were drowning and I was too stupid to know.

"Okay," she said quietly.

I felt James watching me as we walked to the car. Not accusing but wounded, like a puppy someone had kicked. I hated myself a bit more.

We drove to Wal-Mart in silence, and I wondered how she knew where the store was. Maybe that was where she'd bought the groceries that morning.

"Mom, can we go see the fish?" James asked.

She glanced at me, and I shrugged. It felt weird knowing that if I threw a fit, she'd make him come with me instead. Powerful but in an ugly way. "I'll be looking at the clothes."

The smell was better here, but there were a lot of people. Everyone trying to find last-minute items for school. I'd found a pair of jeans and a pair of boots at one of the used clothing stores, and what I really wanted were some warm tops. With Mom harping about the cold, I needed to be prepared. Maybe I'd be better off buying a jacket, but I didn't think we had the money for that, unless it was used. I sighed and headed to the girls' department. I was still small enough to fit into most fourteens and even some twelves there, and they tended to be less expensive and more abundant than the size zeros in women's. The problem was finding something without a cartoon figure on it. I didn't want to look like I was James's age.

My brother hadn't asked for clothes, and I figured he really didn't care. He'd wear the same pair of pants all week when Mom wasn't paying attention. Sometimes even when she was. Mom wasn't too picky about things like that. As long as they didn't stink or have a noticeable stain, clothes simply weren't dirty in Mom's book. I guess it made clothes last longer. She still wore clothes I remembered from ten years ago.

The color caught my eye before anything else about the T-shirt. It was that special blue that was somewhere between aqua and the color of the summer sky. Long sleeves and a cool wavy design in white swirled with black. I knew from the cut it would hug my waist and make a lot of girls envious. I picked it up and looked at the price tag. Thirty bucks? How could they want so much for a simple T-shirt? Oh, it came with a sweet silver necklace and a nice pair of jeans. Jeans with several artfully arranged holes in the legs. Frayed ends. These would look awesome with the new boots.

I wondered if Mom had the money. It wasn't an awful lot, but I'd already spent ten dollars that morning, and she hadn't started her job yet. She probably wouldn't be able to buy the sweaters she kept harping about.

At least I could try it on. I edged down an aisle where brightly colored underwear in a package beckoned to me. I needed those desperately, so I grabbed my size. I gathered a few more shirts and a couple jeans and headed to try everything on, folding the blue shirt under the rest to hide it.

"How many?" asked the lady when it was my turn.

I made a show of counting. "Six."

"You can't try on the underwear."

"Oh, I won't."

"Just leave it out here, then."

I went in a little irritated, but at least she hadn't counted my items. Once in the privacy of the little dressing room, I was amazed to see that the jeans and the blue shirt fit even better than I'd hoped. Awesome. One of the other shirts for five bucks wasn't bad either.

I stared at myself in the mirror with determination. Mom wouldn't buy it all, but there was more than one way to make it mine. I was wearing shorts, and there was no hope of hiding anything there, but I'd thrown a baggy T-shirt over my halter just in case everyone in Utah stared at me the way Allia had. Now I was grateful.

Carefully, I folded the blue shirt into the jeans and wrapped them around my lower waist. The elastic in the shorts held them well enough, if I didn't move too suddenly. I gathered the excess of my T-shirt and tied it in a knot. I looked fatter than a few minutes ago, but I didn't think anyone would notice. It took what seemed like forever to arrange all the other clothing on hangers and hide the hangers to the blue shirt and jeans inside the leg of the other jeans.

The lady didn't look at me when I exited. "You can leave them here if you don't want them," she said.

"That's okay. I do." I swooped up the underwear and headed back to the girls' department, where I dropped them off at the first opportunity, except for the five-buck shirt. The hangers inside the pant leg fell out, but no one seemed to notice. I kicked them under the hanging clothes. I was a little uncomfortable when the clothes under my shirt slipped a bit, but by clamping one arm to my side, I felt better.

"There you are," my mom said. "Find anything?"

James held up a bag. "Look, I got a goldfish. Mom says I can use a big pickle jar to keep him in. Isn't he great? I think I'm going to call him Goldy."

"Wow, looks more like a Fred to me."

James laughed. "Okay, Fred Goldy."

Sometimes it's sad how much he worshipped me.

"Is this the top you want?" Mom asked, her eyes going to the price tag. "It's not very warm, is it? What about this sweater?"

Miracles of miracles, she pointed to a long tan sweater with a big button in front that actually looked cool. My friends always said my mother had good taste. Maybe they weren't that wrong.

"It's twelve dollars, but you could wear it with all the T-shirts you already have, right?" Mom said.

That's not how it worked. If you wore a sweater one day, you couldn't wear it again until the next week, unless you weren't going to see any of those kids. But she didn't need to know that. "Right. Okay, let's get it."

"I think that will have to be it for now," Mom said. "I have to get James a pair of jeans. He only has one that still fits. I can cut off two for shorts, but the others we'll have to get rid of."

I nodded. "That's fine. I don't need any more." I didn't care what happened once the blue shirt and jeans were mine.

"Aren't you going to try the sweater on?" She shoved it at me, and with a little effort I managed to get my arms into it without dislodging my cargo.

"Oh, that's perfect. You look so grown up."

Which was pretty silly given that we were still in the little girls department. "Can we go home now?"

"After I grab some pants for James. Is there something wrong with your arms?"

"No." I shoved the sweater and the package of underwear at her. "Just feeling a little sick. Can I wait in the truck?"

"Sure. Let me get you the keys. Do you want me to go with you?"

"No. I'm fine."

I hurried away from her as quickly as possible, holding my

arms against my stomach. I nearly stumbled into a group of black-haired children clinging to their mother. *Just walk. Keep walking.* No one had seen me put the clothes under my shirt, but I still felt eyes on me. I'd only stolen a few things from stores in the past—candy, jewelry, a pen. My friends had made it fun, but it didn't feel fun now. Had someone noticed the hangers on the floor? Had the lady at the dressing room known what I was up to?

I walked past the registers to the entrance, my heart slamming in my chest. What if these clothes had a hidden security device and I beeped as I left the store? I picked up speed, ready to make a run for it.

Nothing beeped. Finally, I was out the door.

"Miss," someone called.

Was that my heart skipping a beat?

I glanced behind me and saw that the man was talking not to me but to a woman whose bag of dog food had fallen from the shelf under her cart. "Thanks," I heard her say.

Still, it had been too close.

I started to run.

When I arrived at the truck, my hands shook so much I almost couldn't get the door open. When I did, I jumped inside and locked the doors.

I'd made it. No one was around. No one had come after me.

When my heartbeat slowed, I worked the clothes out of my shirt and stuffed them under the seat. Then I unlocked the door, opened it, and threw up on the blacktop.

CHAPTER TEN

Rikki

I came home from work, exhausted from the mind-numbing tedium of data entry and worried about what I'd find. Kyle was acting strange. For the past two nights, she'd come into my bed at night, sobbing. When I asked her what was wrong, she shook her head and clung to me.

She couldn't know. Not yet. Something else had to be wrong.

I found her in the kitchen heating up a pan of packaged noodles. Not exactly nourishing, but I felt too beaten to care. James was at the table drinking a glass of milk, a bowl and spoon in front of him.

"How was your day?" I asked them.

James was full of stories. He loved his teacher. He loved his class. The only thing he didn't love was going to a different class to read. "We're all kind of dumb, I think," he said.

I sat down beside him. "No, honey. You aren't. Never. For some reason reading's just harder for you, that's all. You're good at so many other things." But I knew reading affected all his classes. How could you learn history, science, and math if you couldn't read? I'd known about his problem for the past six months, but those had been difficult months for me, and I hadn't been able to figure out how to help him. Now it was time to do something.

"You should talk to Allia's mother," Kyle said, opening the package of flavoring to pour into the boiling noodles. "Allia told me she's homeschooling her brother. Not Travis. The other one. Can't remember his name."

"Cory," James said.

"Yeah, him. He was having problems or something, so she took him out to catch him up. I think she went to school to be a teacher but didn't finish. Maybe."

That didn't go with the garden design dreams I'd heard from her, but I didn't know enough to say. After my last conversation with Becca, I didn't think she'd be overjoyed to hear from me, but it would be a good thing for James if she could help or even point us in the right direction. James needed her or someone like her, and I didn't know where to begin. "I'll talk to her," I promised. "So, Kyle, what about your day?" I blinked to push off a sudden wave of dizziness. Had I taken my seizure medication? I thought so.

She shrugged. "The same."

I hadn't received any text messages about her missing classes, so she'd at least been there. "Is there anything you need for school?" Was it wrong to hope she said no? I was down to the last sixty bucks in my account and two weeks from a paycheck that would include only a week of work. I wondered if it was true about Mormon bishops being able to get people food. Well, I'd see how it went. We still had a few leftovers from what the ladies had brought on Monday.

"I don't need anything." Kyle managed a smile.

"Tell me what's wrong, honey. You've always been able to talk to me."

Kyle jumped up from the table. "Stop it already! There's nothing wrong! Besides, I can't talk to you anymore. You've changed." Turning on her heel, she fled down the stairs.

"Oops." In less than a second my nagging headache had gone from its familiar pounding to sharp daggers and blurred vision.

"She's probably on her period," James offered.

I blinked at him twice before laughing. "Maybe that's it. How's Fred the Fish doing?"

"He's okay. I'm not giving him too much food."

"I'm sure that makes him happy."

"I saw Lauren at school," James said. "She's in the third grade, not the second. I wish she was in my class. We played together at recess. She's my bestest friend."

"Isn't she a little bossy?"

He shrugged. "I'm used to Kyle bossing me."

"That you are." I rumpled his hair, the swelling in my heart reminding me how much I loved being his mother.

James touched my hand. "Mom, what's wrong? You're looking at me funny."

That's because there were two of him. "Just a headache."

"Better take your pills."

"Yeah. I'd better." Not a good sign to have to take them so early.

I wrestled a bit with the bottle before I got it open and swallowed a pill. My hands didn't want to obey—another reason I was better off not working at a restaurant. I'd dropped too many trays the past couple months. I told myself it was because of the headaches, but I knew better.

I need to lie down.

A few minutes later James found me in bed and climbed up beside me. "Mom? I have to read this, but I don't know how. Can you help me?"

I couldn't even see the paper because of the headache, but in ten more minutes the pills should kick in. "Let's rest a minute and then I will. Tell me some more stories about your day. I love hearing about it." I wished I didn't have to work. I'd stay with him every second, watch as he grew before my eyes.

"Okay. The best thing was at recess when Lauren told Junior to let me go first down the slide . . ."

I dozed as he talked, and it was a long time before I could help him with his homework.

CHAPTER ELEVEN

Becca

Travis came into the kitchen, car keys in hand. "Mom, can I go to BG's and watch a movie?"

"Is your homework finished?" I asked, looking up from correcting Lauren's math. It was always a huge adjustment for the children to go back to school. What they didn't know was that it was every bit as difficult for me. I had to correct homework, talk to teachers, make sure they got to and from school. The good news for me was now Travis had his driver's license and we'd found an affordable car so he could drive himself to school, and eventually maybe he could even pick up Allia at the junior high. I wasn't sure about that yet. Maybe after a few months of experience going solo. He wasn't allowed to drive friends for at least six months, a law I was grateful for.

He tossed his keys into the air and caught them. "I don't have any homework."

"What about the history thing you told me about?"

"Not due until Tuesday."

"That's not very far away." There'd been a time when he'd at least started his projects on the same day or the day after they'd been given. The last few months of tenth grade, however, he'd become a procrastinator, which often sent the whole house into convulsions as he frantically tried to beat a deadline. Dante and I had discussed letting him crash and burn, but his GPA destined him for a scholarship at BYU, and we were reluctant to withhold our help and end up footing the college bill ourselves. We hoped the stress of doing it last-minute would teach him something.

Apparently not.

"We have family night on Monday," I said, "and we don't do homework on Sunday, so when exactly are you going to do this paper?"

He gave a one-shouldered shrug. "Tomorrow. She's giving us time in school on Monday, and I can do it before family night."

"I've heard that one before."

"I got it covered, Mom. I promise I'll get an A. What more do you want?"

"I'll tell you what I don't want. I don't want Monday night to roll around and have you frantically searching for information because you didn't find enough already. You can go tonight, but tomorrow I want to see a strong rough draft before you go anywhere."

He gave me a pained looked. You'd think I'd told him to take Lauren with him to hang out with his friends. "I was going job-hunting."

"Your job is to get that scholarship."

"I will. I promise. Anyway, I'm only going to work a couple days a week. To get some extra cash."

Lauren grinned. "You just want to meet girls."

He gave her an irritated look, where once he would have laughed. "Stay out of this, midget."

"Travis, we don't say things like that."

He sighed. "She's such a pain."

"She learned it from you. Now, have you cleaned your bathroom?"

His irritation increased, but he turned on his heel and stomped down the hall.

"I take that as a no," Lauren said, sounding exactly like her older siblings.

"Guess so." I looked down at the math problem. "That's right. Now you need to color this picture for your English class, and then you're finished."

"What color should I use on her coat?"

"Whatever color you like."

"I can't decide."

I didn't understand it. When she was with children her age, she bossed them around, but in other situations, she couldn't seem to make simple choices.

"Well, figure it out." I started toward the stovetop where my potatoes awaited mashing.

Allia breezed into the kitchen. "Look, Mom, I finished." She extended her hand with a plaid scrunchy.

"Wonderful. I'm sure Kyle will love it."

"I also made her this flower with the scraps we had in the material box." She held up a flower with burnt edges whose blue color matched the plaid. "That way she has a choice. You know, for if she's at home or school or going somewhere nice. She can wear them together or separately. Only I'm not sure she uses this kind of thing, you know? She wears her hair all swooping down over her face. "

"It's perfect." I put an arm around her, feeling proud of my daughter, despite my own reluctance about Rikki. "I'm glad you're trying to befriend her. I think she's really lost."

"She's not even baptized. At least she doesn't remember if she is. Maybe she can take the missionary lessons."

"Good idea. When her mother's records arrive, wherever they are, we can ask your dad to check into it."

Allia nodded. "Thanks, Mom."

Lauren waved Allia over to the table. "Come look. What color should I make this guy's coat? And what about the dog?"

"Black coat," Allia said. "No, do it blue because black will make the picture too dark. Do the dog brown. Maybe mix a little gold in it. You have gold, don't you?"

"Yeah." Lauren set down her orange crayon, grabbed a blue one, and started coloring.

No wonder Lauren couldn't decide. She had all of us to do it for her. I wondered if she made decisions with her friends, or if she asked their opinion and then made them follow through. I'd have to keep an eye on that. I wanted all my children, especially my daughters, to make their own choices in life.

I finished the mashed potatoes and put the butter back in the fridge. Leaving Lauren at the table, Allia walked over and leaned against the counter by the sink. "You know, it was kind of weird," she said in a voice too low for Lauren to overhear, "going over to Kyle's on Monday and her showing me all my old clothes. Her mom didn't tell her where she got them."

I opened the oven to check on my meatloaf. "You didn't tell her, did you?"

"No. But it was still weird."

"Think how you'd feel if it was you."

"Yeah, but what if she finds out now? Will she think I was lying to her?"

"I see what you mean. But no, hopefully, if she does find out, she'll see you were trying to be sensitive and kind."

She sighed. "I guess."

"What about the man's boots?" Lauren asked, her forehead scrunched in concentration. "What color should they be?"

The doorbell saved either of us from answering. "I'll get it." Allia shot from the kitchen, while I followed at a more sedate pace, hoping it wasn't school kids selling something to raise money for this or that. I hated the schools using children as salesmen, and I opted out of it for my children, instead making them earn what they needed around the house or at my sister's, who often had work available at the small advertising firm she ran with her husband. Since Dante was the bishop of the ward and I was in the Primary, every child in the neighborhood who sold anything always stopped by our house. At some point, we'd had to start saying no. I hated disappointing them, though, and there were a few families I'd sponsor, regardless, because I knew the children wouldn't have any other way to participate in the activity.

I was surprised to see Rikki at the door with her two children in tow, James with his bright smile and Kyle with her sullen stare.

"Hey, Kyle," Allia said, "look what I just finished. I was going to ask Mom if I could walk over and give them to you." She held out the scrunchy and the flower. "The flower is for maybe a dressier place, like church. You could use them both. You know, hold back all your hair with the scrunchy and put this flower right here on the side, kinda toward the front." Allia demonstrated. "Want to see in the mirror?"

"Sure, I guess." Kyle's sullen look had vanished but not because of Allia. Her eyes were focused beyond all of us.

I turned and saw Travis. "Can I go now?" He used an aggrieved tone that was worse than nails on a chalkboard. I'd never thought I'd be happy to see my precious boy leave home for school or a mission, but now I was beginning to understand the old saying that teens became annoying specifically so their mothers would be willing to let them go.

"You don't want dinner first? It's almost ready."

He shook his head. "I'll eat at BG's."

"His mother is going to be home?" Friday night was date night for a lot of couples. It was for Dante and me when there wasn't an emergency in the ward.

"Yeah, of course."

"Okay. You call me if you go anywhere else and come home if no adults are there. No driving other kids."

"I got it, I got it." He disappeared through the kitchen.

"Sorry about that." I gave Rikki a smile.

Lauren appeared in the kitchen doorway. "Come on, James. You can help me with my homework. Do you know how to color good?"

The kids scattered, and still Rikki didn't speak. She was dressed in jeans that were probably a size too big and a fitted pink shirt that showed she wasn't all skin and bones. As usual, her blonde hair was everywhere. She looked fragile, as though a breath might topple her.

"Tough day?" I asked, feeling sympathy despite my worry about her intentions toward Dante. I didn't invite her to sit down, however. I wanted her gone and the kids fed before he came home.

She gave a weak laugh. "I had no idea repetition could be so . . . so, well, draining. Look, I'm sorry to bother you, but I have a question, and I don't know who else to ask. It's about James."

"Oh?" I asked, interested despite myself. James was adorable, and the fact that he couldn't read was tragic.

"Kyle says you homeschool Cory, so I thought you might know something that would help." She glanced behind me and lowered her voice. "James has always had trouble reading. I was working a lot when he started kindergarten, so I didn't know there was even a problem until the end of first grade, but we've worked on his letters a lot in the past months, and it hasn't seemed to do any good. Now he's in resource and hating it. He feels stupid."

They'd wanted to put Cory in resource, too, but he'd improved considerably over the summer, and I was confident I would have him at or above his grade level by Christmas. "Have you had him tested for dyslexia?" I asked. "Or something else?"

"No one ever recommended that, though one teacher wanted to give him drugs once, to keep him still."

I shook my head. "James isn't hyperactive. He was fine in Primary. Anyway, the school should have a way to test him, or I have a friend who works for a private school in town who's good at finding the reasons for delayed reading. She tutors a lot of children."

"I'm afraid I wouldn't have money to pay her. I'll have to depend on the school."

Her despondency was as touching as James's problem. "I can try a few things with him myself, if you want. Maybe it's not anything serious. In fact, it's probably not. I didn't graduate from college, but that's what I went to school for, elementary education. There are a few tricks I could try."

"I'd be grateful for anything you could tell me."

"Okay. But it'll have to wait until Monday. Dante and I have plans tonight, and Saturdays are crazy around here. We try to get the house cleaned."

Her eyes ran over the room. "Looks pretty good already, I'd say, but Monday's perfect. Except I'm working until five-thirty, and I usually don't get home until almost six."

Dante had a similar schedule, except on most days I was lucky to get him home by six-thirty. Mondays he made an effort to get home earlier.

"Actually, Tuesday would be even better," I told Rikki. "Say, Tuesdays and Thursdays. On Mondays I'm usually hurrying to get everything ready before family night. Could Kyle bring him over after school?"

"Sure. Yeah. Thanks. I really appreciate it." She paused. "He adores Lauren, you know. They've been playing together at recess."

I hadn't known that, but Lauren had been full of all kinds of information about the new things happening to her at school, so she must have forgotten to tell me. "She likes him, too." I wondered what time it was. Dante should be home soon, and I needed to get the kids fed so I could be ready to leave.

Lauren and James appeared at my side. "Mom, can James eat with us?" Lauren asked. "The meat smell is making us hungry."

"I'm sorry," Rikki said quickly. "He just ate. He can't be hungry."

"I didn't finish my noodles, Mom, and we didn't have meat." James spoke without guile, simply stating a fact.

I suspected she'd fed the kids packaged noodles, which had a lot of fat and little in the way of nutrition. Not a good choice when James was already so thin. He needed protein during these growing years.

"We'll make some when we get home," she said, To me, she added, "Kyle made him something earlier. You know how kids are—food goes right through them."

"Yeah," I said.

She looked about ready to drop, not like someone able to go home and cook a meal. Pity sprang up inside me. What must her life be like, working all day and then coming home to try to take care of her children? All alone. Dante wasn't around nearly as much as I'd wanted since he became bishop, but he was here occasionally to lend a hand.

This isn't my problem, I thought, knowing I should simply agree and let them leave. I'd already promised to help James with reading.

Except James *was* my problem, at least in a gospel sense, and so was Rikki. My parents had raised me better than to think any other way. A ward meant family, and for better or worse, Rikki was in our ward. For now. I needed to get over my insecurities.

"There's plenty of food," I said. "Why don't you come in for a bit? We can talk while the kids eat."

Rikki looked like she was going to say no, but James and Lauren went whooping into the kitchen without waiting for her approval. "I'm sorry," she said softly.

"It's okay, really." Suddenly it *was* okay. If I knew anything about my husband, it was that he wouldn't be home for at least another half hour, and if he was, so what? Rikki was a member of the ward, nothing more. I was still worried about Kyle's influence on Allia, but my daughter seemed to have her head on straight—for now.

"Allia," I called. "Time for dinner."

The girls came out, Kyle's hair pulled back in the scrunchy, the large blue flower on one side by her eye. She looked adorable—or would have if it weren't for that heavy coating of black around her eyes, and how did she get her eye shadow to go on such a heavy blue?

"Nice," I said, hoping they didn't notice how I choked on the word. "I like seeing your face under your hair." Now if only I could see her eyes.

Kyle actually laughed. "It smells really good in here."

"Thanks. I'm afraid it's meatloaf. Do you like it?"

"I like just about everything."

"Mom puts a really good sauce on it," Allia said. "Come on, let's get the plates."

I went to the top of the basement stairs and yelled, "Cory, dinner!" He didn't delay a moment. Meatloaf was his favorite dish.

Kyle and James started eating the minute their plates were before them—until Lauren reminded them about the prayer. "Oh, yeah," James said. Rikki was staring out the window. I doubted she even saw the plate I put in front of her.

Allia's prayer seemed to shake her from her reverie. "Oh, thank you. This is beginning to be a habit. Us eating here, I mean."

"Cool. You could eat here every day," Lauren said. "Hurry, James. Allia's going to babysit me and Cory, and that means you can't stay. Mom doesn't allow friends when she's not home. So we have to go outside and play fast."

"Sorry, another day, Lauren." I poured them both more milk.

She pouted. "At least I get to watch a video tonight."

In five minutes everyone was finished, even Rikki. Amazing how long it took to make a meal in comparison to how long my family took to devour it.

"Thanks," Rikki said. "One of these days you'll have to come over, and I'll make you guys a dinner. I make pretty mean spare-ribs."

She looked significantly recovered, and I was grateful I'd followed my intuition. "Sure, why not?" I'd make sure it was on a night Dante had church business. Guess I still wasn't above feeling jealous. Crazy. I'd never been jealous of anyone in my entire life until now.

"Oh," Rikki said, as I walked her to the door, "I saw this and thought you might be interested." She pulled an ad ripped from a magazine for a garden show in Saint George. "It's like a home show, only for gardens. Not too far from here, really, and the gardens should be really nice this time of year, after having all summer to grow. It's on for a few weeks, I think."

I found I couldn't speak past the lump in my throat. She was the only one I'd ever told about my gardening dream. Silly, really, yet she'd remembered. "Thanks." I made my voice purposefully light. "I'll look into it."

Her eyes met mine for a long moment, and I felt exposed, as if she could see into my soul. I didn't think I was fooling her at all. I think she knew how much it would mean for me to see the show, and how touched I was that someone, anyone, had remembered.

Rikki grinned. "If Dante can't go with you, maybe we should take the kids and go. You know, for a day or two."

Right. A day or two with my husband's former fiancée. "Maybe," I said.

"Well, thanks again. I'll make sure Kyle brings James after school on Tuesday."

I nodded. "See you at church."

Of course Dante had to arrive as they were leaving the porch. He waved and left his car on the driveway instead of pulling into the garage. "Hi, guys," he said, offering James his hand. "How's it going?"

"Good!" James pumped Dante's hand with enthusiasm.

"Fine." Rikki seemed taller and more vivacious now, though I didn't know if it was because of my dinner or because she now had a male audience.

Kyle didn't stop to talk but made a beeline to her mom's truck. I wished Rikki would follow her example.

I'd trailed Rikki down the sidewalk, and Dante smiled at me. "You two have a good visit?" Could he sound any more like a bishop? One thing was sure: he didn't sound like Dante at all.

Rikki folded her hands across her stomach. "Actually, I came here to ask Becca for some help with school for James. And we've been talking about visiting a garden show in Saint George. It's supposed to be really good." She turned and smiled at me as though we were best friends. "I meant it when I said I'd go with you if Dante can't. It'd be fun." She looked pointedly at Dante. "We could let our hair down." With a little wave, she grabbed James's hand and started for her truck. "See you later."

Dante watched her go. "Let your hair down?" He shook his head. "Knowing Rikki, that doesn't sound at all good."

"Next time, be home earlier," I said. "Or I might just take her up on that."

Dante drew me into his arms and kissed me. I could smell a hint of his aftershave, the detergent I used to launder his shirts, and the other bit that was all him. For a moment, I forgot all about Rikki and the garden show.

"Mom." Allia stood on the front door, a phone in her hand. "Cydnee just called me, and she says she saw Travis at the 7-Eleven with a whole bunch of boys. He was driving. I thought he couldn't drive friends yet."

I looked at Dante, whose face had gone stiff like my own. So much for trusting our son.

"I'm going to kill him," Dante growled.

CHAPTER TWELVE

Dante

I should have seen it coming, but I guess a parent never does. I could look at the children in my ward and see what they needed—anything from a little extra parental attention to drastic measures like drug intervention. But I hadn't seen any indications of disobedience from Travis. Maybe with your own child it was different. Maybe I'd trusted him too much, maybe I had expected him to do the right thing simply because my hands were too busy with everything else.

"Dante," Becca tugged at my sleeve, "he hasn't robbed a bank, and he's not on drugs. You don't have to kill him." She spoke with a completely grave expression, which poked more fun at my overly dramatic thoughts than anything else could have done. My Becca knew me too well.

"Fine. I'm just going to make him *think* I'm going to kill him."

"That's okay, then. As long as I don't have to visit you in prison." She started for the door, reaching for the phone in Allia's hand.

"I'll call." I quickly dialed his number on my cell. Travis had a phone, but it was what we called the family cell phone, and we had given it to him to use when he got his license. There was no texting, and we had to pay by the minute, but it worked. That meant he didn't give out the number and he only called us. When he could pay for his own phone, it would be a different matter. For now he was on our dime.

He'd complained. So had Allia, because she wanted a phone, too. But Becca and I both felt that until they were at least sixteen *and* could pay for it themselves, they had no need of a cell phone for personal use. On the other hand, we needed to have a way to contact them and the peace of mind that they had a way to call in case of an emergency. Thus the compromise.

"Where are you?" I said when Travis finally answered.

"At BG's. Didn't Mom tell you?"

"If you're at BG's, tell me what your twin was doing in your car—no, my car—at 7-Eleven driving a bunch of friends."

Silence. Just as I thought.

"We just went to get some snacks."

"What's the rule, Travis?"

He didn't answer.

"Travis, what is the rule?"

"Six months of no driving friends."

"Exactly. And guess what? That six months started when you got your license last month, but now it starts over. No, it starts when I decide to finally let you drive again. Now, get in the car and drive yourself home—slowly."

"But, Dad, I didn't mean—"

"Now." I hung up and smiled at Becca. "He's coming home."

The corner of her mouth twitched. "Your canines are showing." She took my hand and pulled me past Allia into the house.

"This is all my fault," I said.

Becca shook her head. "No, it's Travis's."

I turned back to give my daughter a kiss on the cheek. "Don't ever do this to me, okay?"

"Okay. Hey, Dad, can you check to see if Kyle's baptized? She says she's not, and if she isn't, I'm going to try to get her to listen to the missionaries."

I smiled. "Not a bad idea. That must be why you're my favorite child."

"But, Daddy, I thought I was your favorite child."

I looked up to see Lauren in the kitchen doorway.

"No, I am," Cory said from behind her.

"We're all his favorites," Allia said, rolling her eyes. "Except Travis. He's in the doghouse."

Lauren frowned. "We don't have a doghouse."

"No, but that's what Dad always says when someone's in trouble, and Travis drove friends in the car when he wasn't sup-posed to."

"Never mind that. Come here, you guys." I opened my arms, and the younger children attacked me with hugs. This was my favor-ite part of the day, to come home and find Becca and my children waiting. They were what I lived for. Travis used to wait for me, too. I pushed the thought away, not wanting to spoil the moment.

Becca headed into the kitchen. "I'll just put away the rest of dinner so we can go."

"James ate with us," Lauren told me. "He eats more than Cory."

"Really?" We called Cory our carnivore because he loved meat more than pretty much anything else. Becca told me he often searched the fridge for a spare pork chop or chicken leg after school.

"It's true." Cory seemed a little put out about losing to James, so I tickled him until he screamed for mercy. Sometimes a father's job is tough, but someone's got to do it.

When the kids finally opted to abandon me for the video Becca had rented for them, I slipped away to change my clothes. "We go-ing to see a movie?" I asked Becca.

"Dinner. Then I thought we'd do a round of miniature golf."

I laughed. "So you can kill me again?"

"What's with all this killing talk?" She sidled up to me and put her arms around my neck. "If I didn't know you better, I'd think you've got killing on the brain."

"Hardly." I kissed her because she was in the perfect position for it, and I could kiss Becca all day, especially after an entire day of writing about software. She tasted like sunshine and a hint of mint.

A slamming door interrupted our moment. "Must be Travis," Becca said. "Now, Dante, talk to him like you're in the bishop's office."

Whenever I was really angry at one of the children, she said something to that effect, and for what it was worth, it did calm me down. Not that I was prone to angry outbursts, but it was easier to be hard on your own children. I felt Travis had let me down in a big way, that by his disobedience he was discarding everything I'd ever taught him. If he sneaked around behind my back in this matter, what else had he done? What else would he do?

We went to the kitchen and looked in the garage, but instead of Travis, we found Allia on the back porch talking with one of her friends on the phone. "That movie's a little young," she said to us. "I told the kids I'd be out here if they needed me. How come you aren't gone yet?"

"Travis hasn't come home." He'd had plenty of time, and I wanted to get those keys from him. I took out my cell and started dialing. No answer.

Becca frowned, a worry line appearing between her eyes. "Why isn't he home?"

"He must be afraid," I said, my voice again nearing a growl. "For good reason."

"I hope nothing's happened to him."

Why did women do that—automatically jump to the worst conclusion? "I'll go look for him." I started for the door.

"Maybe we should go on our date and let him come home when he wants." That's what she said, but her eyes were agreeing with me. "Okay, you go. I'll wait here in case he comes home. But, honey, please don't drive too fast."

"I won't."

"What a pain," I heard Allia say as I left. I couldn't agree more.

I drove to BG's and then to each of Travis's other friends' houses. None of the parents had seen Travis, and when they called their children, none would admit to knowing where Travis was.

Now I was really going to kill him when he got home, or at the very least ground him until he went on his mission. Or so I told myself. Inside, I was worried.

CHAPTER THIRTEEN

Rikki

I felt a lot better after leaving Becca's. I'd done something about James, given Becca the information about the show, and eaten supper—I hadn't been able to resist Becca's meatloaf or her sauce. I suspected eating was what had made energy kick back in. Or maybe the migraine pills were finally doing their job.

"How about renting a movie?" I asked James.

"Yay! Can we rent the same one Lauren got? It's about a dragon that can fly."

Flying sounded good to me right now, too. "Sure. Whatever you and Kyle decide."

"Okay, but you go get her. She's cranky."

I went downstairs, my steps slowing as I heard the music. Kyle was in the unfinished family room dancing on the bare cement. It wasn't a dance I recognized, and I thought I'd seen all the ones she'd learned from her classes and her videos. It was a mixture of ballet and modern, the steps difficult, but she went through them easily, as if they'd been written for her.

If I'd had half her talent, I might have done far more with my dancing. Problem was, she didn't have a chance. Not really. I couldn't afford the right kind of lessons. She might have them eventually, though. That was part of the plan.

She came to an end of a difficult pass and stopped before trying a few different steps, shaking her head and substituting new ones. Beautiful, elegant, graceful—all contrasting with her tiny size and the layers of dark makeup. I'd never minded her makeup, feeling it was an expression of her teens, but for a stark instant, I saw her how others must see her—how Dante and Becca and Allia must see her. They wouldn't perceive talent but only her dropout potential.

Kyle rewound the music to the place where she'd left off and began with the new steps. That's when I realized she was making up the dance, with a beauty and maturity I hadn't known she possessed. I sat down on the bottom step and watched, entranced, as my little girl danced her heart out. There was longing and heartache in her expression, in her steps.

You don't even know how much you've lost, I thought. Yet it was there in the dance.

I had to get out of there. I stood and started up the steps, but she'd finally sensed my presence and shut off the music. "Mom?"

"James and I are going to get a video. Want to come?"

She shook her head, still completely caught up in a world I didn't share—could never share again. Not now. "I'm almost done, though, so I'll watch it with you when you get back. I have some popcorn."

I knew about her stash. I'd seen it once, but no matter how desperate I became, I never, ever touched it. "Great. I'll see you in a little while."

Once I'd had dreams. I had nothing now. For a moment, I didn't know why I was back in Utah, or why I thought I could make anything happen, much less a plan that hinged on a boy I hadn't seen for twenty years.

I was worse than pathetic.

I couldn't hate God, because I wasn't exactly sure He existed, but I could hate myself. I was at fault. Me. I shut my eyes and let myself go inside the pain. Just for a few moments, until I heard James's footsteps.

"Is she coming?"

"She's practicing. But she'll watch it with us, and we'll eat popcorn, too, so that'll be fun."

He laughed. "And I get to pick the movie all by myself!"

"Yay!" We ran out to the truck together.

While we were out and about, I'd pick up another gallon of milk and a few other odds and ends that we would be needing. Life wasn't so bad.

"Mom, I forgot to tell you I need a light for my nightlight," James said when we'd found a Redbox movie he wanted. "It's busted again."

"There's a K-Mart over there," I said. "Let's get it now."

"Remember, only up to seven watts."

"I remember." This was our third nightlight, so we were being careful.

Apparently, K-Mart was quite a hopping place on Friday night in Spanish Fork. Not as packed as the Wal-Mart Supercenter in nearby Springville where I'd taken the children shopping on Monday but more crowded than I expected.

"Hey, Rikki."

I looked up, surprised to see one of the supervisors from my work. He wasn't over my section, but I'd noticed him because of his beautiful green eyes. I've always been a sucker for beautiful eyes of any color. He wasn't wearing a wedding ring, but that could mean anything these days.

"Hi," I said, smiling.

"I'm Quinn Hunter."

"From work, yeah."

"So how're you liking it?"

It's killing me. "Fine." He was broad in the way that Kyle's father had been but taller so he didn't look blocky. He had dark blond hair, a tan, and thick eyelashes. His other features were a little too plain to be handsome in a movie star way, but the eyes and that smile made up for a lot.

The smile reminded me of Dante. Not in a painful way but in a way that made me want to smile back.

"Good." His eyes fell to James. "This your son?"

"Yeah."

"Hi, there," he said to James.

"Hi." James cocked his head and held up his DVD. "We're going home to watch a movie and eat popcorn."

"Sounds great." Quinn grimaced. "All I'm doing is changing my oil."

I laughed. "I need to learn how to do that myself."

"It's a skill you grow up with here in Spanish Fork." His eyes went to my hand, though he should have known I wasn't married because it was on my application. Maybe he hadn't known he was interested until now. Or maybe he didn't have much say in who was hired.

"You grew up here?" I asked. "So did I. What year did you graduate?"

He'd graduated the year before me and kicked around the army ten years before coming home and marrying his childhood sweetheart. They were divorced last year, and he'd quit the army so he could have more access to his three children. "I don't believe I've just bored you with all of that," he said. "You have a way about you that makes me tell you things."

People told me that all the time. It was an instinctive balance of telling them about my own life and asking questions about theirs. To tell the truth, I was more interested in his oil-changing skills than anything else he'd told me. I'd learned to take care of myself, but I wasn't above having a man help me simply because he was attracted to me.

Counting on any kind of a future was not on the table.

James tugged on my hand. "I'd better go," I said.

"Well, it was good talking to you. Let me know if you need help with that oil."

"Oh, I'll need help. No doubt about that." I knew later he'd ask me at work, and I'd let him come over to help. I'd kept putting oil in the truck, but I hadn't changed it for a year. Or more.

"Bye, buddy," he said to James.

"You could watch the movie with us," James offered with the innocence that had attracted many family-oriented men to me in the past.

"James," I said.

"If your mother invites me sometime, we'll do it then." Good save. It left things open but didn't back me to the wall tonight, which was a good thing because pursuing him wasn't exactly on my to-do list.

He watched me go. Forty years old and I apparently hadn't lost all my charm. *Fat lot of good it does me.*

"Mom, look! There's Travis," James said as we left the store.

So it was. Looking at Dante's boy took me back in time—except back then it had been only Dante and me. Travis was with two other boys and a girl with short brown hair, who seemed to be attached to one of Travis's friends. They were in a huddle outside the store, crowded around their cell phones. "Dude, they're looking for you big time," said a teen with black hair and a bad case of acne. "You should just go home and face the music."

I would have walked right past them without speaking, but Travis's expression stopped me. He looked—well, he looked like Dante had on the night his father had forgotten the fathers and

111

sons' campout. Again. Broken, sad, lonely, and angry. Travis also looked a bit frightened, and that did something to the mother in me that wasn't related to my past with his father.

"Hey, Travis," I said.

His eyes met mine. "Oh, hi."

His friends smiled at me. "Hey, I know you," the black-haired boy said. "You were at church on Sunday." His voice was admiring.

"Yep, I was."

"I'm Travis's friend, BG."

"Rikki Crockett, and my son, James."

"You mean like Davy Crockett?"

"My great-grandfather."

"Really?"

"No."

He laughed. The other two teens were texting on their phones, only half aware of what was going on around them. Travis still looked like he'd lost his best friend. "Well, we'd better go," he said.

"Wait. Are you driving them?" He had to remember that I'd been at his house when Becca had told him not to drive his friends.

His face flushed. "Yeah."

Now I understood. "I'm not going to tell your parents, but don't you think someone's going to? This isn't a very big town." Especially within the Mormon community where his father was well-known.

BG barked a laugh. "They already did. He's busted. Now he doesn't wanna go home."

"Hey, guys," the girl said. "Ben and Jeanie are coming here to get us. We're going to their house. Later, Travis." They started toward the entrance to the store.

"I wanna come," BG said.

"What about me?" Travis asked.

BG shook his head. "I don't want to be around when the bishop catches up to you. From what we hear, he'll be over at Jeanie's soon. He knows where we all live."

"Sounds like Dante," I said.

"I hate being the bishop's son," Travis muttered.

"Hey, he's a nice guy." BG started toward the store entrance where the others had already disappeared. "Later."

Travis sighed and began walking to his car alone. James and I tagged along since we were parked in the same direction. "I'm never going home," he said. "Never."

"I said that once."

He looked at me.

"And I didn't. Not for twenty years."

"I wish that could be me."

"I wish I had those twenty years back. I never got to tell my mother goodbye."

He stared at me, saying nothing.

"You look so much like your dad," I ventured.

"That's what my mom says."

"Well, she's right. I bet you're close."

"He doesn't have time for me."

I blinked. "That doesn't sound like Dante."

"All he cares about are his rules and the ward. I'm sick of rules. I just want to be myself."

Travis definitely needed help, but I suspected what he needed was easier than what Kyle would need. "Go home, Travis. Your parents love you."

"My dad's going to kill me."

"He's not going to kill you. He's just going to ground you, and I know it might sound really stupid to you right now, but your dad would have given anything in the world if his dad had grounded him just once. You know why? Because that would mean he'd actually seen him and knew that he existed." I blinked away tears I hadn't known were so close.

"You mean my grandpa?"

"Yes. Go home, and when your dad starts yelling, you ask him what happened at his last fathers and sons' campout. Your dad isn't perfect, but he's trying. That's far better than he ever had. Now go home."

He stared at me for a long time, but I met his gaze without flinching, and gradually the fire in his eyes subsided. "Okay."

"Do I have to follow you?"

He shook his head.

"Promise?"

"Yes."

"Okay, then. I'll take your word for it. I know you won't go back on your word." I smiled at him. He was so dejected that it was all I could do not to pull him into my arms and hug him. Not him, really, but the boy Dante had been. What a mess!

James and I watched Travis get into his car. "Do you think he'll go home?" James asked.

"I think so."

"Maybe we should follow him." James's voice showed excitement. "Like on the TV shows."

Travis wasn't my responsibility, yet in a strange way, because of my plan, he was, and it would ruin everything if something bad happened to him. At least that's the reason I gave myself for caring.

"Well, we're going home, so we have to go somewhat in the same direction anyway," I said. "We'll see if he's at least heading the right way before we turn down our street."

At first it was easy enough to follow Travis, but at some point I had to let him out of sight or risk his seeing me. Or risk James understanding and telling Lauren that I really had been following him. In the end, I took a different street and drove by Dante's. Their garage was shut, but Travis's car was in the driveway. I breathed a sigh of relief.

Be kind, Dante. But it wasn't my place to tell him that. If it needed saying, Becca would have to do it. Who was I to preach anyway? I'd made so many mistakes that whatever Dante did could not compare.

Without stopping, I turned the corner and drove home.

• • •

The pain brought me from a sound sleep where I had not been dreaming. I came from a delicious blackness where I knew and felt nothing, a kind of death, really. All I could do against the pain was to clutch my head and try to find rational thought. Impossible. The agony was huge, horrible, all-encompassing. I wouldn't survive another minute.

Yet I knew I would. I had so far. The pain didn't dim, but somehow I found the courage to drag myself from bed and move slowly down the hall. I tried not to cry out, but my breath sounded loud and tortured in the dark hallway. Hurrying the last few steps, I grabbed my bottle of pain pills from my purse on the counter, identifying it by the way it fit into my hand, and slumped to the floor as my vision darkened and a renewed agony sliced into my skull. Unseeing, I uncapped the bottle and swallowed a pill. Then another.

How many had I taken? Too many, and it really would be all over. I didn't want that. Minutes ticked slowly by. How could I hold on?

Somehow I would. I always did.

I moaned. Tears wet my face, but I hurt too much to wipe them away.

Gradually, miraculously, the pressure in my head eased. I felt as though a day or more had passed, but I knew it hadn't been more than a half hour. On wobbly legs, I stumbled back to bed, hoping for the delicious relief of sleep.

I had almost reached that sweet blackness when I felt a movement by the bed. Kyle's thin body slipped under the covers, pressing against me like a small child in need of comfort. Tears ran silently from my eyes as I drew her into my arms. *I love you.* I didn't say the words aloud, but I knew she knew.

I wondered again how long she would hate me when I was gone.

CHAPTER FOURTEEN

Kyle

Mom and James were still sleeping when I left the house. I wasn't surprised. James had stayed up far too late, and Mom, well, she had her own problems. As for me, I felt beaten and exhausted, but I couldn't sleep. My mind was going a million miles an hour.

I grabbed a piece of bread from the cupboard, and for a moment I could see my mom as she'd been last night in nearly this same spot, curled up in pain, unseeing. Should I have called 911? I didn't think so because she recovered, but what if one of these times she didn't?

I could never sleep alone anymore, and I didn't understand why. The past few nights I'd gone to my mom's room. She never pushed me away, but she wondered what was up with me. So did I.

During the day, I was so mad at her most of the time for bringing me here, for not making dinner, for not cleaning the house like Allia's mom did. But at night, there was a terrible darkness that threatened to eat me alive. Only Mom could make it go away.

I was little more than a baby. I disgusted even myself.

Allia had put the bike outside her garage as she promised. It was a nice bright blue one that made me think of the sky by the ocean on a cloudless day.

"Oh, good, you're here." Allia emerged from the depths of the open garage. "Look, if you're going inside anywhere, you'll need to lock the bike up. Make sure you put it through both tires and around the bicycle rack. There's been a lot of stolen bikes around here lately."

"I know what that's like. My bike in California had so many pieces stolen, I didn't bother to bring it." That was the truth, but it was also a little girl's bike, which hadn't made me feel too bad. It was nowhere near as nice as Allia's.

"I hardly use it anymore," Allia said.

She was staring at me oddly, and I realized I still had in my nose ring that so far I'd remembered to put in each night. I'd thought about putting it in at school, too, but not many others wore them here in the eighth grade and I felt surprisingly self-conscious. I reached up and slipped it out and into my pocket.

She followed the movement with her eyes but didn't comment. "Are you sure you know where you're going?"

"Yeah." For a moment, I wished she'd volunteer to go with me, but she'd probably be bored. "Thanks a lot. I'll be careful with it."

She shrugged. "Okay, well, have fun. As long as I'm up so early, I might as well get to my chores."

"See ya." I climbed on the bike and rode away.

The morning breeze felt cool against my arms, and I wished I'd brought a jacket, though I should warm up soon enough with the effort of pedaling. At the end of the street, I slowed to consult the map I'd printed at school. I really hoped it wasn't as far away as it looked because I might not get there before nine.

In the end I was there in plenty of time, which was a good thing because it took me a while to figure out that a house was the right address and that the studio was around the back and down some stairs. A sign above the door read La Belle Dance Studio. The door was locked, and I sat down to wait. There was no bicycle rack, but the bike was probably safe enough here behind the house in this quiet neighborhood. To be sure, I edged it behind some bushes where it was mostly out of sight.

The morning sun felt good on my skin as I sat against the wall, dozing. When I heard the lock on the door click open from the inside, I practically jumped. I waited a bit longer before the girls began to arrive. They were my age, I figured, between twelve and fourteen, though all of them except one was taller. They wore tight black stretch pants, and leather jazz dance shoes dangled on their fingers by their laces. I ignored their curious glances as I followed them inside.

They went to a dressing room and then into the studio, while I stayed outside the wall of glass that separated the studio from a row of chairs meant for viewers. Unfortunately, that's what I was. My dance teacher at school had told me about the classes here, and though I knew Mom couldn't afford them yet, I couldn't stay away. The instructor was supposed to have danced on Broadway or somewhere just as important. I didn't know what she was doing here in Spanish Fork, but I wanted to see if she was any good. And the girls. Would they be good, too?

The music began, and a woman hardly bigger than my mother walked into the room from an inner door, clapping her hands twice sharply. "Okay, class, everyone on the floor. Let's begin our warm-up." She had brown hair and dark eyes and wore no makeup. Her face and body looked strong and beautiful. Most of the warm-up exercises I already knew, though these girls took them far more seriously than I'd ever seen students do before. Minutes later they were dancing, and as they launched immediately into complicated, difficult moves, I understood why they'd warmed up so diligently.

I should have brought a pencil and paper. How was I ever going to be able to memorize it all? I'd have to come back. It was beautiful.

I recognized the different forms of dance they used, though I couldn't say what they all were. I felt carried away to another time and place. One particular move had me backing away from the window so I could try it out myself. Mostly I sat on the edge of my seat and watched—until that wasn't enough and I had to stand next to the window. More than anything, I wanted to be in that class. Usually I was the best in any school class and confident in the other classes I'd taken that I'd soon be the best or close enough. Not so here. Could I even fit in? Maybe if I practiced the moves at home they'd let me into the class once I found the money.

What I needed was a job. But who would hire a thirteen-year-old? I could babysit, if anyone would trust me and if I wasn't already babysitting James every day.

I hate my life.

No, I couldn't hate living in a world that contained the beauty inside this studio. A simple studio in someone's basement. Gold.

Want rose up within me, far stronger than when I'd gone clothes shopping with my mother. I wanted this more than I wanted anything.

I hadn't worn the clothes yet. In fact, I felt sick to my stomach every time I thought about wearing them, but I couldn't explain to myself why. I'd stolen before and never had a problem. Was there a way to return the clothes without a receipt and get money to help pay for the dance class? Probably not. I was pretty sure you had to be an adult and give them ID.

The class was two hours long, and after the girls left, another set of girls arrived. Several had mothers with them who sat on the chairs to watch. I stayed for that class, too. Not as good as the first, but some of the moves were the same, and the teacher led them through more repetitions, which helped me memorize different steps. My body itched to copy the moves, but with the mothers there, I couldn't do anything. When the girls filed out an hour and a half later, no new girls arrived, which was just as well since my stomach felt tight with hunger. I started for the door.

"Wait."

I turned to see the instructor emerging from the door to the studio. Up close her thick eyebrows seemed to dominate her narrow face. "I'm Miss Emily. I see you've been observing today. Did you come to watch someone you know?"

I shook my head. "My teacher at school told me about this place. I came to see what you were teaching." *Please take me into your class,* my heart begged.

She smiled. "Ah, that would be Mrs. McKain."

"Yeah." I toed the floor and didn't meet her gaze.

"She sends me all the girls she thinks have talent."

I looked up. "She does?"

She nodded. "She can't do a lot on an individual basis. Not like here. I hold three group lessons and one private lesson for my students each week. Usually after the first year or two of high school they are accepted to a dance school in New York, or I send them to another teacher I know in Provo who helps them prepare a little more. My classes are only for very serious students. I require two hours of practice minimum per day and preferably more. Some of the girls aren't up to that, so they have to find other studios."

To me it sounded like heaven. But four classes a week at that level wouldn't be within my reach ever. Not even if Mom worked overtime, which, given her headaches, I didn't think was a good idea.

"Could I . . . could I just watch?" It hurt to say the words since I wanted so much to be in her class, to come every day, to practice as if I belonged.

Her head leaned to the side as her brown eyes considered me.

"You're welcome to watch as long as you don't distract the girls. You are also welcome to try out a free class. You could bring your mother, if you'd like, so she can see what we do."

"A free class?" I tried not to sound as eager as I felt. "When?"

She smiled. "I usually like new students to come to the younger class when we meet on Thursday at four, but you can come and observe the other classes before then, if you want. Group lessons are on Tuesday and Thursday afternoon or evening, depending on the age group, and on Saturday mornings. Monday, Wednesday, and Friday I keep open for private lessons. I should tell you, however, that I let the girls choose whether or not they want their private lessons observed, and I pull the curtains inside the studio if they want privacy."

"Do many do that?" It would be a long bicycle ride for nothing.

"About half."

"Okay, I'll come on Thursday for sure." I'd come the other days too, even if I had to bring James. I'd bring him books and a snack.

She walked over to the wall near the exit where a small table held a sheaf of papers. "This paper shows our entire schedule and the dates for our performances. And this sheet has our tuition information. Take it home and show your parents."

"Okay. Thanks." A glance at the tuition sheet showed me I'd underestimated the cost of the classes by more than two-thirds. There was no way Mom could pay that much. I'd have to find somewhere else to take lessons.

I didn't want someplace else.

"Thanks," I told her, carefully folding the papers and putting them in the pocket of my jeans with my Internet map.

She smiled, and her strong face looked a bit softer. "Thank you for coming. I hope we have what you're looking for here."

She did, but it was far beyond my reach. Unless I could figure something out. I rode back to Allia's much more slowly than I'd come. The sun beat down on me until I felt smothered in sweat.

At Allia's, the cars were parked in the driveway instead of inside the garage, and her brother Travis was carrying a plastic tote box of balls toward where two other similar totes sat on the front lawn.

"Hi," I said, feeling suddenly brighter.

He nodded. "Hi."

I wondered why he looked so miserable. "Will you tell Allia I brought her bike back?"

"Just leave it there. I have to take all the bikes out anyway to sweep."

"Chores, huh?" I said. He was so cute.

He shrugged, and even that was hot.

"Want some help?"

He set down the box and gave me an actual smile. "You're volunteering? Allia hates doing anything out here."

That's because she's your sister and doesn't care how hot you are. "I don't mind." My stomach took that moment to growl—loudly. Yeah, I guess bicycling a million miles on a single piece of bread wasn't exactly a great idea.

His brow rose. "Hungry?"

"A little. I've been for a long ride."

"You'd better go eat. I'm almost done getting stuff out. Besides, I have a pretty good idea that my dad wants me to do this on my own."

I felt disappointed even though I was ready to drop. Then again, how romantic could cleaning the garage be? If he liked me, he wouldn't *want* me to help. Besides, I'd been gone all morning, and there was the rare chance that someone at home might have woken up and missed me. Even so, I was reluctant to leave. It wasn't every day you had the opportunity to hang out with a guy like Travis.

"Weird our parents knowing each other," I said. "My mom says they used to hang out together when they were our age."

"Yeah, it's weird. Your mom seems kind of nice, though."

I heard the admiration in his voice. Teenage boys always dug my mom for some reason, whether for her confidence or the way she talked—I didn't know. Certainly couldn't be for her looks, especially if the people who said I looked like her were right. I didn't have a million boys lurking around wanting to pledge undying love. Or even asking me out. If most kids here really didn't date until sixteen, things would probably be even worse for me.

"Your dad seems kind of nice, too," I said. "And your mom. She's an amazing cook, and her house is so . . . . clean."

"I'd trade you," he said with a short laugh. I couldn't tell if he was serious, but his expression did seem to indicate that everything in his life had gone wrong.

I leaned against the back of his mother's van. "You wouldn't if you knew my mom. Her dad was abusive, you know, and she's sort of the opposite. No rules or discipline—for me or James. Or for herself. I never know if she's coming home at night. Or at least I didn't used to. It's been better lately." For the past months she'd been acting weird, but it wasn't all bad. In the bugging category, she'd been a little more like I imagined other mothers were. I didn't exactly hate it.

He glanced into the garage but didn't return to work. "So do you have any rules?"

"Nothing really, as long as I go to school. She used to not care if I cut boring classes, but she does now. What I really hate is when she forgets to go grocery shopping."

Surprise and something I suspected was pity flashed across his face. I'd said too much. "Doesn't really matter. I just go myself."

He studied me a moment before saying, "Sounds tough."

Great. Things had gone from bad to worse. I didn't want to be a charity case.

"After I'm not grounded anymore," he said, "I could go to the store for you, if you ever need it." That made me feel more lousy until he added, "I'd drive you, but I can't drive anyone for six months."

"Rules, huh?"

"Something like that."

"So why are you grounded?"

His smile dazzled me. "I was driving my friends."

"Oh, I'm sorry."

He shrugged. "I'm still waiting to see what they're going to do to me." We stared at each other for a few more minutes in awkwardness—but a nice kind of awkwardness, if there was such a thing. He thumbed toward the house. "You want me to get Allia for you?"

"Naw. Just tell her thanks for letting me use the bike. I'd better get home. Good luck with the garage."

"Thanks."

I felt his eyes following me. I hoped that was a good sign.

The walk home seemed longer than the bicycle ride to the dance studio. Couldn't I have said anything more interesting to Travis? He must think I was the most pitiful, boring creature in the world. Yet he'd offered to go to the store for me. That said something, didn't it?

James was watching TV when I walked in the door, lounging on the one piece of furniture we had in the living room—an old chair someone had given Mom a few years back. The rest of the living room furniture hadn't been worth renting a bigger trailer to bring. Personally, I thought our tiny kitchen table was in worse shape, but I guess it took less space because you could pack boxes under it. Or maybe a table was simply something Mom didn't want to do without.

"Hey," I said to James. An empty cereal bowl lay on the carpet next to the chair, so I knew he'd eaten.

"Hi." His eyes didn't move from the cooking show, which meant all the cartoons must be off the air. For some reason the kid loved cooking shows.

"Where's Mom?"

"Sleeping."

I snorted in disgust. She could have been up cleaning or helping James with reading. What was up with her? Rage building inside me, I stomped down the hall to her bedroom.

When I saw her huddled under her sheet, curled as she had been on the kitchen floor last night, the anger seeped through the cracks in my soul and disappeared. "Mom?" I said.

Her head moved toward me, and her eyes opened. "Hi, Kyle. Are you okay?"

I knew she was talking about my coming into her bed last night and the other nights as well. I didn't want to talk about it. "I'm fine." It came out more roughly than I intended. Suddenly, I wanted to either curl up in bed with her and find comfort or shove the dance papers under her nose and scream at her for not being able to help me.

Instead, I turned and stalked from the room. *I hate you!* I thought. *I really, really hate you.*

Not true at all. I simply wanted to feel normal, and I wanted to stop feeling like she was hiding something. I wanted not to worry about money or about James. I wanted to know for sure that she wasn't going to leave again.

The six weeks she'd been gone earlier this year had been a kind of torture to me, though my friend's mother had been nice enough, and Mom had come back from her job once a week to visit. It still felt wrong, and I'd worried every minute that she might never come back. I don't know why. Before that, she hadn't left us for years.

She always comes back, I reminded myself. Besides, if she decided to leave, there was nothing I could do about it. It was ridiculous to worry.

Better to dream about joining that dance class. Somehow I had to find a way. If I couldn't dance, there was no point at all in living.

CHAPTER FIFTEEN

Travis

Maybe that girl Kyle wasn't as weird as I'd thought. Today she'd been wearing normal jeans and a normal shirt that didn't make me feel uncomfortable when I looked at her. I hated when girls wore clothes they appeared ready to burst out of. I mean, I was every bit as eager as the next guy to talk to cute girls—any girl, really—and I certainly appreciated a good figure, but it was embarrassing when girls looked cheap, like the ones who made out with guys in the lunchroom or behind the school.

Probably my Mormon upbringing, but I knew what I felt when I saw girls dressed like that, and it wasn't respect or friendship. Better to look the other way or to make some snide comment about their heavy makeup. Raccoon eyes. Kyle would look much better if she ditched that junk.

Not that I was interested in her. She was way too young, like a little sister.

That stuff about her mom made me feel terrible. Here I was angry at having to clean out the garage as part of my punishment, though I usually had to do it once a month anyway, and she was worrying about her mother coming home at night or having food in the house.

Her mother. Now that was one good-looking woman. Her eyes could see right into your soul. You knew she really thought about what she was saying when she talked to you. It was hard to reconcile the mother Kyle told me about with the woman who'd sent me home last night and trusted I would go.

When I'd come home last night, Dad and Mom had been waiting. Mom hadn't spoken a word, but the disappointed look on her face had left no doubt that I'd let her down. Dad had extended his hand for the car keys and asked me to go to my room. "I'm taking your mother on a date, and we'll talk about this tomorrow—after you clean out the garage and do your other chores."

What a relief, because the veins had been standing out on his neck, and I knew he wanted nothing more than to lay into me.

Hey, they should be grateful I'd come home, right? Late, but I had come. Because of Kyle's mom, but they didn't need to know that.

Now I wasn't sure if waiting had been a good thing. I kept going over everything in my head, from the law being stupid and their not trusting me to plans of groveling in abject humility so they'd forgive me. It was awful, going back and forth, being furious one minute and feeling like dirt the next. In the end, I had no one to blame but myself.

Couldn't they see that waiting six months to drive other kids was too long?

It was the law.

I couldn't get around that. Dad would say something like, "Do we go forty in a twenty-five mile an hour zone because we think it's stupid? Do we take something from the store because the price is too high?" No. Obviously.

Still, he didn't remember what it was like to be a kid.

Rikki Crockett had told me to ask him about the fathers and sons' campout. I hadn't even known he'd gone on a fathers and sons' campout. His dad hadn't been active, but the ward members back then had probably invited him. Something must have happened. Anyway, I didn't know what it had to do with disobeying my parents.

They were never going to give me the car keys again.

I should have taken Kyle up on her offer to help with the garage. Come to think about it, she looked kind of like her mom, pretty underneath the makeup. She was nice, too.

The door to the house shut, and my eyes jerked toward it. Dad? No, it was Allia.

"Hi," she said.

"Hi." I went for Cory's bike, not looking at her. "Kyle returned your bike. It's out there."

Allia grabbed the handlebars to Lauren's bike and pushed it out of the garage. "So, are you okay? Did Dad yell at you? I was downstairs when you came home."

"Not yet."

She parked the bike and looked at me. "It was me. I told them."

"What?" I let Cory's bike fall to the cement and glared at her. I'd wondered how they'd found out so fast. I knew someone had to have ratted on me.

"I'm really sorry, but I was afraid you'd get pulled over by a cop. Or that you'd get in an accident because of all your friends making distractions." Tears gathered in her eyes. "I'd rather you be grounded and mad at me than dead."

My sister couldn't help who she was—a Molly Mormon, though a good-looking one, according to my friends, who were never above flirting with her. "I wish you hadn't done that."

"I'm sorry," she said again.

I shrugged. "They would have found out anyway." Rikki had

pointed it out last night—it was a small community. As children of the bishop, we were watched more closely than any other children in the ward or the stake, for that matter.

She grabbed the broom. "I'll help."

Now I knew how bad she really felt. I wanted to be angry at her, but worrying all night long about what Dad might do to me made it difficult to hold onto any emotions besides regret.

"No, thanks." I took the broom from her. "I want to do it."

Her face crumpled.

"No, really," I said. "It helps me think. I'm not exactly happy about what you did, but it's nice you didn't want me to die."

Allia sniffed. "Okay." She watched me working for a few minutes before going back inside the house.

As I worked, anger once again flared in my heart. Not just at Allia but at my dad. *I bet he knew I'd worry all night long,* I thought. *I bet he thinks it's wonderful punishment. What a loser. Well, I'll show him.* There was a lot I could do to embarrass him. I could stop going to church, flunk a class or two, even steal the keys and drive somewhere. I'd show him and Allia, too, the little skunk.

With anger riding me, I finished sweeping the garage in record time. I used the snow shovel to scoop up the dirt and put it into the garbage can. I dragged the totes and the bicycles back to their spots. Usually, I'd move in the cars, too, but Mom had moved them out and hadn't left the keys. I hunched my back and stared at them, my thoughts black and angry.

A hand on my shoulder made me start. "Son."

Ah, time for the talk. I turned to my dad, wiping my face clean of expression, though maybe I should let my regret show through. Somehow I couldn't—maybe my pride was getting in the way.

"Let's go inside to my office."

Not the office. That felt too much like church. "Can't we talk out here?"

He looked up and down the street. Several neighbors were out in their yards but not close enough to overhear. "How about in the backyard, then? I'm a little tired, and there's a place to sit."

"Okay." I followed him out to the back, not to the picnic table on the deck but over to the play set he'd put together two years ago—the play fort, as Lauren liked to call it. I'd been planning to help, but it hadn't worked out that way. He sat on the end of the slide, so I took the grass several feet away.

Silence. He glanced toward the top of the slide, as though seeing something he'd forgotten. A smile tugged on his lips. He was a million miles away. As usual.

"Dad? Can we get this over with?"

His attention snapped back to me. "Sorry. Just remembering something."

"A meeting you have to go to?" A guy could hope.

"No. Something that happened a long time ago when I was about your age."

Who was he kidding? He was *never* my age.

"Look, Travis. I'm not at all happy about what you did last night. Well, not so much what you did but that you deceived us. A lie by omission is still a lie. Breaking a rule is still breaking a rule, even if you aren't caught."

I kept quiet. Sometimes that made him think I agreed.

His gaze felt hot on my face, so I looked away. What did he see? He sighed. "I never expected to have to talk to you this way. I trusted you to do the right thing. I always have. I don't even know what to say."

I almost laughed out loud. That was a first. My father the bishop, a paragon of virtue, fount of wisdom, speechless. He'd come up with something, I was sure. *Wait for it.*

After a minute I grew uncomfortable. I knew it was a minute because I counted. A minute is a whole heck of a lot more time than people understand, and it seems like ten or more when you're waiting to hear your fate for the next few weeks or possibly months. I thought about apologizing but knew it couldn't be that easy. After all, he'd trusted me.

Trusted me.

I sneaked a peek at him, but he was staring at the ground looking . . . well, sad. Tears threatened behind my eyes, and suddenly I did feel sorry. Sorry I'd let him down, sorry I'd broken the law, sorry I couldn't be as good as Allia.

He took a breath. "It's a lot of pressure being the oldest and the bishop's son. I'm sorry."

He was sorry? Wow, if that was what happened when we waited to talk, I hoped he always waited. I wonder if, like me, he'd gone through a thousand scenarios in his head as he thought about what he would say to me. That made me feel powerful and scared all at once. Powerful because he was just like me, and scared because if my dad, the bishop, didn't have all the answers, who in the world did?

"I won't do it again," I said.

He lifted his eyes to mine. "I hope not."

If he believed me, he would have said, "I trust you, son." But I'd lost that trust.

"This is really going to put a burden on your mom." He held my eyes with his own. "With you not being able to drive, she'll have to take you to school, and she's got enough on her plate as it is with teaching Cory and taking and picking up the other kids."

Rats. That meant I was grounded from the car.

Dad wasn't finished. "It's not the end of the world. You're a good kid, Travis, and I'm so proud to be your dad. You're intelligent, you work hard, you're good to your siblings." He cracked a smile that was still sad and made me feel about an inch high, though what he was saying was positive. I didn't like seeing my father upset. "Well, most of the time. You have so much going for you. Unfortunately, that makes when you do screw up rather noticeable."

"I said I won't do it again." *What do you want from me?* But I knew. He wanted an apology I wasn't ready to give. It seemed too much like letting him win—even if he was right.

"You made a choice, and not driving is the consequence. We talked about this before you started driving. If I don't follow through, then I'm no sort of a parent at all. Consequences, good or bad, are the natural result of all our choices. I would rather you learn on this than on something far more damaging to you or someone else."

Like sluffing school, drinking, or worse. I understood, but it still stank because I *was* a good kid. All my friends would often say, "I don't know if that would be okay. Ask the bishop's kid. If he says yes, we'll do it." Not exactly unpleasant because they did listen to me, even if it put me on the spot more often than not.

"Is there anything you want to say?" Dad pulled out a few strands of grass from the overly long lawn that begged to be cut. I usually mowed the front lawn and he took the back, but he'd been busy. No surprise there. "Anything you want to talk about?"

My cue to say no and end this torture. Except that I wanted to know how long I'd be grounded. I opened my mouth and words popped out. "I want to know what happened at your last fathers and sons' campout."

His hand stopped tugging at the grass. He stared at me, his eyes darker than I'd ever seen them. "Where did that come from?" he asked slowly.

I lifted my right shoulder and dropped it. "I ran into that new woman in the ward at the store last night. She told me to ask you."

"Rikki?" He glanced toward the top of the slide and back to me, which told me the earlier memory had been related to her.

"Why would she—" He broke off, his stare intensifying to the point of definite weirdness. "Travis, I . . ." His jaw worked but nothing emerged. Twice in one day my dad was speechless.

I was beginning to feel uncomfortable. "Did you and Grandpa go to the campout? I thought you said he wasn't active."

"He wasn't. And no, he never went with me to any campout—Scouts, fathers and sons', whatever. I always went, but he didn't."

I wondered if that was why Dad always attended every campout with me, though he was often so busy with the other boys in the ward that for me he might as well not have come. I almost wished he'd stay home once in a while. "Then why would she tell me to ask?"

"Because the last time I planned to go I was fifteen, and he told me he'd go with me. I was so excited. I'd tried everything to get him to notice me—I got good grades, I did the dishes, kept my room clean." An odd note had entered my father's voice, a longing that made me sad. "I was excited because my dad scarcely seemed to know I was around, but finally we'd be together like the other boys and their dads."

"I know how that feels," I muttered. My friends seemed to talk with my dad more than I did, what with interviews and church activities and all.

"What?"

"Nothing. What happened?"

"He worked late that night. Didn't come home until after everyone left for the campout. I don't know if he forgot, or if he'd only told me yes to get me off his case. I unpacked and went to bed early. I didn't go on any more campouts after that."

"I didn't know Grandpa was such a jerk."

"He wasn't a jerk. He was just very sad. After my mother died, it was like he couldn't go on. Not in any way that meant anything. He simply survived."

I hadn't known my grandfather, though I had a few memories of him from when I was a very young child, the most vivid from his funeral. Dad's face had been so white and frozen that day, except for a single tear that snaked down his cheek. I'd gripped his leg tight, not knowing what else to do.

"He was so sad, he didn't have room for me. It wasn't his fault."

Yes, it was, I wanted to say. My dad had graduated at the top of his high school class, and according to his former companions he'd worked harder than any missionary they'd ever known. Every weekend he'd gone over to Grandpa's to do his yard work before doing his own. All this time he'd been searching for something Grandpa would never give him. What? Attention? A campout? I didn't know, but it made me want to cry.

Had my dad ever wanted to give up? Sluff school? Stop trying to be good? Maybe. But he hadn't. I'd seen that myself. He'd worked hard and become someone, despite his father's neglect. I couldn't believe I'd actually considered skipping school or stealing the car keys to show my dad I wouldn't be controlled. That seemed awfully juvenile now.

"I'm sorry, Dad," I said, my voice choked with tears. "I'm sorry about letting you down. I'm sorry about you not trusting me. I'm sorry for being angry with you and thinking you're always gone." Because he wasn't always gone. He went camping with me. He drove around looking for me when he should have been on a date with Mom. He cared enough to call my friends. He sat here and talked to me when the lawn needed cutting.

"Oh, son." He reached for me and hugged me tight, and then we were both crying. "I don't want to make the same mistakes my father did," he said. "I never want you to feel that way. You mean more to me than any other boy or girl in the ward. You know that, don't you? God has given me stewardship over them, but you're my son, and that means you're my first priority. You and your mom and your brother and sisters are my reason for living. I would do anything to protect you, to keep you safe."

"Last night—I just wasn't thinking." I felt stupid. Stupid for adding to his burden when I should have been helping him and helping the kids in the ward. Being more diligent instead of so selfish.

. "We all make mistakes." Dad was still holding me, and I could feel his tears mingling with mine on my cheek. "What sets us apart is what we do next. Travis, I promise to spend more time with you. I promise to be a better dad. To listen more and be slower to anger. To help you become the great man I know you already are becoming." His chest convulsed with a sob. "If your mother hadn't stopped me from talking to you last night, I don't know how this would have played out."

Probably not good. I might have felt I had good reason for making poor choices. Who would those choices have hurt in the end anyway? Me or my parents? If I failed a class, my father certainly wouldn't have to retake it.

I didn't know what to say next, but I knew that for the rest of my life, I was going to be grateful my dad went camping with me and that he cared enough to ground me when I did something stupid. Maybe knowing he cared enough to be watching would make me think twice about what I did.

What choices would I have made if I'd grown up with Grandpa instead of Dad? I really didn't know. But from here on out, I had a choice. It was up to me.

"My life," Dad continued, loosening his hold on me, "growing up wasn't . . . it wasn't good, but I don't want you to think too poorly of your grandfather. When I needed advice the most, he was there. Because of him I went on a mission, and because I went on a mission, I was still single when I met your mother. For that alone, I forgave him everything a long time ago."

"If you hadn't gone on a mission, would you have married Rikki?" My turn to pluck at the grass. Was I afraid of what he would say?

"I believe so."

"She doesn't seem too bad."

"She wasn't ready to raise a family in the Church, and that's the only way I know that people can be happy. I don't know if she's ready to do that even now. I hope so." He waited until I looked him in the eye again before continuing. "Two months into my mission, I began thanking God every day for letting me serve and for not letting me marry Rikki. I said the same prayer every day for two years, and I still say that prayer when I think about the direction my life might have taken. The gospel is true, Travis—I know it. A mission was my duty to my Father in Heaven and the greatest blessing I'd ever received up to that point in my life."

"It's sad for her. She's all alone."

"We'll do our best to help her find her way."

I nodded. "Her daughter wouldn't be so bad if she didn't wear all that makeup."

He laughed. "If only girls understood that."

Suddenly things were okay again. I was grounded, Dad was still a bishop and likely wouldn't have a lot of free time to do things with me, but I knew he loved me, that he'd be there if I really needed him. I wouldn't let him down this time, but if for some stupid reason I did, I knew he wouldn't give up on me, that he'd give me yet another chance.

"Well," I said, feeling lighter inside. "You need a hand with this lawn?"

He arched a brow. "You offering?"

"I guess—if you'll take me out for ice cream after." When I was little, that was my favorite thing to do with my dad.

"You're on." We shook hands.

He glanced once more into the play set, seeing something I couldn't, but it didn't bother me now. He had a lot of ghosts in his past, but I knew he was glad to be where he was now—with Mom and the rest of us.

I felt different somehow. More responsible. Before today I'd felt younger, like a child seeing how many pieces of candy he could take while his parents weren't looking. But my future was up to me, every bit as much as Dad's had been up to him. I'd done a lot of things I wasn't proud of during the past few months. Things that would likely horrify my parents a lot more than driving friends before the law said I could. That ended now. I was no longer a child. I was a young man with conscious choices to make. A young man with the priesthood, Dad would say.

The future was in my hands.

CHAPTER SIXTEEN

Dante

My wife and daughter sat across the desk from me in my office at the church, Allia staring down at the brown carpet. "I just wanted to see what I'd look like."

Becca's lips tightened. "You said yourself she looked like one of those girls who sleep around. Why would you want to look like that?"

Becca had found Allia that morning in the bathroom, eyes laden with blue, Kyle-like eye shadow. She'd made her wash it off and then come early to church to tell me about it. After my experience with Travis yesterday, I cleared my schedule fast. Allia's actions, though, surprised me far more than anything Travis might do. Allia was so rigid in her beliefs that sometimes I had to stop myself from telling her to lighten up and live a little. She'd learn that soon enough after she got past these dangerous teen years.

"I don't want to look like that. I wasn't going to wear it out anyplace. I was curious how I'd look, that's all." Allia bit her lip, fighting tears.

Becca and I exchanged a glance. "Okay," I said, taking my cue from my wife's face. "It startled us, that's all. You've always been such a strong person, and when we see you following someone who's weaker in the ways that really matter, well, it's a concern."

"I wonder what Kyle looks like under all that makeup." Allia shifted in her chair. "I bet she looks normal."

"Kyle needs a lot of support," Becca said.

"I don't mind helping her. Is she coming to my class today? I don't think she'll go at all if she doesn't."

"I've talked to the teachers and told them that might happen, but I want to talk to her mother first to see how she thinks Kyle would do on her own." I glanced toward the door. "We'd better get to the chapel. It's almost time to start."

"You go ahead, Allia," Becca said, also standing. "I'll be there in a minute."

She waited until the door shut before continuing. "I'm worried about Allia. She's always been strong, but she's also young and vulnerable. I don't know if I like the idea of her being an anchor for Kyle."

"I know, believe me." How many times had I gone through that thought process when considering other members for callings? I wanted to use strengths but not to the point of endangering the faith of the strong. Everyone had a limit. "We'll keep an eye on it. I'll talk to Rikki about Kyle's clothes and the makeup, at least for church."

"I'm doing everything I can to help her, Dante. I'm going to work with James, I'm willing to let Allia befriend her up to a point, but my first responsibility as a mother is to my own children."

I came around the desk and took her in my arms. "I know. It should be. We're going to get through this together, I promise."

She melted into me. I loved it when she did that. "Just so you remember who you have to come home to each night."

"Get to, not have to." I kissed her, feeling a flare of annoyance when someone rattled the doorknob. "Guess we'd better go. I'm not sure my counselors would approve of us making out in the bishop's office."

Becca's laugh rolled over me before she kissed me again. One night at a stake Relief Society event, a psychologist had talked about marital relationships and had mentioned that a kiss between a husband and wife wasn't a real kiss unless it lasted at least five seconds. Becca had taken his advice to heart, and I silently thanked that man every day.

"By the way," she said sometime later as she turned to the door, "you have lipstick on your face."

As I scrambled for a napkin and a mirror, she opened the door and left the room. I could hear the prelude music signaling that I should hurry to sacrament meeting. When I emerged from my office a minute later, Rikki and her two children were walking across the foyer.

"Can't we sit in the back?" Kyle said with a whiny voice I'd bet she didn't know was being overheard.

Rikki tossed her head exactly in the way she had as a teen. "Huh-huh. Those chairs are way too hard."

They were both dressed more moderately this week. Kyle was wearing a plaid skirt that seemed vaguely familiar with a T-shirt that was tight but not immodest. Her hair was pulled back, and she had a blue flower in her hair. Rikki was once again wearing her red gypsy skirt but this time coupled with a white frilly blouse that seemed to have come from another age. On her it was exactly right.

"Dante," she said, pausing. "Can I talk to you for a minute?"

"That's about all we have before church starts. Would you rather make an appointment?"

"No, a minute's fine." She turned to the kids. "Go on in, guys. On the soft seats, though." Her gaze swung back to me. "I'm sure the hard seats haven't changed since we were here."

"Actually, they aren't the same metal chairs. They're plastic now, but every bit as hard. What's up? No water problems, I hope?"

"It's Kyle. She's acting weird, and I'm not sure what to do about it. I mean, I know it's hard moving here and starting a new school, and being one of the youngest in her grade never helps, but it's different this time. She disappeared for hours yesterday and wouldn't say where she'd been, and she keeps coming to my bed at night, crying, but she won't talk about it. I'm not sure what to do."

"I'll talk to her, if you'd like me to." Little did she know this worked into my own plans. I needed to figure out how to help Kyle not end up like her mother. The sadness in Rikki's eyes was all too apparent, and I didn't want that for her daughter.

"I would. Thanks." She sighed. "She never knew her father, and there's never really been a man in her life. I didn't think it mattered, but now I'm not so sure."

"I'll be glad to talk to her. That's what I'm here for, Rikki."

"I don't mean as a bishop, Dante. I mean as my friend."

I lifted my shoulders, extending my hands toward her, palms up. "It's the same thing, Rikki. I am who I am."

She didn't speak for the space of several heartbeats, but then she nodded. "Okay. I'm not averse to having her taught the gospel. I think good values will help keep her steady until she's grown."

"They help keep us steady all our lives."

She nodded. "Maybe."

"I wanted to thank you for talking to Travis on Friday."

"He would have gone home eventually, even if I hadn't told him to."

I hadn't known about that part. "I meant for telling him to ask me about the campout. We had a good talk. I haven't told him much about how I grew up, and I should have."

"He needs you, Dante. Just like you needed your dad."

"I know." I felt grateful to her, and it wasn't a comfortable place.

Stop it with the pride, I told myself. "We'd better go in." I started past her when she spoke.

"Are you going to Saint George with Becca?"

I paused and turned. "What?"

"To the garden show."

"Oh, I asked her about that. She said it was nothing."

She snorted. "Are you really that blind? Ask her about it, and this time listen."

"I did." I tried to stifle the irritation I felt at her insinuation.

"She wants to go. Remember how much I wanted to dance?"

I remembered it well. Rikki had been good, but too much was against her. Her dad would never have paid for the private lessons she needed to go somewhere great. I didn't kid myself that Rikki had shed more tears over that than losing me.

"Well, she wants it, maybe like that. Or she will."

I couldn't believe Becca would feel that strongly about anything and not tell me. I wanted to tell Rikki that my wife was her own woman and free to pursue what she wanted. But suddenly I was thinking of the riotous flower beds outside our house that screamed to be noticed. "I'll talk to her again."

She grinned. "Good. Because if you don't, I'll go with her, and you might not like what you get back."

I matched her teasing tone. "Becca can hold her own. Even against you."

"The question is whether she can hold her own against you."

I laughed. "I'm not so tough. But you know that."

"I remember." Her voice was so soft it could have been a fleeting touch. "You made the right choice, Dante. Don't ever forget that."

"I won't."

There was pain in her face and something more in her eyes, yet I wouldn't lie to her. If she was going to be in my ward under my care, I had to be completely honest. I would help her as I would any

144

ward member but not at the risk of my family. Even if I hadn't been totally and absolutely in love with Becca, which I was, I was committed to her and the kids.

"Kyle can go to class with Allia, if you think that would be better," I said. "I've already talked to the teachers, but I wanted to see how you felt about it."

"She already told me she won't go to the other class alone."

"Okay, tell her to go with Allia." Now probably wasn't a good time to bring up makeup and clothing. I still wasn't sure I should be the one to do that on any day. *Maybe Becca has an idea how to go about it.*

I nodded at Rikki and hurried up the aisle to the stand, where my counselors Brother Paul Thorley and Brother Steve Mendenhall were already seated. But eyes weren't on me. They were on Rikki, who swished across the back of the chapel and up the other aisle to where her children waited for her on the same bench they'd occupied last week. Several ward members smiled and waved at her. It had always been like that, even in the old days. Rikki had a certain way about her that made people gravitate toward her. Given her upbringing, she could have been suspicious and bitter, but she'd always accepted people for who they were. I suspected that was another reason I'd loved her so much. Yes, she'd been fragile and needed someone to help her, but in return she'd accepted me just as I was. Not like my father.

• • •

I pulled Kyle aside after sacrament meeting, promising to take her to Allia's class later. "Have a seat," I invited when we reached my office.

She slumped down on one of the chairs, not meeting my eyes, her face sullen. I knew the look well enough, both from my past experience with her mother and with other youth in my ward. She didn't want to be anywhere near me or my office.

"I like to get to know all the new members in my ward," I told her. "That's why I asked you here."

"I'm not a member."

At least it was a response.

"Well, your mother is, and I guess you'll be here for at least a while."

"Till she moves again."

"Yeah, but for now you'll have to make the best of it."

She shifted uncomfortably. The skirt she was wearing really did seem familiar. I wondered if Allia or Lauren had something similar.

"How are you liking it here?" I asked. "You seem to have made friends with my daughter."

Kyle shrugged. "I guess. I'd rather be in California."

"If you're thinking that now, you'll probably really think that once it starts to snow, though if you've never been skiing, that might make up for the cold. I never really picked it up, but my kids love it."

She met my eyes with an expression that said I was nuts, though whether I was nuts to think she'd like snow or because of my lame attempt to talk to her, I had no idea. I was usually better than this. Of course, most kids I talked to I'd known both them and their families for years. I knew something about them. I knew nothing about Kyle except in her face I saw a younger Rikki—hurting, vulnerable, defiant. *Please, Father, help me reach her.*

"I guess you've heard that I knew your mother when we were about your age."

She nodded.

"She was my best friend for a lot of years. I don't know what I would have done growing up without her. We did everything together." I gave a short laugh. "Of course if my son or daughter

146

started hanging out with someone of the opposite sex all the time, I'd be worried, but Rikki and I, well, we were more like siblings most of the time. Neither of us had any brothers or sisters."

"And your parents were lousy."

"I take it your mom told you about her family."

"Everything. I'm glad I didn't know them."

"Your grandmother wasn't all bad. She'd give me cookies sometimes when I came over."

"She did?"

When her husband wasn't home, but I didn't have to add that. "Yeah. I liked her. She reminded me of my own mother."

"She died, didn't she?" Kyle shivered.

"When I was really young. Younger than your little brother."

She was silent a long moment, as if digesting the fact that I had ever been so young. "I bet that was horrible."

I nodded. "A lot of horrible things happen to good people, to children. What's sad is when there's nobody around to help. That's one reason why the Lord has us come on Sundays to be here together as a kind of an extended family. We call it our ward family. Growing up, your mother and I didn't have much support at home, but we had our ward family, and they helped us. It wasn't perfect, but it was enough." For me, it had been. It could have been for Rikki as well, if she'd let it. If she'd stayed. "What I'm trying to say is that no matter how rough it gets, there are people here who will look out for you."

She snorted. "No one here even knows me."

"Not yet, they don't, but even so anyone out there would help you if you asked. I would. For as long as your mom is living in that house, I'm your bishop, whether or not you come to church. That means if you need me, you can call, and I'll try to help." Warmth spread through me as I spoke. I remembered my own dear bishop and his counselors and how often they'd filled in for my father. The only way I could begin to repay them for their service was to live the gospel and to reach out as they had done to me.

Kyle's freckled nose wrinkled. "So that's why you helped us move in and those women came to clean?"

"That's exactly why. It's like having a bunch of extra relatives. For a lot of people, helping is a highlight of their week. Problem is, a lot of times people need something, but they keep it all inside and don't ask for help. They think they're a burden. Take Sister Gillman, one of the women who came to your house. Last year she was fighting cancer. For a lot of that time she was in bed, and the sisters not only brought in meals but had to spoon-feed her. She kept worrying about being a burden, but the sisters practically wrestled each other for the privilege of taking her dinner."

Was that a small smile on Kyle's face? Whatever it had been, it was gone now.

"What if someone didn't have money for food?"

I met her steady gaze. "Kyle, if you or anyone in this ward ever needs food, you call me personally. We take care of each other."

She seemed to relax marginally, but I still hadn't found out anything about her. Not really.

"Kyle," I said. "Is there anything I can help you with now?"

"No." But her eyes no longer met mine.

"If there is, you can always give me a call. Anytime, day or night, okay?" I jotted down my home and cell phone numbers on one of the three-by-five cards I kept in the desk for that reason. "If I can't help you, I'll find someone who can." It was hardly my regular interview, but her situation was not normal. How could it be with Rikki as her mother? Wild Rikki, whom no one could pin down for long.

Kyle studied the card for longer than it merited. Then she folded it once and closed her hand over it. "Can I go now?"

"I'll take you to class."

She frowned, and I wondered if she'd planned to make a run for it. At the door she hesitated and turned back. "My mom used to dance when she was my age, didn't she?"

"Every moment she wasn't hanging out with me." Or toilet papering someone's house or forging a note to get out of class. Or hiding from her father.

"Was she . . . any good?"

"I thought she was. But it was hard without her parents' support. She didn't have proper lessons. I heard she danced after she left Utah." Actually, I'd heard she did a stint as a stripper. Did Kyle know that? I hoped not.

"She danced a lot when I was little," Kyle said. "I only saw a few of her shows. Her best one was in New Orleans, but I wasn't living with her then."

"Oh?"

She shrugged with elaborated casualness I could see was faked. "I sometimes stay with friends." The way she spoke called up the memory of Rikki sleeping outside in the bushes at my house, too afraid of her father to go home. Rikki might not have kicked her daughter out, but to Kyle it had felt the same.

Poor child. Aloud, I said, "I've never been to New Orleans, either."

Kyle smiled unexpectedly. "I'll go there someday."

"I'm sure you will." I reached past her and opened the door. "Come on. Let's go find your class."

"You mean Allia's class, right?"

"Right. But yours now, too. You have permission to attend her class for as long as you want."

CHAPTER SEVENTEEN

Becca

On Tuesday, Kyle appeared at my house with James shortly after three o'clock, barely beating me to my house after I picked up the children and stopped off for milk at the grocery store. The day had already been busy, and I still had dirt under my nails from planting bulbs in the backyard flower bed. Next year, I hoped to have a new crop of lilies.

"James," Lauren said, "you shoulda just ridden home with us."

"Is Allia around?" Kyle asked, her eyes not quite meeting mine. "She said I could borrow her bike."

"Somewhere." I turned and called into the house. "Allia, Kyle's here for you." To Kyle I added, "Do you want to stay for a snack?" Since James's school got out at 2:45, I knew neither had gone home first.

"No. I have to get going."

"Where're you headed?"

"To a friend's. We're doing a project."

A lie. I could tell by the way she wouldn't meet my gaze, but that was her mother's responsibility.

Allia appeared from the hall and took Kyle through the kitchen to the garage. "See you in an hour," I called to Kyle pointedly.

"Okay."

"I'm glad I don't have to go with her," James said as the door shut behind them. "Yesterday she made me walk like forever to her friend's house."

"What friend?" I asked.

He shrugged. "I don't know. I stayed outside. They have a really cool playground in the backyard, and Kyle said I could play there if I didn't leave."

"She left you there alone?"

"She checked on me. There were a whole bunch of girls going in and out of the basement. They dressed kinda funny."

This didn't sound good. "Funny how?"

"I don't know. They had black socks on their legs. I think."

Tights or leggings? A lot of girls wore leggings these days. Allia had some, but I still made sure any skirt she wore them with came to her knees. Well, whatever Kyle's problem, Rikki would have to deal with it.

"Come on," I said to James and Lauren. "Let's get to work."

James was adorable. He was eager to please, and he could take anything Lauren could dish out without getting upset, which was nothing short of amazing. How he'd managed to retain his innocence was remarkable given the worldly wear on the female members of his family. He attacked his problem of reading the same way he attacked his ignorance of the gospel in Primary—with numerous questions and pleas for examples.

Unfortunately, he could tell me only what a few of the letters were and seemed to have no concept of telling a story from a picture. Kyle didn't return on time, so I kept trying until even James began to show cracks in his patience. I was beginning to suspect a severe learning disability that was far beyond me, when Lauren,

151

after drawing a picture of a tree house with a black marker, began telling a story and James jumped in.

"And the boy climbed up to the highest point right here—"

"That's not the highest point," Lauren interrupted. "The highest point is here." She pointed to a lighter line a little higher up.

James frowned and said softly, "Okay. From there, then."

"James, can you see that line?" I asked.

He nodded. "Yeah, I know it's there."

"Which way does it curve? Can you put your finger on it?"

"Yeah."

"Okay, now follow the line."

He moved a little, and then looked at Lauren's face and moved his finger. When she frowned, he started going the other way.

I realized he might not be able to see the line at all. "James, what if I draw this? Can you tell me what it is?" I drew a big letter A.

"An A?" he asked.

I drew all of the letters bigger with a black marker. The first time through, he couldn't identify any more, but the second time through, he got a few more. Stringing them together was also a big problem.

"Very good, James," I said when I was satisfied. "You two can go outside and play."

"Finally." Lauren rushed toward the door.

He still needed testing, but I believed James had a mixture of dyslexia and farsightedness, with the dyslexia coming first and the farsightedness coming on more suddenly and preventing proper diagnoses. I doubted any of his teachers in the past had spent as much time with him in one block trying to resolve this situation. I didn't blame them—most teachers I knew were overloaded. When it came down to it, this was Rikki's responsibility, though her economic situation and lack of education wouldn't have made it easy on her. Either way, I was determined to help James.

I didn't know much about dyslexia, but I could ask my friend Gretchen from the private school what I could do to help him, and farsightedness was easy enough to fix—as long as that's. what it was. While I watched the kids out the window, I told myself if Rikki couldn't take James to the eye doctor, I would. He deserved a chance. I'd call her tonight to explain my findings.

Allia wandered into the kitchen as I cleared away the kids' papers. I was glad to see that today her eyes were normal—in fact, she might not have put on any makeup at all. "What's up?" I asked.

She shrugged. "I don't know. Kyle keeps asking to use my bike. I don't know where she's going."

"Keeps asking. Isn't this only the second time?"

"Yes, but she wants it again on Thursday and Saturday."

"Are you worried about her damaging the bike?"

"Not really. It's a little small for me, anyway, but I saw her with some kids this afternoon at lunchtime. They were scary-looking. I'm just hoping she's not hanging out with them."

"It's a tough situation. How do other kids act around her?"

"I don't know. But she's a little embarrassing. Her clothes, you know." Allia blushed. "I don't like being with her when my friends are around."

I sighed. "I know what you mean." A part of me was happy to hear my daughter didn't want to be with Kyle, but I'd learned enough about Kyle to pity her as well. "That's why I might have overreacted about the makeup on Sunday."

"Maybe it was good you did." Allia gave me a tight grin. "I feel really stupid."

"I should record you saying that."

She laughed. "Yeah, and play it the next time I do something stupid. But, you know, when it's just us two, Kyle's okay."

"We need to remember that she's had a completely different upbringing."

"It's so sad. Maybe if she was baptized, she would be more . . . more normal."

I laughed. "You mean normal for us. For the world, I'd say she's pretty normal."

"You know what I mean. I feel bad I can't even invite her to Mutual tonight since we're going to the temple."

"There's nothing we can do about that. The leaders planned this activity before she arrived. I'm sure they'll work temple trips in on other days so Kyle can come to Mutual."

Allia frowned. "Maybe since Kyle is coming over to drop off James, you could talk to her. All the Young Women think you're really cool, so maybe she'd listen to you about clothes."

"All the Young Women think I'm cool?" This was news to me.

"Yeah. You don't dress like most of the other moms. I mean, you look good."

I was flattered. I did my best to look nice, but I wasn't a fashion hound by any sense. I loved a good pair of nice-fitting jeans. Maybe since that was what the girls mostly wore, they identified with me.

"Dad should call you to be in the Young Women," Allia added.

I laughed. "So I can check up on you? You might get sick of that."

"Never." Allia hugged me, and I returned the gesture, holding on perhaps a bit too long. They grew up so fast.

The timer on the oven rang, and I went to check my lasagna that I'd packed with enough extra beef to satisfy even Cory. Another ten minutes and I would take off the tinfoil, add a bit of cheese, and turn it off to cool a bit before dinner. "I wonder what's keeping Kyle?" I said, taking out the cheese and the grater. "She should have been here by now. Your father will be home before too long. The boys have already been in here twice looking for food."

Allia shrugged, glancing at the clock. "Five-thirty already? I have some homework to do before dinner. I'll be in my room. Call me when we're going to eat, okay?"

"Okay."

I took a moment to check on Travis, who was on the computer in the downstairs family room working on an English essay that was apparently going to be a weekly occurrence. Cory was sprawled on the couch across from him, reading a book. That was a good sight, and I couldn't help smiling.

Kyle finally arrived, out of breath from her exertion with the bicycle. "Sorry I took so long." She mumbled something about her friend, but I didn't pry.

"Your mother will be home soon, right?" I asked.

"Yeah."

"Tell her I'll call her later about James, would you?"

"Sure."

"It's important." I said this because Kyle had a distant look, as though she were in another world.

I watched her and James leave. For all Kyle's distraction, there was a spark to her step that I'd never seen before. *Well, I thought, wherever you've been, it made you happy. I only hope it wasn't with those scary-looking kids Allia was telling me about.*

CHAPTER EIGHTEEN

Dante

As usual, my stomach reacted pleasantly to the smell of cooking food as I walked through the door, and even more so today because I'd worked through lunch, eating only a sandwich from the stack in the refrigerator that Becca had made for me and the kids to take that morning. We were responsible for whatever else we wanted, and usually I had time to heat leftovers from dinner, but today I'd wanted to leave work on time.

Becca was surprised to see me home so early. "Hey, you're home," she said, greeting me with her customary kiss.

"I didn't want to rush dinner." Tuesday night in a way was one of my favorites, but it was also one of the most exhausting. I had most of my youth interviews on Tuesdays, mostly because the kids were already there for Mutual activities, other interviews, and a meeting with my counselors. I enjoyed interacting with others as I fulfilled my calling, but now with my increased sensitivity to Travis's situation, I worried that he'd resent one more night that I wasn't home. Making a solid appearance at dinner should go a long way to establishing my presence.

"It's basically ready. But I need someone to set the table."

"How's Travis?"

"Okay. He's doing homework, which is a good sign. He's down-stairs with the rest of the kids. If you'll call them up, we can eat."

Nodding, I headed for the basement stairs, going over my daily checklist in my mind. I needed to ask Travis how his homework was going and if there was anything I could help with—then try to fit it in my schedule if he did. I had to keep my promise to him. His brother and sisters were also on the list. I hoped this would eventually become habit and I wouldn't have to actually itemize my tasks. Yesterday morning I'd realized I had no idea what homework they had or which classes they were taking. I could claim that was because the year had only begun, but Becca would know them all, and if I didn't learn all I could within the next week or two, I would be letting my children and myself down. At the very least, I needed to make sure I was taking the time to participate in more of their activities. When was the last time I'd tossed a ball with Cory and Lauren?

Then there was Becca herself. What with Sundays being so busy for me, and Mondays being family home evening, I'd had no time to approach her about the garden show. Rikki had said it meant a lot to her, but if so, why didn't she bring it up? It was all enough to make me wish I were back in the simpler, black-and-white world of work.

"Daddy!" Cory and Lauren attacked me, and I hugged them tightly. When had they grown so big? Only yesterday, Lauren had been a baby. "Mom says dinner's ready," I announced. "But she needs help setting the table."

"I'll do it!" Cory yelled. "It's lasagna!"

I upgraded Cory in my mind from carnivore to omnivore.

Lauren ran up the stairs after him, always willing to help—es-pecially if it meant getting in the way. At least this was something she could actually do.

I went to stand behind Travis, who was focused on the computer. "What are you doing?" I asked casually.

"Essay for English." He turned around to look at me. "What would you call a sacrifice? I mean a real sacrifice. I was thinking of stuff like, you know, studying hard to get scholarships, obeying rules, being nice to your siblings, paying tithing, that sort of thing. But after we talked about it in class and now that I'm reading about it on the Net, it seems none of that is really a sacrifice because you get something back, and the definition of a sacrifice, a real sacrifice, is giving something important and not getting anything back."

"Not getting anything back or not expecting something back?"

"Ah," Travis said.

"Because sacrifice always brings blessings. Some sacrifices you know will give back in physical benefits—like studying and saving and working hard. Others, like giving to the needy or paying tithing, also have blessings attached but are sometimes far less obvious. It depends what you are sacrificing and why. Think of Christ. He sacrificed His life. Do you think He got a return?"

"He got us?" Travis asked.

"Yeah. Would you sacrifice your life to save Cory or Lauren?"

Travis grinned. "Maybe them but not Allia."

"Right." I laughed. "It may not be in this life that you get a reward, but I can't think of a single instance when sacrifice doesn't bring some kind of blessing, even if it's just building your character."

"But if sacrifice always gets us to a sweet place in our career, or makes you strong so you can do more things, harder things—get farther in life—or if God blesses you for helping someone, then doesn't that mean sacrifice really isn't a sacrifice?"

"Oh, sacrifice is real, but it requires giving something that is a challenge for you to give. It's not a small thing. But you are also correct when you say the nature of sacrifice is that it brings blessings."

Travis tilted his head as he stared up at me. "Is that why you don't mind being a bishop?"

I sat on the edge of the computer desk. "I see lives change. I see miracles. It makes it worth it." I grinned. "Most days."

Nodding, he turned back to the computer. "I'll be right up. I want to write this all down while I still remember."

"Okay."

Fifteen minutes later, we were at the table in the kitchen eating. Cory was already on his second helping, but Lauren was pouting at something he'd said and wasn't eating at all.

Travis downed his food, and before I could ask him about school, he was out of his seat and heading for the stairs. "Remember Young Men's tonight," I said.

"'Course. We're doing baptisms at the temple."

The children cleared out, and I was left wondering what I had accomplished by being there. Well, at least Becca was still here. She'd been so busy dishing up and helping Lauren that her plate was still half full.

She set down her fork to take a drink, and I grabbed her hand before she could pick it up again. "You know I love you, don't you?"

She smiled. "Yeah. You, too."

"Look, about that garden show." I felt almost stupid bringing it up. I knew my wife a lot better than Rikki did.

She pulled her hand away and picked up her fork. "That's Rikki's nonsense." The flippant way she spoke didn't ring true. Not that she was purposefully lying, but more like she was trying to convince herself.

"I think we ought to go."

"To Saint George, for a garden show?" Her voice was flat. "You'd be bored out of your skull."

"No more than you were at that writing seminar, and you went with me." Two years ago I'd begun exploring the option of freelancing in my free time—self-help topics, adventure, products. Topics that didn't take as much know-how as my day job writing about software but that used the same skills. Except I'd become the bishop shortly after the conference and that was the end of any free time. Since I still did what I loved every day, I hadn't been disappointed. I could always go back to it someday.

"The hotel had a nice spa," Becca said with a smile. "And it was our first night ever away from the kids."

Had it been? "You hate leaving them."

"Well, they're getting older."

"So let's go to Saint George next weekend. For one night. I'll get off early from work, and we'll go, just the two of us. That is, if the show is still on."

"I think next week is the last week for the show, but what about the kids? We can't exactly leave Travis in charge."

"We'll find a sitter."

"Who?"

"We're in a ward where half the people have all their children grown and gone. I'll find someone."

She laughed. "No, I'll find someone."

"That's probably a good idea." She was pickier than I was, and I didn't want her to worry about the kids.

"Maybe my sister will watch them," Becca mused.

The more I thought about the trip, the more excited I was. Maybe I could get tickets for a play somewhere. Didn't they have an outdoor theater there? We could go somewhere romantic for dinner, sit in the hot tub afterward. Enjoy ourselves with no interruptions.

Becca picked up her plate and started for the sink, though her plate was still half full. "We'll have to hurry to fit in all the gardens. It'll be a bit of driving, but the gardens should be fabulous."

Oh, that's right. Saint George wasn't a romantic getaway, but a chance for her to see gardens. I grimaced internally. Rikki had been right that I hadn't been listening. Not even now. I'd changed the trip into something else entirely. Something for me. "Great," I said.

Becca returned to the table and put her arms around me. I turned and met her lips. Well, maybe Saint George wasn't a romantic getaway, but whatever I'd done had made Becca happy, and I wanted her to be happy.

"You'd better get going," she said. "Or you'll be late for your meeting."

I hadn't done what I'd wanted with all my kids yet, but there was always tomorrow. I stifled a wave of guilt as I gave Becca another kiss and headed out the door.

CHAPTER NINETEEN

Rikki

I'd dropped the kids off at their separate schools on my way to work. I was feeling all right today, better than usual, though I wasn't making any bets on it lasting. Part of why I was feeling okay was that I'd slept better. Not only had I slumbered nearly all night, but Kyle hadn't come into my room crying. Maybe because she'd been practicing her dancing so hard. She was still uncharacteristically silent, though, and that worried me. Once we'd shared everything. Was I being too demanding? Did she feel I was trying to control her life?

I was, just a little. Though I'd sworn to myself I'd never be that kind of parent, I was running out of time with her.

My phone rang as I walked into the building. "Hello?"

"Hi, it's Becca. Do you have a moment to talk about James?"

"Yeah, but only that. I start my shift in a few minutes."

"I would have called last night, but things got a little crazy with the kids. Allia forgot her temple recommend for Young Women's last night, and Lauren suddenly remembered that she had volunteered to take cookies to class."

I laughed. "My kids would know better than to even ask." I'd meant it as a compliment to her sacrifice as a mother, because I'd tell my kids that was their tough luck for not remembering, but the coolness in Becca's voice showed that she'd taken offense. Add insensitive to my list of qualities.

"Anyway," Becca continued, "I wanted to tell you that I think James needs his eyesight checked. He can hardly see the letters on the paper. I think he's farsighted. Badly so. That he's come so far at all is really a sign of his intelligence."

She liked James, as I'd known she would. Everyone always loved James. There was a hitch in my voice when I spoke. "Thanks, Becca. I'll check that out right away. I don't know why they wouldn't have noticed this in his last school." Though actually I suspected it might have happened when I was away and the kids had stayed with friends. He was having trouble in school when I returned.

"Well, it sometimes happens fast. You just need to make sure that there isn't an unusual cause for the farsightedness, and once he has the glasses, it'll make testing so much easier for him."

"Do you think he's dyslexic?"

"I think maybe a little, but like I said, it's hard to tell until his vision is corrected. I'm going to talk to my friend today about some activities to do with him. Meanwhile, you should talk to the school."

"Okay, I will." The lump in my throat was gone, and I could breathe again. I couldn't see through my tears, though she couldn't know that. "Thanks, Becca."

"You're welcome. Well, have a good day at work." The relief in her voice was palpable.

"Wait?" I didn't hear her hang up, so I plunged on. "The garden show. It's the last week, isn't it? Are you going?" So help me, if Dante hadn't spoken to her, I was going to kidnap her and take her to Saint George myself.

"It's still on next week. Dante and I did decide to go then. Well, provided there are no ward emergencies."

"That's wonderful. Good for you! I can watch Lauren and Allia, if you want." I knew there was no way she'd let the boys stay with me. Even if they weren't ultraconservative Mormons, having a teenage boy stay in a house with a thirteen-year-old who imagines herself in love with him wasn't the best idea. "James would be thrilled to have Lauren."

Dead silence. "Uh, I already arranged things with my sister. But thanks anyway."

"Oh, I see. Well, maybe Lauren could come over this weekend and play. Give you a break."

Another hesitation. Too long. "I don't mind. I like to have her close. I'm kind of paranoid that way."

I knew then that no matter how much she liked James and let him play with Lauren at her house, she was never going to leave Lauren in my care. Probably not Allia, either. Not that I blamed Becca, exactly. She probably thought I was a recovering drug addict—which I was, though the recovery had taken place years ago. Funny how my Church upbringing had made me understand the dangers of alcohol and cigarette smoking, both of which I'd rarely touched, but somehow I hadn't managed to avoid falling into the despair of drugs. But I was clean now, and no one was better than I was with young children.

I'd known a lot of parents like Becca when Kyle was small, and I'd never let it bother me because I knew I was eons ahead of them in the fun department. Let them have their stuffy tea parties in their scratchy, expensive dresses. Let them drive their new SUVs and keep their noses in the air. My children would dig in the dirt, bake their own cookies using their own recipes, and sleep outside under the stars.

Yet this time it was different because Becca was part of the plan. To hide the hurt I felt at the discovery of her mistrust, I said brightly, "Well, maybe when you know me better." If there would be enough time for that to happen. "Thanks for calling, and if something happens and Dante can't go with you, I'm so ready for a road trip. Just give me a call."

"Yeah, sure. Thanks. See you later." The line went silent.

Probably she'd call—if I was the last person on earth. Oh, well, at least she was loosening up, taking that first step. Dante had listened to me. He always had, except that last time, and he'd been right then.

I'd stopped inside the hall and was frowning at my phone, so I didn't see Quinn coming. When he tapped me on the shoulder, I started. "Oh." My eyes flew to his. He looked good today, in dress slacks and a green polo that set off his tan and complemented his eyes. I didn't like polos as a rule, but for him I was willing to change my mind. "Hi."

"Bad news? You were staring at that thing like you wanted to smash it." He gestured at my phone with a hand that held a large soft drink cup.

"No way. Then I'd have to find money for a new one."

He laughed, and as we walked toward the elevator together, he asked, "So, how was the movie?"

"Okay—I think. Don't tell my son, but I fell asleep in the middle."

"That good, huh?"

"We don't have any couches. What do you expect when you put a working mother on a pile of blankets and pillows?"

He laughed again, a nice sound. "You really don't have a couch?"

"Our old one wasn't worth bringing, and I haven't had time to find anything else. I'll pick up something second-hand eventually." I didn't actually believe I'd be here long enough to worry about a couch, but maybe that would encourage his lesson on changing the oil. That was overdue.

"They have great couches for sale on KSL all the time."

"KSL? Isn't that a TV station?"

"Yeah, but they have this whole online website with free classifieds ads and the like. Much easier to find what you're looking for than in the newspaper."

"I don't have a computer set up yet." I'd had one but it shut down a few months ago, and I hadn't bothered bringing it. If we needed a computer, there was always the library.

"Check it on your lunch break or something."

"It'll have to wait. First, I need to worry about school clothes and buying a dryer." The last occupant of my parents' house had actually left an ancient washer in a corner of the basement, which seemed to work fine once the kids and I wrested it into place and figured out how to hook it up. No dryer, though, and hanging clothes over the line I'd nailed into the tree and the side of the house was going to get old fast in the winter. Then again, come Christmas, I might be long out of here, depending on how things went.

That thought made me want to throw my phone at Quinn, who, poor thing, was doing nothing more than making conversation.

"Hmm." He beat me to pushing the button on the elevator—probably because my fists were clenched at my sides. "KSL has a free section, too, and I'm always surprised at what people are offering."

"Free? You gotta be kidding." Free was my kind of deal, and I wasn't ashamed to admit it.

"No, I'm not." He smiled, and for no reason I could explain, the tension flowed from my body. "People haven't been able to sell something, or they simply want to get rid of it. Whatever. Usually you have to pick it up."

"As long as it's not too far away. My truck eats gas like my kids guzzle pop."

"Haven't you heard that's not good for them?"

"Life's too short to worry about those things."

"I agree. I drink way too much soda myself." To underscore the point, he sipped at the end of his straw as we entered the elevator. His green eyes watched me as he drank, and it was a strangely intimate moment, one that brought a rush of . . . something to my heart.

The spell was broken as a man's hand stopped the elevator doors from shutting. "Sorry," he mumbled, his gaze never straying from the newspaper folded in his hands.

"No problem," Quinn said.

No problem at all. In fact, I was glad the man had shown up. I liked Quinn. He seemed like a nice man, but I was through with men. Forever.

My stop came first. As I hurried from the elevator, Quinn's voice followed me. "Tell you what. Give me a few days, and I'll see what's out there. You'll be staying awake during movies before you know it."

My turn to laugh. Because the hint was that I could invite him to share one of those movies. "Right. Well, you know that some problems aren't worth solving."

"I can do it." He squared his already broad shoulders.

"We'll see." Let him be a Boy Scout. It couldn't hurt.

I didn't stop to watch the elevator shut, and I could feel his eyes on me. Checking my phone, I saw I had just enough time to look up a few eye doctors and make an appointment for James.

CHAPTER TWENTY

Ryle

Thursday, the day of my free dance class, finally arrived. Though it hadn't exactly been torture watching the other girls dance all week, I was dying to step out on the floor myself. First I had to drop off James and get Allia's bike. I was worried Allia would change her mind about the bike because no matter what, I couldn't be late today.

"Is Allia here?" I blurted the second her mom opened the door.

"She had to stay after school for a project, but she said you could use her bike. Come on in for a minute, and I'll open the garage."

I followed her into the kitchen where small plastic bags of homemade saltwater dough sat on the table. The house smelled wonderful, as usual, and for a fleeting second I was tempted to stay if she offered me a snack, especially if Travis appeared. Maybe I could still be on time. No, better not to risk it. *Hurry,* I thought to Allia's mom. Or Sister Rushton, I guess. That's what James called her—and everyone else at that stupid church.

James couldn't take his eyes off the dough. "What's that for?"

"A game we're going to play."

Lauren frowned. "I thought we were going to teach James to read."

"This is a reading game. It'll be fun."

"Mom took me to the eye doctor this morning," James said. "She got off work and got me at school. The doctor did lots of stuff to my eyes. I didn't like it."

"So do you have to get glasses?" Lauren reached toward the bags of dough but hovered over them indecisively.

"Yeah. But they're not ready yet." He grimaced. "I can't see up close or far way. The doctor said I need more tests."

Sister Rushton looked at me as if asking for an explanation, but I shrugged. The fewer words the better. I edged toward the door leading to the garage.

"I'm sure everything will be a lot easier once you get glasses," Sister Rushton told James. "Did your mom talk to your teachers at school?"

"Yeah, about tests." He gave me a glum look. "I hate tests."

I felt sorry for him, so I said, "It's just to help them figure out how to help you read."

"Oh. That's okay, I guess."

Sister Rushton looked thoughtful, and I wondered if she was surprised that Mom had taken James to the doctor and talked to his teachers so quickly. She did have a tendency to put things off. *But she loves us.* I felt a little sliver of resentment toward Sister Rushton. She shouldn't judge my mom without knowing her. She probably judged me, too, which made me feel a little sad since I thought she was probably more beautiful than the mothers of any of my friends in California.

"Which color dough should I take, Mom?" Lauren asked.

"Whichever you want."

Lauren pushed her dark hair from her eyes. "What do you want, James?"

"Blue. No, green."

Lauren gave him the green and placed the blue and pink in front of her. "I'll use one of these, but I don't know which."

James opened his bag and began rolling out a snake. "What are we doing with this?"

"We're going to make some words and sound them out, that's what," Sister Rushton said. "Why don't you make an A? As big as you want. Lauren, you make an S and I'll make a T. Do them nice and big now so James can see them. Then we'll make more letters so we can learn more words. James, do you remember what sound an A makes?"

"I can't decide what color to use," moaned Lauren.

"Blue," James said.

Lauren took the pink instead. Whatever. That kid was a little funny.

Sister Rushton looked relieved that Lauren had made a decision. She gave a little start. "Oh, sorry, Kyle. I forgot about the bike. Come on."

Finally. The two minutes I'd been there felt like ten. I followed her into the garage and went for Allia's bike as the door lifted. "Watch for cars, okay?" Sister Rushton called after me. I didn't know whether to be amused or annoyed, but when she added, "And be back in an hour," I opted for annoyed.

No. Freaking. Way.

When I arrived at the studio, there was still plenty of time, and I waited impatiently. Finally the class was over, and I went inside. Right away I wasn't thrilled with the girls, who stared at me until I felt self-conscious. Since this was the nine to eleven class, they were all younger than I was, and I felt big and awkward, though I was small for my age.

"Don't mind them," a tall, slender girl with red hair told me when three of the girls burst into laughter as they eyed me from across the room where they were warming up. "It's all about the dance. That's all that matters."

"Right." I appreciated her comment, but I experienced a rare kind of jealousy at the strong and sure way she moved. Not the simple jealousy over a sweater or the kind of house someone lived in, but the jealousy of seeing someone do something you love so much and doing it better than maybe you will ever be capable of. That kind of jealousy bites deep and hard, and tears I couldn't shed stung my eyes.

I felt this girl existed solely to dance her way through life. I could tell she came from a well-to-do family, from the name brand jeans she'd shimmied out of earlier to the sneakers that probably cost more than my entire wardrobe. Her parents could obviously buy her any teacher, and that she had talent made her comment to me more precious—and my jealousy that much more poignant.

I told myself nothing mattered but learning everything I could. I didn't fool myself that the teacher would be so amazed at my talent, she'd give me lessons for free. That kind of thing didn't happen to people like me.

Yet as we practiced moves, I forgot about everything but the dance. I *was* the dance. It was beautiful—the floor, the mirrors, the music, the movements. I loved the sturdy-looking teacher, loved how she ordered us about, loved how demanding she was—and I loved that I'd practiced enough all week on my own not to feel like a total idiot. I enjoyed the grudging acceptance of the younger girls, the genuine smile of approval from the redhead. Not that I did all that great—I couldn't do great without real training—but I wasn't so bad as to feel embarrassed if I was to run into these girls at school or in some other public place.

The class ended too soon. How could it be over? I wanted to throw myself on the ground and cry and refuse to leave. I wanted to plead with the teacher to let me into the class and when I was older, I'd repay her double.

Silly.

I nodded to the redhead and made my way to the changing area with the other girls, where I pulled on my jeans over the black tights without feet like those I'd seen the other girls wearing at other lessons. Not pink because this wasn't ballet and with bare feet so we wouldn't slip and the teacher could see what we were doing with our toes. Sometimes she'd have them put on their jazz shoes, but she hadn't today, and I was glad because mine were a little tight.

I stayed to watch a bit of the older girls' class, but I finally made myself leave to pick up James. I still didn't arrive until after five-thirty. Sister Rushton wasn't pleased at how late I was, but I couldn't tell her why. She probably thought I was smoking pot out behind the school or something.

Let her think it. What do I care?

When James and I finally got home, I was carrying both him and my dance bag. It was nearly six, and I was afraid I wouldn't beat my mother to the house, so I was trying to run. I sighed a breath of relief when she wasn't there.

"Come on," I said to James. "I'll make you some mac and cheese."

"Goody. I'm starving. I think I'm growing."

"Good thing. You're a guy. You don't want to be short." I made the noodles without really thinking, my mind still caught up in the dance. Maybe if I hurried and finished my homework, I could practice a few of the more difficult moves I'd learned today.

Mom came home before we'd finished eating, her face flushed and happy. She looked pretty, like she used to when she'd dress up to work at the restaurant. As usual, she smelled like a garden of flowers. I wished she smelled the way she had when I was younger. Less like flowers and more like herself.

"Guess what?" she said in singsong. "We have a couch. Two of them actually."

"A couch?" James leapt up from the table and followed Mom out the front door.

Sure enough, loaded into the back of our truck were a couch and a love seat. "Where'd you get that?" I asked.

Mom gave us a conspiratorial smile. "I mentioned to a guy at work that we hadn't brought our old couch, and he found these online. Free to anyone who would pick them up."

"Was that the guy we saw when we got the movie?" James asked.

"Yeah. He helped me load them in the truck." She looked down the street. "He should be coming any minute now to help us get them inside."

"We could call the bishop and his son," I said. It would be the perfect opportunity to see Travis since he hadn't been around when I'd been at the Rushtons' today.

She laughed. "We three should be able to take care of it."

"Four," James said. "Don't forget me."

Mom bent down to kiss him. "I wasn't. It was me I wasn't counting. I'm a weakling." James giggled at that, and even I smiled. Mom had her moments.

"There he is now," Mom said as a dark green convertible turned down our street. It was a cool car, and I felt a thrill of excitement despite my disappointment about the dance classes. The man who emerged from the car looked a lot like the kind of men my mother usually dated, only taller, and the way he carried himself reminded me faintly of the bishop, though this man was decidedly broader, his muscles bulging in his snug shirt. His blond hair was also longer, and his eyes green instead of brown. Okay, he didn't look at all like the bishop, except he had that clean air about him, which I liked. I knew at once that he wasn't a smoker, and maybe he wasn't a drinker, either. I liked him better for that already.

"This must be Kyle," he said.

I nodded. "That's me."

"I'm Quinn Hunter. I work with your mom. Think we can get this couch in?"

I liked the way he talked to me, as though I were an adult. "Yeah. I think so."

We did manage, though it wasn't easy, and James got in the way more than he helped. My mom acted a little giddy, laughing too much and too easily. I could see she liked the man, and I could tell he felt even more strongly about her. I'd seen it many, many times. My mother might not be as beautiful as Allia and her mother were with their dark hair, but men always fell for her. They seemed fascinated by everything she did.

Quinn was nice. If allowing James to sit on the couch while we moved it around the living room wasn't enough, when he returned to his car for the take-out burgers he'd stopped to buy on the way over, he completely won my brother's admiration. I wasn't above eating the fries or the shakes myself, since the best thing after a hard workout was to load up on carbs. Only Mom picked at her food. I wondered if that was because she had butterflies in her stomach the way I did when I talked to Travis.

I thought so.

At the same time, she didn't invite him to stay or ask me to watch James while she left with him. That made me both happy and uneasy. I didn't want to see my mom hurt again, and mostly that's what boyfriends meant, sooner or later. At least for her. And James was getting to the point where a man leaving might really mess him up.

Mom didn't kiss Quinn when he left, which meant they were

only beginning their relationship or that she considered him a friend. There'd been plenty of that kind of man, too. Those who appeared to do something to the car or apartment and just as soon disappeared. Those who took James to fly a kite or to Disneyland and didn't return after they brought James home. I'd learned those guys were safer for all of us because they were never around long enough for us to really care.

"Nice guy," I commented as we watched him drive away.

"Yeah," she agreed. Her face was too still, and I had the feeling she was fighting tears. Man, we were all a bunch of hormones. Did being a woman always mean so much emotion? Or did most women only feel this way where men were concerned? I for one was thinking way too much about Travis, and I still wasn't sure he even realized I existed.

Mom kept staring down the road, not into the dark or at a sunset, and it made me feel jittery rather than romantic. "So," I said. "Are you going to date him?"

"No." Nothing more. No explanation or shaking her head but a simple and final no.

"I thought you liked him."

"He's a co-worker, that's all."

"Married?"

She finally took her eyes from the road and looked at me, a smile growing on her face. "No, silly. It's just that a man is the last thing I need right now."

Actually, a man to earn a bit of money, fix things, help out with James, and take us out to dinner every now and then was exactly what I thought we needed, especially in light of my yearning for dance lessons, but, hey, you couldn't force these things. Maybe Mom had finally gotten wise to the result of having a boyfriend.

Yet maybe it didn't have to end that way. Maybe she kept picking the wrong kind. Take the bishop, for example. If she'd married him, it might have been me living in Allia's beautiful, clean house, taking all the lessons I wanted. So many lessons I might even get sick of them, and Mom would have to make me go.

"What?" Mom said.

"Nothing."

"Anything happen today?"

"School was boring, as usual."

That seemed to satisfy her. She went into the house, smiling, and sat on one of our hand-me-down couches. They were a pale floral but not too ugly.

James cuddled up to Mom, and she started tickling him. "Maybe we should sleep right here tonight," she said. "You know, have a campout on our new couches."

"Yay!" shouted James, bouncing so hard he would have fallen off the couch if Mom hadn't caught him. They collapsed on the couch again, tickling each other and laughing, and for a minute I felt that strange sort of happiness I sometimes felt when we were together. The world could fall away and it wouldn't matter because we had everything we needed right in this very room.

Even without dancing.

My stomach started to ache. "I have homework," I said.

"You didn't do it already? You had all afternoon."

"She was dancing," James said. I glared at him, hoping he wouldn't say where I'd been dancing.

Mom frowned. "Kyle, I told you. Homework first."

"I'll do it," I said. My mom the homework police. That was still weird. So many years without really saying anything, and now she was always on my case.

Mom rubbed her temple. I knew that meant a headache coming on, maybe a migraine. I followed her into the kitchen and watched her down a pill, replacing the bottle in her purse where she always kept it. I took the discarded bowls of mac and cheese and put them in the sink filled with water to soak off the mess, a little bit amazed and proud at my actions.

"Thanks, honey."

"Come on, Mom!" James yelled. "Let's get the blankets!"

I went downstairs and really did my homework, practiced dance for a bit, and then read a book until late so maybe I would be too tired to dream about dancing when I finally slept. Too tired to wake up worrying with tears on my face or feel the need to climb into my mother's bed.

CHAPTER TWENTY-ONE

Becca

Tuesdays were usually good days. I had the house in order after Sunday's activities, and I often made time to go to the temple after I'd finished teaching Cory his lessons for the day. Afterward, he'd come with me to do errands. I was really enjoying the one-on-one time with my little boy, who usually wasn't as demanding as the rest of the children and who I sometimes suspected I overlooked.

After school, Kyle dropped off James for his lesson and asked to use Allia's bike. Allia came out and talked with her for a few moments, but she had no more luck finding out where Kyle was headed than I had last week. Except for Saturday, Kyle hadn't asked to borrow the bike on the days James didn't come here. I wondered if she was heading to the same place she'd taken him and if she was still going with him on days he didn't come here. I made a mental note to ask James about it. I still hadn't told Rikki that both times James had come last week, Kyle had picked him up late. I hadn't really minded because James was such a sweetheart, but if Kyle wasn't on time today, I'd get to the bottom of it one way or another.

"Don't forget about Young Women tonight," Allia said as Kyle got on the bike. "Remember we're making chili and bread sticks."

"Oh, yeah. Right." Kyle couldn't have looked less thrilled. "Not sure I can go. Depends if my mom gets home."

"It's not until six-thirty. Usually it's seven, but we're doing it early because it's dinner."

"Okay." Kyle nodded without smiling and rode away.

Allia sighed. "That is just weird."

"Yeah, she's been really cranky lately," James said, bouncing as he talked. "Hey, are we doing more letters with that dough?" His glasses still hadn't arrived, but he was making progress. The bigger we wrote the words, the better he could read them. Better still if he could feel them with his hands.

I rumpled his blond head. "Maybe later if there's time. I have something else planned today. Come on, let's go out back." I led them to the sandbox where we scratched letters in the sand with the small end of my old wooden spoons. We spelled all the words on James's spelling list and then anything else we could see in the backyard, including the names of a few flowers.

An hour and a half later as I was reading a Magic Tree House book to Lauren and James on the living room couch, the phone rang with the tone I'd programmed for Dante.

"Hi, honey," I said. "I hope this call doesn't mean you're going to be late. I have a roast in the oven." Roast was one of the easiest things to make as I sat and did homework with the children, but he didn't need to know that. And why wasn't Kyle back, anyway? This was beginning to be a bad habit. On the other hand, James was making beautiful progress, and I'd enjoyed myself, too. At least here he wasn't being exposed to any of Kyle's questionable friends.

"I just got a call," he said. "From the police station."

"The police station?" A knot of fear formed in my stomach before I remembered that all my children were home and safe. Cory was downstairs playing his half-hour of Nintendo with Sean from next door, Travis had come home and gone straight to the computer in the family room, muttering something about another essay for English, and Allia was washing her hair for Young Women's tonight since she hadn't had time for a shower that morning. Now that I'd stopped reading, Lauren had taken out my homemade dough from last week and was making bird nests with James at the table.

"It's Rikki's daughter, Kyle. The police caught her shoplifting at K-mart."

"Ah, that would explain why she hasn't come back to pick up James. I told her an hour."

"Look, I can't leave for at least a half hour more, and that means I won't get there for another forty-five minutes. But she needs someone there now, and they can't get hold of Rikki. She's not answering her cell. I could call Steve or Paul, but Kyle doesn't know them. Same for any of the other leaders. But she knows you, and you have a way with kids. What do you say?"

I turned off the oven. "Okay, I'll go." On Tuesdays the younger kids and I often spent time in the yard after dinner, with me in the flower beds and them on the play set, while the older kids were in Mutual and Dante in interviews, but tonight didn't look promising for any of that.

"Thanks, hon. I'll meet you there as soon as I can."

"I love you," I said.

"You, too."

Part of being the bishop's wife was pitching in when needed, and that meant a lot of late dinners and unexpected opportunities to serve. I had never really minded. I'd grown up seeing my parents give their all to the Church, and I loved our ward members. However, Kyle and Rikki were hitting too close to home. It was hard knowing that Rikki and Dante shared a past that didn't include me, and I suspected she at least wished things had turned out differently between them. For my part, I wished she'd chosen any place but Spanish Fork to live. Yet she'd been at church again last Sunday, with both children, and Kyle had been decently dressed. Mostly. They appeared to be making an effort, and I knew I should befriend her like any sister in the gospel, not wish her away.

"Why don't you two go outside and play in the fort?" I said to Lauren and James.

"Okay." Lauren jumped up. "I get to be Spiderman this time."

"You mean Spidergirl."

"Yeah."

I shoved the dough back into the bags, noting that they were drying up a bit. Nothing a little water wouldn't help. I dribbled some in and stored the bags in the fridge. If I remembered, I'd give one to James so he could practice forming letters at home.

"Travis, I have to go to the police station," I called down the stairs. "Tell Cory to tell Sean he has to go home now." I didn't allow neighbor children over when I wasn't there to supervise. We'd have to make an exception for James, of course, as he had nowhere else to go. I certainly wasn't going to take that innocent little boy to the police station. "You and Allia will have to keep an eye on Lauren and James. They're in the backyard."

Travis appeared at the bottom of the stairs and started up them, two at a time. "Did you say the police station?"

"Kyle's been picked up for shoplifting, and they can't find her mother."

He shook his head. "Poor thing."

"Poor thing? She's obviously stolen something."

"Yeah, I know, but why?"

"Maybe she wanted something new."

"I guess." One shoulder lifted in a shrug.

I didn't have time for this. "Tell Allia I'm going, okay? When she gets out of the shower."

"All right."

I left him staring after me thoughtfully.

Poor thing, I scoffed as I backed out the driveway. Little weasel, more like. The more I thought about it, the more I didn't want Kyle anywhere near Allia, possible conversion or not, unless they were at church around the other ward youth. A mother had to draw the line somewhere, and Allia had already proven more susceptible than I'd expected. At least they hadn't had much contact that I'd seen, except for this constant borrowing of Allia's bicycle.

Not that I entirely blamed Kyle. Rikki was ultimately responsible for her daughter.

Like I was responsible for Travis breaking the law by driving his friends? Would I have been responsible if he'd become distracted and caused an accident?

That's different, I thought.

Why? Because he doesn't wear a nose ring?

Most intelligent people talked to themselves, I'd heard, but I bet only geniuses argued with themselves. My IQ was probably off the charts. I rubbed my temple, feeling the beginnings of a headache.

At the police station, I wasted no time in stating my business to the female officer the receptionist called to the front desk. "Are you her mother?" she asked.

"A friend of her mother. A neighbor."

"We can release her only to a parent or guardian."

"From what I understand, you haven't been able to contact her mother, which was why she called us."

"That's right."

"Well, can you release her to her bishop? That's my husband. He'll be here in a while."

"I'll check, but we'll probably need verbal approval from a

182

parent, who will have to come down sometime tonight and sign some papers, anyway."

I nodded. "Can I see her?"

"Sure. Come this way."

I could see our night dwindling away, and I tried not to be resentful. Boy, that girl was going to get an earful. She'd better be repentant.

"Was there a bike?" I asked. "She borrowed my daughter's."

"We have it outside. It's locked up."

"Thanks."

The officer led me down the hall to an open door. Inside, Kyle made a tiny, tragic figure, her hands folded on the table in front of her as she stared blankly at the wall. Two officers passed us in the hall, talking loudly. Kyle didn't flinch or look toward the door, which told me she'd been here long enough to stop hoping someone was coming for her any time soon.

As we approached, she turned her heart-shaped face toward me and something flared in her eyes and was gone before I could tell what it was, but it certainly didn't look like remorse.

"I'll try her mother again," the officer said. "And talk to the chief about releasing her. But, like I said, I'm sure we'll need at least an oral approval from a parent."

"Thanks."

Kyle was no longer looking in my direction, but as I regarded her, the sharp words I'd been practicing in my head fled. Her lips were pursed, the makeup on her eyes smeared from crying, though she was dry-eyed now, and her hair was a wild mess like her mother's always was, which was actually an improvement over the way it normally fell lank over much of her face.

Father, I prayed. *What am I supposed to do now?* At least I no longer wanted to slap her silly. Well, mostly I didn't.

I took the seat opposite her. "My husband couldn't get away

from work, so he gave me a call. He didn't want you to be here alone. He'll be here as soon as he can."

That got her attention, but she didn't speak. One of her eyes had almost no makeup, and without it she looked about eleven instead of thirteen trying to be thirty.

"So?" I said. "James spelled out some words today. I think once he gets his glasses, he'll be reading in no time. He's a smart kid to have come so far on his own."

She didn't reply.

"I hear you guys have been going on some long walks lately."

Her eyes widened. "What'd James say?"

"Something about a place you've taken him several times. He stays outside to play while you go in the house." I waited several seconds before adding, "You didn't take him someplace dangerous, did you?"

"I wouldn't take him anywhere like that!" she shot back. "I wouldn't even take him to some of the places my mom would."

Righteous indignation. So where had she taken him? An inkling of an idea appeared in the corner of my mind, trying to work its way into my consciousness, but even as I tried to pinpoint it, the feeling disappeared.

Anyway, I wasn't getting anywhere with this indirect approach. "Kyle, why don't you tell me what happened?"

"Because it doesn't make any difference."

"It makes a difference to me."

"Why? Because my mom was your husband's friend?"

"No, because you're a neighbor, and you're in my ward."

She snorted. "I don't care. Besides, you wouldn't understand."

I sighed. *Father, I have no idea what I'm doing here. She obviously doesn't want or need me.*

Still I stayed, because as defiantly as she stared at me now, I remembered the shrunken figure I'd seen upon entering the room.

"I understand one thing," I said. "No. Two things. One, your day has been a lot worse than mine. Two, if we don't get out of here soon, you may never learn the secret of Sister Flemming's chili. Now that would be a major tragedy."

Kyle stared at me as though trying to determine if I was serious.

"Maybe we can steal the recipe from Allia," I added. "That is, if I get home in time for her to go. She's babysitting Lauren and James."

I thought I detected a hint of a smile at the corner of Kyle's mouth. Maybe we were finally getting somewhere. Her anger gone, the shrunken look had returned, and she was a child who desperately needed a hug. I wished I could give it to her.

All at once something clicked inside me, something that didn't come from me but from above, and I knew where Kyle had been taking James, where she'd been going on Allia's bike, and what it meant to her.

CHAPTER TWENTY-TWO

Kyle

Allia's mom was trying to make me feel better, even though she didn't know that I really did have a reason for trying to steal the candy and the fancy markers. It wasn't that I wanted something new to wear or that I felt any weird compulsion to take things that didn't belong to me. I had a reason.

Yesterday at school, I'd manage to sell the jeans and the cool blue shirt with the necklace I'd stolen the Monday before school started. It wasn't like I could wear them, anyway. I felt sick even thinking about it. That might have something to do with those lessons in Allia's class at church and that annoying teacher who kept smiling at me, but regardless, they did me no good at home under my bed.

I'd gotten fifteen bucks for the set of clothes—half the original price. It wasn't a lot, but if I took more, I'd have more to sell. I might begin to make enough.

Enough to pay for the lessons.

Except I'd been caught, and now there was no hope at all. There was nothing except watching and longing and dancing alone when Mom was upstairs with James. My muscles already hurt from hours of practicing the new moves—and from riding that bike. Muscles I never knew I had.

Something inside me was breaking, and I felt I couldn't hold it all together. More than anything at that moment, I wished Allia's mom were really my mom and that she could take me in her arms and hold me and tell me everything was going to be okay.

My mom would be here soon, and she'd hold me and say those things, but I wouldn't believe her. She was hiding something from me. I think I knew why she'd come here, out of all the places we could go, and why she'd wanted to find her old friend Dante. I didn't like knowing, and I didn't think they'd be pleased when they found out either.

Sister Rushton came around the table and sat in the chair next to me. Her hand reached out to my arm. "Kyle," she said. "You dance, don't you? Like your mother? I remember her saying something like that the first day we met you."

A huge, impossible lump formed in my throat. I nodded.

"You took James to a dance class, didn't you? Are you taking dance?"

"No." I tried to hold them back, but the tears fell, in large drops. Her face was distorted, but I could tell she wasn't upset, and that made it okay. "Well, I had one free class, but that was all."

"So all these other days you've just been watching?"

I nodded. "I practice the moves later. I thought if I could sell some things, I could pay to really be in the class." I rushed on, explaining how my teacher at school had recommended the class and how she only recommended it to girls with talent, how good the new teacher really was, how wonderful the lesson had been, and how much I wanted to attend. It all tumbled out. Even if I'd wanted to hold it in, I couldn't have.

Her eyes widened, blue eyes like my mother's, but darker, more oval-shaped. Or maybe the dark lashes made them seem that way.

Pretty. She hadn't connected dance with the shoplifting before I told her, but I wanted her to know I had a reason. I wasn't just scum.

Except maybe in the end that's all I really was.

"Oh, Kyle." Tears shone in her eyes now. "I'm sorry. I'm so sorry."

"It won't ever be enough." I could barely push out the words now. "Never. And I'm getting older, and soon I'm going to be exactly like my mother." Washed-up, a has-been, or in her case, a-never-quite-there. Why hadn't I seen it before? That was my destiny. What I'd been born to.

I wanted to die.

"Kyle," Sister Rushton slid a hand over my shoulder. "I—I know what it's like to want something."

How could she know? With her rich house and a husband who supported her? Then again, she was looking at me as though she did.

"I didn't know what else to do." I didn't want to add that Mom couldn't come through, that she would try, but it wouldn't happen. Not this. She would want to, but there was too much else. There were her headaches, the medicine, the tears in the night. She'd feel terrible, and I would feel worse for wanting so much. I was a lousy piece of garbage. I wanted it all to end.

"It's going to be okay. Everything's going to be okay." She pulled me close to her. James was right that she smelled good. Not sweet like that cheap perfume Mom kept putting on lately, but she smelled like food, like the earth, warm. She smelled like safety.

Stupid.

But I let her hold me as I sobbed. I saw the woman police officer peek in and leave hurriedly. Still, I cried.

Sister Rushton kept holding me, and when I peeked at her face, I saw she was crying, too. Dante had said in his office that the ward was a family. For the first time, I dared to think it might be true. Maybe we could stay in this place. Maybe long enough for me to grow up. Mom would be happy, and James wouldn't be around scary people.

Yet if I couldn't dance, I didn't know if I really cared.

The tears finally stopped, and Sister Rushton found tissues in her purse to wipe my face. "You are so beautiful without that black stuff," she said softly, almost in a dazed voice. I knew she wasn't saying it to hurt me but because she thought it was true.

Dante came through the door with the officer before I was finished mopping my face. Or the bishop, I guess I should call him. He wore dress pants and a shirt, but no tie or jacket today. He looked from me to his wife. "Are we ready to go?"

"They're letting us take her?"

He nodded. "Rikki's on her way. She gave permission, and they're releasing her to me. Thankfully, the store isn't pressing charges since it's her first offense."

"That's a relief," said Siser Rushton.

I agreed. Such a relief that I wanted to cry again.

Sister Rushton put a hand on my back. "Ready?"

I nodded. The bishop put a hand on my shoulder as we walked out. It felt weird to have a man there, a man who wasn't hung up on my mom. Well, he might be, but I didn't think so, not with the way he looked at Sister Rushton.

He walked us to her van, where he put Allia's bicycle in the back. "I'll meet you two at home."

Home. I wished it were my home.

An old blue truck drew our attention as it squealed into the parking lot. Mom. She didn't park properly before she hopped out the door and ran toward us. "What were you thinking? Kyle, you are in so much trouble I don't even know where to begin!"

Okay, this was weird. I'd expected *her* to be sympathetic and the Rushtons to be disgusted.

"Maybe you could begin by signing the papers inside," Dante said.

Her glare didn't leave me. "This is so not what I need right now. You have to be more responsible, Kyle. Shoplifting? Is that what I've taught you?"

"Come on," Sister Rushton touched her arm. "I'll go in with you. Dante will stay with Kyle."

Mom's face swung between the bishop and his wife for several seconds before she nodded. "Okay. But don't go anywhere, Kyle."

I watched them walk across the parking lot. "Don't worry," the bishop said. "Becca will help her calm down. That's not saying this isn't serious, because it is. I'm glad to see your mother's upset about it. I would be far more worried if she weren't. It means she cares—about you and about doing what's right." He paused. "But I want you to know that we'll get through this, and things will be okay again if you're willing to make amends. I'm glad you had the officer call me."

I didn't have anyone else to call when Mom didn't answer her phone, but he probably knew that. Silence stretched out between us.

"Did you know my dad?" I asked. It was worth a shot.

"No. I never met him."

"Me either." It wasn't something I thought much about, but at the moment it seemed huge. I ducked my head to hide fresh tears.

"He was someone Rikki met after she left Utah."

After she left him, he meant.

"She only wrote me once on my mission," he added.

I'd learned what a mission was on Sunday. "You went on a mission?"

"When your mother and I were nineteen. That's when she left Utah."

I'd had it all wrong. I thought my mother had left him, but it looked like he'd been the first to go.

"I knew she wouldn't wait," he said, "but I think a part of me always hoped." He chuckled. "That single letter she sent me cured me of that notion. She'd told me she was married. I was glad she'd found someone."

Someone who'd eventually left. Mom had been married twice, and both times had ended in divorce. Neither time had been to my father or James's. She would have been better off waiting for the bishop. Of course, then she'd have had religious junk shoved down her throat each week. He was high on that sort of thing.

The bishop's cell phone rang, and he answered. "Hello? Hi, hon. Yeah, go ahead and feed them if it's finished. We'll be a bit longer. Kyle? She's okay." He paused to listen. "Okay. Love you, too, honey. Bye." He put the phone away and smiled at me. "Allia. She says the boys are dying of hunger. Can't have that."

I smiled. But how could I smile when my world had ended? When a few minutes ago, I wanted to be dead?

More seconds ticked by, and I couldn't help focusing on my own stomach that burned with hunger. "Do you think I could still go to that class tonight? Young Women's?" I hadn't eaten my free school lunch today, having sold it to someone else who'd forgotten his. Every little bit for my dancing fund. Homemade chili and bread sticks sounded better than anything my mother or I could whip up from a can.

He smiled. "That'll be for your mom to decide."

She'd probably ground me, and though most of the time that made no difference because she wasn't around to enforce it, it would make a difference tonight.

His eyes went beyond me. "Ah, here they are—finally."

My mom hadn't been gone long enough in my opinion. My muscles clenched, the sore ones screaming in objection, ready for what she would do. This time Mom hugged me, enfolding me in her arms and her flowery aroma, and I didn't mind the smell. Tears threatened to fall, but I didn't want to cry anymore. Crying was exhausting.

"I'm sorry, Mom," I muttered. A part of me hoped Sister Rushton had told her why I'd done it, but another part of me didn't want her to know. I knew it'd hurt Mom that I hadn't gone to her, even though she'd always taught me to depend on myself. That's the way life worked.

Mom turned me toward the truck and gave me a little shove. "I'll be by in a minute to get James," she told the Rushtons. "Thank you for coming."

"No problem," Dante said.

Sister Rushton's hand went out to my arm, and she leaned down to whisper in my ear. "It's not over yet. Something will work out. Give it a few days."

I nodded and tried to smile, but it hurt too bad. She was only being nice. I hurried to the truck and watched them as my mom drove away. The bishop was hugging his wife. It made a beautiful, safe picture in my head. Allia was lucky for more than just having a hot brother.

"So," my mom said after a few moments of silence. "Why did you do it?"

That meant Sister Rushton hadn't spilled everything, maybe because she thought I should tell Mom on my own or because there hadn't been enough time inside the station. Unless Mom was playing one of those parent's traps on me. "It was stupid, that's all. I'll never do it again. I promise."

"Honey, if you need something for school, you need to tell me."

"I know. It was just a few pens."

"Eight packages?"

I shrugged.

"Kyle, this is serious—uh, stuff."

I couldn't help smirking inside. She'd been going to swear again. Old habits and all that.

"I know."

"I don't want you to grow up and go to jail."

"I won't."

She pulled over to the curb and killed the truck. When she spoke again, there was a coldness in her voice that made my stomach twist. "Your dad and I broke up because he couldn't keep his hands off things that belonged to others."

"I thought you said he just left."

"He did, but only because I told him to choose us or stealing. I was tired of bailing him out, of people banging on our door looking for him. He didn't make the right choice."

The knowledge stunned me. "My father was a criminal?"

"He had a compulsion. I always thought he'd love us enough to overcome it and come back."

"But he didn't."

"No. And I don't know what happened to him. I looked for him a few months ago, but I couldn't find him. He might have died. Or maybe he's in prison."

I stared at her. There went my dream of finding my dad and having everything be miraculously okay. "And when were you going to tell me all this?"

"I'm telling you now. How could I bring up something like that out of the blue? Look, Kyle, I made a poor decision when I chose him. He wasn't ready to be a family man. Maybe he never would be. He was exciting, handsome, and kind of dangerous-looking. I thought it was love. I was wrong. He wasn't a good person inside, where it counts. He felt the world owed him a living and he had every right to take what he wanted if he could get away with it. But what he did doesn't reflect on you or me."

"Then why did you even look him up? If he's such a jerk." Maybe she was lying.

She sighed. "I thought you might be curious. I was hoping he might have changed." She started the engine again. "We'd better get James."

"I can't believe you! You should have told me." I folded my arms across my chest and glared out the window. I was never going to talk to her again. Hiding information about my father like that was lower than low. Worse, she probably wasn't lying, and that meant I really did have a criminal for a father. My mind was in turmoil, and my stomach was still churning something awful, though that might be partly because it was empty.

Mom started the truck, and when I glanced at her she seemed small and sad. *I don't care,* I thought. But I did, and a little piece of me hated my father for hurting her, and I hated myself for being exactly like him.

Except right now my stomach seemed more important than almost anything. I didn't want to think about my mom's feelings, about my dad, or how I would never be able to get the money I needed. "They're having a meeting for the church girls tonight." I tried not to sound angry as I spoke, but I failed miserably. "They're learning to make chili and bread sticks, but I guess I'm grounded, right?"

She didn't immediately say no, so I pressed. "It's not like it's going to be any fun with those girls. More stupid church. But I need to learn how to cook." I thought about adding something about how she never taught me, but that might be going a bit far.

I waited as she thought it over. "Okay," she said at last. "You can go, as long as you come right home afterward, but otherwise you are completely grounded. I'm letting you go only because it's religious and because right now I'm rather upset with you, and I think it's best that we aren't together for a while. But this isn't over by a long shot, Kyle. We're going to have a serious discussion about a punishment when you come home. And so help me, if I ever catch you stealing anything again, I will make your life miserable. We may be poor, but we are not cheats."

Not that kind of cheat, she meant, because I'd heard her lie plenty to get something she wanted for us or for herself, but if I wanted that chili and bread and to get away from her, arguing wasn't going to get me far. Besides, I really didn't care what she did to me. I couldn't have what I wanted most, so what else mattered? "Okay," I mumbled.

At the Rushtons' house, James came running out and Allia as well. "I'm about to walk over to Young Women's," she said as I opened the door for James to climb in. "I'd like you to come with me. Uh, that is if it's okay with your mom."

I glanced at my face in the mirror. I looked horrible since I'd been crying. Big surprise there.

"You can wash your face inside," Allia said. "I'll do your makeup."

That wasn't promising—not that it really mattered what I looked like.

"She can go," Mom said to Allia. "What time is it over?"

"We should be finished by eight or so. I think. Plus walking home time."

"Be home by eight-thirty or call," Mom told me. "We'll talk when you get home."

"Okay." With relief, I slipped down from the cab of the truck and started to follow Allia, but James threw his arms around my waist.

"I love you, Kyle."

I smiled. "I love you, too, James."

He released me and climbed into the truck. I saw Mom's face over my shoulder, staring at me with an expression I didn't understand. I never understood her anymore. Was that because I was growing up? I used to think I was lucky to have the best mom in the world, like James still believed she was, but different things were important now that I was growing up. I saw differently.

For a moment I wished I could be seven again, that I could adore my mother without reserve. *I love you, Mom,* I thought.

Turning, I followed Allia up the walk.

It wasn't until the door closed behind me in that wonderful, roast-smelling house that I began to worry why my mother had chosen now to search for my father. I wondered if she'd searched for James's dad, too.

CHAPTER TWENTY-THREE

Dante

Becca was looking out the window as Allia and Kyle ran up to the walk. "Looks like Rikki is letting Kyle go to Young Women's."

I couldn't tell if that was approval or disapproval in Becca's voice. In fact, I didn't know if I thought Kyle should be allowed to go anywhere except to her room. On the one hand, a church activity should be a good influence, something Kyle decidedly lacked, but on the other it would be fun—and after what she'd done today, she should receive some punishment. As a father, I wouldn't let my child out of his or her room if I'd had to pick them up at the police station, but as a bishop, I wanted Kyle at the activity.

The girls breezed past us with hardly a look. "This won't take long," Allia was saying, "but we have to hurry. I have a shirt you can borrow, if you want. It'd look good with those pants."

So they were exchanging clothes now? I lifted an eyebrow, and Becca gave me a wry smile. "Allia's conscious about the tightness," she said in a low voice. "They've been hitting modesty issues pretty hard in church lately. Remember what the stake president said last month?"

197

I nodded, remembering it well. In a mother-daughter fireside, he'd complimented the women and girls for trying to maintain modesty, but he'd ended with the plea for everyone to "loosen up." Allia had taken that to heart and had begun wearing the snugger tops only under looser ones. Her pants, however, were one area I felt we could work on in that respect. Allia was definitely getting some curves, which fact made me vaguely uncomfortable. I still saw her as somewhere near Lauren's age.

"You left work early," Becca said as we moved to the kitchen to see what the kids might have left us in terms of food.

"What else could I do?" I took down two plates from the cupboard as Becca uncovered the roast.

"You could have sent one of your counselors. If Kyle's here for the long haul, they'll need to develop a relationship with her as well."

"I promised her a couple Sundays ago that I'd be there for her."

"Are you sure you didn't go because you see Rikki in her?"

Where'd that come from? "I'd go if it was any of our youth, you know that." I did see Rikki in Kyle, and I felt the need to protect her, but what I'd said was true as well. My youth, my responsibility.

She sighed. "Of course you would. It's just, well, something Rikki said when she first got here has been bothering me—that she sometimes leaves her kids to go somewhere on her own. What if that's what she plans on doing here? Something's odd about her coming back right now and suddenly showing up at church when those children have barely heard of the Bible and don't know what Mormons even are. What if she's planning to take off to, say, Monte Carlo or Japan or somewhere and can't take the children? Maybe she isn't looking for religion so much as a place to dump her kids."

"I don't see how we can stop her, if she leaves them with someone responsible. She'd even have a few willing volunteers here."

"At least for James, and as long as she came back." Becca put several slices of roast on my plate as she spoke.

"I know Rikki, or at least I knew her, and she loves those kids. That's not fake. As for the religion part, you know how the Lord works. Something may have happened in Rikki's life to bring her here, but maybe it's a good thing, not a negative one."

She sighed. "You're right. And you were right to send me to the police station tonight. I found out why Kyle took those things. Or at least the reason she gave me."

As we ate, Becca explained about dance classes and Kyle's dream, keeping a sharp eye out for any small, listening ears. There was an understanding of Kyle's longing in her voice that I hadn't expected. Unlike Kyle and Rikki, Becca had taken advantage of every opportunity while growing up, from singing and piano lessons to volleyball and soccer. Her many abilities and talents still floored me, though she'd never been inclined to pursue any of her talents on a professional level, which was fine by me. She'd mentioned finishing her teaching degree in the future, but since she planned to remain home with the children, it hadn't been a priority to either of us.

"I'm going to call the school and find out the address of those classes," Becca said. "I want to be sure this isn't a story she's feeding us."

"That's a distinct possibility."

"My gut tells me it's true." She moved her food around on her plate. "So, did leaving early today mean you can't leave early on Friday?"

"Why would I leave—?" Oh, Friday, the day we were leaving for Saint George. How had I forgotten? I'd even reserved both Friday and Saturday nights at the hotel. We'd be back before church, but I'd told my counselors I was going to miss our morning meetings. "No, not at all. I'll go in a little early tomorrow. Stay a little late."

There was gratitude in her eyes, which made me feel uncomfortable instead of pleased. I leaned over to kiss her.

"Gross." Travis emerged from the basement stairs, carrying a stack of dishes. Lauren and Cory were close behind, also carrying dishes.

"Were you eating downstairs again?" Becca said. "Just because I'm gone doesn't mean you don't eat dinner at the table."

Travis put the dishes in the dishwasher. "Uh, I was doing a project on the computer. I put a sheet out for the kids."

"Don't eat anywhere but in the kitchen," I said.

Cory frowned. "You guys do." Same old argument.

"That's because I own the house. I can eat wherever I please." I picked up my own plate and went to rinse it in the sink before placing it in the dishwasher. "When you own a house, you can eat wherever you want. Don't do it again."

"Okay, Dad. We won't," Travis said.

The children usually followed the rule, but every now and then, if we didn't remind them, they grew lax. Playing stern usually got them back on the right track, and a little object lesson couldn't hurt.

Before I could open my mouth, Cory said in a bored tone, "I know, I know. We remind you of the Nephites in the Book of Mormon, who always needed a reminder to obey the commandments."

Becca threw me an amused look.

"That's right," I said. "Travis, it's almost time for Young Men. Aren't you guys doing a service project for the Sagers?"

Travis nodded. "Cleaning up their backyard. I'll finish up on the computer and go over. Can I take the clippers?"

"Sure. But this time remember to bring them home, okay?"

"Right. I'll do that."

Allia and Kyle rushed into the kitchen. "We're going to be late, I think," Allia said. "Can someone take us?"

Kyle's eyes went to the rest of the roast on the stove, which was probably a good thing because I did a double-take at her appearance. Her makeup, if she was wearing any, was tasteful, and wearing Allia's shirt, she looked like a girl even Becca wouldn't mind Allia hanging out with.

Travis was also staring, a puzzled expression on his face.

Kyle dragged her eyes away from the food. "Hi," she said to Travis.

"You look different."

Kyle smiled. "Thanks. I think."

"She looks great, doesn't she?" Allia said.

Cory leaned in. "Yeah, no more raccoon face. I don't know what girls see in that crap."

"Cory, we don't say crap!" Becca said.

"You just did!"

Becca frowned. "One more word, and you'll be grounded tomorrow."

"Can someone take us?" Allia repeated, bouncing from foot to foot.

"I will," I volunteered. "I have to go to the church for interviews tonight anyway. I'll drop you on my way."

"Not before Kyle has something to eat." Becca was already putting food on a plate. How she could have seen Kyle's longing and acted on it while correcting Cory, I'll never know.

"We're going to have chili there," Allia said.

"It's not finished yet, and Kyle's had a long day." Becca handed Kyle the plate.

"Can she eat in the car?" Allia asked.

"I can," Kyle said. "If you don't mind."

"I don't. Come on." I grabbed my keys.

"Okay, so how come she doesn't have to eat in the kitchen?" Cory grumbled.

Travis slapped him on the back of the head. "Because she's a guest. Duh!"

Cory hit him back and darted down the stairs, with Travis close behind. Lauren rolled her eyes. "Boys," she said in a decidedly adult voice tinged with long-suffering. "I'd better keep an eye on them so they don't kill each other."

I could barely stop from grinning as I grabbed my suit jacket from the closet and hurried to the door. If the Lord blessed me any more, I might feel guilty. "See you later, honey," I called over my shoulder to Becca.

"What about a tie?"

"I keep a few in my desk at the church."

"Okay." Her voice was distracted, and I stopped to see why. She stood at the counter, looking at a sheet torn from a magazine, folded enough times that the edges were beginning to show wear. A picture of a garden filled the back.

Rikki had certainly known what she was talking about.

The girls were silent as I drove to the Flemmings', Kyle gulping her food in the backseat and Allia staring out the passenger side window in the front. Memories assailed me as I pulled up at the house. Joel Flemming had been first the Young Men's leader and then the second counselor in the bishopric for much of my youth. All the young men had spent many hours with him at his house and at other activities. I'd often secretly wished he was my father. He'd also taken the place of Rikki's father on Young Women daddy-daughter activities, and I'd been as grateful for her sake as for my own. How ironic to be dropping Rikki's daughter off here now.

"Have fun, girls," I said.

Allia leaned over and gave me a kiss on the cheek. "We will."

Kyle set her empty plate on the backseat. "Thanks." She hesitated as though wanting to say more, but then slammed the door and hurried after Allia. Running up the sidewalk, Kyle looked more like Rikki than ever. Or like the Rikki I'd known.

What had Rikki's life been like all these years? I hoped she'd found some happiness along the way.

I felt restless. Strangely, a part of me wanted to go over to Rikki's to make sure she was okay, but we were adults now, and she'd learned to take care of herself. Besides, I had to get to the church to be on time for my first interview. After that, I'd go straight home to Becca and the kids. That was where I really wanted—and needed—to be.

CHAPTER TWENTY-FOUR

Kyle

I was grounded, of course, but I still went to watch the private dance classes on Wednesday. No way was I going to miss them, and since we didn't have a phone at home, it wasn't like Mom could check up on me. James wouldn't say anything, because I'd promised him a package of licorice from my stash and let him play in the backyard at the house where the lessons were held. No one seemed to care that I was bringing him, and I hoped my luck held.

After my time at the police station, I'd told myself I'd accept whatever punishment Mom gave me, and I really intended to go straight home from school to clean the kitchen, as she'd ordered me to do for the next month, and even to have dinner ready. But the idea of missing out on learning new dance moves for an entire month—well, I couldn't stay home.

I hated myself for being weak, for wanting something so much I couldn't accept a punishment I knew I deserved—no, that was way less than I deserved.

The redhead who'd befriended me last Thursday had her private lesson today. Last Wednesday, she had pulled the curtains and

I'd only been able to watch the lesson before and after hers, but today she left it open. I waved at her.

Watching today hurt worse than I'd thought it would, given that now I knew there was absolutely no possibility of paying for lessons myself. My chest felt tight, and I struggled to breathe. *Concentrate on the movements,* I told myself. *I can do this myself at home.*

I bit my lip and tried not to cry. Before her lesson ended, I slipped into the small bathroom off the changing room to fix my face because I hadn't been all that successful at not crying.

When I emerged, I saw Sister Rushton in the observation area. James was with her, and my face reddened as I came back to myself and remembered that I wasn't supposed to be here but at home serving out my punishment. She'd tell Mom. Maybe I even wanted her to. Maybe if Mom knew about the lessons she could find a way.

No. She couldn't. She'd enroll me in something less expensive, and I might not be allowed to return here even to watch.

I walked toward Sister Rushton as a redheaded lady came in the door, probably here to pick up her daughter.

"Kyle, look who's here!" James said. "Lauren might be taking dance like you. Isn't that cool?"

Of course that was why she was here. I'd have laughed if it hadn't hurt so much. "I'm not taking dance. I'm just here to watch a friend." I kept my voice low so the redheaded lady and her daughter, now coming from the dance floor, wouldn't hear.

The redhead waved at me as she left. I smiled, though my face felt frozen. Maybe Sister Rushton wouldn't tell my mom. She couldn't know the details of my punishment, and I'd be good. I wouldn't even come back tomorrow to watch the group lessons. But I knew I was lying to myself about that. I would do everything I could to make it here.

"I didn't see a bike," Sister Rushton said. "Do you guys need a ride home?"

"Sure!" James grabbed her hand. "It's a long ways home, and I'm hungry. We've been here forever."

The teacher was coming my way, probably to ask if I was planning on actually taking real lessons instead of watching all the time. I felt like a fraud.

"Come on. Let's go." I hurried out the door, feeling eyes gouging into me as I left. I blinked hard to keep back fresh tears.

Sister Rushton and James came outside with the teacher. James walked over to me where I waited by Sister Rushton's van, while Sister Rushton lingered. Probably discussing how talented Lauren was. An ache blossomed in my chest.

Help me. I didn't know whom I was asking. Wait, I did know. *God.* Would He care for a disobedient girl who was also a shoplifter and a lousy sister who left her brother all alone in a stranger's backyard? A girl who was jealous of a redheaded stranger because she could dance?

Probably not.

The sound of Sister Rushton's laughter floated to me on the light breeze that felt cold and clammy on my skin.

James and Sister Rushton chatted on the drive home, and though she tried to include me by asking about last night's Young Women activity, I felt too depressed to talk. I'd enjoyed the activity, and the girls seemed much nicer to me than they'd been on Sundays. I even understood why Allia loved it so much. I almost felt as if I belonged. Until we'd left and the reality of who I was set in.

Shoplifter, grounded, poor, jealous, greedy, angry. Angry.

Maybe I would tell Mom where I'd been. Dump it all in her lap. Accuse her of not taking care of me.

Except I'd heard her crying last night, when I'd awakened

myself, drenched in sweat, tears on my cheeks. I'd dreamed about my father, the man I knew only from a picture. He'd come to visit, but instead of helping me, he'd stolen the seventeen dollars I'd saved toward my lessons.

"Here we are." Sister Rushton brought the van to a halt.

"Thanks," I said.

"I'll talk to your mother about taking dance, okay?"

I shook my head. "No. Please."

She tilted her head but didn't reply. "Never give up hope. Never."

I watched her drive away, and the only thing that gave me the strength to go up the walk and open the door was what she'd said.

Mom came home after I fed James a grilled cheese sandwich and put him in front of the TV with the licorice I'd promised him.

"Hi, kids."

"I saved you a sandwich," I said. "Just needs warming up."

She reached for the plate but closed her hands just short of it. "This darn headache," she said. "Makes me see double." She picked up the plate and fumbled with the door of the microwave before getting it open.

"Aren't you supposed to clean the kitchen?" she asked.

"I had homework," I said quickly, glad James wasn't there to contradict me. "I'll do it now."

"Okay." She took her sandwich from the microwave, sat down at the table, and stared out the window, though I was pretty sure she was seeing nothing. When her phone rang, she fumbled for it. "Hello?" Pause. "Oh, hi, Quinn."

Quinn, or the Couch Man, as I thought of him. Maybe he'd come over with more hamburgers and fries.

"Friday? Oh, I can't. I have something planned with the kids. But thanks for asking. Some other time. Yeah, maybe next week.

Yep. Thanks. Okay, bye." She heaved a sigh and laid her head on the table. "Can you bring me my purse?"

When I did, she popped a pill from a bottle and swallowed it without water before laying her head again on the table next to her plate. "Thanks."

Uneasiness stirred in my stomach. "Are you okay?"

"It was a busy day at work. How was your day?"

"I'm grounded. How do you think it was?" All the bitterness came flooding back.

"Not today, Kyle. Please, not today."

Fine. "So why don't you go out with him?"

She sighed. "Because there's no future in it."

"How do you know unless you try?" I'd thought a lot about Travis and the comment he'd made about me last night after Allia had done my makeup. "You look different." Bad different or good different? I still didn't know for sure, but after Allia's encouragement and what Cory said about raccoon eyes, I thought it meant good. I'd considered doing my own makeup that way this morning, but in the end chickened out and went with what made me comfortable. What if the kids I was friendly with at school said something? I wasn't ready for rejection or to try to fit in again somewhere else.

Truth was, I didn't know where I fit in. I felt unsettled. I wished I could tell Mom and she could make it all better—my mixed feelings about Allia, my so-called friends at school who were willing to buy my stolen items or my free lunch, my attraction to Travis, and especially the dance lessons I wanted more than I wanted air. Except none of this was like kissing my owie when I was small and had fallen down and skinned my knee.

Mom didn't answer my question about how she could know there wasn't a future with Couch Man, and I knew she hadn't heard.

I'd finished cleaning the kitchen by the time she stirred. "Oh, I feel better," she said. "Where's James?"

She'd passed him when she came in. Didn't she remember?

"Watching TV."

"Oh, right. Let's go watch it with him."

I stared for a minute at her untouched sandwich before replying. "Okay." I grabbed my backpack and hurried to the living room with her. James made way for us on the couch.

After a while Mom seemed normal again, so I left and went downstairs to practice dance. I kept the volume low so I wouldn't bother Mom and James, though they were probably too busy with the TV to notice.

Hours fell away, and when I finally collapsed to the ground, exhausted but feeling good, I was drenched in sweat. The hair that had escaped my ponytail was matted to my head, and my body felt in desperate need of cool water. Plus, I was famished and once again craving carbs to replace the energy I'd used.

Upstairs the house was dark and quiet, so I moved carefully as my eyes adjusted. My foot hit something by the table, and I bent to pick it up. Mom's purse. I set it next to her still-untouched sandwich and took another step, landing on something tiny—no, a whole bunch of tiny things. I scooped up a few and opened the door of the microwave for a little more light. In my hand were small white pills. On the floor by the table lay Mom's pill bottle, fallen over on its side, more white pills spread out on the floor.

Hadn't I seen her put them away? I'd have to tell her to be more careful. James might pop them in his mouth just to taste them. I brushed the pills back in with my fingers and secured the child-proof cap, placing the bottle next to her purse on the table.

The darkness felt heavy now. Oppressive.

In the living room Mom and James were curled up together in front of the couches, bringing to mind a picture of big cats I'd seen in science a few days back. They looked peaceful. I could hear James breathing softly, but Mom's breath came so faintly I almost couldn't hear it.

Forgetting all about food, I lay down next to her, my hand against her back to feel the thumping of her heart, and listened to the soft in-and-out whooshing. It was a long time before I slept.

CHAPTER TWENTY-FIVE

Dante

I punched in my home number, knowing Becca would be wondering where I was. "Hi, hon," I said.

"Are you on your way? Remember, we still have to drop the kids off at my sister's before we head to Saint George."

"Uh, yeah. About that."

She sighed, knowing what was coming. I had a good reason for canceling our trip, and she would forgive me, but I felt terrible anyway.

"I'm at the hospital. Joel Flemming's had a heart attack. Steve and I gave him a blessing before they rushed him into surgery, but it's not looking good." My stomach twisted at the words. Joel Flemming, the man who'd been like a father to me. I wasn't ready yet to let him go.

"Oh, no." Becca's voice showed genuine concern. "Is Kate there with him?"

"Yeah, and their children and her three sisters. You don't need to come down, not yet. There are too many here as it is. I'll give the Relief Society president a call so she can see about meals and such."

"When will the doctors know anything?"

"He's in surgery now. It'll be hours before we have news. I'm coming home to grab something to eat because it looks like it'll be a long night. I'd also like to contact as many ward members as possible and ask them to start praying, maybe even fasting. The next few hours are crucial."

"I'll start calling now," she said. Becca, my rock. Not one word of regret about the trip, though I knew she had to be disappointed.

"Thanks. I'll see you in a few."

Leaving Steve with the Flemmings for the time being, I hurried to my car. I needed to be back as soon as possible; I wanted to be there for Joel and Kate.

As I pulled into my driveway fifteen minutes later, Rikki's truck came down the street, sounding rather loud. *The muffler must have a hole.* I couldn't remember if I'd heard her truck when the engine was on before and if had always been that way, or if it was something new.

I pulled the car in the garage next to Becca's van but left the door open. Rikki pulled into the driveway. James jumped from the truck and ran toward me. "Look, Bishop! I have my glasses."

"So you do," I said. "Very nice. Can you see better?"

"Yeah. It's so cool. I can see the letters in my books, I can see the board at school, and everything. I can't wait to show your mom. I mean, Lauren's mom. Um, Sister . . ."

"Sister Rushton."

"Yeah."

"She's in the house. Go right ahead." I indicated the back door, and he ran toward it.

Rikki was moving a little slowly, but she finally made it up the driveway. "How are you?" I asked.

"Good. Thanks. You?"

"Fine." So this was what we were reduced to. The whole conversation seemed wrong somehow.

"I'm glad to catch you and Becca before you head off to Saint George. I was worried you'd be gone already. James was excited to show off his glasses to Becca and Lauren."

"We're not going to Saint George, after all. Joel Flemming's had a heart attack. He's in surgery now. I can't leave him and Kate."

Rikki frowned. "That's terrible. I'm so sorry. From what I remember, he was a decent guy."

"He really is." All at once the awkwardness vanished. I knew she understood exactly what Joel meant to me for all the years he'd been there when my own father barely recognized that I was alive. A few seconds of silence ticked between us. Comfortable silence, like we'd shared in our youth.

Rikki gave her head a little shake. "Becca should go anyway. This is the last week."

"She'll want to be here with Kate."

"I seem to remember the Flemmings having a lot of relatives, and there are plenty of people to hang out with Kate tonight and tomorrow. Becca going for one day won't affect anything, will it?"

"I don't know that she'd be able to enjoy herself knowing Joel's life is in danger."

Rikki snorted. "She's not going to get through it any better sitting here and worrying. The real work will come in the recovery afterward, or . . . or in comforting Kate if . . ."

"You're right, but Becca won't leave. I know her. She'll want to know what's going on."

"That's what cell phones are for."

"She won't want to drive by herself."

"Are you sure about that? Are you sure you're not just saying that because you don't want her to go without you? So she can be here when you come home from the hospital tonight? You depend on Becca far too much, Dante. Just like you depended on me."

That took me by surprise. "Depended on you?"

"Yes, Dante. On me. Except for all that homework, you couldn't do anything without me—go to school, church, the mall. You asked me what you should wear, what classes to take. You couldn't make a decision until we talked about it."

Who was this woman who could walk into my life after more than twenty years and think she knew me so well? Problem was, I suspected she was right. Next to the gospel, Becca was everything to me. I hoped I didn't repay that trust by smothering her.

"Becca makes her own choices, Rikki."

"Are you sure it's not you or the Church who makes them? Becca needs to do something for herself every now and then, and putting things off time and time again gets old. It makes you wither inside."

Where was all this bitterness coming from? First toward me and now the Church? Well, she could say all she wanted about me and I wouldn't complain, but the Church was true, and the ward family had saved both our lives. They were a large part of who we became.

"Don't blame the Church, Rikki. The gospel is true. If you'd only understand that, it'd bring you peace."

Her lip curled. "Don't give me that. The only reason you left me and went on that mission was because your father said you should go. The first time he actually notices you and it's to tell you to do something you didn't even want to do. You bent over backward all through high school, getting straight A's, never sluffing class, even trying to make him dinner most nights just so he'd spend time with you. Don't think I don't remember that burnt spaghetti or that stinky fish. Let's be honest. If he'd told you to be an astronaut, you'd have applied to the space program. If he told you the moon was made of cheese, you'd have believed it as fact. You were so starved for his attention, you would have done anything to please him. That's why you went on a mission, and you can't say it wasn't.

You can't say it was because you believed in the gospel. Because I knew you, Dante. I knew you as well as I knew myself."

I was quiet a moment as I took in her words. "You're right. I did go on a mission because of my father—and because of others as well—Joel Flemming and our bishop among them, but that is absolutely not why I stayed. I realized that first month that being a missionary wasn't going to change anything between me and my father. He wrote me only once the whole time I was gone."

"Then why did you stay?"

"I stayed because I learned the importance of the gospel for myself, because I believed with all my heart in what I was doing."

Rikki frowned. "I'd thought you'd leave after a few weeks and come search for me. I'm not talking about romance, but we were everything to each other back then. Everything."

"I couldn't. I'd promised God to serve."

"So God came first. Before me."

Her lost tone twisted something in my heart, but there was only one answer. "He always comes first, Rikki, and when He does, everything else falls into place."

Her eyes held mine, but she didn't speak. We didn't need to. Like siblings raised in the same household, she understood that I believed with everything I was. I had told her the truth.

"Everything else falls into place," she repeated. "You mean like it did with Becca."

I nodded.

Her lost expression was so like the child I'd known that tears pricked behind my eyes. "Will you tell James to come out?" Rikki said, turning on her heel. "I'll be waiting in the truck."

"No, come inside for a minute." I didn't want to let her leave like that. Maybe Becca could make her feel better somehow.

Silently, Rikki followed me to the back door, which was slightly ajar. Though we had automatic hinges, I'd adjusted the threshold last winter to prevent the heat from escaping, and now it never closed all the way by itself, a thing I'd been meaning to fix for months.

I pushed open the door and found Becca standing by the refrigerator, an open cooler on the floor beside her. Food for the trip, I guessed.

"Hi, honey."

She met me halfway across the room, and I gave her a hug and a kiss. "Any news?" she asked. She didn't hold my gaze, and I wondered what that meant.

"No."

She pulled away. "Hi, Rikki." No mistaking the lack of enthusiasm there. "James looks great in those glasses."

"He loves them. He had to come and show you." Rikki was holding on to the back of a chair with whitened knuckles. "Where is he, anyway?"

"With Lauren and Cory downstairs," Becca said. "I let them play an extra half hour of video games since they're so disappointed about not going to their cousins' house. Have a seat, Rikki."

Rikki sank into the chair. "That's tough about, uh, Brother Flemming. I'm sorry."

"He'll pull through." Why did I feel so panicked as I said it? *Calm down,* I told myself. I knew my fear wasn't only for Joel but also for Rikki's spiritual welfare. That glimpse into her bitterness had been far too revealing and left me wondering anew why she'd returned to Utah at all—and especially to the Church. She was right when she said we'd been everything to each other. That we both had others now, more important in our lives, didn't take away the past. It also didn't mean I had any clue as how to proceed with her now. *Father,* I prayed, though I wasn't sure what exactly I was praying for.

"We have leftovers from last night," Becca told me. "Do you want me to heat them up?"

I grabbed her hands. "No. I want you to go to Saint George."

She blinked. "What? I can't leave now, and I'm certainly not going alone."

"I know how much you've been looking forward to it. This is the last week of the show, isn't it?" I could feel Rikki staring at me from her chair, her eyes urging me on.

"I have to be here for the Flemmings."

"You'll only be gone until tomorrow night or Sunday morning at the latest. Others can fill in until then."

Her eyes glistened. "I couldn't."

"You can," Rikki said. "You should. There's nothing you can do for them right now."

"There'll always be next year."

"Next year something else could happen to stop you from going," Rikki countered. "And the year after that. Something that always seems more important. Isn't that always the way it is? Something with the kids, or the ward, or"—Rikki shot a black glare at me—"with Dante."

"Well, we are kind of busy," Becca said.

I could see as clearly as if she were shouting that she believed Rikki's scenario would come to pass. She was probably right. Something always did seem to pop up.

"You could take Allia," I suggested. "She'd probably like that, and if she didn't, there's always the hotel pool. I'll keep you updated by cell phone. The Flemmings will never know you weren't sitting here worrying the entire time."

Becca was shaking her head, but she was smiling. "You're nuts."

"About you." My hands tightened on hers. A movement from the corner of my eye caught my attention: Rikki looking away.

"Maybe I will," Becca said.

I felt a little internal resistance at that, but I squashed it. Rikki was right. I wanted Becca here for me, not for the Flemmings. I counseled people all the time that often making a better marriage was a matter of moving just a bit toward your spouse, each giving a little, no one giving too much. Becca had been giving too much, and I'd been blind to it. Maybe this could help begin to right that wrong. "I'll take care of the kids, or Travis will when I'm not here."

Becca was shaking her head. "You have no idea when you'll be back, and I don't want to leave Lauren so long with the boys. I'll take her, too. It'll be girls' night out. Maybe you could take the boys next month."

Not a bad idea.

Becca went to the basement stairs. "Kids, I need to talk to you! Please come up now."

I took yesterday's leftover beef stew from the refrigerator and ladled some into a bowl.

"Grounding is just around the corner!" Becca threatened. "Push pause now!" Magic words. Seconds later Travis, Cory, and Lauren, trailed by James, came up the stairs. Lauren went to get Allia from her bedroom.

Allia was more than excited to go to Saint George, and Lauren was ecstatic. "Can I eat chips in the car?" she asked.

Rikki smirked at that, and I wondered why she was still there. Didn't she have somewhere else to go? Shouldn't she be checking up on Kyle?

"You'll be able to eat some things in the car," Becca said, "and boys, you can go somewhere with Dad next month."

"It better be somewhere fun," grumbled Cory. "I don't want to see any gardens."

"James does." Lauren put her arm around James. "Can James come, Mom? He won't get food on the floor."

"No, honey, he can't. He needs to stay with his mom."

Everyone looked at Rikki for confirmaion. "Actually," she drawled, "I'd like to come, too. I think a girls' night out is exactly what I need."

We all stared. "It is?" Becca asked, ever polite.

"Yeah. I meant what I said when I gave you the flyer." Her gaze brushed mine. "It'd be fun to let your hair down. Kyle could come too, so Allia has someone to hang out with."

Becca took a breath and knowing her as I did, I knew she was going to say something about spending alone time with her girls, but Allia beat her to it. "That would be fun. If the little kids get sick of gardens, we can take them to the pool or something." As if Becca would let anyone take Lauren to the pool without her, though Lauren was fishlike in her ability to swim. "Or to a park."

"Or watch cartoons in the room," Lauren put in. For some reason, that was always her favorite part of going to a hotel.

Rikki laughed, and Becca joined in. "Okay," Becca said. "Why not? If you really want to go, Rikki, you're welcome." I heard the strain in Becca's voice even if no one else did, but I felt helpless to step in. Besides, a part of me thought maybe Becca could do something to help both Rikki and Kyle.

"Yippee!" Lauren shouted.

James frowned. "But it's a girls' night out. I'm not a girl."

"You could stay here," Cory offered.

"No," Rikki said. "You're coming with me. It's girls' night out plus kids under eight."

"Okay." James's smile was back. "Let's go."

Lauren held up her hand. "No, silly. You have to go home and get your clothes. You can't go without clean underwear. I have my bag ready since I was going to my aunt's. I'll get it!" She was off and running.

Rikki came to her feet, that crazy smile still on her face. "I'll go home and get ready. Won't take more than fifteen minutes."

"I'm ready now," James insisted. "I don't need underwear."

A typical boy. Much to their mother's dismay, my sons would go an entire week on a Scout campout without changing underwear. Partly my fault, she always said, for forgetting to remind them.

Rikki pulled James toward the door. "We'll be back."

"I'll come by to get you," Becca said. "I'll take the van so we have more room. Dante will need his car, and the one Travis drives probably wouldn't make the trip."

The van ate more gas than Cory ate meat, but I couldn't care less. Becca was happy.

After Rikki left, the children scattered, and I downed my food as Becca repacked the cooler. "You'll have enough leftovers for today and tomorrow," she said. "But if you're not home tomorrow afternoon for Cory's soccer, you'll have to unground Travis so he can take him."

"Probably should unground him anyway, don't you think? It's been two weeks."

"Probably."

"I think he learned his lesson."

She gave me a lopsided smile. "What do you bet another one is just around the corner?"

"Isn't it always?"

She scanned the kitchen, hands on her hips, her blue eyes sparkling. "I guess I'm ready, then."

I jumped up from the table and wrapped my arms around her. Every time I did this, I had the sense of coming home, that she had been made for me and I for her. I didn't know if she felt the same. "Are you sure about this? Taking Rikki, I mean. I think you are a good influence on her, but I know how you feel about Kyle and Allia."

She tilted her head, studying me. "It's Rikki I'm mostly worried about. There's something odd about her."

"Odd as in serial killer odd?" I joked. "Or just strange?"

Becca shook her head. "I'll let you know."

"It's still not too late to get out of it."

"I want to go, Dante, and Rikki is the one who found the show for me. She listened."

Her words hit me hard. *She listened.* Rikki had always been a good listener. What's more, she was pretty good at talking, too, since she'd succeeded in getting me to listen as well.

"I love you, you know."

"I know." She relaxed against me, but an odd note in her voice caught me unaware. "I'm not afraid of the past. I know what kind of man you are."

"Good." I kissed her.

"I love you, too, Dante."

I left her then, but my thoughts had difficulty returning to the Flemmings. This trip of Becca's was either going to be a huge success or a roaring failure.

CHAPTER TWENTY-SIX

Becca

I hadn't meant to eavesdrop, but after James came running inside with his glasses, I'd been curious about why Rikki didn't show up after him. The back door was ajar, and I'd hesitated as I'd heard Rikki and Dante arguing, sounding much like siblings, though Rikki's words made it clear she'd expected much more from Dante all those years ago. I'd been proud of my husband for standing up for what he believed, yet with Rikki around to continue muddying the waters, I worried the tension would only get worse.

So I'd allowed her to come with me to Saint George, not because I wanted her company, but because I wanted to find out why she was really here in Utah. Another part of me also wanted to help Kyle, to encourage her to tell her mother about the dance lessons so we could begin to look for resolution. It wasn't going to be easy, and I understood why Kyle was afraid to tell Rikki. The lessons were expensive, more than I paid for piano, guitar, gymnastics, and karate for all my children. However, the teacher was the very best, and her students always excelled.

Despite Brother Flemming's illness, I felt excitement about my plans for the future, for what I would do when my children were off living their own lives and didn't need me so intensely. Already the older two were mostly independent, taking care of their schooling, their own schedules, even their own laundry. I'd always wanted to finish my teaching degree, but now other choices stretched before me, as sparkling and full of promise as they'd seemed when I was twenty. I owed some of that to Rikki.

First she and I needed to talk so we knew exactly where we stood. I hadn't overheard their entire conversation, but Rikki seemed to still want something of Dante, and if he couldn't tell me, I'd find out for myself.

When we pulled up at Rikki's, she and her children were ready, each with a small backpack or duffel, unlike Allia, who'd somehow needed an entire suitcase for the two days. But they weren't alone. A broad, blond-haired man about Dante's height stood in front of the porch talking to them. Nice-looking and, by the way his eyes followed her, obviously fascinated with Rikki. I didn't blame him. She looked small and frail, like someone who needed looking after.

James saw us and said something to the man, who gave him a high five before James came tumbling toward the van. Kyle flushed at something the man said and followed her brother almost as quickly.

"Stay here," I told my children as I opened my door.

Rikki and her friend met me on the sidewalk. "Ready?" I asked.

"Yeah," Rikki said.

I stared at her friend, and she started visibly. "Oh, right. Becca, this is Quinn Hunter. We work together. Quinn, this is Becca Rushton. She's a friend in my ward."

Of all the things I'd expected her to introduce me as, friend wasn't at the top of my list. James's tutor, the wife of her childhood friend, the bishop's wife, or even a sister in her ward. We weren't exactly friends.

Quinn turned his gaze on me, and for the first time I saw what might have attracted Rikki to this man. Not only did he have a nice smile but he had kind emerald eyes that seemed to peer into your heart. "Nice to meet you."

"You, too," I said.

He thumbed over his shoulder. "I knew Rikki had plans with her kids tonight, but I came to see if I could help her change her oil before they left. Didn't realize she was heading off to Saint George."

Ah, he'd hoped to worm his way into whatever plans she'd made by offering help. Not a bad strategy. I knew changing her oil wasn't going to be high on Rikki's list, especially after paying for James's new glasses.

"Guess next week will have to do." He glanced at Rikki, his eyes lingering. What's more, I could see she wasn't immune to his charms.

The tight knot around my heart eased. *Rikki has a crush*, I thought, grinning to myself. That was good news. "We'd better go. We're already going to get to the hotel kind of late."

"Not if you drive fast," Rikki retorted.

She turned to leave, but Quinn grabbed her hand. "Can I call you?"

The Rikki I was coming to know would probably say something like, "It's a free country, isn't it?" But she gave a quick nod. "Sure."

He winked. "I confess, I was looking forward to seeing you under that truck."

Rikki laughed, and I found myself laughing too. "Nice guy," I said as we drove down the street.

"Yeah, he is."

When nothing more was forthcoming, I asked, "So, are you dating him?"

"No. I just need him to change my oil."

I glanced in the rearview mirror, but the children, involved in their own world, weren't listening. "You're kidding, right? He couldn't take his eyes off you. And you weren't much better."

Rikki sighed. "I know." She fell silent, almost brooding. I'd never seen this side of her before, and as the miles passed, I kept throwing her sidelong glances.

"Would you stop that?" she asked after a while, but despite the words, she smiled. "Okay, he's cute, but there's no future in it."

"How can you know that?"

"Because I'm not going to be here much longer."

In my view that was also good news. Why, then, did I feel a pang of regret? My next thought was, *What about the kids?* I didn't say it aloud, though. Time enough for that later.

From that moment on, being with Rikki in the car reminded me of trips with my family, particularly my sister. We sang songs with the kids, played the Alphabet Game and I Spy, and later as the children dozed, we told stories of the past. She told about dancing gigs, about the time when she'd met Celine Dion, when James had escaped his preschool teacher and been found in the park feeding the pigeons with a kind homeless man. I talked about growing up as a mission president's daughter, of serving a mission under him when I was only eighteen, of going to college. The first time I'd set eyes on Dante.

I still shivered when I thought about that moment. I'd dated several dozen guys by that point, but when his eyes met mine, I couldn't look away. He was good-looking, and I'd expected him to be full of himself. I'd turned him down for the first date and the second, but when he asked me a third time, I couldn't find any more excuses.

"It was his name that finally made me go out with him," I told Rikki. "Dante. Someone had just brought up the Italian poet Dante and his unrequited love for Beatrice. I was curious about his name." Dante had later told me that like the Italian Dante had fallen for

Beatrice, he'd fallen in love with me the moment he'd seen me. I took more convincing, but I never turned him down for a date again.

"I told him his mother must have named him after that poet," Rikki said.

"You know about the Italian Dante?"

"Yes, and what's more, I'm probably one of the eighty-six people on the planet who actually likes reading his poetry. Or any poetry, really. Anyway, back in high school, in one of our classes, maybe American heritage or psychology or something, we had to tell how we got our names. Dante didn't know. His mother was dead, and his father didn't talk much. The teacher mentioned the poet Dante, so I did a little research. Dante—the poet—first saw Beatrice when she was eight and he was nine."

"Yeah. Pretty odd that he could think himself in love with her as an adult even after not talking to her for nine years."

"Maybe he worshipped from afar."

The story from there went downhill. Dante and Beatrice both married others, and Beatrice died at twenty-four.

Rikki must have been thinking along the same lines. "Well, his love inspired all those poems. The teacher called them master-pieces."

"The greatest Italian literary work, I think my teacher said." I was beginning to feel uncomfortable with the conversation. Did Rikki see herself as Dante's Beatrice? Dante was a writer, but not of fiction, and he certainly didn't write poems about Rikki and his childhood.

Silently, I scolded myself for what was plainly jealousy. I had everything compared to what Rikki had—Dante, the gospel, a stable life. She wasn't the sort of person I would normally choose as a friend, but she had helped Dante through a difficult period of his life, and for that I would try to like her.

Wait. The freeway exit in Saint George was rapidly approaching. How had the time passed so fast? It was already after ten, and I'd been so occupied with Rikki that I hadn't once worried about the boys.

"Mom, I'm hungry. Really hungry." Lauren had slept half the way, and now she looked ready to party. "Starving. My insides feel like they're sticking together."

"Me, too," James said.

Allia laughed. "How could you guys eat anything more? We've been eating the whole time. I think I'm going to puke."

I hated that word. "Allia," I said.

"Well, I just want to get to the hotel."

"Me, too," said Kyle.

"Do they have enough beds?" Lauren asked.

"I didn't think about that. Probably not, since just Dad and I were going before."

Rikki and I looked at each other and burst into laughter.

"I'll see if they have another room," Rikki said. "I planned on it anyway."

"No," groaned Lauren. "I want to watch TV with James."

In the end, our rooms at the Budget Inn were next door to each other. Though they did have a suite with three queen beds which would have accommodated all of us—Lauren and me, Rikki and James, and Allia and Kyle—Rikki paid for her own room. I had a coupon we both used, so it wasn't overly expensive, but the children were disappointed at the decision that seemed so unlike Rikki's free-spirit attitude. I was secretly relieved.

We fed the children snacks from my cooler and from a bag of food Rikki had brought, and when that didn't have everything they wanted, we visited the hotel's snack machine. All the while, the TV was blasting. Lauren and James were content, and I didn't mention the crumbs all over the carpet between the bed and the TV, though I felt a secret delight that I wouldn't have to clean them up.

Rikki, sitting on the floor with James in her lap, ate nothing. She smiled and interacted with James, but her usual vivaciousness and energy were absent. Kyle was the one who paid attention to what her brother ate, gave him a drink, threw away his wrappers. Her solicitousness surprised me, though not as much as her skill with him. This was a Kyle I'd never seen, never suspected existed. Every so often, I caught her staring at her mother, a blank expression on her face.

James and Lauren were nearly asleep when we called it a night. Lauren barely stirred as I changed her into pajamas and put her into bed, and Allia fell asleep not long afterward. Flipping off the TV, I looked up the garden sites on my map, though I'd already done it earlier in the week and I'd borrowed my sister's GPS so we wouldn't miss anything. Still not sleepy, I called Dante for the third time on our trip to find out about Joel.

"He's finally out of surgery," Dante reported. "There were complications that deprived him of blood to his brain, and we're still waiting to see how he is when he awakes—if he awakes."

"Okay. Let me know."

"I'll call you in the morning. Love you."

Feeling a little guilty for the fun I'd been having, I prayed for Joel and for Kate, too. I knew how I'd feel if it were Dante in that hospital room.

I'd barely turned out the light when a quick, frantic knock sounded on my door. I jumped to my feet and peered through the peephole before opening the door. "Kyle, what is it?"

Tears marked her cheeks as she staggered under the weight of her little brother's sleeping body. "It's Mom. She's hurting, and I don't know how to help her."

"Come in here." I took James from her and laid him on my bed.

Kyle extended a bottle of pills. "Maybe she needs these." She started sobbing.

Taking the pills, I reached for her, held her shaking body. "It's going to be okay. Look, you lie down and rest. Don't worry about anything. I'll take care of your mom. If you need me, come next door, but don't open the door for anyone."

"Okay." Her voice was so lost and forlorn that I had to force myself to leave her. *Poor child.*

Rikki's door was open, and she was in bed in the dark, moaning. I turned on a lamp to the lowest setting and shut the door. "Rikki?" She only moaned and grabbed her head. The pillow was wet with her tears. My brother-in-law had migraine headaches, but I'd never seen him like this.

I looked at the bottle in my hand. "Do you need one of these?"

"Yes," Rikki whimpered. Then, "No. It's too soon. Tomorrow."

"Do I need to take you to the hospital?"

"Nothing they can do."

"They could put you out."

"I just need to sleep. In the morning, I'll be fine."

There was no emotion in her voice except for the pain, and I realized this was nothing new to her. No wonder she'd insisted on separate rooms.

I sat on the bed. "Okay, then. Keep your eyes closed and try to relax." She whimpered, and I pulled her head onto my lap and gently rubbed her temples, rotating my hands in circles. I had no idea if this would help, but when I had been in labor with my children, just having Dante rub my back or hold my hand had been a great comfort.

As I would with one of my children, I smoothed her hair and whispered comforting words. "Think of your favorite place in the world," I told her. "Think of being there with those you love. The sun is shining, and everything is warm and full of light. You can hear laughter, the sound of the ocean, or maybe the wind blowing through the mountain trees. You can smell delicious food, or maybe salt, or maybe the rain on the wet pavement." On I went, not so much caring what I said but keeping the tone steady, something for her to focus on.

After long minutes, the tension began easing from her body. I drew my fingers over her forehead to smooth out the furrows. "Relax," I said. "Let the pain roll through you and out the other side."

I was stiff when I realized she was finally sleeping. She looked like a child under the blanket, except for her face, which was deeply furrowed even in sleep. Still-drying tears stood out on her cheeks. This wasn't normal. Why hadn't her doctor given her something more helpful?

I looked at the bottle once again, but I wasn't familiar with the medication. As I put it back, my hand hit against her purse on the nightstand, knocking it to the floor where it wedged between the nightstand and the bed. Sighing, I leaned over and tugged it loose, pulling too hard and sending the purse and the contents flying in all directions.

The first thing I noticed were the prescription bottles, at least three. No, four. None of the names were familiar to me. What was going on here? I looked at Rikki. She looked so normal lying there, and for a moment I imagined the little girl she'd been when she knew Dante.

Replacing everything inside the purse, I went next door to check on the children. All were asleep, and since I didn't dare leave Rikki alone, I decided to let them remain where they were. I could check on them again later.

Back in Rikki's room, I headed to the bathroom, gagging over the mess I found there on the floor. Someone had been repeatedly sick and hadn't made it to the toilet. I turned on the fan and began cleaning up the mess. Not exactly the way I'd planned to spend my night away from home.

Afterward, I slipped into a fitful sleep on the other bed, waking twice to check on Rikki and the kids. Rikki didn't stir, though once she cried out in her sleep.

In the morning I awoke to more gagging in the bathroom. "Rikki?" I asked outside the door. "You okay?"

"I will be. Just a moment." The toilet flushed, and she came out, a smile on her face. A smile I might have believed if I hadn't lived through this night with her.

I held out the pills Kyle had given me. "Need these?"

"Thanks." She opened the cap and downed a pill without water.

"So," I said. "Are you going to tell me what's really wrong?"

She blinked. "Nothing's wrong."

I folded my hands over my stomach. "Try again, Rikki. You have a bagful of medicines with names I can't pronounce. And you look like death warmed over. What's wrong?"

Rikki sagged against the wall. "I have seizures sometimes, that's all. But I'm fine. Honest. By breakfast, last night will be nothing but a bad memory."

She didn't look healthy enough to go anywhere. "But—"

She raised a hand. "Please, Becca. I want to do this. I want to see the gardens with you, maybe stop and do a little shopping somewhere, and then we'll come home and get in the pool with the kids. It'll be our last real outing for a long time."

Her eyes begged, and it was a relief to let her persuade me. If Rikki said she was fine, who was I to object? "Let's wake up the kids, then. There's still plenty of time for breakfast before we go."

She gave me a wide smile and pushed off from the wall. "Great."

The children were already awake and waiting for us—but not one of them was happy. We had no sooner opened the door when Lauren and James burst outside their door, Lauren in her day clothes and James still in his pajamas. "Mom, James is being rude," Lauren exclaimed. "He's not my friend anymore, and I'm not going to play with him."

"I'm not playing with you, either!" James marched into Rikki's room.

Allia poked her head out the door. She was dressed. "Good, you're here. Kyle's locked herself in the bathroom, and she won't come out. How am I supposed to get ready? It wasn't my fault she saw the shorts that matched one of the shirts we gave her. I didn't realize she'd guess we'd given her the clothes."

Rikki and I exchanged a glance. "You take the little kids," I told her. "I'll deal with the older ones." I'd rather juggle a childish argument over the TV or how to split a granola bar than mediate between teenage girls any day, but Rikki looked dead on her feet so I couldn't hand that off to her, even if her daughter was the one upset.

"She won't come out," Rikki said. "Not till she calms down. I've tried begging her before. It doesn't work."

I smiled. "Then you'll have plenty of time to get James and yourself dressed. Allia, you watch Lauren. Take her for a walk or something. We'll have breakfast in a bit. Don't go far."

Rikki shrugged. "Suit yourself. If it doesn't work, we'll eat breakfast and then I'll talk to her."

"Okay." I turned into the room.

I knocked on the bathroom door, faking a bravado I was far from feeling. "Okay, Kyle, everyone's gone. Open the door and let me get ready. I'm here to see some gardens. I want them every bit as much as you want your dancing, so open up."

I waited. Aside from forcing the lock, there was really nothing I could do.

Moments ticked by. "Please," I said.

A tiny click, and the door opened.

CHAPTER TWENTY-SEVEN

Kyle

I opened the bathroom door because Sister Rushton had been nice to me and hadn't ratted on me to Mom about why I'd been shoplifting.

I started past her, but her voice stopped me. "Kyle, what's wrong? You know what happened the last time you wouldn't talk to somebody. We ended up at the police station."

I whirled toward her. "Someone should have told me those clothes were from Allia!" My voice was louder than I intended. "It's just weird using her stuff, like I'm some sort of charity case." Face flaming, I stalked to the bed where James and I'd slept last night. Mom should have told me, I meant, but I didn't want to say that.

Sister Rushton came after me. "Is it really so bad? You and Allia are friends. You wore one of her shirts to Mutual the other night, and when she grows out of it, she'll probably give it to you. If you had something that was too big, and Allia wanted to wear it, wouldn't you let her?"

That made me stop and think. Yeah, someone should have told me so I didn't look like an idiot showing off to Allia the clothes she'd given me, but I wouldn't have refused them if I'd known. I probably would have worn them more often. Allia was so beautiful and popular and—

"She hates my makeup," I said in a low voice. We'd been in the bathroom together when I'd noticed the shorts that matched my hand-me-down shirt at home and finally made the connection. Maybe I wouldn't have reacted so badly if I hadn't forgotten to pack my nose ring to wear last night. That meant the hole was going to close and when Mom finally let me wear it again, I'd have to go through all that pain to get it done again. Even the idea made my eyes water. *Don't think about that now,* I told myself. "Anyway, she keeps bugging me to do it different."

Sister Rushton thought for a moment. "What do you want to do?"

"I want to be normal. I don't want to feel . . ." Feel scared all the time. Not anything I'd tell her, but maybe I could say something. "Mom's acting weird. She's taking a lot of pills. I looked one up at school, and it's for seizures. I didn't even know she had seizures."

"I just learned that myself. Why don't you ask her about them?"

"I don't know." That wasn't exactly true. I was afraid, I guess. She'd changed so much this year. What was it with Sister Rushton, anyway? One moment we were talking about makeup and the next about my mother. It was like I couldn't keep anything from her.

Sister Rushton sat down beside me. "Kyle, it may not make sense, but I'm sure there's a reason for the pills and for your mother's behavior. I mean, she doesn't act like she's drugged, does she? Talk to her—about the pills and about the dancing. Tell her how you feel. Whatever is up with her, you won't have to handle it alone."

"You mean that ward family stuff." These people were seriously weird if they thought they could help me handle my mom.

Sister Rushton smiled. "Not exactly. I meant that everyone in your life may let you down at one time or another, but the Lord will never let you down. Not ever."

Then why don't I have a father? Why is my mom crying in the night? Why am I so afraid? For that matter, why am I so ugly? Right. Like I could say any of those things aloud.

"You understand?" Sister Rushton asked. "We go through things, difficult things, so we can grow and learn, but God doesn't abandon us to do it alone."

I was listening, but the feeling in my chest was odd, almost uncomfortable. The idea of God watching me was a little unsettling. I was glad when Sister Rushton fell silent. An idea occurred to me then, and I blurted it out before I could stop myself. I'm like Mom a lot that way. "Do you think I wear too much makeup?"

Sister Rushton pursed her lips. "Do you really want to know?"

Duh. She was the most beautiful older lady I knew. "Yes."

"I think you're beautiful, like your mom, and all that makeup hides your beauty. Makeup should enhance assets, not cover them up. Makeup also marks you as a type of person, and even if that's not the real you inside, people see the face you present to the world and treat you accordingly. It's not fair, but that's the way it is." She reached over and tucked my hair behind my ear.

I didn't care that she was ruining my hair that I'd arranged so carefully over my face. She thought I was beautiful? "Will you show me?"

"Sure."

Why not let her do my makeup? It wasn't as if any of my new friends from school could see me, and it would make Allia happy.

Maybe I could ask my Mom about the pills. Maybe I would dare to confront her about how she'd left them all over the kitchen floor where James might have found them. Maybe Sister Rushton could also convince Mom to not leave us again the next time she had something mysterious to do.

Well, I wasn't going to hold my breath. Not yet anyway.

CHAPTER TWENTY-EIGHT

Rikki

I was surprised when Becca emerged from her room with Kyle. Allia, back from her short walk with Lauren, rushed inside to get ready, but I stared at my daughter. She was so beautiful and so young. Helpless. Sometimes she acted grown up, but at that moment I knew she'd need me for years and years.

Her eyes ran over me. "You feeling better?"

"Perfect." They didn't have to know how much I was fighting to stay on my feet. A little food should help, though.

Kyle leaned on me, and I put my arm around her. I felt weepy, but I told myself it was the medication.

"Come on," Becca said. "I'll go hurry Allia so we can eat. Oh, and Dante called. Joel Flemming is awake and stable. He doesn't seem to have experienced any brain damage."

I smiled. "That's a relief. He's a good man." He'd never been anything but kind to me, though enduring daddy-daughter activities with a child who wasn't his daughter couldn't have been all that comfortable for him.

At breakfast, James and Lauren promptly forgot their battle and began playing so much that Becca had her hands full keeping them at the table. She didn't seem to mind.

We left the older girls at the hotel's playroom with the room keys, instructions for the lunch in Becca's cooler, strict orders not to swim in either of the two pools until we returned, and a cell phone in case of emergency.

The first garden was easy, with even paths and uniform beds. The next was tougher—a hilly patch of ground with ups and downs that made me sweat. The flower beds here were overgrowing with apparent abandon, but Becca pointed out how carefully the garden was tended, from the aerated soil to the tiny ties that trained the vines. As she talked, she glowed, and not for the first time I could see what Dante loved about her. I was beginning to love her myself.

I had to rest frequently. "Sorry," I muttered once, sinking onto a decorative metal bench. "Still a bit under the weather, I guess."

"Don't be. Gives me more of a chance to *feel* the gardens."

I smiled. "Getting any ideas?"

"Yeah. I think I should use some trellises. I've always been a little scared to try, but it doesn't look all that hard after all."

"Yes, it does."

She laughed. "No, it's kids that are hard."

"You can say that again. Speaking of that, I was really surprised when Kyle came out with you this morning." I didn't add that once I'd known everything about my daughter but suddenly she'd become a bit of a stranger. Becca understood the way teens grew up better than I did. "I like what you did with her makeup."

"She's a beautiful girl."

"I wish you'd tell her that."

"I did."

I felt a rush of gratitude toward her, knowing how far that would go with Kyle. We sat on the bench in silence for several minutes. A bird flitted overhead, its shadow passing over the cobblestone walkway. I found myself wishing for the courage to finally confide my secret to someone, but a group of people came toward us and the moment passed.

Swallowing a bout of nausea, I jumped up from the bench—or tried to. In the end it was more a rolling up out of the seat. "Let's go to the next garden," I said. "Isn't that the one by all those outlet malls? We should stop there and see if they have any specials. You should buy something to remember your first garden show."

Becca laughed and followed me down the path.

I wished I believed in God so I could pray. I needed a miracle.

CHAPTER TWENTY-NINE

Becca

I had fun—a lot of fun. The gardens were luscious, succulent, and creative, and Rikki was marvelous company. Every time I got out my camera to record some flower or arrangement, she insisted on taking one of me. She refused to be in any of the pictures, though. "I don't believe in pictures," she said. "Tomorrow, I'll no longer be who I was today." Only once did an older couple convince her to stand in front of a beautiful, ten-foot lattice of miniature roses with me. At the last moment before the picture snapped, I felt Rikki's hand inch behind my back. I threw my arm over her shoulder, and we leaned in and sang, "Cheese."

I was happy. I didn't think I could feel so content at something so unrelated to my family, but it was nice, peaceful, inspiring. Whatever the future held for me and Dante, I was going to get away again, and I was going to drag them into this new world as well. I wanted to share this beauty with them, not keep it all for myself.

At the factory outlet stores, I bought a pair of sunglasses and a red blouse that Rikki made me change into in the van. "That's more like it," she said. "You look like a rose."

Despite the fun, I found myself worrying about the kids and

also about Rikki, who had begun to drag. At one garden, I tried to encourage her to wait in the van for me. She refused but did agree to wait in a long line for the snacks some enterprising children were selling in front of their parents' garden while I perused the plants alone. I thought cutting corners might make me upset or feel cheated, but it didn't.

I would have, though, if it had been Dante here with me, dragging along. I'd be resentful that he wasn't worrying about the children and that he hadn't planned for them during the trip. I'd be upset inside that he would every so often call one of his counselors.

Since when had I begun to think of Dante as not pulling his weight? The seed of resentment had been growing for a long, long time, if I could judge by my feelings now.

All at once I was angry. Angry at Dante, at the monotony of my life. So angry I tightened my hands into fists to stop myself from screaming. One stiff foot in front of the other, I walked the garden, seeing nothing. At the end of the path was a large fountain, where little stone children played in the water under the watchful eye of two women, both carrying urns from which water poured out regularly. One statue child stood close enough to put a hand in the falling water.

The anger drained from me, and I sank to a bench. Was I really angry at Dante? Was it Rikki? I just didn't know.

I did know that I was finished seeing gardens. They were beautiful and had given me more ideas than I knew what to do with, but at the moment, I had bigger worries—like Rikki and her children and what to do about my relationship with Dante.

It was time to go back to the hotel and then home. I had a lot of thinking to do.

"What's wrong?" Rikki asked when she saw my face.

"We're going back to the hotel," I said.

"Why? You love this stuff."

"We need to be with the kids."

Rikki rolled her eyes. "I knew we shouldn't have brought them." Yet I could see the anticipation in her face.

"I've had fun," I said. "Thanks to you."

Rikki grinned. "You just needed a little loosening up."

Within the hour, we were at the hotel pool with the kids. Though I knew Rikki was exhausted, she made a heroic effort with James, who didn't notice anything different about his mother. Only Kyle watched her when she thought no one was looking. I wondered if she was thinking about the dance lessons or about the pills in Rikki's purse. I hadn't seen Rikki take any more pills, and she'd seemed normal all day, if a bit tired, which was understandable given her migraine last night.

Rikki floated over to me and pulled herself from the water. I stifled the urge to ask her if she was okay.

"See that guy?" she said, indicating a large thirty-something man, obviously a body-builder, who was walking into the pool area with a woman who resembled a toothpick. "James's dad is like that. Or was. With that build, I thought he would protect me forever."

"Guess he knew he looked too good, eh? No time for anyone but himself."

Rikki laughed. "Exactly." She sobered. "What about Dante? What kind of a father is he?"

I opened my mouth to tell her how wonderful he was but something else came out entirely. "He's preoccupied a lot of the time. Travis and Cory suffer with that, I think."

"But he doesn't hit anyone, and he doesn't yell."

"No. But he needs to spend more time with them."

Her eyes gleamed. "And with you."

I nodded.

She sighed. "To tell the truth, I couldn't get rid of him when we were kids. He was always trying to take care of me." She paused. "Becca, maybe if you were a little less capable—"

"What?"

She shrugged. "Dante seems to rush to the aid of everyone he sees. Why not you?"

"I'm not going to pretend to be helpless so my husband will pay attention to me."

"Well, I would. But that's not what I meant. I meant you should tell him about the gardens and take a class at school. He can step in and be your hero."

My hero? Where did she get this stuff? I didn't need a hero. I needed a husband who was there more. A husband who . . . knew my dreams. Goose bumps popped out all over my skin. I didn't even know my own dreams, so maybe I needed someone to help me figure them out. A hero.

I stared at Rikki, and she held the stare, a smile coming over her thin face. "He'd be with the boys more whenever you went to see gardens. Like he is now." She frowned. "Well, if he's torn himself away from the hospital."

"He has. He went to Cory's soccer game."

"When was the last time he did that? What good is being a bishop when you miss your own kids' lives?"

I'd thought the same thing but never dared voice it aloud. While I was growing up, my father had missed a lot of our activities, and I thought it was a way of life. But maybe there was a compromise. Maybe putting things right between Dante and me wasn't a matter of huge changes but of each of us moving, just a bit, toward the other. Giving a little. Taking what was offered.

I slung my arm over Rikki's shoulder. "I really like you."

"You sound surprised."

I laughed. How odd was it? Here I was talking to my husband's former fiancée about things close to my heart, things I'd never share with my own sister. "A little," I said. "I'm usually too busy to think about these things."

"You're thinking about them all the time. You just don't talk about them."

She had me there.

"But you have to talk about them." Rikki was looking out at her children playing together in the water. "You never know how much time you have. You must live every day as if it's your last. You know, I never came back to see my mom, not even when she was sick. I was too afraid of my dad. I don't know why. He couldn't have hurt me anymore. I've never forgiven myself for not coming. No matter how weak she was or how she refused to stand between me and my dad, she loved me, and I wasn't there for her in the end. I always thought there would be more time, but now I know that's only something we tell ourselves so we don't have to do the tough things. Until you run into something that you can't put off."

Something like dying, she meant. I thought about Dante and all that he'd done for his father, right up to the very end. Though his father had never changed in all that time, never given Dante what he'd been craving, Dante had no regret for his own actions. I'd fallen in love with my husband a little more as I'd watched him serve his father, though sometimes in my heart I'd regretted the attention it took from me and our children.

I leaned closer to Rikki. "Thanks for coming with me. I don't know that I really would have come alone."

"Yes, you would have."

"Well, it wouldn't have been as much fun."

She grimaced. "Last night was a hoot."

"I meant today. It was fun."

She lay back on her elbows. "It was, wasn't it? Next time come a day early and schedule time for a spa, too. Now that would really make it worth it."

I didn't tell her I would worry about missing the kids too much, though since they were growing up, they'd all be leaving me soon. "Why not?" I said instead. I noticed she hadn't included herself in any future plans, though that was probably more from politeness than any slight in my direction. She didn't have much of a feel for nuances, I'd learned.

"So how about some dinner?" Rikki called out to the kids. Her suggestion was met with enthusiastic cheers. "Guess that's a yes." Rikki tried to stand and lost her balance, nearly falling into the pool. I steadied her quickly. She giggled. "Thanks. I got up too fast."

The rest of the evening was fun. We ate dinner at Denny's and then cruised around to a few stores. We all ended up buying silly cheap earrings that were more glitter than taste—except for James, who opted for a few smooth rocks to put in with his fish, Fred.

We laughed a lot. Several times teenage boys passed by, and the girls were all aflutter with their attention. I was glad to see that the black leather-clad kind didn't seem to look their way.

The only blemish on the evening was when I helped Kyle pick out her earrings. Allia had to snap our picture wearing the silly things, so we threw our arms around each other and hammed it up. Behind Allia, Rikki's face grew white, and I didn't think I imagined the anger in her face. Hatred, almost. For me. The next instant it was gone, and Rikki even let Allia take her picture, which, from Kyle's reaction, was something bigger than I'd realized.

Shoving away what felt like an invisible smothering hand, I erased the incident from my mind.

CHAPTER THIRTY

Dante

It was nearly time for church, and I was pacing in and out of my office at the ward building, checking for the missing female members of my family. Becca and the girls should have been here by now. I stifled irritation that stemmed more from worry and a lack of sleep than from any upset she'd caused by her absence. How strange the house felt without her, how empty our bed. How needy the boys. Did she feel this way when I was gone?

The thought made me smile. Becca didn't worry about things like that. If she was awake when I was at late meetings, she did laundry or cleaned the house, made kids' lunches, or prepared something for Primary. I grimaced at how dull that all sounded. No wonder she'd jumped at the chance to go to Saint George.

No, you idiot. You convinced her to go. Truth was, Rikki was right. I took Becca for granted, and I suspected if I didn't do something about that right now, it might become a problem. Sending her to Saint George for a well-deserved day off was a step in the right direction, though in the possessiveness of my soul, I hated the very idea.

Then again, with the girls and Rikki's kids, it probably hadn't been all that much of a vacation. Rikki shouldn't have forced Becca to take her. What had they talked about? And where were they, anyway? The trip didn't take more than five hours, even with the necessary rest room stops.

What was taking her so long? Maybe I shouldn't have let her go. Let her?

As though it was up to me to give her permission.

While she'd been gone, I'd been busy every second—most of which had nothing to do with my calling as a bishop. There had been dishes to wash, counters to wipe, homework to deal with, and all kinds of unimaginable cleanup that I normally took for granted. And to think I'd only had half the children, and I hadn't had to prepare food from scratch. I was amazed at how easily Becca handled everything in the house. I'd done my best, but the kitchen already looked rumpled around the edges.

I'd spent my rare evening alone at home replacing a broken light switch in the main upstairs bathroom and fixing the door to Cory's room, which had mysteriously fallen off its hinges. Mysteriously. Right. Things tended to self-destruct where Cory was concerned. Too bad he was so dang cute or I might hold it against him. When I was finished, there'd been no one to ooh and aah over the job. The boys hadn't seemed all that impressed.

What if Becca never came back? Though I knew the idea was ridiculous, it made me feel ill all the same. I couldn't imagine life without Becca, yet I was starting to believe that she was nowhere near as happy as I was in our relationship. And why should she be? When was the last time I'd surprised her with a night away? When had I last made reservations somewhere just because I loved her?

I was about to call her when I heard Lauren's loud voice in the foyer. "Mom, can I sit by James?"

"No, you'll sit with the family."

I rushed from the office, and there was Becca, wearing a bright red blouse I'd never seen before with a black skirt. She looked fabulous, and if we hadn't been at church, I would have grabbed her and kissed her like a drowning man. Was it the red that brought that color to her cheeks?

"Hi," she said a bit breathlessly.

"I was getting worried," I said.

"Worried about us getting in an accident, or about us being here on time?"

What kind of a question was that? My confusion must have shown in my face because Becca gave a quick shake of her head. "Never mind. We'll talk later." Her hand touched my cheek, and suddenly everything was right with my world.

Behind Becca, Rikki caught my eye. She was smirking at me, but I didn't show my irritation. Kyle, on the other hand, was almost unrecognizable. Someone had pulled back her hair, and her makeup was tasteful. I knew somehow Becca was responsible. I shook Kyle's hand. "Good to see you," I said.

She smiled shyly. "Thanks."

"And me?" Rikki said.

"Always nice to see you, Rikki. But you'd better go in now. It's starting." I took my own advice and hurried up to the podium. As usual, the members noticed when Rikki came in, and hands were raised in friendly greeting. Sister Gillman briefly grabbed onto Kyle's hand, her mouth moving. I hoped whatever she said didn't destroy all Becca's good work with the child. But Kyle smiled and went on her way. Rikki sat on the same row as Becca, with James and Lauren next to each other. Becca would have her hands full. She didn't seem to mind, though. The smile on her face made her seem dreamy and young and a bit like someone I didn't know very well. A tremor shuddered up my back, but when Becca caught and held my eye, I was okay again.

Silly, I thought and pulled my mind back to what I was going to say after the opening hymn.

CHAPTER THIRTY-ONE

Kyle

Church was different today. I didn't know if it was because I was getting to know everyone, because I was dressed more like the other girls, or because Allia and I were really starting to be friends. I didn't catch her staring at me anymore, and if someone called her over to speak with her, she motioned for me to come along.

We had a visitor in the Sunday School class today, a kid named Monty Earl, and he smiled at me. It wasn't just a regular "hi" smile, but one that seemed, well, really interested. That had never happened to me before. Never. Not from a boy who looked like Travis, only younger. I'd seen this boy in the hallways at school. In fact, we had a class together, though I doubted he knew that since it was a big class and I always hid in the back, while he sat in the front. If he smiled at me at school that would be the real test, since everyone was supposed to be nice at church. Butterflies danced in my stomach, but good butterflies, not the kind that made me want to throw up.

I still felt sad about dance, but every time I thought about it, I remembered Sister Rushton's advice to wait and see. She'd also told me to talk to Mom. Should I? Being with Mom in Saint George had been almost like old times. Mom had been fun. Herself. Maybe she wasn't planning on leaving. After all, she seemed pretty happy at her new job, and maybe Couch Man would keep coming around.

I held my breath. Allia bumped her shoulder to mine and whispered. "That guy is so staring at you."

"Maybe," I said.

"Don't be offended if he doesn't ask you out. Remember, he's a Mormon. You'll have to be just friends until you're sixteen."

For some reason that made me laugh like crazy. I danced so much, it wasn't like I could become obsessed with a boy, but there was a strange sort of comfort in knowing that becoming steady dates wasn't expected here. Some of the girls I'd been hanging out with were doing things with the older boys at the high school, things that made me uncomfortable. For the first time in my life, I was glad to be only thirteen.

Church was over all too soon, and I headed out to the truck with Mom and James. Mom could barely keep her eyes open, and I was tempted to ask her to let me drive. I knew how. Mom had taught me earlier in the summer, just for emergencies. I didn't know what emergency she might have been talking about, but no thirteen-year-old in her right mind turned down driving lessons.

We ate ravioli from a can. James loved the stuff, but I didn't. I wondered if Sister Rushton or Sister Flemming of chili fame made ravioli from scratch that tasted better. Of course, Sister Flemming was probably still at the hospital with her husband, and Sister Rushton wouldn't have time since she'd just arrived home, like us. I wondered what she was making and if she was dreaming about her gardens while she cooked.

"Mom," I said, trying to be casual.

"Yes?" Mom looked up from her plate. The wrinkles around her eyes were more prominent, and the way her forehead creased,

I knew she was fighting a migraine. Not a good thing since she'd already taken her pain pill after church. Still I pressed on.

"About dancing. Do you think I might be able to have lessons now?" Now she could ask if I had someplace in mind, and that would at least open the door to the possibility.

She shook her head. "Not yet, honey. Give me another couple months, okay? I promise we'll look into it. I need to pay off James's glasses and the doctor appointments. But you're next, okay?"

"What about me getting a paper route or some other kind of a job?" It was worth a shot.

"I need you to watch James. Besides, I don't know what you could do, especially while watching him. A paper route requires adult supervision these days. It snows a lot here, and I don't think I'll be able to get up at five in the morning to drive you around."

Something inside me froze, and all the joy I'd felt earlier in the day vanished.

"We'll do something about dance," Mom continued. "Just wait."

I felt like she was telling me to wait to breathe. In a few more months, all those girls would be far ahead of me, and I'd be stagnant, watching James while my chance passed before me. While I suffocated.

"Wait? Wait?" My voice was rising. "James is your responsibility, not mine. Why do I have to watch him?"

Her eyes widened. Blue eyes that reminded me of my own. She hated it when I talked this way about James, and truthfully, I didn't exactly mean it because I loved James and wanted him to be happy. But what about *my* happiness? Since she was going to be angry anyway, I might as well get it all out. "And why do you have all those pills in your purse? Are you some kind of druggie?"

"Why are you snooping in my purse?" Her angry tone matched my own.

I jumped to my feet. "Because the other night you left pills all over the floor. James could have gotten them."

"No, I wouldn't." James's eyes were big, and he looked close to tears.

"I picked them all up and put them in your purse. I had to look to find the right bottle. I looked one up. Why are you taking seizure medicine? Is that why you're so different now? I feel like I don't even know you anymore."

Mom stared at me from her seat. Emotions raged in her face but what they were I couldn't tell, though they didn't seem to be just anger. That made me feel worse. A girl should be able to read her own mother. "You shouldn't have snooped," she said. "There was a coldness in her voice now, one that scared me.

"You shouldn't hide things. You never used to." Unable to stand it any longer, I ran toward the basement stairs. "Forget it. I can see that as long as I live with you, I'll never reach my dreams." I fled before I could see her reaction.

"Kyle!" Mom called after me.

I didn't stop. I ripped open my door and drove the lock home before throwing myself on my bed and sobbing, my face buried in the pillow. I hated Mom. I hated her. I hated our life. I wanted to be Allia, to have her parents, to be able to dance. To not have to worry about James, or at least not so much.

I heard knocking on the door and Mom's voice begging me to open up. But I didn't want to see her because I knew that she'd talk and talk and somehow make me feel okay when really nothing would have changed at all. I didn't want to feel okay. I wanted to be mad at her.

I wanted to dance.

I put my head under the pillow and screamed.

Eventually, I must have fallen asleep, and when I awoke, the house was dark and quiet. My stomach was growling—probably the reason I'd awakened at all. On the table were the remains of dinner. Mine and Mom's plates were barely touched, and James's was empty. He'd had milk, too, I was glad to see.

Remorse fell over me, streaming out my eyes and down my cheeks. What had I done? Mom had responded the best way she knew how, and I'd reacted like a two-year-old. Yes, I couldn't depend on her for lessons, but I could ask neighbors to let me rake their leaves or do odd jobs. Something. Fleetingly, I thought about shoplifting again, but I didn't want to be like my lousy, no-good father. No, I'd do it the right way. Maybe Sister Rushton or Allia would have some ideas about earning money.

I could also pray. I didn't know if I believed something like that could really work, but Allia seemed to believe it. Bishop and Sister Rushton, too. Maybe if I prayed, and there really was a God, maybe He could help me find a way.

I turned on the light, and the first thing I saw was Mom's purse on the counter, her bottle of pain pills open, the white pills in a loose mound on the counter. *Not again.* At least there seemed to be none on the floor.

I went to check on James, but he wasn't in his room. He was probably with Mom, and I knew there'd be room for me, too, despite my outburst. Mom would take me in her arms and smooth my hair and whisper that she loved me, and I would believe it was true.

James's soft snores filled the room. I waited until my eyes adjusted to the dim moonlight filtering through the open window. Mom was curled away from James, her face toward the light, and she was lying so still that for a moment I thought she was already awake. I waited for her to hold out her arms.

She wasn't moving. I took several more steps. Her face looked odd. I leaned over her and heard nothing. I shook her. "Mom." Then more urgently, "Mom, are you okay? Mom, wake up!"

"What's wrong?" James mumbled. "What are you doing?"

"Mom won't wake up."

"So? It's night."

"She's not breathing. James, go turn on the light!"

He hurried to do as I asked, and even that had no effect on Mom. I didn't even know if her heart was beating.

Everything angled into sharp focus. If I didn't do something, Mom was going to die.

If she hadn't already.

CHAPTER THIRTY-TWO

Dante

My cell phone buzzed from the nightstand, and I came awake more quickly than usual since I had been in bed only a few minutes. I glanced at the number without recognizing it. There was no name.

"Hello?" Next to me, Becca rolled over. I could see her open eyes gleam in the darkness as she waited to see who it was this time and if I'd be leaving. With meetings and dinner and all the bustle with the children, there'd been no time to discuss her trip. Except for what she and Allia told us at dinner, I had no idea how things had gone at the gardens or with Rikki.

"It's my mom," came a strangled voice. "She wasn't breathing. I called the ambulance, and they're here, but—"

"Who is this?" I demanded.

"Kyle."

"Are they helping your mother?"

"Yes." Her voice was barely a whisper. "But I'm—James is really scared."

"I'll be right there." I was up and stumbling to the closet. Becca jumped from the bed to help me find my clothes. I shoved one leg into my pants and then the other as I explained. "It's Rikki. Kyle said she wasn't breathing. The ambulance is there."

"Oh, no." Becca tossed me my shirt. "She had a scary episode on Friday night, too, but she seemed okay last night. I'll wake Travis and tell him he's in charge. You go ahead. I'll come along in a minute."

"Okay." I leaned in and kissed her. I loved her even more for being ready to drop everything and help me in my calling without any notice.

The drive to Rikki's was too long, though the clock on the dash said only a minute had gone by since I'd started the engine. The ambulance was still outside, as were a fire truck and a police car. Several neighbors stood on the sidewalk in front of the house. I nodded to them as I bounded up the few steps and pushed open the door that was already slightly ajar.

In the back bedroom, Rikki lay on the bed, surrounded by four paramedics and two police officers.

"Excuse me," said an officer with dark hair. "Do you live here?"

"I'm her bishop. I'm here for the kids. Is she going to be okay?"

A female paramedic kneeling on the bed by Rikki's head looked up at me. "She's breathing but not conscious. We don't know what's wrong. We'll transport her as soon as she's stable."

"I think it's her pills." Kyle stood by the window, holding her little brother, who clutched her tightly, tears wetting his cheeks. "She always takes them when she gets home, but I saw her take them once, and they weren't spilled. They're all over the counter now."

My heart sank. *Rikki, what have you done?*

Kyle's comment interested the paramedic. "Were there a lot of pills missing?"

"I don't know."

"We'll need to take all her medications with us," said another paramedic. "The doctor can look at the date and the dosage and how many pills are missing to see if it relates to her collapse. Could be she needs a different dosage." His voice was calm and soothing, a tone I knew I needed to adopt as well, though the ten-year-old inside me wanted to shake Rikki awake and demand to know what she'd done.

"I'll get you the bottles." Kyle put James down, but he started crying.

"Come here, James," I said, going to meet him halfway.

He shook his head but then seemed to change his mind and came toward me. No, not toward me but toward Becca, who'd come in the door behind me. He started sobbing loudly, but Becca scooped him up and held him tight, whispering soothing things and rocking him until the tears lessened.

There are a lot of good reasons why bishops need to be married, and I knew this was one of them.

I followed Kyle into the kitchen, where she handed me an open bottle of pills. "They're for her headaches," she said. "She has really bad ones sometimes."

Four more bottles followed the first, and with each my trepidation grew. At least they all seemed to be prescribed medications. With Rikki you could never be sure. She'd never bothered with alcohol when I knew her, but even as a teen she hadn't been able to understand why a little recreational weed was off-limits to me because of my belief in the Church. She didn't understand why I cared if I gave my father one more reason to overlook or despise me.

Kyle stood as though dazed, and in my mind she was Rikki as a young child—before there'd been any real differences between girls and boys. I put a hand on her shoulder. "They're taking care of her, Kyle. They're doing everything they can."

"She's been acting weird. We had a fight. Maybe if I hadn't—"

"It's not your fault. Come on. Let's give them these bottles, and then you and your brother can come to our house."

"I want to go to the hospital."

"I'll call you when there's news."

"No. I'm going with you."

I had two daughters who often used that same stubborn tone, and I knew better than to argue—especially about this. "Okay, you can come with me, but I need to call someone first." Becca wouldn't want to drag James to the hospital or leave our children alone so long, and I didn't want to take Kyle to the hospital alone without another priesthood holder. I pulled out my cell and called my first counselor Steve Mendenhall, who answered after two rings and promised to be right over.

In the bedroom, the paramedics were moving Rikki onto a board they would carry into the ambulance. Her eyes fluttered, but she didn't awaken. She looked far more frail this way, as though she might easily break.

Becca's hand was on my arm. "You go ahead. I'll lock up here and take the kids home."

"Kyle wants to go with me. Steve's on his way."

Becca studied Kyle. For a moment I thought she would try to talk her out of going, but instead she secured James with one arm and put the other around Kyle. "If you need anything, tell the bishop to call me, and I'll be right there. I'll come, anyway, when I can find someone to stay with James and the other kids. Okay?"

Kyle nodded, her face crumpling as she buried it into Becca's shoulder. For several long moments she simply sobbed while Becca held her. I felt grateful for whatever experiences they'd had in Saint George and at the police station that made Kyle able to turn to Becca for comfort.

"I'll go ask where they're taking her," I told Becca, swallowing the lump in my throat.

Outside, there was a growing crowd of neighbors and ward members. The questions started the moment they saw me, but I held up a hand for them to wait while I talked to the paramedics. After receiving the information I needed, I briefly explained to the neighbors what little I knew.

"How can we help, Bishop?" Daren Godfrey asked.

"We'll let you know," I said.

"What about the children?" This from Julene Tuft.

"Kyle's going with Steve and me to the hospital, and Becca's taking James home."

Steve had arrived, so with a few brief comments, I extricated myself and went to tell Kyle I was ready to go.

• • •

An accidental overdose of prescription medication was the diagnosis the doctors agreed upon. "The medication is a very potent painkiller," Dr. Samuelson, one of the young doctors on call, told me. He was on the high council of our stake. Tall, thin, and stately looking, he was a good doctor and an even better man. "I can't elaborate on her condition without her consent, but I will tell you that she must be suffering some major migraines or she's been prescribed the wrong medication. When she's a little more with it, I'm going to suggest a change to see if we can't get her on something safer, though with her other problems, that may not work out. One thing for sure, if that little girl hadn't found her and acted as quickly as she did, her mother would have died." He sighed. "Some of her other vitals still aren't all that great, and some of the blood tests look odd. I'd suspect drug abuse, but I don't find anything like that in her system, though I'm still waiting for a few more tests."

"Let me know, okay?"

Samuelson smiled. "I really won't be able to talk to you about her condition, Bishop. Unless she gives permission."

"She will."

Except that I really didn't know Rikki anymore. Had she taken the extra medication on purpose? If I asked her straight out, she might admit to it.

"You can see her in about ten minutes," the doctor added, "but only two at a time. She's asking for her daughter."

Steve nodded. "We'll wake her up and tell her, the poor thing. She's been waiting all night."

"See you in a bit, then." Dr. Samuelson strode from the room, his blond hair reflecting the fluorescent light overhead.

I made my way toward Kyle, who'd fallen asleep on three chairs in the ICU waiting room. "Kyle," I said, touching her shoulder.

She jerked awake. "Is she okay?"

I nodded. "She's awake, and she's doing much better. They're going to let you see her in a minute. She's still kind of groggy, though. They think she might have accidentally taken too much medication."

"I thought it might be that. She gets sort of goofy sometimes after she takes it. Once, she told me it's like her brain stops working. She might not remember taking the pills. She doesn't usually take them that early, I don't think. Maybe she thought if she took some before we went to bed, she wouldn't have the pain at night."

"Does she wake up a lot at night?"

"Yes."

I didn't ask how she knew. Anger boiled inside me. Rikki had said something was bothering Kyle; maybe I'd found out what. Rikki was going to hear a thing or two the second I felt she could physically handle it. Not from me, her bishop, but from Dante, the friend she'd grown up with. We'd told each other a million times that we'd never do to our children what our parents had done to us, but Kyle and James were suffering from her actions every bit as much as she'd suffered from her father's. So help me, if she didn't change her ways, I would act to protect her children. I'd told Kyle we were a ward family, and I'd meant it.

"Will you go in with me?" Kyle sounded about six years old—exactly like her thirteen-year-old mother had sounded when she'd asked if she could sleep in my dad's bushes.

If I were a swearing man, I'd have made good use of a few choice words. As it was, I simply nodded. "Sure." I thought a minute and then added, "Kyle, has this happened before? Your mother collapsing, I mean." Kyle had shown remarkable calmness in the face of what had happened. If it was a repeat, Rikki might have a problem with substance abuse.

She shook her head. "No."

"Becca mentioned that your mother sometimes leaves you and James with friends."

"Yeah. Sometimes."

"When was the last time?"

"Earlier this year, but the time before that was longer, and only once more that I remember since James was born."

"How long was that?"

Kyle stared down at the ground. "Three months?"

"Three months? You didn't see your mother for three months this year?"

"No, that was the time before. This year it was six weeks. We stayed with one of my friends, and she came to see us a few times. She had a contract job that wouldn't let her take kids. It was fine."

Her face didn't say it was fine. "Is she going to have to leave again?" I asked.

"No!" Kyle shook her head emphatically. "She said she'd never go again. She hated going. But . . ." I heard the uncertainty in her voice. "I think maybe she will have to eventually."

"Well, probably not with her current job." That earned me a smile. Underneath her smeared makeup she was a frightened little girl. I hated the idea of children growing up frightened, but it was worse knowing Rikki was the one responsible for making Kyle afraid.

"Can we go see her now?"

"I'll check and come right back."

I met Dr. Samuelson coming from the ICU, and within a minute he escorted us inside. The lights were much dimmer than I'd expected, though I should have remembered it was nighttime after all. Rikki lay in her bed, a fragile, tragic figure. My anger started to flicker out as it always had when I was with her, but I stoked it, egged it on. Righteous indignation. Someone had to tell it like it was, and that seemed to fall to me, in both my capacity as her bishop and as her once-best friend.

"Mom!" Kyle ran to her and put her head next to her mother's, her hand going around Rikki's neck.

"I'm sorry, honey."

"It's okay. I know it was an accident." There was a question in her voice.

"Of course it was. These headaches, they just . . . I couldn't remember how many pills I'd taken. They think I took two or three more than I should."

"You have to be careful!" Kyle drew back, a stern note in her voice. "The pills were spilled on the counter again. James could have gotten them."

Rikki's brow creased. "Where are they now?"

"We gave them to the ambulance workers."

"Just those? Not the others?"

"We gave them all the bottles in your purse," I told her.

Rikki looked at me and then away. She grabbed her daughter's hands. "They say you saved my life."

"I guess. It was scary."

"I know, baby." Rikki pulled her head to her chest, and for a long moment no one moved or spoke. I felt like an outsider, which was a strange thing to feel around Rikki, because even after all these years, I felt I *knew* her like she was family.

Which was also why I knew she was up to something. She hated living in Utah and had left the Church, making it clear she'd stopped believing, and now she suddenly comes back? Back to Utah, to church, to my ward? Maybe she was down on her luck and needed a place to stay, but selling the house, even for cheap, would have put her life back together, at least temporarily, and she could have gone anywhere. So why was she here?

I suppose she could have found religion, but wouldn't she have shared that joy with her children?

I didn't fool myself that she'd come back for any connection she and I had shared. Rikki knew my dedication to the Church and my family. If I'd chosen the Church at nineteen, she'd know my conviction would only be that much stronger now. Besides, she'd likely had many other friends during her life. So why was she here?

Becca's fears about her leaving the children to pursue some personal dream returned to my mind, but even after Kyle's confirmation, I found that hard to believe. If that was the reason, she could have left them with other friends in another state. Better than uprooting them first.

Unless she had no more friends.

Ridiculous. People had always gravitated to Rikki.

I vowed to get to the bottom of this—today—but not while Kyle was here. I cleared my throat. "Kyle, Sister Rushton texted me, and she's on her way. Do you think you'd like to go home with her after you talk to your mom? You can see she's going to be fine."

"Will you give her a . . . a blessing?"

I was surprised she knew the terminology after so few Sundays—and even more amazed that she believed in it enough to ask.

This miracle showed me once again how teachable young people really were. "Of course—if she wants one. I can see if they'll let Brother Mendenhall come in here with us for a while. Your mother is supposed to have only two visitors at a time."

"Well, Mom?" Kyle asked.

Rikki's hand had fallen back to the bed, as though she was too exhausted to hold onto anything. "Yes, give me a blessing. It can't hurt."

"It might help," Kyle said.

"Sure." Rikki's eyes were wide, but she didn't seem to be focusing well.

Kyle stared in dismay at her mother, rubbing her arms as though she were cold.

"It's the medication," I told Kyle in a low voice. "She's going to be out of it for some time longer. Stay here while I get Brother Mendenhall."

I asked the nurse if Steve could come in for a few minutes to assist with a blessing, and she went to get him herself. A short time later, Steve placed his hands on Rikki's head to anoint her with the oil, and then I joined him to give the blessing. She would go home, I promised her, but there was something odd looming in my mind as I spoke, something just out of reach, something I could feel rather than see. "Take the opportunity to get your life in order," I said, "and everything will be all right."

Her life in order. Rikki was *not* going to appreciate that.

Kyle blew out a breath. "Thanks. That was . . ." She nodded, but I knew what she meant. I could feel the Spirit as well. Whatever was going on with Rikki and her children, God was very much aware of them.

Rikki said nothing, but I could feel her studying me intently behind half-closed eyes. I knew she wanted to say something, but whatever it was, she didn't want an audience.

Kyle cracked a yawn. The child was practically asleep on her feet. "You should go home and get some sleep," I said.

"What about school? It's almost morning."

"Do you have classes you can't miss?" I asked this because convincing my older children to miss school for any reason was such an unpleasant ordeal that Becca had changed dentists twice so they could go later in the day. They hated missing any class that would be hard to make up later.

Kyle blinked. "I could miss every class, every day. It's all a waste. Well, except dance, but they're mostly way behind me in that class anyway."

"Are you sure? Isn't there a class or two that would be easier to attend and get the assignment in even if you're tired?" I was wasting time, practically speaking a foreign language. Kyle hadn't been taught that education was a privilege and responsibility but rather something to be endured.

"Well, we are starting a project in English," she said, stifling another huge yawn. "Fourth period." I don't know who she startled more with the admission, me or herself.

"Tell Sister Rushton. She'll get you there and excuse you from the others." Becca would know who to talk to for that to happen.

"Okay." Kyle turned back to her mom, but Rikki's eyes were closed now and her body limp. Kyle leaned down and kissed her cheek. "I love you, Mom."

"Wait with Brother Mendenhall until Sister Rushton comes, okay?" I exchanged a look with Steve, who nodded subtly.

"I don't need a babysitter."

I grinned. "Not a babysitter. A ward family, remember? You'd do the same for us if someone at our house was in the hospital."

"Don't be too sure." But she said it under her breath, with a happier lilt to her voice than she'd used all night.

She disappeared with Steve, and I turned back to Rikki. Not

that I really expected to have a decent conversation with her now, seeing her condition. Yet her eyes were open again and her expression clear. Ah, she'd been faking it these last few minutes, waiting for Kyle to leave.

"So," I said.

"So."

Infuriating as usual. "Why did you really come to Utah, Rikki?"

"Because you were here."

No joking gleam, no teasing grin. Uneasiness shivered through my body.

CHAPTER THIRTY-THREE

Rikki

ante shook his head. "That doesn't make sense."

Genuine puzzlement. I almost felt sorry for the man. "A lot of things don't make sense, but they're still true. Fact: I looked you up on the Internet and found you'd moved back into our old neighborhood. I felt it was a sign, you being here with your family and me still owning my parents' house. I looked up the time the meetings started and went. I didn't know you were the bishop, though."

"Why, Rikki?"

"Because of the children. I have to make sure they're taken care of. Like you said in the blessing, I have to put my life in order. That means finding them a good place to stay."

His eyes flashed, and he looked every bit as dark and dangerous as any of my former boyfriends. I hadn't known he had such passion. If I had, maybe . . . No, better not to go there.

"So, you're going to up and leave?" he demanded, his voice harsh. "You're a mother now, Rikki. That means responsibility. Those kids deserve stability. They deserve discipline. They deserve a mother. You can't desert them. Kyle's still hurting over how you left them earlier this year and the time before that. Three months, Rikki? That wasn't what we agreed all those years ago. We both promised we were going to take care of our children, not ignore them or abuse them like our parents did."

I glared at him. "There's a lot of things we don't plan on, Dante. Maybe your life has been a sweet ride without major bumps. Maybe I'm the only one with the crappy life. But I do love my children, and they know it."

"Then stay."

"I don't have a choice."

"There's always a choice, Rikki."

"Not for me."

"I can help you. What is it? Money problems? Substance abuse? Spousal problems? As your bishop I can help with all of these."

"I don't need a bishop, Dante. I need you."

"I don't understand. You can't be saying—"

"I'm dying."

That stopped him good. He opened his mouth and then shut it and sat down in one of the straight-backed visitor chairs.

"About eight months ago, I was diagnosed with a brain tumor. Inoperable." I sighed. "When I left the kids earlier this year, it was so I could do an aggressive chemo and radiation therapy. Six weeks of hell." Even the memory made my bones ache and my stomach sick. "I lost a lot of hair, and every time I went to visit the kids, I wore a wig so they wouldn't find out. They laughed, thinking it was just a new style, another strange phase I was going through. But the treatment didn't work, didn't stop the growth. I'm still taking pills that are supposed to slow it, but they don't do enough. The symptoms are worse—headaches, nausea, muscles that won't work right. I have seizures because of the growth in my brain. I drop things." It would only get worse, or it would if the pain didn't make me so crazy that I accidentally took too many painkillers—again. "If this is the type of game your God plays, Dante, I'm glad I left. I'm glad I didn't have to hope for anything so stupid as eternity."

"I don't know what to say," Dante whispered. "I'm so sorry."

I tried to smile, but it probably looked more like a grimace. Too often these days, I only saw a skull staring back at me from the mirror. Most women would love to have lost so much weight. But not like this. Never like this. "There's nothing to say."

"The kids—have you told them?"

Irritation swept through me. "Of course I haven't told them! What would I tell them? That I'm dying, that I can't find Kyle's father, and that James's father has a wife and a new son and doesn't want anything to do with him? That there's not one of my friends I feel could raise them properly, even if they had the means? That I don't know what's going to happen to them?" The anger died as quickly as it came, leaving me weepy and afraid. "Look, I've left my children before—a couple times for jobs when Kyle was small and once for drug rehab a few years ago—but this is different. This is permanent. I won't be able to call and make sure they're okay. I won't be coming back for them. Ever. There's no second chance at getting this right. I have to be sure they'll be with someone who will treat them the way they should be treated. Maybe even love them."

I was crying as I pushed out the last words. This was the hardest part of all, not knowing what would happen to my kids. Not knowing if someone would ever love and care for them as much as I did. As much as they deserved. If I'd known years ago that I would die before my children, would I have chosen to have them at all? I'd once thought that I would never, ever give them up for anything. Not for riches, or fame, or success. But what if it was for their well-being? If I hadn't had them, would they have been born to another, more worthy mother? Or someone even worse?

Good mothers didn't leave their kids forever.

"So you came home," Dante said. His voice was hushed, almost reverent.

"I came home to you. I want you to help me find someone to take my children, Dante. I want them raised in the gospel. That's the real reason I came home to die."

He blinked. "You want them raised in the gospel?"

"Don't get me wrong—I'm not a believer. Not in visions or baptism or any of that. But it's a good way to raise kids. It was a steadying influence on me, and the ward members were, too. I don't want Kyle to sleep around. I don't want James to join a gang or father a bunch of children he's not going to take care of. I want them to go to school and not get into drinking and drugs. I want someone watching out for them, helping them get jobs so they can make something of themselves. Please, help me find someone you'd trust with your own children, and then promise me you'll keep a good, close watch on them. Promise me, Dante."

Was what I asked even possible? Why would a perfect stranger be willing to take on that kind of work for next to nothing? Kyle was a handful, and James was long past the cute baby stage. Two children cost a lot to raise, and though the state might give money to a foster family, I didn't want a foster family or a series of temporary homes for my babies.

Of course, having Dante find me a family wasn't really what I'd wanted. I'd hoped he would be in a position to take Kyle and James himself. But he already had four children, and in this world, that meant far too many already. Besides, something in me couldn't ask; I was too afraid he'd say no. That he'd reject me. Reject my children.

He rubbed a hand across his face as he always had when he was stalling for time. I knew it was a lot to absorb, and I hadn't meant to dump it on him like this. I'd meant to have Becca fall in love with James and want to help him when she heard about me.

I'd hoped to have Kyle impress the family in some way, or at least become good friends with one of Dante's children, so they'd all want the best for her. I hadn't meant for Kyle to develop a crush on Travis and get picked up for shoplifting or for Becca to realize the truth about how much extra work James would be for anyone who adopted him.

I bit my lip, trying to see past the tears. I was pretty sure Dante wouldn't be thrilled with even my simplified request, but coming here really was my last hope. The fact that he was a bishop might make it harder for him to refuse. I hoped.

Dante had said something and was waiting for an answer. That was happening to me more and more. I told myself it was the medication, but the truth was my brain wasn't working the way it once had. I was often distracted and couldn't seem to hold on to two threads of thought at the same time.

"What was that?" I asked.

"How long do you have?"

I snorted. That was always the question. "I don't know. No one knows. In January the doctor said six months, a year. I could drop dead tomorrow. But it will get worse first. They'll want to put me in the hospital."

He shook his head, and I took some comfort in knowing I didn't have to tell him I didn't want to die in a hospital.

He rubbed his face again. It made me want to laugh, but what came out was a sob. He placed his hand on my arm, and his fingers felt warm against my flesh. "We'll figure this out," he said in a soothing voice that made me more angry than comforted. I imagined he used it on all the members of the ward who had problems.

His hand was bigger than when it had held mine twenty-odd years ago, but it was more than the extra pounds he carried because his fingers were also longer. Either he'd had a growth spurt since I knew him, I was shrinking, or my memory was faulty.

What if all my memories of him were faulty? I was trusting him to do the right thing for my children despite his religious fanaticism. Maybe I was wrong.

There was no other choice.

Dang, I was a mess.

Dang? That made me smile. I was finally getting the hang of controlling my language, even to myself. Not that it mattered anymore.

He thought the smile was for him, and I let him think it. Most males were genetically programmed to assist and protect, and a little show of trust helped them follow through. Too bad the men I'd fallen in love with had let other drives overcome those better instincts. All but Dante, but that had been my own fault.

No, the Church's. I had to keep believing that for a little while longer.

"You going to be okay?" Dante asked, his voice gentle.

"I'm fine. Well, except that I'm dying." In a weird way it had been therapeutic to tell him. Now there was at least one person I could really be myself around, deep, dark secret and all. "Please don't tell the kids. Or anyone else." I didn't think he would, but I had to make sure.

"Of course not." He stood. "Can I at least tell Becca?"

"I want to be the one. Please? Don't you have some sort of bishop's oath that you have to keep my private life confidential unless I say otherwise?"

He gave me a pained look. "It'd be better to tell people. Easier to find a family."

"The kids have to know first, and I'm not ready to tell them." I didn't know if I would ever be ready, but I would have to do it eventually. I already knew James was going to be devastated, and Kyle would never, ever forgive me.

"As your bishop, I'll do what you ask, but you'll have to tell

Kyle and James soon. They deserve to know, to have time—" He broke off, but I knew he meant time to say goodbye, to prepare to be without me.

I covered my face with my hands, my heart shattering.

"I'm sorry, Rikki. I really am."

No apology in the world could make anything even marginally better. As I'd told Becca, there were some places you simply couldn't take children, and I was heading to one of them. Worse, no power on earth could stop me from leaving.

"I'll do everything I can to make sure your children have what they need," Dante said.

It wasn't enough, and if I thought it would help, I'd throw pride to the wind and beg. I needed Dante to be my last and greatest hero, to take care of my babies the way he'd taken care of me all those years ago. As long as they were with Dante, a part of me would always be with my children, the part I knew he carried in his heart, the same as I carried part of him. A sweet bond forged by children in desperate need of something to cling to.

For a sharp, agonizing moment I hated Dante. Hated him, while at the same time I needed him more than I'd ever needed him in my life. I hated him for the chance he had of being with my children—if he would only open his eyes—and for the fact that he might never see what great kids they were, which meant they might end up with no one to love them.

The only thing worse than dying was knowing how vulnerable my children were. My life choices had made them that way, but I was going to use my last breaths to give them the life they deserved. Even if it ripped my heart in pieces.

Now that Dante knew the score, it was time to go back to working on Becca.

CHAPTER THIRTY-FOUR

Becca

On Monday morning Dante came home for a quick break-fast before work, looking weary and beaten. I felt the same way. James had been too worried to go to sleep on the inflatable mattress I'd set up in Cory's room. I'd had to rock him for an hour before he fell asleep, the tears still drying on his cheeks. For the rest of the night, I'd called the hospital every hour until I heard that Rikki was going to be all right. By five, Charlotte Gillman was installed at my house to watch the children while I went to the hospital to collect Kyle.

A long night for me but worse for Dante. At least I'd been able to doze between phone calls.

"The doctor said she'll probably be released later today," Dante said, the worry line between his eyes deeper than usual. "But I'm not sure she should be alone."

"It's that bad?" I wasn't privy to the details of her condition, only that she'd be all right.

"I guess we'll have to wait and see." He was hiding something, and I didn't press, as a good bishop's wife shouldn't. He had to keep secrets, even when he didn't want to. That it was Rikki's secret, though, made it harder for me not to pry, given their past relationship. I wondered if she'd tried to kill herself, and after trying futilely to comfort James last night, the idea made me furious.

"Are the children going to school?"

I knew Dante meant Rikki's children, not ours. "James seems fine," I said, glancing at the table where Lauren and James were eating letter-shaped pancakes. "Since I told him his mother's going to be okay, he's not upset anymore. I thought we'd go by the hospital to see her before taking him to school, though, so he could see for himself."

"They were moving her from ICU when I left."

"That's good, then." I stopped myself from probing because I sensed Dante wanted to talk about it. I'd have to be strong to help him keep his word.

Darn that Rikki anyway.

Dante kissed me and went toward the door, stopping to kiss Lauren on the way. He also rumpled James's hair. "You okay?"

James nodded and continued eating his pancakes. Dante remained watching the boy, an expression of sadness on his face. A fear cut through me. Why was Dante acting so strangely? Was Rikki's condition more serious than it appeared? Or had Rikki told him something that involved James?

A second later the expression passed, and Dante was heading for the door. I shrugged off the creeping feeling of unease.

"Come on, kids," I said. The older kids had already gone to our next-door neighbor's to catch a ride to school. Sister Gillman was downstairs watching the morning news and would keep an eye on Cory and the sleeping Kyle. Not only did I not trust Kyle, I didn't want her to be alone yet. She'd had a rough night.

"Are we going to be late to school?" Lauren asked. "Because I don't want to miss math."

"Just a little late," I said. "We'll only stay a minute for James to hug his mommy."

"Okay. Hurry, James."

James picked up his bowl and chugged down the milk, wiping his mouth with the back of his hand. He was wearing some of Cory's hand-me-down clothes that I'd kept for some reason, just as I'd kept Allia's and Lauren's. Keeping Allia's made some sense because I could save them for Lauren, at least the classic ones, but Cory was eleven, and we hadn't planned on more children. Maybe it was time to let it all go.

The children chatted on the drive to the hospital, but inside the building they fell silent. "Mom, do people die here?" Lauren asked.

"Yes, honey."

"That's sad."

"It can be really sad, especially for the families, but you have to remember that people go back to live with Heavenly Father when they die, and all their parents and grandparents are there to meet them."

"Like a family reunion."

"What's a family reunion?" James asked.

That was something Lauren knew. "It's when you get together with your family, like cousins and aunts and uncles and grandparents. And you eat a whole bunch of cake and pies and stuff, and you play all sorts of games and laugh a lot."

"I don't have any family, just Mom and Kyle."

"Well, your mom's fun, but you can't have a reunion without cousins and stuff."

James frowned, so I took his hand. "Don't you believe that. You can have something just like a family reunion with close friends. It's basically a party."

"Oh," James said.

"Well, don't you at least have grandparents?" Lauren asked him.

"They're dead," James said. "They used to live in our house. Can I come to your family party, Lauren? The next time you have it, I mean."

"Sure. You can pretend to be my cousin."

James and his family would probably be long gone the next time we had another family reunion at my brother-in-law's parents' farm, but nothing would be served by bringing that up now.

As we approached the room, James began to walk slower. I could feel his fear and resistance, and I hoped it was because he was remembering the last way he'd seen his mother, not because he felt frightened at what he might see now. "It's okay," I told him.

"If you see any blood, just close your eyes," Lauren said.

Sometimes that child simply begged for a good swift kick. Fortunately for her, I possessed a lot of restraint. Restraint was one of the first rules of motherhood. "There isn't any blood," I told James. "Your mother is fine."

"Knock, knock," I called, though the door was open.

"Come in," Rikki answered. She was lying in bed watching TV, but she immediately switched it off when we came in. "James, baby!"

He ran to her, climbing up the side of the bed and into his mother's open arms. All the tension had left him now, and he began telling Rikki everything he'd done that morning, including how we'd practiced the alphabet with pancakes.

Lauren surveyed the room with interest that quickly turned into boredom. No blood, no doctor shouting commands, and no needles, except for Rikki's IV, and that was obscured by tape. Her hand slipped into mine. "Can we go?" she said in a whisper that was loud enough to carry. "I really don't want to miss show and tell."

"In a minute." I approached the bed, having to plaster a smile on my face as I remembered Dante's behavior. "How're you doing?"

"Much better. Thank you. Well, except for this IV. I told them if they didn't get in here to take it out, I was going to do it myself."

I laughed, hoping she wasn't serious but suspecting she was.

"I'm really fine, Becca," Rikki said. "They're going to let me go today. As soon as they can get me cleared."

"You do look good." Well, except the too-thin part, but that seemed to be her normal.

"Thank you so much for looking after James and Kyle. I don't know what I'd have done without you."

"No problem. You're lucky Kyle was there. It was she who called 911."

"So I heard." Rikki looked past me. "Is she here?"

"No, she's at my house with Sister Gillman. She was asleep when I left. She was up most of the night, but I'll get her to school before her English class."

"Thank you."

"James and me are going to school, too." Lauren tugged a little on my hand.

"James and I," I corrected.

"James and I," Lauren said, pulling harder.

James gave a huge yawn. "That's right."

Rikki's arms were still around James, and she looked reluctant to let him go. "I could take Lauren to school and come back with James," I said. "Or leave him here if the nurses don't mind."

"Oh, no, he should go to school. They've been testing him because of the reading, and I don't want to mess that up." Rikki bent her head to kiss James. "You go to school, sweetie. If I'm out of here before you finish school, I'll pick you up. If not, Kyle will come to get you."

"I'll pick them both up," I said, "and we'll make sure you have a ride, too. Sister Gillman's already planning on bringing dinner."

Rikki laughed. "Good old Sister Gillman."

There was a bit of derisiveness in her tone that made me say, "Charlotte's glad to have a chance to give back. There was a time not too long ago when the sisters brought her family dinner for months."

"She had cancer," Lauren said importantly. "We made her cards in Primary. We all thought she was going to die, but she didn't."

Rikki's smile faded. "I didn't know. So that's why she's lost so much weight from when I knew her."

"She hasn't gained enough back yet. It still seems strange to see her like that. She's a good woman."

"Yes, she is." Rikki buried her face in James's neck, hugging him tightly. "Go with Becca," she said. "I'll see you later. I love you, honey." I couldn't see her face, but I heard the catch in her voice.

"I love you, too, Mom."

"Oh," I said, remembering the shopping bag in my hand. "Your purse is in here. Kyle and I stopped by your house to get it and a change of clothes when I picked her up here this morning. She put my number in your phone, so call me when you know what time they're letting you go. That way Charlotte or I can pick you up."

Rikki took the purse from the bag, her lips clenched tight. For a moment, I thought she was angry. "Do you always take care of everyone else, Becca? How is there ever time left for yourself?"

I laughed. "Some things simply matter more."

"Priorities?"

"Something like that."

"What about Saint George?"

I shrugged. "I'll get the pictures developed and go from there." I could tell my answer didn't satisfy her.

The children were more talkative than ever as we drove to

school. I walked with them into the office to sign them in, staying to talk with the principal to let him know what had happened to James's mother.

"She's going to be okay, right?" he asked.

I nodded. "I think so." An emotion filled me—thankfulness that James hadn't lost his mother last night. It had been far too close. Hopefully, that meant James would remain as happy as he'd been seeing his mom at the hospital. I was beginning to really care about that child.

Kyle, however, was a different story. I still didn't know what I was going to do about her. Last week at the dance studio, it had been plain that Kyle longed to be in the class, and when I'd talked to her dance teacher at school, she had raved about her raw talent. I'd gone through a phase as a child where dancing had been my life—lasting for all of about three months—and I'd enrolled both Allia and Lauren, who'd both shared my short attention span, but not one of us could begin to approach Kyle's dedication. According to James, Kyle had been dancing all her life and practiced for hours every day.

That she'd tried shoplifting to get enough money for the classes made me want to weep. Most parents would love to see their child go after something with so much passion, yet to watch her stoop to illegal means was painful. Not having the classes was clearly punishment enough for Kyle for the shoplifting, but such a drastic and permanent punishment was surely overkill. The dying of a dream went deeper than sad, deeper than I had words to describe.

The cost of the special dance lessons was staggering, and when I'd told the teacher about Kyle's situation, she seemed willing to work with Rikki in regards to payments, but I had no idea what that would mean in the end. As far as I knew, Kyle still hadn't talked to Rikki, and I felt I would have to do so. I hoped Kyle didn't feel betrayed when I did. Even so, if there was any way to help Kyle achieve her dream, I had to act. At least dancing would be a start to keeping her out of trouble.

• • •

When I arrived home, I found Charlotte sitting at my kitchen table with a cup of hot chocolate. "Well?" she asked, taking her eyes from the window.

"Rikki seems to be doing well."

"But?"

I couldn't tell her that Dante was hiding something, though she probably knew how it worked better than I did. At her request, he'd kept her cancer a secret for weeks until the chemo and radiation made her too weak to hide it any longer. Why did we do that? Hide our troubles from those who could help?

"I don't know," I said. "No one's talking much about what's wrong, but she's taking an awful lot of medication for someone who's supposedly going to be all right."

Charlotte looked out the window again with more intensity than even the beauty of my flower beds demanded, her nose more prominent in outline. I shifted position so I could see what she was looking at.

"She's been out there since she woke up," Charlotte said. "I don't know anything about dance, but I think she's really very good."

When Kyle was moving, she didn't resemble the questionable-looking girl with the too-tight clothes and the short skirt but became something else entirely. Something flowing, vital, alive. I could almost see the music that she must hear in her head.

"Her mother was like that," Charlotte said in a reverent voice. "A waste, really. I wished then that I'd had the means to help her, but the kids were all at home and money was tight."

I knew what she meant. "The lessons she needs cost more than all the lessons my children take."

"Means she's good. Maybe I can help."

I knew her battle with cancer had seriously depleted her savings, and her husband had delayed his retirement to try to make up somewhat for that. I sighed. "It would take more than just one person."

Charlotte pulled her hand away from her mug and sat up straight. "Good thing we have more than that available to help. I, for one, am not ready to watch history repeat itself."

Tears welled up in my eyes. "No," I said. "Neither am I."

CHAPTER THIRTY-FIVE

Rikki

ife stinks. I never let my children say that, and all my life I've always corrected any friends or strangers who said the phrase. After all, I'd been the child with the verbally abusive father and frightened mother. I'd been the girl whose best friend was a boy whose father barely spoke to him. I'd been left by men I'd thought loved me, and I'd made more wrong choices than I could count on all my finger and toes. If anyone had the right to complain aloud, it was me. Up until now, I hadn't.

But you know what? They were right. Life does stink, but even then it is ultimately precious. I'd do anything to cling on to my rotten, stinking life.

Not that I was left much time alone for reflecting upon my woes. Teri Bunk, my old Primary teacher, showed up shortly after Becca left, her eyes large in her lined face, and her gray hair curled, if anything, more tightly than usual.

"Hi, dear," she said, shuffling in, her hands carrying a brown shopping bag with a rope handle that had obviously been used many times. "Brought you a few magazines and some *MacGyver* videos. Sometimes he gets a little too free with his lips, I know, but I think I threw out the bad ones."

She thought *MacGyver* was too racy? Was that a dig about my own life? No, the woman didn't have a subtle bone in her achy old body. I was an ungrateful wretch.

"Thanks," I said. "How did you hear?"

"Oh, I use a hearing aid these days."

"I meant about me being here."

"Charlotte called me. You poor thing. I came over as soon as I could."

"I'm okay. I think they're going to let me out soon." After the doctor confronted me about my many medications, I'd told him about my tumor, and he insisted on consulting a specialist before signing me out. If he didn't come soon, I could always leave on my own.

"Well, I'll stay and watch this with you." Teri put a gnarled hand in her bag and pulled out not a video after all but a DVD. "My favorite episode is on this one."

I wanted to give an excuse so I didn't have to watch it, but what else was I going to do? Sit here and worry about how well Becca was taking care of my children and how I'd never in a million years be able to pay for this hospital room?

Besides, it felt nice not being alone—and MacGyver was kind of cute, I had to admit. His hair reminded me of Dante's before he cut it to go on his mission. Dante's hair had been lighter, and the resemblance didn't stretch much further, but it made me smile. In case I missed anything, Teri kept up a running dialog during the show, which was every bit as fascinating as the plot.

An hour later Debra Lungren arrived, her makeup perfect, including the outdated blush, and her brown hair ratted three inches off her scalp. She carried a romance novel and a box of chocolates.

The women talked ten minutes before Teri left us with a bright smile that finally put some color on her pale cheeks.

I was beginning to see a pattern. These were two of the women who'd come to help me clean my house when we'd moved in. Did they do most of the service in the ward, or did Becca and Charlotte call them because they thought I'd feel more comfortable with them?

During my visit with Debra, she assured me the sisters would bring dinners in for the next few nights.

"Actually, I'm fine," I said. "I'll be back at work tomorrow." The doctor didn't say I could go, but he didn't have to worry about my bills, either.

"Well, then, for tonight at least. You need to rest."

My next visitor was Charlotte Gillman herself. It was only when she walked into the room that I remembered what Becca had told me about her cancer. This woman with the big nose and sagging cheeks had faced death. Maybe not certain death but the very real possibility. She'd spent months in recovery.

For the first time since Dante, I wanted to tell someone else, someone who would understand. But could she really? Her children were grown and had been when she'd fallen ill. She couldn't know the ache of leaving behind helpless babies.

"Are you in pain?" Charlotte asked.

I blinked away the tears. "Just a bit tired, I think."

"Well, no wonder."

"The doctor should have been back an hour ago. I'd really rather be home."

She plopped into the chair. "Yeah. That's what doctors do, but he'll get here in the end. Why don't you rest, and I'll sit here and read a bit?" She picked up the romance novel Debra had left.

I wouldn't be able to sleep with her there, but I didn't want to tell her to leave. What was up with me? I guess it's true that dying changes a person.

The next thing I knew, Charlotte was touching my shoulder, and I jerked awake. "Huh?"

"Sorry to wake you, but it's been a couple of hours and someone's here to see you."

Instead of the doctor, it was Quinn from work. He smiled at me uncertainly. "Heard you were here, so I thought I'd stop by."

I checked the clock and saw it was barely one, so he was on his lunch break or he'd cut out early. "I hoped to be out of here already," I said, my voice croaking from disuse.

Charlotte cleared her throat. "The doctor stopped by, but he wouldn't let me wake you. Promised he'd be back at two, but that probably means three." She looked from me to Quinn pointedly. "I'm going for a walk. I'll be back soon."

I wanted to ask her to stay because I was starting to like Quinn, and that was the worst thing that could happen now. To me and especially to him.

Of course he hadn't changed my oil yet, so maybe I could hold off alienating him for another week or two. I could barely afford groceries, much less someone to change my oil.

He brought his hand out from behind his back and handed me a bouquet of roses. Red. I loved red roses, and I really appreciated the gesture. He couldn't possibly know I loved sunflowers more. "I know it's kind of cliché," he said, "but at least I came prepared." His other hand held a vase, which he filled at the sink in the corner before settling the flowers inside.

"Thanks." I didn't know what else to say. I felt overwhelmed. When I'd come to Utah, my solitary goal had been to find Dante, to get him to love my children so I'd know they were taken care of. Here, suddenly, I had a lot of other people looking after me, and they didn't even know the terrible secret. I felt guilty for hiding it, for letting them think there was something to look after, to protect. No one could protect me from this.

People often talked of miracles, but I knew my body. I'd tried everything I'd heard about these past eight months, from chemo to natural remedies I bought on the Internet. I'd seen three doctors and four alternative caregivers, and every single one, except the man who wanted me to sign over the life insurance policy I'd bought when Kyle was born to pay for his radical treatment, told me the same thing: there was nothing they could do. At the end, I'd exhausted the tiny savings I had and pulled in every favor from anyone I knew. I owed everyone money now, money I'd never be able to repay.

So here I was, staring at Quinn and wishing for time, feeling angry that I even cared. For my children, yes, but not for romance or a man. Men were nothing but trouble.

Quinn sat on the chair and picked up the *MacGyver* DVD. "No way. I loved these growing up. They were my favorite. Should I put it in?"

What could I say? No, because I'm dying?

I let him. He scooted the chair closer to the bed and laid his hand beside mine. Next to his strong and healthy hand, mine looked fragile, and more so because of the IV. My heart thudded in my chest.

After about ten minutes, he looked me in the eye and took my hand, his thumb rubbing my skin softly. "What happened? Can you tell me?"

"I have these headaches," I said, debating how much to say. The last thing I needed was to lose my job before I absolutely had to. "They were bad yesterday, and I had a reaction to the medication. It's never happened before." The doctor had mentioned taking something else, but that was before I'd told him about the tumor. Nothing else worked, or at least nothing that was less dangerous. I would simply have to be careful, maybe work up a system where

I wrote down when I took the pills, or maybe I could time them when Kyle was around so she could double check.

More responsibility for my little girl. I sighed internally.

"I'm sorry it happened," Quinn said. "Is there anything I can do?"

You can make me better. You can support my children. Or give me a million dollars. But of course he could do none of those things. "Well, you did mention something about teaching me how to change the oil."

He laughed. "That's easy. Why don't I do it this time, and I can show you the next?" He should have let go of my hand, but he didn't, and I didn't pull away. It had been so long since I'd let any man get this close. I hadn't put on my perfume that morning, and I wondered if he could smell death on me, the death I imagined was always emanating from my body, despite the perfume. I wondered, too, if I should tell him my truck would probably never need another oil change. Not while I owned it.

His attention swung back to the TV, and I let myself float. Float. Let go. Just for now I wouldn't worry about telling my children. I wouldn't worry about Dante and Becca loving my children. I would feel Quinn's warm hand on mine and let myself pretend.

• • •

When Charlotte came back later with my doctor and his specialist in tow, Quinn was gone. I must have fallen asleep. My head was hurting again, and I had to ask for something for the pain. Charlotte waited outside while the doctors talked to me. Nothing new. Nothing they could do.

Sometimes I really hated doctors.

I blinked back the tears as Charlotte returned to the room. She took one look at my face and sat silently in the chair next to the bed, giving me time to recover. Her eyes were on the tray where my medication bottles stood like small sentinels.

"They said I could go," I said, swallowing hard. "I guess I should change so I'll be ready when the nurse comes to bring me the paper and wheel me out. Becca brought me an outfit."

She didn't speak for the space of several more heartbeats, and then, "This isn't something you have to do alone, Rikki."

"What?"

"The cancer."

I searched her face. "How long have you known?"

She motioned to the pill bottles. "Those are names I'll never forget. But there are other signs, too. What kind is it?"

"It's a tumor. A brain tumor. There's nothing more they can do." My voice broke at the words.

"Oh, Rikki." Charlotte's eyes watered. She seemed lost for several moments but then straightened her back. "It's going to be okay. God loves you, Rikki. Don't ever forget that."

"God loves me," I sneered. "That's a good one. If there is a God, He certainly doesn't care about me."

"Oh, honey." Charlotte leaned over, her hand on mine. "He brought you back to us, child. He brought you back to people who love you and who will take care of you and your babies. He put me here to share this time with you. If He didn't love you, He wouldn't have bothered."

Tears escaped my eyes. "I thought Dante . . . I wanted him to . . . take the children. But I couldn't ask . . . He seems so overwhelmed."

"Give him time, Rikki. You've had a lot of months to come to accept what's going to happen and what your children need. He's only had a day. He may be our bishop, but he's also just a man."

She was right. Heroes weren't made in a day, especially not one who'd begun as broken as Dante.

"Look at me." Charlotte's voice was gentle. "Don't you ever again doubt the Lord is here for you. Pray, child. Pray as you have never prayed before. He will answer."

Her eyes held mine, both of us tearful. My mouth worked. "I—I don't know how."

"You can learn." She took both my hands and held on tight while she said a prayer aloud, not stopping even when the nurse came in.

I clung to her helplessly and tried to believe.

When the nurse finally wheeled me to the hospital entrance for my release, Charlotte was outside in her car waiting. "If you're feeling up to it, I'd like to take you somewhere before I take you home."

"I'm pretty tired." I was always tired.

"It's about Kyle. She's been going to this dance studio to watch. I thought you'd like to see it. She's there now."

"She's supposed to be grounded." Though since she saved my life, maybe I should give her a break.

"She is? Well, Becca thought you'd be okay with it. Just a few minutes."

Well, if the perfect Becca thought so, then by all means. "Okay, let's go." I felt bad at my bitterness. Both Becca and Charlotte had been nothing but kind.

It wasn't far, but I was surprised the studio was in a residential area instead of downtown. I recognized Becca's van outside. It was already five-thirty, and I wondered that she wasn't home making dinner for her family. Had she brought James with her?

All at once, I wanted to hug my children, both of them. And never, ever let them go.

"Need a hand?" Charlotte asked, coming around her car.

My heart felt as if hands were squeezing it inside my chest. "No. I'm fine."

We went up the walk and down a flight of steps to a basement studio, where Becca waited for us. James wasn't with her. "Good, you're here. Don't worry. James is at my house playing with Lauren. Allia's watching them. Come closer. Over here is the best view."

The curtains in the observation area were open to the dance floor, though the girl inside with the teacher didn't look our way. It took a few seconds for me to realize that the girl was Kyle. I didn't recognize the moves or the eager way she watched the teacher.

I must have made a sound because Becca and Charlotte both reached for me. Ignoring them, I sat down on the chair closest to the observation window and watched my little girl who no longer seemed like my little girl but someone else, all grown up. I recognized a step or two from the dance she'd been choreographing the other night, but there was far more I didn't recognize.

Charlotte sat down next to me. "She has a lot of talent."

"Yes." I felt a deep sadness. Why couldn't Kyle be content with crushes on boys and a longing for a horse or something? Instinctively, I knew these lessons were as far from my budget as I was from owning a Porsche.

"The teacher is willing to take her at a discount," Becca said. "It's still a lot of money, but Charlotte and I and a few others would like to sponsor her. If you're okay with that."

A few others? Embarrassment flamed over my face. Had they gone through the ward list and asked everyone to donate to poor Rikki Crockett, the new, barely active member with the daughter of baptismal age? Had they hinted that baptism for Kyle was likely if they donated? How many of the ward members had refused?

"I know what you're thinking." Becca's fingers felt like feathers on my arm. "But she's been coming here every day after school to watch the other girls dance. She brings James when he's not at my house, and he plays in the backyard. Look at her. She's so happy."

She was. Every part of Kyle glowed. Not with happiness but with pure joy.

I didn't want her to hope and then to fall without me around to catch her when I was gone, and that meant I couldn't accept their offer.

"The shoplifting," Becca added softly. "She was trying to find enough money for the lessons."

I'd suspected there'd been more to the incident than simple greed, but Kyle had been so belligerent of late and I'd been so tired that we hadn't gotten around to that conversation yet.

"You were like that, Rikki," Charlotte said. "I couldn't help you, but we can help give Kyle the chance you didn't have."

They were wrong. I'd had chances, and I'd pursued them. Though I hadn't taken lessons on this level, I'd gone as far as I could alone. I'd practiced, I'd sweated, I'd worked hard. Now I saw that effort as a useless, stupid thing. What good did dancing do for me when I was destined to die? I should have found a stable life, a job with good insurance, a husband who wouldn't leave me. My children were the best thing that had ever happened in my life, and dancing was part of the reason I wasn't able to assure their future, or at least the monetary part of it. Some dreams were a waste of time.

Yet there was Kyle, my baby, and I knew how she felt. I knew it intimately. And I didn't care if I had to knock on every door in Spanish Fork, if I had to milk every bit of sympathy out of my tumor, no matter how I had to debase myself, I wanted her to have the chance to fulfill her dream. Maybe her dream wouldn't end as bitterly as mine. I had to believe that.

"Okay," I said. "Okay. But I pay a share, too, and I want to know who's helping us." I didn't want to wonder, to look into everyone's eyes and think, "Is this person sending a check each month? Are they wondering why I didn't make better choices to support my daughter?"

I'd taken charity before—from the government, from friends, from boyfriends, from strangers. This was different. It wasn't food or clothes or shelter. It was what my daddy would have called a waste of money. Hardworking people throwing away good money on a hobby that would never bring in a decent paycheck. The pressure inside me built until I could hardly breathe. Maybe I was setting up Kyle for as hard a fall as I was suffering.

"I feel exactly like Kyle," Becca whispered so softly, I knew the words were meant only for me. "You were right. I needed to see those gardens in Saint George."

Just that easily, everything was all right. Becca understood. She didn't look down on me or judge my past—at least not so it mattered. She saw a girl with a dream and wanted to help, regardless of who that girl was. She knew what it was like to dream. And dreams sometimes kept people alive.

I had a dream. A dream that I was healthy, that I'd married one of the nice men I'd met in my life, the ones without the nice cars but with the steady job and the ability to commit. I didn't dream of dancing.

Well, sometimes. But in those dreams I was always dancing with Kyle and James, and we were together. Always.

"Rikki?"

I looked at Becca, startled for a moment. There I was wandering again.

"You okay?"

I was nauseated and exhausted, and I was dying. "I'm fine."

"We didn't tell Kyle anything, just that the teacher was willing to give her a free private lesson," Becca added. "Apparently Kyle attended a group lesson last week with the younger class. Anyway, the teacher had a couple girls move on to a dance school in New York at the beginning of school, so she has openings. Probably not for long, though."

New York. That was impressive. Hope for Kyle blossomed through me. Maybe if she had this, she wouldn't be so angry at me. After.

"Come on," Charlotte said, a hand on my shoulder. "Let's get you home."

"I'll bring Kyle and James in a bit," Becca said. "Kyle's almost finished here."

That was too long. I needed my boy now. "I'd like to stop and get him."

Becca regarded me silently, compassion in her eyes. Did she know? Did Dante break my trust? No. He wouldn't break his word.

"We can do that." Charlotte went for the door, holding it for me while I concentrated on placing one foot in front of the other.

At Becca's, James ran into my arms joyfully. "Look, Mommy. Look!" He showed me a plastic container full of chocolate chip cookies. "They're letters. Lauren's mom helped us make the dough and cut them out. We made words from them and baked them in the oven. We got to keep all the words we could read. Cool, huh?"

I felt gratitude toward Becca once again. "That's great, sweet-heart." I hugged him tightly. He felt so good in my arms, so right.

Already James was making a lot of progress. The school had re-tested him and diagnosed him with minor dyslexia, but like Becca, they suspected that the glasses would do the most for him in the long run.

That started me worrying about the additional tests the op-tometrist wanted in two weeks. He worried James might have a more serious degenerative condition because of how rapidly he'd lost sight. What if something was seriously wrong? It was going to be hard enough to find someone to take care of my children, and if James was going blind, it would be that much more difficult. It would also be one more thing ripped from him.

Another part of me felt guilt. Guilt because I'd been so focused on my own fight these past eight months that I hadn't made my son's increasing eye problems a priority. Logically, I knew there was only so much I could process, but it still meant I'd failed him.

Bad mother.

Becca would do it all.

No, I must not resent her. Dante knew about my problem, but he hadn't swooped in and become my hero like I'd dreamed he might. Becca was my real hope now.

James tugged my hand. "Mommy, are you listening? I said I also played video games with Cory and Travis. They're so good, but they didn't care that I always got killed."

"That's so cool!" Once I would have asked him to show me and take a turn myself, but I was barely standing upright at the moment.

"You'll get better like me," Lauren told James. "I'd be even better if Mom let us play more." She gave a surprisingly teenage-like sigh. Dante and Becca were going to have full hands with that one.

Travis came into the living room from the kitchen, as though drawn by his name. "Oh, hi." He paused a minute, looking awkward. "Glad you're okay."

"Thanks."

He flushed and stood staring at me with that abashed look I'd seen in far too many teens I'd waited on in restaurants. The boy had the definite beginnings of a crush. One more reason for Kyle to hate me and Dante and Becca to back away.

Nothing I could do about it now.

The drive to my house went far too fast. To my surprise, Charlotte didn't leave us but came inside. "My husband will be here in a few minutes with your dinner," she said as we went up the steps. "I hope you like lasagna. It's really the best thing for him to cook while I'm not home."

"Your husband cooks?"

"Goodness no. Or nothing besides steaks on the grill, anyway.

He's from my generation, not yours. I made the lasagna, and he put it in the oven for me."

James laughed. "I'm going to learn how to cook."

"I like the sound of that," Charlotte said. "You come over to my house, dear, and I'll teach you."

She meant it, too. Tears made it hard for me see James's face, but I could tell from his bouncing that he was happy.

Happy.

All at once I was fiercely glad I'd come home to Utah and to this house. It was the right thing to do for my babies. Never mind that I didn't want to face what was ahead. I had to be strong for them. For once in my life, I had to do the right thing.

"Oh, there he is." Charlotte moved back through the doorway to meet her husband, who climbed out of the car. I didn't remember him from before, but I recognized his rotund figure from church. "Come on, James. You can help."

Within minutes, Charlotte and her husband had a full meal on the table, including milk, garlic bread, a salad, and the makings for root beer floats in the fridge and the freezer. "Do you want me to stay to put things away?" Charlotte asked.

I made a show of strength, reaching up to get James a plate from the cupboard. "I can do it. Thank you so much, Charlotte, for everything."

"Don't mention it. I'm happy to help, and I'm so glad you've come back to us." Charlotte surprised me by hugging me, and I surprised myself by letting her. Who knew that I would ever crave human contact the way I did now?

Charlotte went on. "You'll have to tell me all about Kyle's reaction when you tell her about the lessons. Oh, and I'll be the one gathering the funds since I'll put the lesson on automatic deduction from my checking. That way we'll never be late."

It also meant I could never spend the money on anything else.

I was being ungrateful again.

"I'll tell you all about it," I said. "I'm sure she'll be crazy with joy."

I walked her to the door, and when I returned, James had still not started in on his food. "Mom, we have to say a prayer. They always do that at Lauren's."

That was new. "Okay. Do you want to do it?"

He nodded. "You have to fold your arms like this."

Standing next to him, I obliged.

"Heavenly Father, thank you for this food. Thank you that my mommy's not sick anymore and that she came home 'cuz I really missed her. Thank you for my best friend Lauren and for my cookies and for Lauren's mommy, who is always nice to me. Thank you for our new couch and my glasses. Amen. No, in the name of Jesus, amen."

He smiled up at me, apparently expecting approval. I ran my hand through his hair before squatting next to his chair. "I'm glad to be back, too, James. I'm sorry I scared you."

"I was scared." His voice came out a whisper. "Really scared. Lauren's mommy rocked me, but it wasn't you." His face crumpled, and I gathered him into my arms. For long moments he sobbed, clinging to me, but after a time his tears dried, and he regained interest in his lasagna.

"Aren't you going to eat, Mommy?" he asked, sitting on his chair again.

"Sure." I wasn't hungry, but if I didn't eat, I would only get worse.

How long, I wondered, would he cry when I was really gone? Maybe I didn't want to know.

"How about we sleep in the tree house tonight," I said. "Would you like that?"

CHAPTER THIRTY-SIX

Kyle

For a day that hadn't started out so well, it was ending perfectly. I'd dared wear my new makeup to school for the half day I was there, and my friends hadn't said a word. What's more, Monty, the visitor from church, talked to me in the halls and said he'd look for me in our tech class the next day. Two of his friends had stopped to chat with me, too. I was about ready to die from happiness. School suddenly looked brighter. Even Allia said she'd looked for me at lunch, not knowing that I'd eaten at her house before arriving at school.

The crown on the day was when Sister Rushton picked me up from school and told me that not only was my mother coming home from the hospital but the dance teacher had agreed to give me a free private lesson. I could hardly contain my excitement. I didn't ask how it happened—probably she'd been talking to the teacher about Lauren and had mentioned me—and I didn't care. A private lesson. I could do a lot with that.

And I did. I think I might have even impressed the teacher, though she didn't invite me to any more free lessons. At least I'd learned enough to keep me busy for a few weeks, and I'd learn more if I kept watching the other lessons. I couldn't wait to get home, eat something fast, and do a little more practicing before getting to my English homework. I'd finished most of it in class, though, so I was confident I could do the rest tonight.

I practically skipped up the steps to my house, almost forgetting to wave to Sister Rushton. She was weird that way. All her kids waved to her or kissed her cheek or something whenever she dropped them off. She waved back to me but didn't leave, waiting to see if I got inside okay. I didn't need her to wait. I'd left my bedroom window open a crack and taken off the screen in case I got locked out someday and Mom forgot to leave the key under the front mat. Today the door was unlocked.

A heavenly smell hit me as I walked into the house, and for a moment I stood there, taking it all in. It reminded me of Allia's house the times I'd picked up James. My mouth watering, I hurried across the living room into the kitchen.

"How about we sleep in the tree house tonight," Mom was saying to James. "Would you like that?"

"Yay!" James cheered. He forked another mound of food into his mouth. Lasagna. My stomach rumbled, reminding me how starving I was. But not starving enough to notice that Mom's plate was still empty.

"Outside? No way." I sat down where Mom had left me a plate. "Mom, you just got back from the hospital. You need to be in a real bed. James, don't be selfish. She can't sleep out there yet."

"I can too. I'm fine." Mom had a bright smile, but I could see the strain around her eyes. Was it only because of what had happened last night? I hoped so.

James studied her. "We should sleep in your bed instead."

Mom sighed. "Whatever. But I'm fine. It was an accident."

Silence. I'd been thinking a lot about how to avoid another

of these "accidents," but I didn't want to talk about it in front of James. He'd been so scared last night.

I plopped a big spoonful of lasagna on Mom's plate. "There you go."

"We have root beer floats for after," James told me. He was such a kid. What did root beer floats matter after the time I'd just had at my dance lesson?

"Yummy." I was dying to tell Mom about the dancing, but I wasn't about to bring it up again, not after what happened last night.

"Look, Kyle," Mom said, without warning. "I know about the dancing."

My hand stopped with my fork halfway to my mouth. I stared at her and then at James.

"Hey, it wasn't me," James said. "I didn't tell her."

My gaze swung back to Mom. "How?"

"How? I can read it in your eyes. See it in the way you walk."

"Sister Rushton told you, didn't she?"

Mom nodded. "Yes." Was that a tightening of her lips?

"I'm okay just watching. I can copy it at home. When I'm older, I can get a job and pay for lessons." Never mind that I'd probably never be able to make so much while I was young enough for it to matter.

"Sister Rushton and some of the other women want to help you with the lessons, and the teacher has an opening. She doesn't take just anyone, so that means you're pretty special."

The words felt huge, as though they took up the entire universe. I blinked, hardly daring to believe. My fork dropped from my hand. "Really? You mean I can . . . I can . . ." If I was so happy, why was I crying? Why did my chest feel ready to explode?

"Yes." Mom was crying too. I launched myself at her and hugged her tight.

"I can't believe it. Oh, I swear, I'll never do a mean thing again. I'll clean the whole house every single day. I'll get straight A's, I'll babysit James without complaining, and I'll pay everyone back when I'm older."

Mom laughed, her arms hugging me tight. "Whoa," she said. "You should stop right there before someone asks for your firstborn child."

I pulled from her grasp and danced around the kitchen. "It's a miracle! I can't believe it! I thought Utah would be the worst ever, but this makes up for everything!" God had heard my prayers, but I didn't say that, not knowing how Mom would take it.

James and Mom both jumped up from the table and began dancing. Mom was really good, and what James lacked in knowledge, he made up for with intensity. I laughed, and the happiness was almost too big to contain. We used to always dance like this together, mimicking moves we'd seen from old movies. How long had it been since we stopped? Eight months, a year? Mom had always initiated it before, and now I felt sad that I'd waited for her to be the one. Maybe she needed someone to remind her how much fun it was.

James banged into the wall. "Oops."

"It's a new move!" Mom called, falling into the wall herself so realistically that for a second fear arrowed down my spine. Then she was up and laughing.

After a while, I sat down to my cold plate of lasagna, not because I was hungry, but because Mom was looking pale and her forehead pinched, signaling one of her headaches.

James and Mom followed me, James eagerly, Mom moving with a deliberate slowness. "I want more," James said. I gave him another helping, which he downed in less than a minute.

"Can I watch TV now?" he asked.

Mom smiled. "Yeah. Why not? I'm going to take a bath." James ran off, and Mom stood to clear the table. I noticed that only half her lasagna was gone.

"Mom," I said, as she put plastic wrap over her plate.

"Yeah?"

"Do you have a headache?"

Her hands stilled. "A little one."

"Are you going to take a pill?"

She sighed. "Not until ten, I'm not."

That meant hours more to wait.

"Mom," I said. "How are you . . . I mean, can I help . . ." How are you going to stop from killing yourself, was what I wanted to say, but I knew that wouldn't go over well.

"It won't happen again." Mom's stare felt heavy, like she could read my thoughts. "Look, honey, is there something going on with you? Besides dance?"

"With me? Naw."

"It's just, you haven't been sleeping well."

She wanted to talk about my nightmares, and I wanted to talk about the pills. That made two of us who weren't going to get what we wanted.

I shrugged, but inside I was screaming, "You're different!" Dancing together in the kitchen made it that much more clear. My mom wasn't the same, and it made me uneasy.

Mom drew her pills from her purse and showed me the sticky note attached. "I'm marking down whenever I take my medication. If I can't see what I've written, I'll ask you to tell me what it says."

"Why wouldn't you be able to see it?"

Mom's turn to shrug. "The headaches make it hard to see sometimes."

"Okay." Relief shuddered through me. She was taking this seriously. "When will the headaches go away?"

"Unfortunately, I'm going to have them the rest of my life. But we'll deal with it."

That didn't sound good, and a wave of pity for my mother surged in my chest. "I'll help in any way I can." I started for the basement stairs, thinking I might practice a bit more, but Mom stopped me.

"Uh, aren't you forgetting the kitchen is yours? You're still grounded. School and dance and places with me. That's it."

I sighed, but deep down I knew I deserved worse. "So when do I start dance?"

"Tomorrow." She grinned at my happiness.

"It's the best thing that's ever happened to me."

"I know."

And I knew she really did.

I hugged her. "I love you, Mom."

"I love you, too, honey." Her voice sounded so strange that I drew back to look at her face.

"Are you okay?" I asked.

Mom nodded. "I think I'll lie down for a bit before my bath." She walked slowly to her room. I stood watching after her, not knowing what to think.

James had reappeared in the kitchen, probably looking for an after-dinner snack. The kid was a bottomless pit these days. He tugged at my hand. "Is Mom going to be okay?"

I looked at his sweet face, those huge eyes begging for reassurance. "I don't know," I whispered. "I just don't know."

CHAPTER THIRTY-SEVEN

Rikki

I'd planned on dropping the kids off at school and then going to work as usual, but I simply couldn't get out of bed on time, so I climbed into the truck with my hair still uncombed. No big deal. I'd bathed last night, and my hair didn't look all that different when it was combed, so fingers could do the trick as I drove. Only by the time James got out of the truck and disappeared inside the school, I was seeing double, and it took me ten minutes of resting in the car before I could drive home.

It was as if telling someone about the tumor had made all my energy and courage flee. As if I didn't have to be strong anymore. Except that I did. The situation with the kids wasn't handled to my satisfaction, and I didn't know how to hurry that along.

I didn't want to die. I wanted to see my little girl dance in New York, I wanted to see James go to college, I wanted to get to know Quinn.

Tears made it even harder to see. I told myself to quit blubbering and go inside the house, but my muscles had decided they were through for the day. I hurt everywhere, and I couldn't remember if I'd taken my pain pill, though I'd tried to be careful about writing it down on the sticky note. All I had to do was open my purse and look. Only somehow my purse wasn't in the truck, and I couldn't walk inside.

I had to, though. I reached for the door. My hand closed on thin air.

Tears came in earnest now, and I laid my head against the steering wheel and sobbed. Charlotte had said the Lord loved me and had brought me home to Utah for a reason, so I wouldn't be alone. Yet here I was, without friends and family, sitting in my driveway too weak and discouraged to go on. What if I died here and now, without telling Kyle and James goodbye or how much I loved them?

I hated God! Or the idea of Him. I hated the false security believing gave people, especially when they were at their most vulnerable, when they faced the end. Was it any wonder I'd stopped praying the night my father had sent his thirteen-year-old daughter alone into a cold November night because she hadn't cleared the table fast enough? I'd known then that God was too far away to care about me and that only Dante could help

Dante had helped. He'd wanted me to sneak inside his house each night to stay, but I didn't like his father any more than my own, and it was warm enough in the bushes with all the blankets and old coats Dante arranged from somewhere.

Yet even Dante had let me down now.

Charlotte had told me to give Dante time. What if I didn't have time? What if right now, this very moment, was the end? What if I never saw Dante or my children again?

Another thought came, every bit as disturbing. What if God *had* been watching all those years ago? What if He'd sent me to Dante's that cold night? What if God had seen ahead and had known what would happen and had prepared him with what I needed?

I needed him prepared now.

For the first time since I was thirteen, I prayed. I prayed for strength, for time, but most of all for Dante to be my last and greatest hero. As I prayed, I cried with a strength I didn't know I had. I couldn't open the door to the truck, but I did a decent job of leaving every bit of water in my body on the steering wheel.

At last I grew quiet, holding the steering wheel and feeling the warmth of the sun coming through the windows and pushing back the coldness in my heart. The heat gave me hope, and I reached for the door again. *Please let me be able to open it.*

That's when I heard the tapping and looked out the passenger window into Becca's concerned face.

CHAPTER THIRTY-EIGHT

Becca

I left Cory his school assignments when I took the children to school, planning to go to the temple after I dropped them off, yet as I pulled up at Lauren's school, my mind felt unsettled. I kept thinking about the gardens in Saint George as I debated what to try first in my own yard. Maybe I should pray about it, but I felt a little silly doing that. I mean, whether I chose a trellis with roses or with ivy, it could hardly make an eternal difference. What I needed was to talk to a friend who knew my heart. Yet no one really knew about my dream, except Dante, who'd acted strangely yesterday during family home evening, bringing up people we hadn't seen for years and asking me how many children they had.

Not that I didn't want to share this new part of my life with Dante, but the trip to Saint George had opened another door. I hadn't had a close girlfriend since I began having children. Oh, there were women at church, neighbors who I knew would drop anything to lend a hand, old college or mission friends who were always enjoyable to catch up with, and even my sister, though we'd drifted apart these last years as we raised our families.

What I wanted was to talk with Rikki. Getting to know her the past weekend had brought it all back. The youthful friendships, the craving to talk things out with another woman, having someone to laugh with and to share moments no one else really understood.

I craved that now. Rikki didn't see things like I did, but she had a way of getting down to the nub of the concern, and even when I totally disagreed with her, she believed my opinion was every bit as good and valid as hers.

She wouldn't be home, of course. She'd be at work now, though she probably should have held off a few days after her brush with death. I went home by way of her house anyway, just to see, because I remembered how fragile she'd been at the dance studio yesterday. It wasn't too far out of the way. One street.

Her truck was in the driveway, and I felt an odd déja vù sensation as I left the van and walked up to the door of the house. I shivered in my sweater because the sun was still hidden behind a large patch of angry gray clouds. Fall had officially arrived.

I was almost to the porch when I saw movement in the truck. I stopped and stared. Rikki was inside, slumped over the wheel. My heart jumped into full alarm as I sprinted to the truck.

I knocked on the glass. Her head came up slowly, her eyes reddened but intent. "Becca," she mouthed.

I took that as an invitation and opened the passenger door. "What are you doing out here?" Crying for one thing, I was sure, but it wouldn't be polite to bring it up.

"Thinking." She looked away again. "How come you're here?"

"I felt like talking to you." Tears pricked the back of my eyes, though I had no idea why. "Are you going to work?"

"I was."

"Maybe you should rest another day." Though she was always pale, her whiteness today was frightening.

"It's not all that hard. I sit a lot. It doesn't take much energy to push a few buttons on the computer."

She was simplifying things, as we women have a tendency to do. "Just being there is stressful," I said. "Do you really need to go?"

"Actually, I don't think I'm ever going to work again."

I froze. "What are you saying?" Maybe she'd say she was leaving. I didn't want her to go.

Her face turned to mine, her fingers white-knuckling the steering wheel. "I'm sorry, Becca. I should have let Dante tell you, but I wanted you to hear it from me."

Except I already knew. I think I'd known the minute I'd seen all those prescription bottles at the hotel, or if not then, when Dante had come home from the hospital looking so beaten. Still, I listened as she told me about her tumor, about dying.

"I can't make my body work," she said, a tear slipping from her eye. Finally, she let go of the steering wheel and sat back on the seat. I scooted over, put my arm around her, and leaned my head against hers.

"I'm so sorry, Rikki." I was sorry for her, for Kyle and James, and for myself, who was losing a friend before I really had time to love her, and for my husband, who would be tortured with helplessness. Having Rikki back in his life was challenging enough, but knowing that she was dying complicated everything.

"I haven't told the kids," she whispered.

I couldn't begin to imagine how she felt about leaving her children, and the little bit I could imagine horrified me. If it were me, who would help Cory catch up with school? Who'd counsel Allia about makeup and boys and teach Lauren not only to make choices but to make good ones? Who would remind Dante to think before he punished Travis? Who would hold Dante at night when the cares of the ward were too heavy for him to bear alone?

That Rikki faced death alone made it that much more terrible. I choked back tears.

"Don't cry," she said. "It can't change anything."

I felt profoundly sad. Rikki was the kind of person people gravitated toward, the kind people told their most inner feelings. She could have done so much good in the Church. She would have made a wonderful Young Women leader or a visiting teacher who mended lives. Instead, her choices had brought pain to her face and left her and her children adrift when she needed help the most.

Not too late. Whether the impression came from my own heart or the Spirit made no real difference. We, as a ward family, could help Rikki be the person God had meant her to be. Sometimes it was only when people were at the most bitter place in their lives that they were finally willing to change. I'd seen it happen on my mission, I'd seen it happen in the lives of ward members. *Please let it happen to Rikki.*

"You need to talk to Kyle," I said. "She knows something's up, and she's terrified. She can see the difference in you. Kids are sensitive to these things."

Once, Rikki might have told me to mind my own business, perhaps adding a few coarse words to make sure that I did, but now she simply nodded. "I know, but I can't tell her. I can't."

"Yes," I said. "You can, and you will."

"She'll hate me."

"Maybe at first, but she's a smart kid, and she'll come around. You need to give her that time."

"Can't you tell her?"

"No, but I can be here if you want."

Rikki sighed. "I hate this. I don't know who I am anymore."

"You're Rikki, the mother of two great kids, and my friend."

She lifted her head from where it still rested against mine. "I know what Dante sees in you, Becca. I see it too. I only wish I had more time so we could really be friends."

Her comment echoed the feelings of my heart, and for a full

minute I couldn't speak. I could only stare at her as I struggled not to cry. "Come on. Let's get you into the house."

She didn't resist as I helped her from the truck, though once outside, she paused and stared up at the gray mass of clouds. "I thought the sun was out a minute ago."

"It hasn't been out at all this morning. Hopefully, the clouds will burn off by noon."

Rikki looked again at the clouds and then at me. A small smile touched her lips. I didn't know how she could smile at all, but there it was. "I feel the heat." Her hand went to her heart, as though holding in the warmth. What had happened in that truck before I arrived?

We went up the drive into the kitchen door and through to her bedroom, moving with a deliberate carefulness. By contrast, my mind was going too fast. I'd have to call Charlotte and the Relief Society president. If she continued to deteriorate, Rikki couldn't be left alone for long periods of time, especially when the children were around. Dinners and homework had to be taken care of. Grocery shopping. Her bills.

As I settled her in bed, I thought of Saint George and how she'd talked of dying. I'd thought it was her mother she'd been talking about, but now I knew it was her own death. I bit my lip to keep myself from crying. If I'd been in Rikki's shoes, I wouldn't have wasted time on any gardens, no matter how beautiful or intricately organized. I'd be with my children every waking second, memorizing their faces and making sure they knew I loved them and how much the Church meant to me so they could hold those precious truths in their hearts long after I was gone.

So why had Rikki gone with me and wasted so much time? Given her rapid decline, it hadn't been good for her health. At the very least, she should be with her doctor, discussing alternate methods or seeking a medical trial to participate in.

Maybe she'd done all that and more. Maybe she was ready.

How could she be ready? She hadn't even told her children.

Then why had she felt inclined to go with me, to help me find my future?

Rikki had closed her eyes and was breathing steadily. I could see the blotches left by earlier tears—tears likely shed as she contemplated leaving her children alone in the world.

All at once, understanding flooded over me. I knew why Rikki had come to Saint George with me and why she'd tried to be my friend. Why she'd searched out Dante and come home to the very ward she'd grown up in. The prodigal daughter returned to the fold to share her past with her children and to trust her longtime friend with their care.

"Oh, Rikki," I said.

She didn't answer, and I knew she was asleep. I stared at her, studied the features that had become so familiar. How could I have missed the fact of how very ill she was? I'd seen the face of death before, but I hadn't wanted to recognize it.

She wanted too much. James was a lot of work all by himself, but he was still young and moldable. Even if his eyes became a serious handicap, Kyle's needs far overshadowed his. Her expensive lessons, her upbringing that had no resemblance to the one enjoyed by my children, her sneakiness, her apparent attraction to Travis, to which he might not be completely immune. There were bound to be arguments about boys, curfews, and schoolwork. Maybe more arguments about drinking and drugs. Her poor influence might risk the eternal salvation of my own children. Not to mention that Kyle would forever remind my husband of his first love. Would Rikki, in dying too young and tragically, become his Beatrice?

Yet Kyle was also a lost, lonely little girl with more talent and passion for dancing than I'd ever dreamed of. That desire might be a stabilizing factor. No matter how hellish the next few years of adjustments, she would eventually go off to New York to study dance, and just that fast the day-to-day conflicts would vanish. By then she would have a testimony—or not—and would make her own choices.

A desire to help welled within me, but I knew all too well how quickly such an emotion could dissolve into duty and an overabundance of nightmares. I'd felt exactly that with Dante's father.

No, I thought. It's too much. Had Dante been hiding this information? Had he expected me to raise Rikki's children alone as I was practically raising his kids?

I dismissed the thought even as it came. I would have seen that in him, and Rikki hadn't told me, either. When would she? Or would she ever say it? Perhaps she'd planned to simply leave them with us one day and slink off to die on her own.

I stood up and paced the length of the room. I didn't know what to do. Wait. Yes, I did. I needed to call Charlotte on my cell so she could get the ball rolling with the Relief Society and compassionate service. For the moment at least, I could concentrate on that.

I'd barely hung up after speaking with Charlotte when Rikki's phone rang. I fished it from her purse lying on the floor next to the bed. "Hello?"

"Rikki?" asked a man's voice.

"No, this is her friend Becca."

"Oh, yeah, the friend she went to Saint George with. This is Quinn, Quinn Hunter. I went to the hospital to see her, but they said she'd been released."

"Yeah, she's here at her house, sleeping right now."

"Will you tell her I called?"

"Sure, Quinn. I'll tell her."

I'd barely replaced the phone in her purse when I realized Rikki was awake and watching me. She gave me a flat grin. "You know the irony of it? I think he might have been the one. After all the men I've dated all these years."

"Quinn?"

"Yes."

"Him and not Dante?" There. I'd asked the question.

Her head swung back and forth ever so slightly. "Not Dante, Becca. You are his Beatrice. Not me. I was never right for him. Oh, I told myself all these years that I was, that it was the Church that tore us apart, but now I see that it was me and my choices that did the tearing. Truth was, I didn't know how to be ordinary back then, to stay in one place and build a future. But all Dante ever wanted was roots. You're together now, and you're in love. Please don't waste your time together. I want Dante to be happy. I want you to be happy."

I leaned closer to her. "I'm sorry, Rikki."

"Don't be sorry." Her hand touched mine. "Help me."

I nodded. "Okay."

What had I agreed to? I didn't know, and neither did Rikki, but she seemed satisfied. I remembered how at the pool when she'd tried to stand and lost her balance I'd had to steady her. It made sense that the tumor in her head would have more side effects than headaches, but what would she do when there was no one to catch her?

Of course that was why she'd come home to Utah. There was no one left. No one but Dante. And now me. No, not just us. The ward was here, too. And God. If only she could believe.

"The sun," Rikki murmured. "Becca, can you feel the sun?"

The sun was still hiding behind the clouds and, if anything, the room was chilly.

"No," I said.

"I can."

Maybe she already believed. Or was beginning to.

I sat next to her on the bed and watched her sleep.

• • •

In the afternoon, I picked up the children—Rikki's and mine—dropped my older children off at the house, and headed back to Rikki's with Kyle, James, and Lauren.

"Thank you so much," Kyle said as I pulled up at Rikki's, a smile on her thin face.

"I guess you're talking about the dance classes." So much had happened since yesterday, I'd completely forgotten how new it all was to Kyle.

"I know it was because of you," she said. "I'm so—I—it—"

"It wasn't just me. I mean, I wanted to help, but I wasn't sure how. It was Sister Gillman who reminded me that a lot of people would be happy to pitch in, that it wasn't something anyone had to do alone."

"It won't be forever." Kyle's words tumbled from her mouth. "I bet if I worked hard the next three or so years, I could learn enough to get a scholarship to a dance school in New York. I promise to work really hard."

Her earnestness touched me. The most emotion my children had shown about lessons was to ask in long-suffering voices how long they had to take piano. The answer was always the same—until they could play hymns well enough to accompany a congregation on their missions—but that didn't stop them from asking.

"Help me take in the groceries," I said.

Kyle looked over the backseat. "These are all for us?"

"Your mom's not feeling well. That's why I'm doing the lesson with James at your house today. If you have homework, I can help you with it before you go to dance."

Kyle nodded, but her smile was gone. She waited until the younger children ran up the steps before saying, "Mom didn't go to work, did she?"

"No."

"It's something horrible, isn't it?"

Her eyes held mine in an almost physical gesture, pleading. I nodded. "You need to talk with your mother. The sooner the better." It was the first thing I could do for Rikki and Kyle—make them talk—but I hated every minute of it.

"But what if she won't tell me?"

"She will. And no matter what, Kyle, remember you're not alone."

Kyle nodded and said softly, "I know."

Charlotte met us at the front door. "Dinner's ready to warm up in a couple hours," she said, "and Teri's coming over at five-thirty to take a shift. Then I'm coming back over later."

Kyle looked back and forth between us. "Where's my mom?"

Under Charlotte's sympathetic gaze, I put an arm around Kyle's shoulder and guided her down the hall.

Rikki was lying on a bunch of pillows Charlotte must have brought. Perhaps they'd been the same pillows that had eased her during her battle with cancer. "Hi, sweetie," Rikki said.

"Hi." Kyle's expression was lost and forlorn.

Rikki's eyes turned to me, pleading.

"It's time," I told Rikki with all the firmness I could muster. "Tell her everything. I'll be right outside if you need me."

I left them then but stood outside the door in case I was needed. There was a muffled conversation and then nothing for a long time except quiet sobs. For the first time that day some of Rikki's imaginary sun reached my heart. Kyle hadn't thrown a fit or run out in anger, as we'd both feared. She had risen to the occasion and stayed with her mother. I wasn't sure Allia would have been that grown up.

Kyle's special, I thought, and that was the real beginning.

CHAPTER THIRTY-NINE

Dante

My friend was dying, and there was nothing I could do to help.

No, I can help by finding someone to take her children. If the Flemmings weren't so old, I'd recommend them, but with the heart attack, that was out of the question anyway. No one else in the ward immediately came to mind. No one who could have enough love while at the same time give Kyle much-needed discipline. There was, however, an old mission companion of mine who might fit the bill. They'd adopted two children already. Maybe they'd be interested in more.

When I arrived home, the table was set and dinner was in the oven, but the house was quiet and no one greeted me at the door. I almost felt I'd walked into the wrong house. I wasn't accustomed to the silence, to Becca not being there. I found her downstairs in the family room with the children, but the TV was off and no one was speaking.

"Hi, everyone."

No one jumped up to hug me, though gazes turned in my direction.

"Oh, Daddy," Lauren said, her voice mournful, "did you hear? James's mommy's dying. She has a tumor in her head. That's a big growth. A mass of tissue."

I met Becca's eyes and was relieved that they were not accusing. "Yeah, I heard." I sat down on the couch next to Becca. Lauren climbed from her lap into mine and put her arms around my neck, giving me much-needed comfort. Allia was sitting on the chair next to the couch, and the boys were sprawled on the floor.

"When did you hear?" I asked Becca. There was a sadness in my wife's face that I wished I could wipe away.

"Rikki told me this morning. She wasn't able to go to work today—she probably won't be able to work again. She told Kyle and James after school. I stayed for an hour after she talked with Kyle."

"How'd Kyle take it?"

"Better than I thought she would." Was that a hint of pride in Becca's voice? "She's known for a long time that something was wrong. In a way, I think it was a relief for her to finally have it in the open. Someone from the ward is there now. We're going to try to have someone there all the time. Rikki's been struggling to keep it together for so long, and now it's like . . . well, like she simply can't anymore."

"That poor lady," Travis mumbled.

Allia sniffed. "Poor Kyle."

"Poor James." Lauren gave a big sigh. "I guess he's going to have to live with us now."

No one said anything to that, but a weight seemed to push down on my shoulders.

"I should never have let her go to Saint George with me," Becca said.

I put an arm around her. "Honey, Rikki does what she wants—always has. There's no way it's your fault."

She frowned. "You should have told me, Dante. About the tumor."

"She wanted to tell you herself."

"No, that's not what she wanted." Becca looked ready to say more, but Allia stood up, drawing our attention.

"I could share my room with Kyle," she said.

I arched a brow. "What's all this talk? Rikki asked me to find a home for the kids, and I think I may have found someone."

"It's us, Daddy." Lauren gave me a scowl. "You can't give James to someone else. He'd hate that."

Becca shook her head. "It has to be you, Dante. Don't you see?"

The room at once seemed too small, and I felt suffocated. "What are you talking about?"

Becca took a deep breath. "Who else, Dante? Who on this earth knows what she went through as a child? Who knows her like you do? No one. Not one single person. Even after all these years, everything that made her who she is took place in those years, and you're the one who lived them with her. You're the only one she trusts to watch over her children when she's gone, the only one who can remind them who she was. That's what Rikki wants. She doesn't have anyone else. You were her brother, her only true friend." Becca was crying now. "She wanted to show us how great they are. She wanted you to volunteer. She wants you to be her hero."

Of course. It all made sense now, and I felt like an idiot. Why else would Rikki want her children raised in the gospel when she didn't believe in it? That time of her life was the only security she'd ever known.

"I think we should do it, Dad." Travis was sitting up tall.

"Whoa, guys," I said. "It all sounds so easy now, but once you're all sharing rooms, fighting over who's going to drive the car, scrimping on everything so we can pay the extra bills, it'll be a different story. Taking on two children would be the hardest thing we've ever done."

Travis shrugged. "If it was easy, it wouldn't be a sacrifice."

Easy for him to say when he'd be out of the house and on a mission in three years. I looked at Becca, who held my gaze. I could see she was also torn. "I couldn't do it alone," she said, her voice soft. "Someone would have to take Kyle to dance lessons four days a week and then pick her up, especially in the winter. There would be more homework projects, and I'm just not that great at math."

"I am," Allia said. "I'm two years ahead of Kyle. Her math is easy. And all her other classes, I've already taken, so I can help with those, too."

"I can help with English stuff," Travis volunteered. "When Dad can't. And I can do some driving."

"Okay." Cory heaved a sigh. "I guess James can sleep in my room, but he has to promise not to touch my Lego collection. We'll have to buy a lot more food, especially when we barbecue. He eats more than I do."

"James can sleep with me," Lauren protested.

"Can't," Cory said. "Girls can't sleep with boys."

"You can if he's your brother."

"Then why aren't you sleeping in my room with me?"

Lauren grinned. "Okay. I'll sleep with you and James. That's fine with me."

Everyone laughed, even Lauren, who would eventually learn that Cory's sarcasm meant she'd be staying in her own room.

I looked at Becca, feeling amazement. Tears I hadn't known were close slid down my cheeks. "You really want to do this?"

"Don't you?"

I nodded. It was the right answer. Not the easy one, but it was the only one that allowed me to remain true to my childhood friendship with Rikki—and to my family, who apparently already looked upon Kyle and James as theirs.

"But as I said, I can't do it alone," Becca said. "You can start helping by picking Kyle up from dance on your way home from work."

I took Becca's hand. "Let's go tell Rikki. Because there's one thing she still has to understand. I can agree to take her children, but I'm not the hero she really needs right now."

"I think," Becca said with a smile, "that she's already beginning to understand."

CHAPTER FORTY

Kyle

I stayed with Mom until both our tears dried. Sister Rushton had long ago knocked on the door and called out that she was going home and that someone named Sister Bunk was with James and not to worry. A bit later, Sister Bunk let us know dinner was ready. I didn't feel like eating. Maybe I would never feel like it again.

Everything made sense now, from the changes in Mom to the decision to return to her childhood home. But what about me and James? Did coming here mean she had plans for us?

No, I couldn't think about her being gone. I could hope for a miracle, right? Besides, I was too afraid of the answer. I didn't want to be a ward of the state and be shuffled from foster home to foster home. I didn't want to lose both her and James.

James came in and lay down with us. I knew Mom had to tell him, but I couldn't bear to hear it again, so I pretended to be hungry. In the kitchen, I ate under the watchful eye of Sister Bunk, whose thin face was kind beneath her round glasses. She didn't say anything but offered me a sympathetic smile. Pretty smart for a wrinkled old lady. Was she one of the sisters who was helping pay for my dance lessons?

After I ate, I couldn't remember what kind of food it had been. I knew I should go back to Mom, but I wasn't quite ready to face her. I needed to feel stronger first.

The Rushtons showed up to see Mom, and while they were talking to Sister Bunk, I slipped out of the house. I wanted to run and run and run to stop the turmoil that was building inside me again, but I had nowhere to go.

I ran anyway, and before I knew where I was going, I ended up on the Rushtons' front doorstep. I didn't remember ringing the bell, but the door opened and Travis stood there. "Kyle," he said in surprise.

I started to cry.

He put a hand on my shoulder. "I'm sorry about your mom."

So, he already knew—from his parents, probably. My tears were coming so fast I could barely see his face. Where did all those tears come from? I thought I'd cried them all out with Mom. I felt empty, alone, and so scared. I needed . . . I needed . . . I didn't know what I needed, except for my mother to live.

I hurled myself at Travis and felt him stiffen. Then his arms went awkwardly around me. "Shh," he said, patting my back like I was three years old. "It's going to be okay."

"How can it ever be okay?" I cried.

"I don't know, but I think it will. It has to be." He sounded really sorry, but hugging him wasn't anything like I'd thought it would be. I didn't feel romantic or anything but grateful that he was there—that anyone who wasn't my mom was there.

"I'm so mad at her for not telling me sooner, but at the same time I wish I didn't know," I sobbed out the words. He probably couldn't even understand them. "I can't even tell her I'm angry because she's dying. Dying! She's already hurting so much." If she was feeling anything like what was in my heart, it was a wonder she kept breathing at all.

All at once Allia was there, pushing Travis away and hugging me tight. A real hug. Exactly what I needed. "Come in," she said. "Move, Travis."

I clung to her as she led me to the couch. Travis sat on my other side, every now and then patting my shoulder. Allia held me for a long time while I mumbled on about Mom, coming at last to my worry about losing James.

"You don't have to worry about that," Allia said in a voice so soft I almost didn't hear through my tears. "We're going to take care of you and James."

I froze. "What?" I looked from her to Travis.

He nodded. "We want to be here for you and James when . . . you know. We talked about it just now. We all agreed."

I glanced back at Allia, who nodded. "We want you to be part of our family."

Relief poured over me as the last piece of the puzzle clicked into place. Mom did have a plan. Now I understood why she'd said Travis was off limits and seemed so worried when I wasn't listening. But I didn't care about him being off limits now. I didn't need a boyfriend. What I needed was a friend and an older brother so I wouldn't always have to be the strong one. Besides, Mormons like Allia didn't date before sixteen, and I wanted to be like her.

"Would that be okay with you?" Allia said, suddenly hesitant at my silence. "Or is there some other place you'd rather be?"

I shook my head. "No," I said. Or tried to. Nothing came out.

She hugged me again even tighter. "We're going to be with you every minute," she promised. "You're never going to be alone."

Yes. I wanted to be just like Allia.

CHAPTER FORTY-ONE

Rikki

It seemed silly for me to begin to rethink my entire past because I felt a little heat where there was obviously none. Or because Becca had shown up after I'd said my first prayer in a very long time. Yet telling Kyle and seeing her struggle to be strong for me made me realize that I'd lived a life of selfishness.

Once I'd thought I had no regrets, but suddenly I had plenty. I should have stayed near people who cared about me instead of seeking love in the arms of strangers. I should have developed a relationship with my mother, even it if meant moving out and seeing her only when my father wasn't around. I should have found a good father for my children, a steady home. I should have thought about the what-ifs and searched out the source of the warmth I'd felt—was still feeling since that morning.

Maybe if I'd stayed I would not only have accomplished all the things I was proud of in my life—having my children, achieving many of my dance goals, visiting numerous cities, reaching out to the people I'd helped over the years—but also much more because I could have avoided more of the heartache and wasted time.

Maybe Dante had been right all along.

But perhaps these regrets weren't all bad. Regrets might give me the courage to make changes for the future. A future I didn't have but could try to create for my children.

Kyle had wanted to ask what was to become of her and James, but she hadn't. Had she held back from fear that I had no plan, or because she didn't want me to see that already she was accepting the inevitable? She was pragmatic in that regard, the way I'd raised her to be.

I had a plan, and though it hadn't gone as well as I'd hoped, the heat and Charlotte's words at the hospital made me able to wait. At least a little longer.

It was then that Becca and Dante arrived, Becca strangely lacking her usual confidence and Dante looking at me with more sorrow than the time his dad had let him down about the campout. Underneath it all was the acceptance I'd been waiting for. I wanted to jump up and hug them. Instead, I lay there inside my weakened body and cried.

• • •

"I want to know more about this feeling," I told Charlotte when she arrived later.

"Shoot. You already know."

"It's been so long."

"Don't worry. It'll all come back." She plumped the pillows she'd brought me, careful not to disturb James, who was sleeping in my bed. "I brought you this book. It gave me a lot of comfort when I didn't know what the future held. Maybe some of the passages I marked will be useful."

I knew the blue book. I'd had one once.

I was still reading an hour later when Kyle slipped into my bed. The redness in her face told me she'd been crying again.

"I love you, Mom," she whispered.

I hugged her tight. "I love you, too. So much."

Shutting the book, I put my arms around my baby girl, and together we slept.

CHAPTER FORTY-TWO

Kyle

I'd thought all I wanted in life was to dance, but now all I wanted was my mother. Still, I danced. I danced for her, because when I danced I was able to become the dance and forget, just for a while.

Things weren't great, but less bad than I expected. I thought I'd die at first when I learned, but while knowing made the fear real, knowing also made my nightmares stop.

None of the adults ever really sat us down and said we were going to live with the Rushtons, though Mom and the Rushtons had many serious discussions behind closed doors, but from the beginning everyone talked as if we were. The relief I'd felt when Allia had first told me never went away.

Except I didn't care anymore about having a nice, clean house, or about having hot dinners at a regular time, new clothes, or a mother who was active in the PTA. When it came right down to it, I'd rather have my mom. Still, knowing the Rushtons wanted us made the fear in my stomach less painful. Sister Rushton suggested we all move in right away, even Mom, but Mom wanted to stay in her own house, and there was no way James or I would leave her.

The ladies in the ward were always at our place, coming and going until I knew them all and their families. It made going to church each week like a big family reunion—or what I thought a reunion might be like. Sometimes I didn't understand how the sisters kept coming, especially on Mom's bad days when all she would do was lie in her bed and cry, but keep coming they did, especially Sister Gillman and Sister Rushton, who asked me to call her Becca for now.

Becca came every day, and sometimes twice a day. She helped James and Lauren with their homework, while Allia or Travis helped me with mine. She took a ton of pictures and videos and wouldn't let my mother say no. Sometimes she and Mom would sit giggling in her bed together, and every now and then I'd hear about them going out to lunch while I was at school.

Not that Mom ever ate much. She was as frail as a dry winter leaf, tossed about in the wind. Sometimes I felt jealous of their relationship, but all I'd have to do was lie down beside Mom and feel her hand on my cheek to know my mother loved me first and best. Me and James.

She gave me an apron she'd made in Young Women's when she was my age. It looked practically new, and I took to wearing it every time Sister Gillman taught me and James to make a new meal. Eventually, I showed Mom my photo album, and she didn't laugh. It felt good showing it to her, like we finally didn't have any secrets from each other.

There were other differences in Mom, ones that had nothing to do with her declining physical ability. She talked more about God and the purpose of life, especially after one of her long talks with the Rushtons.

One day when I was feeling sorry for myself, she took hold of my hand. "I want you to remember something," she said, "and never, ever forget it."

I blinked. She hadn't spoken so seriously since she told me about the tumor. "Okay, what?"

"Call your brother first."

I did, wondering if there was more bad news. But what could possibly be worse?

James came running, as he always did the minute anyone hinted that Mom might need him. He jumped onto the bed and curled into her side, not noticing her wince at the pressure. No pressure at all, really, but anything was too much for her these days. Still, neither of us pushed him away.

"There will be tough days," Mom said, as I sat next to her. "There will be days when you feel all alone, days when you think there's no going back. On those days, I want you to do something for me. I want you to look outside and look at the mountains—to really see them." She pointed out the window of her room where we could see the mountain peaks to the east. I'd noticed her staring out the window sometimes, but I'd never known what she'd been seeing.

"I want you to remember them the way I saw them when we came to Utah," Mom said, her voice now a reverent whisper. "They're God's hands, and they'll always be holding you through the tough times. Then I want you to think of me standing right by Him, watching over you and telling God to hold you tighter when you need it the most."

James gaped at her. "You'll stand right by Him?"

"I promise."

"Will I see you?"

Mom ran her hand through his hair. "No, but I'm telling you now, that's right where I'm going to be. You'll feel it. Maybe someone will say something to remind you, or maybe you'll just know."

"Does God hold you?" James asked.

Maybe it was stupid, but I wanted to ask the same question.

Every day she was slipping further away from me, every day her pain increased, and yet she never complained.

Mom blinked several times, swallowing hard. "Oh, yes. He's been holding me every day since I was born, only no one ever told me. I had to learn it for myself, and I made a lot of dumb mistakes. That's why I want you to know right from the beginning. So you won't have to go through what I did."

"What if I can't see the mountains?" James asked, his forehead creasing with worry.

She laughed. "It doesn't matter. Close your eyes, and you'll see them. Close your eyes, and I'll be right there, watching and cheering and waiting. Don't wait for God to show you He's there. Reach out for Him anytime you need help, and even when you don't."

James dug his head into the side of her chest. This time she didn't wince but hugged him tighter.

"How do you really know He's there?" I asked softly.

"Because I feel His warmth. Because Dante and Becca were ready for you kids. Because I have a second chance to get things right."

I wasn't sure what she meant by the warmth, but I understood about the Rushtons and second chances. "Then is it okay if I get baptized?" I'd wanted to ask for the past few days, but I hadn't dared.

She hugged me. "Yes, sweetie. It's always been your choice. Just make sure you're doing it for the right reasons."

I didn't know what the right reasons were. I might be doing it because I wanted to be like Allia and because I wanted to fit in better with the Rushtons. But I also wanted to be baptized because I loved everyone at church and felt at home there. Funny when I'd hated it so much those first Sundays.

When I told my mom my reasons, she smiled. "That's a start, Kyle. It's what I had when I was your age. But don't stop there. I promise you, there's a lot more. Listen to Becca and Dante. They'll help you understand."

It was my turn to hug her—but gently.

Our house also underwent a change. The Young Men and Young Women came over, with plenty of adult supervision, and painted the outside of our house a bright, clean white. Mom chose red for the shutters, which made the house seem more hers. Men cut the lawn and put chemicals in the back to get rid of the weeds. They said they'd have to do it again in the spring and that it would take a year or more for the grass to be thick, but it looked wonderful to me. They even fixed up James's tree house, which got him so worked up, he went zooming around the yard getting in everyone's way.

I wanted to ask why they were doing this when it was so obvious that Mom might not survive the month, much less make it until Christmas, but when I saw the contentment on her face as she insisted on sitting on the porch to watch it all, I knew. Because they wanted to show her they cared. They wanted to show us.

Quinn the Couch Man came to help, too, and he brought a dryer, which no one else had thought of, or at least not that I knew. I hugged him and thanked him because I was more than tired of hanging out clothes on the line. He wiped at his eyes and mumbled something about KSL, whatever that was.

When the day of my baptism arrived, Mom was able to attend, though Bishop Rushton—who I was now calling Dante—had to bring a wheelchair to take her into the church. Travis had volunteered to baptize me, but I wanted Dante to do it. I guess I felt it would stick more, or something, since he was the bishop.

After I came out of the water, I felt light and wonderful. For that moment, I was clean. It was as if I'd never said or done anything mean or tried smoking out behind the school. As if I had never shoplifted. Warmth filled my heart, every last inch, until I felt so full I wanted to shout and laugh and sing as loud as I could.

Warmth.

Ah, Mom. Now I understand.

After I changed my clothes, everyone waited to congratulate me. Travis was second in line after Allia. "I want you to know," he said in a low voice as he hugged me, "that I'll be here for you, like I am for the other kids. If you ever need me to tell some guy to leave you alone, or want a ride somewhere, or just to talk, you let me know."

"Thank you," I whispered. I hugged him again.

Behind him I could see other people lining up to greet me, even Monty and his friends from school, Allia's friends, who were now mine, and the kids from the ward. Not just the kids but also the ladies who'd been coming to stay with Mom and the men who'd helped paint. I'd never had so many people attend something just for me, and seeing them all brought me to tears.

Shyly, I bypassed all of them and ran straight to Mom. She leaned forward and hugged me as I knelt before her chair. "This is why I brought you here," she whispered. "This is why I should never have left. Kyle, don't do what I did. Don't leave them. Even when you go away to New York, find a ward there. We all need a family like this. It's God's plan."

"I will, Mom. I promise."

"Remember, there's always a way back. Always. Everything for begins today, and I know you're going to do great."

'er confidence buoyed me.

'nk hard a few times," she added. "That's good. Now go let congratulate you."

'd.

CHAPTER FORTY-THREE

Rikki

The week after Kyle's baptism, Becca arrived at my house on a Saturday afternoon as Quinn was leaving. Quinn was a regular visitor, and as he dipped his head toward her in acknowledgment, my heart went out to him. He looked so sad. Though he knew we had no future, he still continued to visit me, and his presence brought me a lot of joy.

"Good day, huh?" Becca said.

I was sitting on the couch, which always signaled a good day. I was sick of my bed by now, and I jumped at any chance to leave my room. Trepidation shivered up my spine, though, because the good days were inevitably followed by the bad.

"No pumpkins yet?" I asked. Dante had taken all the kids to the store to pick out pumpkins to carve for family home evening. Becca had explained that it was still early for pumpkins and they would be rotten and perfectly awful by the end of the month, but that was the way her children liked them—spooky.

"Not yet. They should be here soon. You have a nice chat with Quinn?"

I smiled. "I don't know why he keeps coming."

"He loves you."

"Poor man. At least he gave Charlotte a chance to go home for a bit. That woman is tireless." I was amazed at her service, a thing I could never repay. "So, anything new?" I asked before I became emotional.

Dying made you emotional about everything.

Becca told me about the upcoming parent-teacher conference, the program the Primary was working on for Christmas, and how next week Travis was going on his first real date. When she started talking about the new trellis she'd found on clearance at Home Depot, I grabbed her hand.

"Finally, you got the trellis! What are you going to do about the gardens? You can't let this go. It's a part of you. Please promise me you won't give up your dreams." I felt a little guilty saying this, since I'd added to her burden more than any of her children had.

Becca smiled. "For now I'm going to visit gardens, study plants, and help a few of the sisters with their landscapes. Maybe I'll take a few classes when the kids are older."

"That's all?"

She laughed. "Rikki, I'm grateful to you for encouraging me to go after my dream. I'm going to do it. I promise. I'm going to take care of me. But you being sick, seeing how much your children crave to be with you, how much you want to stay with them, that's taught me what's really important."

I didn't get it. "So basically you're going to continue like always, taking all the responsibility for the children, doing everything for everyone else?" I didn't bother to hide the annoyance in my voice.

Becca shook her head. "Don't you understand, Rikki? My children are the flowers in my eternal garden, and I only get one chance with them. I want to do it right. They aren't going to be small forever. They're already all in school. Going through this with you—suddenly all my so-called unfulfilled dreams aren't as important. My children are. My family is. And you know what? I wouldn't trade my job as a wife and mother for all the exotic flower beds in the world. My children are the flowers I'm helping to grow. Your children are those flowers. Think of it. If you could do anything with the rest of the time you had left, would it be dancing on Broadway or being with Kyle and James?"

I stared at her. She was right. I didn't want dancing. No matter how much I loved it, I loved my kids more. Dancing meant nothing next to them, and I'd give all my years of dancing for even one more day with Kyle and James. I imagined Becca felt the same about her children.

"I'm going to have the rest of my life and eternity to create gardens," Becca said. "But only this little time with my kids. You taught me that, Rikki. You."

I hadn't meant to. I'd meant to teach her to go for her dreams, to put herself first for a change, but I'd forgotten that her first dream was an eternity with Dante and the children.

"It's silly to keep yearning for second best," Becca added. "Which is what my gardening dreams are when I really think about it. I've realized that I'm so grateful for what I have now."

I hugged her. "Well, good," I said, blinking back the tears. "Just so you don't give it up altogether. And keep making Dante pull his share."

"So far, so good. He seems changed. Like he's realized now is every bit as important as someday. He's spending more time with the kids, and he's been making dinner every Saturday, if you can believe that." She laughed. "He and Kyle are developing quite a relationship since he started picking her up from dance."

That hit me so hard it was all I could do not to fall onto the floor in a weepy heap. Dante was going to take care of Kyle. She'd never had a father figure before, and the fact that she wouldn't have to deal with a man like my father made everything worth it.

Thankfully, Dante arrived with Lauren and James before I gave in to my emotion. The kids carried their pumpkins. If I felt up to it, we'd carve them at their house on Monday, or they'd carve here if I had to stay in bed.

"Look, Mom!" James's face was shining as he showed me a tall, narrow pumpkin that had a twisted look in the middle. "My pumpkin's going to be the scariest. Cory helped me pick it out."

"That is scary," I said.

Lauren showed me the perfect round one she'd picked out. "Mine's going to be the prettiest. I don't want it scary."

"Come on," James, said. "Let's go put them in the tree house."

"We can pretend they're our kids."

I stopped myself from grabbing James and hugging him tight. All I ever wanted to do these days was to hold or touch my children, to have them always close by. But sitting at my side waiting for me to die was no way for a child to live.

"I dropped the others off at our house," Dante was saying to Becca.

"What about Kyle?" she asked.

"She's finishing up a bit of math with Allia. Apparently she took it with her."

That was my fault. On my bad days, Kyle refused to go to school and had to make up her homework. Becca had talked to all the teachers, though, and they were going out of their way to help Kyle keep up.

"I'm going to get you something to eat," Becca said to me. "I brought some fruit. Is there anything else in particular you feel like?" I noticed she didn't ask me if I wanted to eat in the first place. Probably I was still alive because of all the food she forced down me.

"No," I said. "The fruit sounds good."

Dante settled on the chair as Becca left, his eyes on my face. "So."

I rolled my eyes. "You look like a nervous ten-year-old."

"I feel like a nervous ten-year-old."

"Look," I said. "I want to thank you for what you and Becca are doing."

He shook his head. "You would do the same for me."

"You're right. I would, though I would never do it as well as Becca. She's going to work hard. She's going to work even harder on my kids than on yours, to try to make it all up to them."

"Probably."

"Don't let her give up on her gardens, okay? Take her for shows, for nights away. Promise, Dante. Even just a little bit will help her stay strong."

"I promise."

"And when she experiments at your house, tell her how beautiful it all is, even if you hate it."

He laughed. "You want me to lie?"

"No. It *will* be beautiful. You'll be the only one who can't see it. Sorry, Dante, but your artistic ability never did extend to the visual. I bet she even picks out your clothes."

"Okay, okay. You don't have to worry. I love Becca. She's everything to me."

I smiled. "Besides God, you mean."

He nodded.

My heart was feeling that now-familiar warmth, and we sat there in comfortable silence, the way we had once sat under my tree in the summer.

"You were right, Dante. All along, you were right." I understood so much more now. Why he'd left me for a mission. Why he'd stayed here and how he'd become the man he was, the man who was there for me and my children.

His emotion showed in his eyes. "God's always been there, Rikki. You only had to reach out."

I knew that, too. God had been there, ready to cradle me in his arms, if only I'd let Him. But I hadn't understood that until I came home, felt the mountains around me, and saw how content Dante was with his life. Until I felt the love of my ward family.

With that knowledge came the understanding that Dante was my hero, and Becca, too, but not my last and greatest hero. My last and greatest hero had held my hand in the night all these years when no one else was around. He'd given me two wonderful children and friends to point the way when I'd been lost and hadn't even realized it. He'd been there during my treatments and when I finally realized there would be no cure. He'd given His life for me and had been waiting, ready to wash away all my terrible choices and the years of pain and hiding. Trusting Him now was the only reason it was remotely bearable to leave my babies behind.

I would see Him soon, and I was no longer afraid.

CHAPTER FORTY-FOUR

Becca

Ten Months Later

W ow, she was fabulous," Allia said as the applause at
Kyle's dance recital finally subsided. "Makes me wish
I'd stayed in dance class."

"No way," Cory scoffed. "You'd never want to practice so many
hours every day."

She sighed. "You got that right. Kyle's a little crazy. In a good
way, I mean." She turned to me. "Mom, I want to go backstage and
tell Kyle how well she did, okay?"

"Guess that means you're not mad at her anymore for losing
your mascara," Travis said.

Allia flipped her dark hair. "Of course I am. But that doesn't
mean I'm not going to tell her how great she was and how Tom
couldn't keep his eyes off her."

Tom, that was a name I hadn't heard before, but I wasn't worried. At the moment, Kyle was still so involved in dance that no boy
stood much of a chance. Good thing, since she still had two more
years before she could even begin to group date.

"Go ahead," I said.

Allia took James's hand. "I'll take the little kids with me."

"I guess I'll go, too." Cory shot out of his seat.

"I'm going to talk with Claire." Travis waved and headed over to talk to BG's sister, whom he'd gone out with twice already, which was pretty much as long as he'd dated any girl. As long as they were double-dating or in a group, that was okay with me.

The auditorium at the junior high was quickly clearing. Dante put his arm around me. "So, are we going to have to build on to the house to keep those girls from tearing each other apart?" There was a hint of real concern behind the casual tone.

"It was just a spat. I'm making Kyle buy Allia a new mascara."

"Would it help if I talked to Kyle?"

"Probably." Kyle listened to Dante like no one else. I didn't know if it was because he picked her up each day from dance and they'd developed a rapport or because he treated her with all the childhood love he'd had for her mother. Regardless, she responded better to him than to anyone. Maybe she simply craved the love of a father. I raised a finger. "But keep in mind, it was just a spat. Not a war."

We'd had wars. Oh, not for the first eight months as a family, though they had been challenging enough. Rikki's death had been followed closely by a successful surgery to align the muscles in James's eyes and Kyle's constant tiptoeing around the house with the frightened look that told us she was worried about being sent away. There had been a sort of stilted politeness in her interactions with all of us.

These past two months, however, challenging had given way to wars, as if we'd finally meshed as a family. The children fought hard, played harder, and loved more. Perhaps they'd all realized we were in it for the long haul. That meant Kyle had begun to demand more, to test the limits—thus the wars. It was a good change emotionally for her, despite bringing substantially more fireworks. They never lasted long, and they were occurring less often now, another good sign.

"Look what I have." Dante pulled a paper from his pocket. "Tickets."

"Oh?" I took the paper and studied it. "The garden show in Saint George?" The memory brought a rush of emotions—and with it the sound of Rikki's laughter.

"You can print them right off the Internet."

"I can't go. The boys have soccer. I have to make sure Travis studies for the ACT."

"Come on," he coaxed. "There are no refunds. It's just one night. I mean, we could go for more, but we'd only have to go for one, if you'd prefer."

I met his eyes, saw the love there.

"Come on," he said again. "I miss you."

I'd been busy melding two families. Too busy. Interestingly enough, these days it was me who was more occupied than even my bishop husband. "Are you sure this isn't because you hate my trellis?"

He laughed and pulled me closer. "I love the trellis. It's beautiful. All the neighbors say so." His lips touched my cheek, making me shiver with the unexpectedness. "Almost as beautiful as you."

Mentally I began rearranging things. The children could stay with my sister, Allia would look over James's and Lauren's math and help my sister keep an eye on them, Charlotte Gillman and Travis would take turns getting Kyle to dance. Travis would take the boys to soccer.

"Okay," I said. "We'll go. Two nights. If we leave early enough, we could see a play the first night." That was my attempt at returning his gift with something I knew he'd enjoy. Give and take—I'd learned these past months that everything good always boiled down to those two things. Neither of us had to give it all, nor did we have to be equal in everything we gave every time. It was enough that we each took a step toward the other, that we tried to make the differences between us smaller.

Dante smiled and kissed me right there in the auditorium. I knew he loved me. He'd shown me every day for the past months as he'd kept his promise to be there for me with Rikki's children— and our own. As for me, James and Kyle had filled a part of me that I hadn't even known was missing. Things weren't perfect, but we would never stop trying to make them better. One step, one compromise at a time.

Kyle called out to us then, waving from the corner of the stage. We jumped to our feet and hurried over. "Well?" she asked, her eyes fixed on us, ignoring the throng of friends around her.

"It was perfect," I said. "All the girls were wonderful, but you were absolutely amazing."

She looked toward Dante. To my surprise he had tears in his eyes. "You remind me of your mother. She would be so proud."

It was the right thing to say. Kyle launched herself into Dante's arms and hugged him. "Thank you," she murmured. Then she hugged me just as tightly and whispered in my ear. "I'm sorry about the mascara. I told Allia, too."

My eyes rose to the ceiling overhead, only dimly lit by the lights along the wall. I could almost hear Rikki saying, "See? You're doing it. She'll be okay. Now go to Saint George and kick up your heels."

"Come on," Dante said, motioning to the kids. "Ice cream's on me."

About the Author

Rachel Ann Nunes (pronounced noon-esh) learned to read when she was four, beginning a lifelong fascination with the written word. She began writing in the seventh grade and is now the author of more than thirty published books, including the popular *Ariana* series and the award-winning picture book *Daughter of a King*.

Rachel and her husband, TJ, have seven children. She loves camping with her family, traveling, meeting new people, and, of course, writing. She writes Monday through Friday in her home office, taking frequent breaks to take care of kids or go swimming with them.

Rachel loves hearing from her readers. You can write to her at Rachel@RachelAnnNunes.com. To enjoy her monthly newsletter or to sign up to hear about new releases, visit her website, www.RachelAnnNunes.com.